SEA OF TIME

Will Hubbell

ACE BOOKS, NEW YORK

SEA OF TIME

An Ace Book / published by arrangement with the author

PRINTING HISTORY
Ace mass market edition / February 2004

ISBN: 0-441-01143-8

ACE®
Ace Books are published by The Berkley Publishing Group,
a division of Penguin Group (USA) Inc.,
375 Hudson Street, New York, New York 10014.
ACE and the "A" design
are trademarks belonging to Penguin Group (USA) Inc.

PRINTED IN THE UNITED STATES OF AMERICA

10 9 8 7 6 5 4 3 2 1

To my parents
James Harrison and Virginia Clements Hubbell

Acknowledgments

I would like to thank the people whose expertise and assistance helped me write this book: Gerald Burnsteel, Richard Curtis, Diane Gummoe, Anne Sowards, Dr. Joanne Stevens, Bruce Younger, and my wife, Carol.

1

WINTERS WERE BRUTAL IN THE MONTANA TERRITORY, and Con Clements's office was chilly despite the cast-iron stove. The windowpanes were coated with a thick layer of frost that numbed her fingertips when she scraped it away to watch the men unloading the wagon in the street. She had waited months for this delivery, and the long delay only heightened her anticipation. With difficulty and much cursing, the two teamsters lugged a large, wooden crate over to her building. Soon, frigid air flowed under Con's closed doorway, as the men entered the outer office.

"God dang ya, Jess!" yelled a man. "Watch ma toes!"

"Where's he want this load of trouble?" asked a second voice.

"*She* wants it in her office," replied Con's male secretary.

Her secretary, Matthew Tompkin, opened the door, letting in a fresh blast of cold. "Pardon me, Mrs. Clements, some men have arrived with your delivery."

"Have them bring it in, please."

The two teamsters carried in the crate. Their clothes were crusted with snow, and their moustaches drooped with ice. The rare presence of a lady subdued them, and the man who had cursed Jess just moments before asked Con meekly, "Where'd ya want it, ma'am?"

"Close to the stove," replied Con. "Could you uncrate it?"

"Ah'd be pleased. Jess, go git the hammer."

Now that he was unburdened, the remaining teamster politely removed his hat. "That was shore some heavy crate, ma'am."

"It's my new desk," said Con, "all the way from New York City."

The man smiled self-consciously. "You women shore like furniture."

"The Clements Mining Company is a growing business. I can't run it from a table anymore."

"*You* run the mine, ma'am?"

Con had heard that question asked so often, it had ceased to provoke her. "I do."

"You a widder?"

"No. My husband's alive," replied Con. "He's more interested in paleontology than money."

"Pale-lee-oh-what?"

"He's a geologist," said Con, choosing the briefest explanation. "He finds the gold. I run the mining end."

The man shook his head in amazement. "Wal, Ah'll be danged."

Jess arrived with the hammer and relieved Con from further interrogation. A few minutes later, the desk stood shining and new amidst the ruined crate. Con stared at it with a stunned expression.

"Ma'am, you all right?" Jess asked.

Con caught her breath. "Yes," she said in a faraway voice. "I . . . I'm fine. Just surprised, that's all."

"It's what ya ordered?"

"Yes . . . yes. Thank you."

The two men hauled the remains of the crate away, shaking their heads as they departed. Con closed the door to be alone. Slowly, almost fearfully, she approached the desk, which now dominated the room. Its pristine rosewood veneer shone softly, a lighter shade than Con remembered. The desk's top was devoid of the minute furrows scored by countless ballpoint pens. *They haven't been invented yet,* she thought. Con reached out and touched the ornate Beaux Arts carvings, recalling how they had fascinated her as a child. The desk had been a prized antique then—the oldest family heirloom.

Con closed her eyes and let her fingers be guided by memory. As they traced the swirl of the carved volutes, what she knew intellectually became concrete. The gulf of time that separated her from her first eighteen years became real. When she opened her eyes again, they were wet with tears. Con opened the top drawer and found the familiar ink stain gone. She wondered who would make it. *Me? One of my children? A great-great-grandchild?*

Gathering her long dress and petticoats, Con crawled into the well of the desk. The space she remembered as so large—the perfect hideaway—was cramped. She peered at the drawer bottom and found what she was looking for. The paper pasted there was white and new. The ornate handwriting upon it stood out more boldly than Con recalled. Though she knew what it said, its meaning was utterly transformed. It read, "Special order for Constance Clements." That was her great-great-great-grandmother's name. Her name, too. It was no coincidence. They were the same person.

DUSK CAME EARLY in February. Rick arrived in the buggy just when it was necessary to light the lamps. The miners and prospectors in Little Hole started drinking at sundown, and the wild streets were no place for a respectable woman. The buggy had no top, and Rick's snow-covered coat added bulk to his muscular frame. The wind whipped his sandy blond hair about his face. Summers spent in the sun and a ready smile had added a few creases around the eyes, despite his youth. Con had been waiting for him, already dressed in her coat and bonnet, and she rushed out the door before Rick could step down to the snowy street. When he saw her, his pale blue eyes lit up. Con clambered into the seat and kissed him passionately.

"Mrs. Clements!" said Rick with a grin. "How you carry on! What will the townsfolk say?"

Con kissed Rick again. "I don't care! Can't a woman kiss her husband?"

"Not in public. Not in 1881."

"I *hate* the nineteenth century!"

Rick laughed. "I've heard that before." He turned to kiss Con and noticed the worried look in her hazel eyes. He had seen that look before, all too frequently as of late. His smile faded. "Was there trouble at the mine?" he asked, almost hoping there was.

"No," replied Con as she snuggled close to Rick. "They delivered my desk today, and it was Daddy's desk."

Rick shifted the reins to free an arm and hug Con. "That must have felt strange," he said, "but didn't you expect that?"

"I suppose I should have," said Con, "but it was still a shock. Sometimes, everything that happened seems like a weird dream, not something real."

"Perhaps it's best that way," said Rick. "This is our home now, the place we'll live our lives."

"Yes," said Con, "I guess it is."

Rick lapsed into silence, knowing Con would talk when she was ready. What she needed for the moment was his presence. The road left the makeshift buildings of the boomtown behind and began to climb a hill that over-looked it. Rick and Con's nearly finished home crowned the hilltop. A mansion by frontier standards, its white-painted clapboards stood out against the shadowed blue-gray of the Anaconda Range. The house's gentility contrasted with the gold mine that funded it. The Second Chance Mine marred a hill on the opposite side of town. Its timber head-frame and piles of tailings spoiled the view from the front windows, where Con sometimes watched the men laboring to push the ore carts.

The stable hand took the reins when they arrived. Rick and Con climbed down from the buggy and entered the house. Rose, the nanny, held Joey in her arms. The toddler struggled to be set down, and when he was, he ran to Con yelling "Mommy!" Con's face brightened as she knelt to embrace him.

"Did you see our snow angels, Mommy? Rose 'n' me made lots 'n' lots!"

"Angels in our yard!" exclaimed Con with exaggerated excitement. "And the best angel in the house!" She lifted Joey up and whirled around the room.

Joey squealed with delight. "I'm not an angel. I'm a boy."

Con hugged him close. "You're *my* angel."

* * *

JOEY WAS IN bed by the time Con and Rick ate dinner by the soft light of oil lamps. Bridget, the middle-aged cook and housekeeper, brought out her standard winter fare— pickled beets, potatoes, canned green beans, and local beef that had been boiled until it was chewable. Con sawed at her gray beefsteak until she was able to cut off a piece. "Mmmmm," she said, still chewing. "Better than night-stalker."

Rick looked both amused and disconcerted by her remark.

"What's nightstalker, Mum?" asked Bridget.

Con swallowed. "Dinosaur."

"Dinosaur? And what is that, Mum?"

"A kind of bird," said Rick quickly. "We used to eat them."

"Never heard of 'em," said Bridget. "Are they from here?"

"They used to be," said Rick.

"They're extinct," said Con.

"Did you say they stinked?" asked Bridget

Con chuckled. "They did," she said, "they truly did."

"Then why would a body eat them?" asked Bridget.

"We were starving and glad to have them," replied Con. "I forgot you and the mister had hard times before you found the mine."

"We lived in a tiny log cabin," said Con. "I panned for gold when I was nine months pregnant."

"Blessed Saints!" said the cook.

Con omitted that their year in the cabin had been a happy time, and their real hardships had occurred 65 million years in the past. Con was well aware of her reputation for eccentricity and did not intend to increase it by speaking of time travel. Yet, her vacation at Peter Green's island resort in the Cretaceous Period and the disasters that ensued increasingly haunted her.

"Would you have a fire made in our bedroom?" asked Con.

"I'll see to it right away, Mum."

When Bridget left the room, Rick rolled his eyes. "Nightstalker?" he said. "You're incorrigible."

"I still dream of them," Con said in a low voice. "Those big eyes staring in the dark."

"They're gone forever," said Rick. "You shouldn't mention them around the help."

"It's *my* house," retorted Con. "Besides, they already think I'm batty, and not because I mention dinosaurs. They can't understand why I run the mine. I've heard them gossip; they say I act like a man."

"There's 180 years between your thinking and theirs," said Rick. "That's a lot of change."

"I'll say! I want to go to work in sensible clothes, not dressed like a doll. And everything's so primitive. What I wouldn't give for some shampoo and a shaver. I'm so tired of scummy hair and hairy legs!"

"They're fluffy legs," said Rick, with a grin.

"You know what I mean!"

"Those things didn't bother you when we lived in the cabin."

"I wasn't hemmed in then. Now it's different."

"We don't have to live here," said Rick. "We can go anywhere and do anything you want."

"Rick, you know we can't do that! We have to . . ."

Bridget's return cut her short. The cook eyed Con's plate and noted Con had added three more potatoes and half of Rick's beefsteak. Bridget, naturally, said nothing. With so many other quirks to ponder, she had ceased to question why her slender mistress ate like a lumberjack. *Rose says the child's the same way. It's a peculiar household,* thought Bridget, *and that's God's truth!*

DESPITE THE FIRE, Rick and Con's bedroom was still chilly when they went to bed. Con changed into her night-clothes and crawled beneath the frigid quilts. Her lithe body, with its metabolism accelerated by genetic engineering, quickly warmed the bedclothes. She snuggled close to Rick more for the comfort of his touch than any need for warmth. He responded by wrapping his arms around her. This was usually the most peaceful time in Con's day, but the arrival of the desk had stirred thoughts that troubled her. "Rick," she said after a quiet interlude, "are you ever afraid our happiness might vanish?"

Rick stroked Con's light brown hair. "It seems to me that, of all people, you have the fewest reasons to worry about the future. Who else knows how their life turns out? That's why they sent us to this century rather than our own—so the future wouldn't change."

"It doesn't make sense," said Con. "How can I be my own ancestor?"

"It's a paradox," said Rick. "But you have to admit it's real. How else could you have known where to find the Second Chance Mine? It was right where you said it would be. And don't forget the desk."

Con did not reply. Her skepticism was ironic, for the strange humans from the future had sent Con and Rick to the nineteenth century only because Con had proven the act was part of their history. The proofs that had satisfied those cold, disdainful people also satisfied Rick, and he was confident their lives would unfold as Con had foretold. Yet Con felt a life of wealth and happiness was far from assured. For that to happen, she must assume the role of Constance Clements, the family legend. The tale of the woman who founded the family fortune had been a staple of Con's childhood. The story also had saved her and Rick. Yet ensuring that tale would reach her ears in the distant future was no easy matter, and the problem bedeviled Con.

"I'll tell you why the desk upset me," said Con after a long silence. "It's a reminder of how much time lies between my birth and now. What if I do something that breaks the cycle? Something that prevents me from being born in 2041? I might disappear!"

"Joe said only the past can affect the future. Nothing that happens in the years ahead can change your present life, including never being born."

"Joe was from our century," replied Con. "He wasn't an

expert on time travel; he just flew the machine."

"Joe knew what he was talking about. He got it straight from the time traveler, the guy he called Sam."

Con sighed. "I just wish I knew what to do. When I was growing up, the family legend was only an interesting story. I didn't know it was a message, so I didn't pay that much attention. Rick, I don't even remember if I'm supposed to have five or four children."

"Everything will work out," said Rick.

"Don't you think we can change our future?" asked Con. "You must. Tonight, you suggested going away."

"I'll do anything that makes you happy," said Rick.

"I *am* happy," whispered Con. "I don't want it to ever end."

"It won't," said Rick.

Rick's touch assured Con more than his words. It reminded her they had faced and overcome formidable odds together. In his loving embrace, the drowsiness that eluded Con finally stole upon her. She was lulled by his breathing, and in her half-dream state, it sounded like waves breaking on sand. Con envisioned herself standing on a beach, placing messages in bottles and tossing them into the restless sea.

2

CON SAT AT HER NEW DESK, REVIEWING A PARTNER-ship proposal with an absorption that would have surprised her in the twenty-first century. There, Con had been planning to study art history at Harvard, not business. Business was her father's passion. As she scrutinized the papers, she paused to reflect on her new role. *I have my father's genes after all,* she mused. An ironic smile came to her face. *He inherited those genes from me.*

A knock on her door broke Con's concentration. "Yes," she said.

Matthew Tompkin poked his head inside the room. He had a puzzled expression on his face. "Mrs. Clements, there is a strange gentleman to see you. He gave me a message, saying you would understand its import."

"What is it?"

"The gentleman said he knows a former traveling companion of yours, someone named Joe Burns."

Con instantly went white. "Give . . . Give me a minute . . . and . . . and then show him in."

A minute later, Matthew ushered in a tall, baby-faced man with vaguely East Indian features. He was well dressed, but his brow was wrapped in bandages. Con remained seated at her desk, her right hand beneath an unfolded newspaper. "Have a seat, sir," she said, nodding toward a chair. "Mr. Tompkin, close the door when you leave."

Without a word, the man sat down. Con waited until Matthew had departed before she uncovered her hand. It held a revolver. She aimed it at the stranger's chest. "All right," she said in a shaky voice, "why have you come to see me?

The man looked at the gun without betraying a hint of emotion. "I believe we have a mutual acquaintance—Joe Burns. He used to call me Sam."

"Joe said you were dead," replied Con, "that Peter Green killed you to steal your time machine."

"Obviously, he was misinformed. Must you point that weapon at me?"

"Your kind pointed enough of them at me."

"My kind?"

"Your species—*Homo perfectus.*"

"And you think I am the same as they?"

"Joe said nothing to make me think differently."

Sam sighed. "You know what kind of man Peter Green was. All our dealings took place in an atmosphere of mistrust."

"You're dancing around the real issue," said Con, not lowering the revolver. "Why are you here?"

"To help you," replied Sam.

Con's expression became one of disbelief mixed with cynicism. "To help *me*? Rick and I are stuck here to preserve *your* precious future."

"And what future would that be?"

"How would I know?" said Con. "You kept us in the dark."

"Before we proceed further," said Sam, "we must clear up a misunderstanding. I am not like the people who sent you here. They are aberrations."

"They looked just like you. You have one of those dots under those bandages, don't you?"

Sam pulled up a band of gauze to reveal a metallic-colored dot in the middle of his forehead. "You mean my implant?" he said. "People like you have them also."

"People like me? They said *Homo sapiens* were extinct. It had something to do with purification."

"*The* Purification," corrected Sam. "A euphemism for an extermination. It should never have happened. It *did not* happen in the normal timestream."

Con did not let go of the gun, but she ceased to aim it at Sam. "I'm confused. You said you were here to help me. If you want to do that, take Rick, our son, and me back to our own time."

"If I did that," said Sam, "it would not solve the problem."

"What problem?"

"I think you already know."

"I assure you, I don't," replied Con.

"Surely you realize the unnaturalness of your existence. A person who is her own ancestor can only be the product of time travel."

"Of course," said Con. "It's a paradox, an infinite loop."

"Oh, it is hardy infinite," said Sam. "Great effort was necessary to achieve a single cycle."

"What do you mean?"

"Time has a natural flow from the past to the future, and

there are forces that constrain its course. Even in your time, people have given names to some of these forces—probability . . . thermodynamics . . . relativity. Your existence runs counter to all of them. It is an artificial event and an unstable one."

"But those people said my existence is part of their history."

"And you believed them?" countered Sam. "Think. It must have occurred to you how difficult it will be to make this happen again. You do not even know which of your progeny will be your ancestor. Your message to yourself is bound to get garbled over time."

"I'm here," retorted Con. "Somehow, it happened."

"But *why* did it happen?"

"How should I know?"

"Others have worked very hard to create your existence," said Sam. "What makes you think they are done with you?"

Con tried to maintain a poker face, but failed. The gun shook in her hands as she imagined all sorts of terrifying possibilities. The only response Con could muster was, "Why me?"

"Your nature makes you useful to them."

"How?"

"As a paradoxical element in the timestream, you are extremely effective as a causal agent."

Con responded with a quizzical look.

"It is a complex phenomenon," continued Sam, "and difficult to explain. Individuals are connected to their time period through countless associations that merge them into the timestream and reduce their potential to change events. These entanglements make free will largely an illusion. You, however, are uniquely free from those connections. That makes you particularly useful to anyone who wants to alter reality."

Con's eyes narrowed. "Including you," she said.

"True," admitted Sam. "And though I am here to help you, I would also like you to help me. The timestream has been distorted. Will you help me set it right?"

Con paused before she answered. "I have a husband and child," she said. "I can't leave them."

"From their perspective," said Sam, "you will be gone only an instant."

"Joe told me that's impossible."

"He learned only the rudimentary mechanics of operating a time machine," replied Sam. "I am free of his limitations."

"I'm sorry," said Con, "but I won't go."

"I am not here to coerce you," said Sam. "You must act freely or you lose your effectiveness."

"Thank you," said Con. "I'm glad you understand."

"I do understand, though others may not."

"I won't help them either."

"They may not even ask," said Sam. "They may alter your reality instead."

"What do you mean?"

"If they were to change your past," replied Sam, "from that point onward, the resulting reality would be the only one you knew. They might erase all who stand in their way, all who are precious to you."

"Are you trying to scare me?" asked Con in a tone that betrayed he already had.

"I am not," said Sam. "It is only a possibility, but you should be aware of it."

Con stared at Sam's impassive face, trying to read it. It was inscrutable. "Thank you for your concern," she said as calmly as possible, "but this is not my affair."

"I accept your decision," said Sam, appearing unperturbed by her refusal.

"Are we done with our business?" asked Con. "If so, I must get back to these papers."

"Yes," said Sam, rising from his chair. "I will show myself out."

After the door closed, Con stared at the papers on her desk. They could have no less meaning if they were written in Chinese. All she could think about was the implications of Sam's words. *Was he warning me or threatening me?* Either way, Con felt utterly defenseless. *How can I guard against an assault that occurs in the past?* All the gold in the Second Chance Mine could not buy her security or allay her fears. The work that had consumed her attention now seemed pointless. She rose and paced about the room. The more she thought, the more her agitation grew. When it became unbearable, Con put on her coat and bonnet, then opened the door to the outer office. Her distraught expression alarmed her office staff, and they stared at her in bewilderment.

"Mr. Tompkin," said Con, "may I borrow your horse?"

"Yes, ma'am, but I don't have a proper saddle for a lady."

"It doesn't matter," replied Con.

CON GALLOPED OUT of Little Hole, her dress and petticoats hiked up to her thighs. Only her long wool stockings covered her legs. She was oblivious to the cold, the wet snowfall, and the catcalls her indecorousness provoked. Her only concern was to see Rick and Joey.

When she burst into the entrance hall, both Bridget and Rose were standing there, convinced their eccentric mistress had finally lost her sanity. "Where's Joey? Where's Rick?" shouted Con.

"Your son's nappin', Mum," said Rose in a frightened voice.

"Mr. Clements is at the mine," added Bridget.

For a moment, Con whirled about in panicked indecision, and when she seemed about to bolt for the door, Bridget stepped in her way. "Should the stableboy go fetch 'im, Mum?"

"Yes . . . yes . . . and have Billy return Mr. Tompkin's horse as well." Con turned and, without a further word, scrambled up the stairs. Soon Joey's wails came from the nursery.

"Go see what she's up to," said Bridget to the nanny. "I'll send Billy after Mr. Clements." When Rose hesitated, the elder woman snapped, "Go on, you ninny, and see no harm befalls the child."

Rose anxiously climbed the stairs and entered the nursery. She found Con clutching her son. Both were weeping.

"Mum, you're frightenin' the lad. Can you let him go?"

Con slumped to the floor and relaxed her fierce grip on her son. He stopped crying and looked solemnly at his mother, who still convulsed with sobs. "Don't cry, Mommy," he said, his tiny voice reflecting his confusion and compassion.

Con stifled her sobs and forced a smile on her tear-streaked face. "Mommy's silly."

"Would you like to change from those wet clothes, Mum?"

"No," said Con. "I must stay with my son."

RICK ARRIVED AN hour later. Con heard his boots clumping rapidly up the stairs and ran to meet him. Before he could utter a word, Con clasped him tightly and began to weep.

Rick held her and let her cry. When her sobs diminished, he said, "You're wet. Why don't you change? I'll make a fire in the bedroom, and we can talk."

Rick built a large fire while Con changed into a nightgown. She sat on the floor in front of the flames and warmed her bare feet. "Sit beside me, Rick, I want you close."

"Will you tell me what's happened? This isn't like you."

"Sam visited me today."

"Sam? Who's Sam?"

"Remember the guy Joe talked about? The guy with the time machine? That Sam."

Rick's face grew grave. "I thought he was dead."

"Well, he's not. It felt so strange to be with a *Homo perfectus* again. It was like being on the island."

Rick hugged Con close. "No wonder you're upset."

"It's more than that. What he said was so frightening."

Con told Rick everything that had happened in her office. When she was done, Rick sat in silent contemplation. He was disturbed by what he had heard, but Con's reaction disturbed him more. During the hard times they faced together, he had come to count on her fortitude and optimism. Both seemed shaken, first by the arrival of the desk and now by the time traveler's visit.

Desiring to reassure Con, Rick kept his speculations to himself. "You did the right thing," he said. "You shouldn't get involved."

"Will you get under the quilts with me?" asked Con. "I need you to hold me."

Rick tenderly kissed her. "Of course," he said. "For as long as you want."

3

CON SLOWLY OPENED HER EYES AND PEERED OUT from under the quilt. Snowflakes fell on her cold face. The wind that howled outside the tiny log cabin had found cracks to blow in the snow. There was a sizable drift in the corner of the room. With no wood for the stove, the drift would linger until spring. Con was too exhausted to move her head, so only her eyes traveled about the room, carefully avoiding the table. She had the feeling she was saying good-bye to the home Rick and she had built together, the site of so much joy and so much sorrow. *Joey was born here,* she thought. *He died here, too.*

She forced herself to gaze at the table where Joey lay. His thin, pale face was as white as a sculpture on a marble tombstone. *How many days has he been there?* wondered Con. *Two or three?* For her, days were only to be endured, not counted. *But not for much longer,* she thought. *It's my turn next.*

Con sensed that turn was not far off. She had not eaten

for days, and her genetically enhanced metabolism had brought her to starvation almost as quickly as it had her son. The genes that had kept her slender had also wasted her body. Con no longer cared. Her sole regret was she could not bury Joey next to Rick. The ground by her beloved's grave was frozen, and frostbite had transformed Con's hands into useless claws.

Con's mind clouded over, and she slipped in and out of consciousness. She relived her Montana days in fragments, some bright and some somber. She recalled helping erect the walls around her. She saw Rick holding his newborn son aloft in this very room, his face filled with rapture. Con remembered the heady night when Rick returned with pockets full of gold and the terrible day when they brought his body slumped atop a mule. For some reason, the image of Rick's pockets turned inside out was more vivid than the bullet hole in his back. She recalled the pitying look on the men's faces when she told them, "It's not supposed to be this way. We're going to be rich."

Con was beyond regretting her decision to stay at the cabin; that was history now, no matter how disastrous its consequences. She realized it had been her downfall, yet she couldn't imagine any other choice. She and Rick had shared a dream, and she had been unable to abandon it. Isolation, hard luck, and winter had doomed her and her son. When Con's breasts ran dry, Joey had slipped uncomplainingly into oblivion. A tear rolled down Con's frigid face. *He was always an easy baby.*

AN ICY BLAST of wind tore at the quilt and through half-closed eyes Con saw a dark shape enter the cabin. *A bear?* she wondered, beyond truly caring. She heard the door slam, then felt a soft tube between her lips. A sweet, aromatic liquid dribbled into her mouth. She found the strength to whisper hoarsely, "Who?"

"A friend," said a voice.

Gentle fingers pushed the tube deeper in her mouth. "Drink," said the voice. "This will help."

Con obeyed. The liquid warmed her body and her mind slowly cleared. After a while, she felt capable of moving her head. She turned it and saw a stranger wearing a long, dark brown robe that reached to the floor. His face reminded her of someone, but she couldn't recall whom. It was a young-looking face, almost childlike, despite the person's tall stature. When the stranger saw Con was looking his way, he smiled at her kindly. "Rest and save your strength," he said.

The room was warm, and Con saw a small, glowing cube levitating a few inches above the stove. The heat seemed to be coming from its direction.

"Who are you?" asked Con weakly.

"We will talk about that when you are stronger," said the man. "All you need to know now is I am here to help you."

"If you want to help me, then bury my child."

"I will."

"Bury him next to Rick," mumbled Con.

The man leaned over and pressed something against the back of Con's neck. Immediately, a pleasant tingling spread throughout her body, accompanied by irresistible drowsiness. As a hand stroked her brow, Con drifted off to sleep.

WHEN CON AWOKE, her hands and feet itched. Her hands were covered by what seemed to be gloves made from a gel-like substance. Her feet felt similarly covered. When she tried to peel the gloves off, someone said, "Leave them on, they are healing your frostbite."

Con turned in the direction of the voice and saw a strange *Homo perfectus* seated in a chair. He smiled at her.

"Who are you?" asked Con.

"Do not be frightened," he said. "I have been taking care of you."

"Yes," said Con slowly. She glanced at the table. "I remember, now. You buried Joey."

"Next to your husband."

Con tried to get up. "I want to see his grave."

"You have no boots. Let me carry you." The man wrapped

Con in the quilt and lifted her as easily as he might a child.
Then he carried her to the side of the cabin. Cradled in
his arms, Con peered about. A large circle had been melted
in the snow. Though drifts had begun to fill the cavity, Con
could still see two graves—Rick's and a miniature version
for Joey. Tears blurred Con's vision. "Bless you," she said
between sobs. "Bless you."

The man carried Con back into the cabin and laid her on
the bed. "You must be wondering who I am," he said, "and,
perhaps, you are frightened also. Others of my species
have not treated you well."

"You're from the future. You're a *Homo perfectus*."

"Correct, though 'Kynden' is the term I prefer."

"I know what you are, but not who you are," said Con.

"A friend of yours called me Sam."

"You mean Joe? Joe said you were dead."

Sam smiled. "Luckily for you, I am not."

"But why are you here?"

"I am going to tell you something that will be hard to
believe, but if you think about it, you will know it is true."

"What?"

"We have had this conversation before, in other circumstances."

"I don't remember. Was I out of my head?"

"You do not remember because we spoke in your office.
You were running the Clements Mining Company. It was a
different reality."

Con simply stared at Sam.

"You were wealthy," continued Sam. "Your husband
and your son were alive. Your life was unfolding as you
knew it should. You were sent to this century to live that
life so the future would not be altered."

Con answered Sam only with silent tears.

"You had a secretary, his name was Matthew Tompkin.
He is not your secretary now. When your husband was
murdered, his reality was changed also. The difference
between you and him is he will never—can never—know
his life should be different. Your husband's murder
affected countless lives and changed history, but only you,

I, and the persons who killed him know reality has deviated from its natural path. Think. You know I am right. Do you believe me?"

Con nodded. "Why?" she asked. "Why did they do this to me?"

"They did not do it to you, they did it to history. Your life—your tragedy—was not a consideration. They were only concerned with twisting the future more to their liking."

"Why are you telling me this? Rick's dead. Joey's dead. It doesn't matter if Rick was killed for his gold or to change history. He's still dead."

"He is dead in *this* reality," said Sam. "Yet now you know reality can be changed."

A glimmer of hope came to Con's face. "You could undo Rick's murder?"

"With your help, I believe we can get reality back to where it should be."

"I think I know where he was shot. Maybe you could go back in time and somehow . . ."

"I am afraid it will not be that simple."

Con's look of hope dimmed.

"The true cause of your husband's death lies in the future. Time travelers murdered him. We will have to change their past to prevent them from traveling back in time to change yours."

Con sighed. "It sounds complicated."

"You want to see your husband and child again, do you not?"

Con's eyes welled with tears. "I'd do anything for them."

Sam smiled. "Of course you would."

4

SAM HANDED CON A VIAL OF LIQUID. "DRINK THIS," HE said. "It will give you energy, though it cannot treat your starvation. For that, we must go someplace safer than here."

"Safer? What do you mean?"

"The people who altered your reality know where you are, in both time and space. I would like to take you downwhen beyond their reach."

"Downwhen?"

"You remember—a destination in the past, the opposite of 'upwhen.' I have a secure base far downwhen. Will you come with me?"

"Sure," said Con, and she started to rise.

"I will carry you."

"I'm not a baby."

"You are still as weak as one."

Con realized it was true. With a sigh, she lowered herself. She had gone to bed wearing every article of clothing she owned, and now her wasted body felt like loose bones in the bundle of rags.

"Are you ready to leave?" asked Sam.

Con looked about her home and suddenly felt melancholy. "I guess so."

Sam gently wrapped Con in the quilt and effortlessly lifted her. When he carried her past the two forlorn graves, he briefly halted. "When you return to this time, these will be gone, for your husband and child will be alive." Then he resumed walking toward the snowy foothills that loomed over the tiny cabin.

* * *

CON DOZED OFF as Sam carried her, and, when she awoke, they were in a box canyon several miles from her home. A time machine stood there on three slender legs. Like the one Peter Green had stolen, it was the perfect image of a flying saucer, except for the black, energy-absorbent panels that covered its upper surface. Upon their approach, a section of the machine's underside fell to the ground like a broad metallic ribbon and transformed into a stairway. Sam carried Con into a hemispherical cabin and set her upon one of the seats inside.

Having been in a time machine before, Con found most of her surroundings familiar. Her seat was one of several that faced a thick, transparent column in the center of the cabin. Within the column glowed a shimmering, immaterial cylinder. Looking at it began to give Con a headache, and she turned her gaze elsewhere. A pilot's console, covered with controls and gauges, faced the cabin wall. The viewscreen before it displayed charts and images of bewildering complexity. The other viewscreens on the cabin walls resembled windows and presented clear images of the canyon outside.

Sam sat behind the controls and began pressing buttons and flicking switches. The sides of Con's seat gripped her; then the viewscreens indicated they were rising. The screens shifted their perspective to show the snow-covered landscape below. Con watched the hills diminish as the time machine ascended. When it halted, even the mountains seemed tiny. She braced herself for what would happen next.

Con had been conscious only on the downwhen portion of her previous voyage through time. That journey had been impossible to remember, except for the terrifying sensation of falling. When glowing tendrils arched into the cabin from the transparent column, Con experienced the nightmare anew. The dazzling entities removed everything they contacted from the realm of the present. When they touched her limbs, she felt as if they had been painlessly amputated. As Con was engulfed, solidity became an illusion, and everything—including her—dissolved into chaos. As before, it was impossible to determine how long the ordeal lasted. Only when Con felt her trembling hands gripping the sides of her seat, did she know the journey was over.

The viewscreens revealed only featureless gray until the time machine descended below the clouds, and Con beheld the surface of a rain-swept sea. They were flying low enough for her to see the foam of the breaking waves. Curtains of rain obscured the horizon, and they were quite near the island before it became visible. Con immediately recognized the rocky mesa that towered over the sea. It was the site of Peter Green's ill-fated resort in North America's Interior Seaway. "Montana Isle!" she exclaimed. She was immediately gripped by conflicting memories of happiness and terror. "Are we back in the Cretaceous?"

"The Cretaceous Period is over. More than a century has passed since the meteor struck."

"So, there are no dinosaurs now?"

"Both the land and sea are virtually empty."

"But the people from the future . . ."

"Have forgotten this place exists," said Sam with such confidence that Con did not continue her question. Instead, she turned her attention to their destination looming in the rain. The tiny, rocky island was not exactly as she recalled it. There was greenery around the mesa that rose in its center, but there were no trees. Con suspected the sea had become shallower, for the beaches extended much farther out than they had before. The time machine settled in a circular landing site and the solid floor of its cabin lowered to become a stairway. Warm, humid air filled the cabin. Sam rose as Con's seat released her. He hoisted her into his arms.

"I am afraid you will get wet, but there are fresh, dry clothes for you."

"I'll be fine," said Con.

Sam exited the time machine into a heavy rainstorm. The large drops that pelted Con felt pleasantly warm. Sam ran quickly down the path, but by the time they reached the shelter of a room carved in the base of the cliff, Con was thoroughly soaked. The room they entered was exactly as Con remembered it. It was carved out of the living rock, with an open colonnade facing the outdoors. The room's only furnishing was a platform that served as a bed. There were two smaller rooms carved farther into the cliff, each with a separate entrance at the rear of the main chamber. Con recalled one was a bathroom, with all its fixtures carved out of stone. The other had served as a dressing room during Con's prior visit. Since Sam had placed her on the bed, she could not see what function the former dressing room served now. She did, however, catch a glimpse of the door in that room that led to a complex of chambers carved deep inside the mesa.

Through that door emerged a *Homo perfectus* woman who smiled at Con as soon as she saw her. She wore a light blue sleeveless robe that reached to the middle of her thighs and a pair of simple translucent sandals. The robe was made of a shimmering material that reminded Con of satin. The woman approached Sam, and they pressed foreheads so their metallic dots made contact. Con had witnessed such behavior before and knew the two had communicated. The woman's smile became tinged with sympathy.

Sam said to Con, "This is my daughter, Katulumamana," speaking the name like a rapidly sung tune.

Con felt awkward, but managed a smile. "I can't possibly pronounce your real name. Would you mind if I called you Kat?"

"Of course not," replied the woman.

Con looked at Kat with interest. She had her father's light tan skin, black hair, and dark, almond-shaped eyes. Like him, she resembled a prepubescent child enlarged to the size of a six-and-a-half foot adult. Con remembered Rick's theory that genetic engineering had produced a species whose adults retained juvenile characteristics. *He called it "neoteny,"* she recalled. Certainly, Kat's body betrayed no hints of the curves Con associated with womanhood. Instead, it had the muscular grace of a child gymnast.

Kat looked at Con with interest also, and Con was suddenly self-conscious about her apparel. She had lived in the same clothes for weeks—a filthy coat, a ratty sweater, a long dress, and two chemises over jeans and wool stockings. Her garments were filthy, and they smelled. Now, they were soaked also. Con felt like a derelict.

Kat said something to Sam in their language, and he departed. "You have suffered greatly," Kat said, "but I will nurse you back to health."

"Then what will happen?" asked Con. "What am I supposed to do?"

"Do not concern yourself with anything but getting well," replied Kat. "Take things one step at a time."

"All right," Con said listlessly. "I'm so tired."

"Of course you are," cooed Kat. "You are frail, and time travel is always exhausting. I will take off your wet, dirty clothes and wash you."

Con felt embarrassed to be undressed like an infant, but she did not protest. When she was completely naked, the sight of her emaciated body shocked her. Her once firm muscles looked like ropes beneath her sagging skin. Her ribs stood in high relief, as did all of her bones.

Kat gently, almost tenderly, examined Con's skeletal body. "This is the result of your accelerated metabolism," she said. "It is a genetic modification unique to your era."

"My parents arranged it so I could eat all I wanted and still stay thin."

"That was ill-advised," said Kat.

Con did not respond, for extreme exhaustion had rendered her completely passive. Kat carried her like a helpless baby into the bathroom to wash her. Slumped in warm water as weeks of grime were gently scrubbed away, Con was overwhelmed with gratitude toward Kat. For the first time since Rick had been murdered, she felt nurtured and protected. Kat lifted her from the tub, dried her, and dressed her in a short robe similar to her own. Then she laid Con upon the bed.

"Since restoring your muscle tissue is painful," said Kat, "I will render you unconscious."

"Okay," said Con.

"Soon, you will be whole again."

"I'll only be whole when I'm with Rick and Joey."

Kat simply smiled and pressed a device to Con's neck that sent her into carefree oblivion.

5

CON SLOWLY DRIFTED AWAKE. EVEN WHEN SHE WAS fully conscious, she hesitated before opening her eyes, for she dreaded seeing her skeletal figure. When she finally looked at herself, she discovered that her body was restored to health. A puncture on her inner elbow was the only evidence of her treatment, other than a complete recovery. The sight of smooth flesh, intact hands and feet, and sleek muscles filled her with an animal joy. She bounded out of bed, delighting in her renewed vitality. Con danced about the room. It was easy to move again. There was no pain or effort in it.

Beyond the colonnade, the sun was low in the rosy morning sky. A breeze rustled the ferns that were the only vegetation. Con stepped outside, passing through an invisible barrier to discover that the air was warm and humid. Memories of Montana's gnawing cold made the mildness of the new day even more special. Con luxuriated in the touch of the breeze upon her skin and the feel of soft earth beneath her bare feet. There were two other rooms carved in the base of the cliff, but both were empty. For the present,

Con seemed to have the island to herself. She wondered if she should go looking for someone, but the attraction of the morning proved too strong. She had been anticipating a frigid death, so this moment felt too precious not to savor.

As Con walked toward the sea, she noted that the air smelled almost sterile. The ferns lent a faint vegetative scent; otherwise, the breeze carried only the smell of salt and weathered rock. The rich fragrance of life, which had been so appealing on Con's first visit to the island, was absent. There were no birds or pterosaurs calling. No insects buzzed about. The only life visible was the monotonous expanse of ferns. For the first time, the magnitude of the Cretaceous extinction hit her. She reached the low cliff where she had viewed a seashore for the first time. The beach, which had once been narrow, now sloped over a quarter of a mile to the water. Con clambered down the rocks to walk to the surf. The pale gray sand she traveled over was almost devoid of shells. The few she found were fragmentary and worn.

When Con reached the shoreline, she shed her garments and waded into the water, confident it was empty of monsters. The sea was as warm as a tepid bath. When the water reached her waist, Con dived into it and swam farther out. She saw nothing swimming or crawling in the clear depths. Con swam until she began to worry she might be missed. She returned to the beach, where she dried in the sun and dressed.

Con slowly headed back, considering her situation as she went. Her initial exuberance calmed and concerns invaded her thoughts. When Con had agreed to come downwhen, she had been frail and helpless. Now that she was healthy, she questioned that choice. The idea of snatching Rick and Joey from death seemed too good to be true, and it seemed likely she had been saved for other purposes. Nevertheless, Con felt beyond coercion. *I've already lost everything but my life,* she told herself. Having once been resigned to death, that prospect held little terror. Con paused on the empty beach to ponder her options. There were really only two—she could be governed by hope or by doubt. At the moment, she couldn't decide which was stronger.

KAT WAS WAITING in the room when Con entered. She looked at Con's wet hair and smiled. "You have been swimming."

"Yes," said Con. "I hope you weren't worried."

"I was not. This place is dull, but safe," said Kat. "How are you feeling?"

"Fine."

"Do you have an appetite?"

Con smiled. "I'm always hungry."

"The result of your genetic 'enhancements,' no doubt."

"Yeah. In the twenty-first century, they called it being 'souped.' It was just catching on then."

"I know," said Kat. "I have studied your century extensively."

"So you're a paleontologist?"

"No," said Kat. "Why would you think that?"

"The last time I met someone like you, that's what she called herself."

"Someone like me? Who?" asked Kat.

"A woman who was a *Homo perfectus,* like you. She said *Homo sapiens* were extinct."

"You must have imagined it," said Kat. "Starving people are often delusional."

"It happened before I went to the nineteenth century," said Con. "I've been here before. After the meteor hit the earth, I was a prisoner on this island. That woman was one of my captors. Didn't your father tell you?"

Kat stared at Con in puzzlement. "*Homo sapiens* are not extinct," she said.

"Your father said others are altering history," said Con. "Perhaps our extinction was their doing."

"That must be it," said Kat.

"Up to now, I always assumed we were just pushed aside. After all, with those computer things in your brains, you're more advanced than we are."

"Computer things? What do you mean?"

"You know, the dot on your forehead that allows you to download stuff."

"You mean my implant?" asked Kat. "All the species have those. You will get one, yourself."

Con paled. "Your father never mentioned surgery!"

"How could you expect to learn all you will need to know?"

"There are ways to learn without changing my brain!"

"It won't change your brain," said Kat. "Getting an implant is a minor procedure. After your training is over, we will hide it."

Con shook her head. "I don't know . . ."

"It is absolutely necessary. You will have to learn new customs, a new language, and new skills. You can only do that with an implant."

Con sighed. "So if I want to save Rick and Joey, I have to get a dot like yours?"

"Yes," said Kat.

When Con did not respond, Kat did not push the point. Instead, she opened a box she was carrying to reveal a flask of liquid and an assortment of variously colored cubes. "Would you like some nourishment?"

"I thought you'd never ask."

Kat handed the box to Con, who wolfed down its contents. All the cubes had a texture that resembled firm tofu. They varied in color and flavor, but the range was limited. Though the meal was less than gourmet, it was filling. Con turned to Kat when she finished and asked, "When do I meet everyone else?"

"There is no one else to meet. Only Father and I live here."

"Just you two? How can two people change history?"

"I collect data that Father uses to calculate the critical events. It only takes one more person to effect the change."

"Me?"

"Yes. You will be our instrument."

"So you want to use me, not help me."

An injured look crossed Kat's face. "I am not uncaring."

"I'm sorry if I sound suspicious," said Con, "but I've been through a lot."

"I understand," said Kat. "I, too, have suffered privations. Thirty-seven years of isolation."

"Thirty-seven years! But you look so young."

"From your perspective, I imagine that is true."

"What have you been doing all that time?"

"Collecting data and waiting."

"Waiting for what?"

"For you."

Con studied Kat's face for some sign she was joking, but found none. "I just turned twenty," she said. "How could you wait for me thirty-seven years?"

"You must think about time differently if you wish to understand," replied Kat. "In day-to-day living, we experience our existence only in the instant we call the present. The future and the past are abstractions. In truth, they have as much reality as the present."

"So, at this moment, I'm also a little girl in the twenty-first century."

"That was true before your husband was killed. Since he was also your great-great-great-grandfather, the girl you were no longer exists. Her ancestor was eliminated."

"You've lost me," said Con. "How can I be here if my childhood has been wiped out?"

"You were downwhen from the change, and therefore not affected by it. The past changes the future, not the reverse."

"If I have no childhood, why do I still remember being a child?"

"Your memories are part of your brain," said Kat. "They traveled with you back in time."

"So I'm here, and yet I was never born? What you say isn't logical."

"Logic only goes so far in understanding the universe."

"Okay, so my childhood's gone. How much of me still exists?" asked Con.

"Everything downwhen from the time my father rescued you."

"So I could go back in time and visit myself during my first trip to this island?"

"No," said Kat, "Temporal Mechanics would prevent you from encountering yourself."

"If you say so," said Con with a shrug. "But how can I be my own ancestor?"

"It is not that complicated. You took a trip downwhen and returned to a time earlier than the one you departed. You had many descendents. One of them was a person who also traveled back in time—you."

"You make it sound normal."

"Simple, perhaps," said Kat. "I would hardly call it normal."

"So if you restore the timestream, won't I be the first thing to go?"

"Your paradoxical existence does not concern Father."

"So what does?" asked Con.

"The purposeful distortion of history. That is what must be stopped."

"How?"

"Father has been working on that problem for decades," said Kat. "Now, he has found the critical event."

"The one I'm supposed to change?"

"Yes."

"What is it?" asked Con.

"Father knows. I just provide the data."

Kat's answer seemed evasive to Con and made her uneasy. She stared out at the empty landscape beyond the colonnade, wondering why she was there.

"Are you having second thoughts?" Kat asked.

"Who wouldn't!" said Con. "I want to stop my husband's murder, not change all of history."

"I know it is a big decision. You need not hurry to make it."

"If you've been waiting for thirty-seven years, you must expect me to say yes."

"It is still your choice," said Kat.

"What if I decide not to help you?"

"We will return you to the future."

"The twenty-first century?"

"You no longer have a place in the twenty-first century," Kat said.

"Or the nineteenth either," said Con, with a sigh. "All because someone shot Rick. It only took one bullet to destroy my world."

"Would you tell me about your husband?" asked Kat.

"How can I explain Rick to you? Your species doesn't fall in love, at least not in the way we do. You go into . . ." Con stopped herself from using the word "heat" and tried to think of a more acceptable term. ". . . into that . . . that condition only periodically."

"You mean love is like the Ripening?" asked Kat. "How could anyone tolerate those emotions all the time?"

Con noticed Kat was blushing furiously. "Perhaps I made the wrong comparison. The last time I talked to a woman like you, she was vague about such feelings."

"I am shocked she discussed them at all," replied Kat.

Con was surprised by Kat's reaction and decided to proceed delicately. "Love is a bond between a man and a woman. There are urges involved, but it is more than that. Being with Rick made me feel complete. He cared for me and protected me. I could be myself with him. We talked together, worked together, dreamed together. Our son tied us even closer. And now that part of me has been ripped away. I . . . I can't . . ." Con slumped her head, as tears rolled down her cheeks.

Kat spoke softly. "This love sounds like a very fine thing. I can see how it would be hard to lose."

When Con lay dying in the cabin, she had lacked the strength to mourn. Now her sorrow burst forth with such force, she became oblivious to everything except her emptiness and grief. She did not notice that Kat appeared unsurprised by her reaction. Kat watched Con sob awhile before leaving her to cry alone.

Con wept until her tears were spent, and her sobs diminished to hoarse shudders. When she rose at last to

wash her puffy eyes, she felt drained of all emotion except
the fierce need to be with Rick and Joey. With the same
decisiveness she had displayed as a businesswoman in a
different reality, Con made up her mind. She swept aside
all her doubts and resolved to regain her loved ones. The
risks did not intimidate her, even if it meant submitting to
surgery or transforming the world. Con was ready to do
whatever was necessary.

6

CON WAS UNWILLING TO WAIT FOR KAT'S RETURN, SO
she went searching for her and Sam. She passed through
the doorway in the former dressing room into a curved
hallway carved into the rock. Con had been there before
and knew the way. After walking a short distance, she
encountered openings to side chambers. The first was filled
with machinery that operated the facility's utilities. The
rest appeared to be for personal use. These austerely fur-
nished rooms were obviously where Kat and her father
lived. They were unoccupied, and Con proceeded down the
hallway. It terminated in a large chamber that had served as
an observatory during the meteor strike.

Upon entering the room, Con saw it had been transformed. Most of the viewscreens that had formerly covered
the walls were gone. Those that remained displayed complex images similar to those at the controls of the time
machine. The floor, which had formerly been clear, was
now crowded with large, intricately shaped objects. Some
of them almost touched the high ceiling. Con could see
neither Kat nor Sam, but she could hear them conversing in
their rapid, tonal language.

"Sam?" called out Con.

Sam emerged from behind one of the large objects. "Yes?" he said.

"I'm ready to help you."

"Good," he replied, appearing unsurprised.

"What will I have to do?"

"You will take someone's place for a while."

"How can I do that?"

"You will find it easy when the time comes," said Sam.

"So, when do I start?"

Sam spoke in his language and Kat emerged from the maze of objects. "You could get your implant today," she said.

"No point in waiting," replied Con.

"Good," said Kat. "We will proceed shortly."

Con looked around her. "So this is where you do your research?"

"Yes," Kat replied.

As she spoke, a flash of light briefly illuminated the room. Con looked up and saw that its source was a tiny point that still glowed against the dark stone ceiling. It faded quickly to a dull red, then extinguished. "That was a miniprobe," said Kat, in response to Con's puzzled look.

"Do you mean a miniature time machine?" asked Con.

"Precisely. I use them to gather data."

"Could I see one?"

Kat went over to a large, rectangular apparatus and pressed a button. A sphere the size of a pea rolled into a tray. She handed it to Con.

Con examined the tiny device. It was smooth and translucent, with an interior filled with intricate, shifting patterns. "It looks more like a gemstone than a machine."

Kat pressed some more buttons on the apparatus, and the sphere appeared to transform into a housefly, though it remained spherical to the touch. Con stared at the device in amazement as she tried to reconcile the conflicting sensations.

"It can assume other guises, also," said Kat. "The insect form is the most intricate." She pressed another button and the "fly" became a sphere again. As Con handed it back to Kat, she noted that Sam was staring at them. Kat became aware of her father's gaze also and suddenly grew subdued. "I must get to work," she muttered. Then she fixed her attention on one of the other devices around her.

Con retreated to her room to wait for Kat. After an hour, Kat entered carrying a small case. Con eyed it apprehensively. "Is that for my surgery?"

"I would hardly call it surgery."

"Then how will you get that implant inside my head?"

"The hole in your skull will be microscopic," assured Kat. "The implant flows through it, then forms along the inside of your skull."

"Will I be conscious?"

"No."

"So it won't hurt?"

"You will get a headache as the connections are established. I am afraid that is unavoidable."

"And in your time, people like me have these things?"

"All the human species do," replied Kat.

"All the species? How many are there?"

"Only three."

Con, trying to distract herself from the impending implantation, asked, "Your father said you call yourselves Kyndens. What are the others called?"

"You are called Sapenes," said Kat. "The others call themselves Gaians."

"What's it like living with different humans?"

"I do not know," said Kat. "I had a sheltered childhood, and Father took me downwhen at a young age. My knowledge about the other species is purely academic."

"So I'm the first Sapene you've met?"

"Yes."

Con smiled self-consciously. "What do you think?"

"It has been an instructive experience."

Kat's response disappointed Con, but nevertheless she replied, "I'm glad I met you and your father; otherwise, I would have thought all Kyndens were cold and arrogant."

Kat smiled. "I am glad you feel that way."

"What surprised you the most about me?"

"You are so changed," said Kat. "It took a while to adjust."

"Changed? What do you mean?"

" 'Changed' is the wrong word," said Kat quickly. "I meant 'different.' Your body is different."

Con regarded Kat and thought she appeared flustered.

"We should proceed with the implantation," said Kat, quickly opening the case to take out a cylindrical instrument. "Please lie down."

Con complied.

"I will make you sleep now," said Kat. "When you awake, the procedure will be completed." She pressed the instrument to Con's neck, causing a pleasant tingling as the room faded into darkness.

CON AWOKE ALONE with an aching head. She was facing the ceiling, which glowed dimly. Her fingers immediately went to her forehead and gingerly touched it. There was a spot that felt smooth and metallic. Although woozy, Con rose to look at herself in the bathroom mirror. Its reflection revealed a quarter-inch circle above her nose about two inches from her eyebrows. It was a light, silvery blue. Con touched it again. She could feel no edge; only a difference in texture indicated where her skin ended and the circle began.

Her pain began to increase, but Kat's remark that headaches were "unavoidable" discouraged Con from seeking help. Also, she thought Kat was likely asleep. "I'll tough it out alone," said Con to herself. The pain made her restless, and she wandered outside into the night. Humid air flowed over her like warm syrup as she moved slowly through the shadowy ferns toward the sea. Con reached the surf and waded into the warm water up to her ankles.

Nothing eased the pain inside her head. Soon it exploded in sharp bursts, like strings of firecrackers. The firecrackers became fireworks, and in her agony, Con feared her head would explode. She fell to her hands and knees and vomited into the surf. She crumpled further and, for a panicked moment, feared she would drown in inches of water. Somehow, she managed to roll on her back. Then she lay still, paralyzed by the searing chaos in her mind.

Ever so slowly, the pain subsided. Con crawled out of the water and collapsed again. She lay with her face on wet sand, steeling herself for more torment. Exhaustion came instead, and Con gratefully slipped into oblivion.

SOMEONE WAS GENTLY stroking Con's shoulder. She opened her eyes to the bright light of morning. One side of her face felt raw. "Oh God," she moaned, "what a night." She turned her head and saw Kat kneeling next to her. Her expression was filled with concern, and her eyes were moist with tears.

"Are you all right?" asked Kat.

Con rubbed the sand from her face. "I guess so. My headache's gone."

"After you eat and wash, we will test your implant."

As Con approached her room, she watched the tenderness fade from her companion's face. By the time they reached the colonnade, Kat's emotions were masked, though Con thought she detected a hint of nervousness. The transformation puzzled Con, but she decided not to mention it. Instead, she said, "I thought I'd feel smarter."

"The implant is basically a data transmission and storage device," Kat replied. "It does not make you more intelligent."

"So people from the future don't have computer brains?"

"No," said Kat, "just very good memories."

"So my implant's empty?"

"For the moment," said Kat.

THERE WAS FOOD waiting in the room. Kat left Con alone to freshen up and eat. Naturally, Con ate before bathing. She emerged from the bath to find fresh clothes. Kat entered the room precisely after Con dressed, making her wonder if she was being monitored.

"I would like to test your implant now," said Kat. She took a cylindrical device from her pocket and touched it to Con's metallic dot, then her own. She smiled. "The implantation was successful."

"What's next?" asked Con.

"You must learn how to use your implant."

Kat touched Con's dot again with the device, and Con experienced the impression that a thought had arisen at the edge of her awareness. Through a series of mental exercises, Kat trained Con to access such thoughts. At first, the training was dull and tedious, but as the session progressed it became more interesting. By the late afternoon, Con was not only able to acquire knowledge rapidly, but physical skills as well. As dinner approached, Con learned a new language called "Norto," which sounded like a blend of English and Spanish. She assimilated its vocabulary and grammar instantly, and after taking a moment to practice the tongue roll, she spoke it fluently.

"Wow!" exclaimed Con. "It took me years to learn French and Italian."

"So, was the implant worth a headache?" asked Kat.

"I'll say!"

Kat smiled. "I am glad you are pleased. One more download, and we will stop for the day." She touched Con's dot with the device. "Now, tell me about your upwhen destination."

"The year is 2693," said Con. "I will arrive on Febre 30."

"Where?"

"El Confederation del Norte," answered Con.

"Describe it."

"El Confederation includes the former United States, Mexico, West Canada, and Quebec. Its government is weak. Transnational corporations wield the real power."

"Where will you live?"

"Outside Chicago."

"Give me some facts about the society," said Kat.

"Genetic engineering has altered the biosphere, but there is still only one species of humans. Time travel is considered possible, but impractical. Global warming has transformed the climate. Experimental implants have just been invented. Women are considered . . ."

"That is enough," said Kat. "You could go on for hours. So now you know where you are going. Tell me—*who* will you be when you arrive?"

"Ramona Eberlade," replied Con. She looked confused. "Who's she?"

"An actual twenty-seventh-century woman," said Kat. "After tomorrow, for all practical purposes, she will be you."

7

AFTER A SOLITARY DINNER, CON LEFT HER ROOM TO wander the island. The sun was setting behind the mountains on the mainland, and she stood on the beach to watch it go down. It stirred idyllic memories of watching sunsets with Rick their first summer in Montana. She recalled the beauty of the rolling foothills, the pleasant tiredness from working outdoors, and the smell of food cooking on a wood fire. Rick would stand behind her, hugging her with hands clasped above her growing belly. The worries that would plague her later had not yet arisen, and the future held only promise. The recollection made Con ache with loneliness. The absence of Rick's touch produced an emptiness that approached physical pain. It seemed fitting to feel her loss surrounded by a nearly empty world.

Con tried to envision her life in the reality Sam had described, the one where Rick had not been murdered. *It would be wonderful,* she thought. Con was not merely speculating. The stories of her great-great-great-grandmother spoke of a long and happy life. Con had even seen relics from that existence. There were old photos taken of the mansion in Butte before it had been torn down. Con recalled playing house as a child in the well of a beautiful heirloom desk specially ordered by Constance Clements. Once, she had visited an aunt and met an older cousin named Constance Brown, who had shown Con a huge collection of fossil ammonites. They were meticulously labeled and stored in the drawers of wooden cabinets. "Great-great-great-grandfather found these," Constance Brown had said in a voice low with reverence. Con had been very young and thought the fossils were seashells carved from stone until her cousin told her differently. Cousin Constance had shown these things with the same excited gleam in her blue eyes that Con had seen in Rick's. The memory of it made Con even more melancholy.

The bullet that had killed Rick had also wiped out Constance Brown. It swept away Rick's son and buried his fossil collection in an avalanche of change that overturned history. It obliterated Con's childhood, leaving her existence on this empty beach as a tattered remnant, a bit of wreckage washed up on the shores of the sea of time.

SAM ARRIVED IN Con's room the next morning immediately after she awoke. He carried a box of food and a metallic instrument the size of a toaster. The device featured a carrying handle, complex controls, and a short cylinder, which was attached to the device by a cord. "I have brought you nourishment," he said.

"What's the other thing for?" asked Con.

"Yesterday, my daughter spoke to you of a young woman named Ramona Eberlade," replied Sam. "This device contains her memories. They will guide you during your stay in the future."

Con looked at Sam with skeptical astonishment.

"I will explain while you eat," said Sam. "Throughout history there have been a few individuals who made great leaps of understanding—geniuses like Einstein, Newton, and Eckmair. Ramona Eberlade was such a person, and that is why she was eliminated."

Con swallowed a bite of a cube that tasted vaguely like
cantaloupe. "And that caused Rick's murder?"

"That single alteration to the timestream caused an
ever-expanding set of consequences. One of them was
your husband's death."

When Con shook her head, clearly dubious, Sam added,
"This conclusion is the result of years of study. I cannot
begin to explain it to you." His voice became gentle. "It is
not easy to possess trust and hope after what you have
lived through."

Con sighed. "It's hard."

"Of course it is," replied Sam.

"So how did you acquire this woman's memories?"

"In the time I come from, it is possible to download a
person's brain activity."

"You mean Ramona's brain is inside that box?" asked
Con.

"Only the relevant parts," said Sam.

The idea made Con both uneasy and curious. "How did
you do it? You said she was eliminated."

"Ramona was killed in a faked accident shortly before
she made her discovery," said Sam. "I was able to extract
her memories moments before she was incinerated in a
fusion explosion."

"If you could do that, why didn't you save her instead?"

"It would have betrayed my presence to my adversaries," replied Sam. "I know that sounds callous, but you
have to understand what is at stake. It is nothing less than
the future of the human race."

"Won't they try to eliminate me also?"

"They have returned upwhen, confident they have per-
manently changed reality. When the timestream is restored,
their reality will no longer exist, and they will disappear
with it."

"But even with Ramona's memories, I don't see how
I'll pull this off. They have the means in the future to detect
I'm a fraud."

"It would seem that way," said Sam, "but societies tend to
rely overmuch on their technology. You have downloaded

information about the Personal Identity Code, have you not?"

"Yes," said Con. "It's based on your DNA. Your body chemistry becomes your ID card and your debit card all in one."

"Precisely," said Sam. "The system is immune to tampering in the twenty-seventh century, but I am not from that time. My daughter has already replaced Ramona's information with yours throughout the system. Everywhere you go, you will be accepted as her without question."

Con looked nervously at the device that contained Ramona's memories. "But will I still be myself with her thoughts in my head?"

"They are only memories," replied Sam. "Your personality will remain intact. It will be a little confusing at first, but you should adjust quickly."

"Once I get this girl's memories, will I know what to do?"

"I will also download a set of instructions that will be triggered whenever the circumstances are appropriate. It will be just as though I am talking to you, except my voice will be inside your head."

"I'm not going to become your puppet!" said Con. "I never agreed to that!"

"There is no cause for alarm. These instructions will be no more compelling than I am now. If I were to attempt to control your actions, it would destroy your effectiveness."

"Aren't you afraid I'll let you down?"

"You know what is at stake," replied Sam. "I trust you to do the right thing."

Con quickly finished the last of her bland breakfast while Sam watched. When she was done, she said, "Well, I guess I'm as ready as I'll ever be."

"Then we will start," said Sam.

Con nervously watched as Sam turned on the device. He asked her to lie down. Then he touched her dot with the cylinder from the instrument while he monitored its displays. After several minutes, he pulled the cylinder away and said, "We are finished."

Con remained lying on the bed, her eyes rolling dizzily.

It took a while before she slowly sat up and peered about the room. When she did so, her eyes widened in terror. "My God! Where am I?" she cried in Norto. When she saw Sam, she started back. "Who the hell are you?"

Sam seized Con's arm to keep her from bolting away. As she struggled in his firm grip, he said, "You are Constance Clements. You know who I am and where you are."

Con stopped struggling and a confused expression came to her face. "I . . . I'm Con. My friends call me Con."

"I am one of them. What is my name?"

Con began to struggle again. "No! No! I should be . . ." She grew passive. "You're Sam."

"I just gave you a new set of memories."

Con slumped down on the bed with Sam still grasping her arm, though he gripped her more gently now. "I don't know if . . ." Con tensed, then relaxed again. ". . . don't know if I can sort this out."

"The brain is a remarkable organ," said Sam. "You will soon be able to distinguish Ramona's memories from your own. Unfortunately, I cannot assist you in that process."

Con tensed again. "Why the hell am I here?" she shouted in Norto.

"You know why," said Sam calmly. "You remember."

"Yes, I . . . I do," replied Con in English. "How long will this go on?"

"I do not know," said Sam. "Not long, I hope."

"Are you going to leave me?"

"There is no point in my staying," said Sam. "All I can do is confine you to this room so you will not injure yourself." Sam spoke a few words in his language, and an immaterial, translucent plane bridged all the openings in the colonnade. It swirled with colors, like an oil slick on a puddle.

The colors stirred up Con's memories of her captivity on the island and sent shivers down her spine. "Is a pain barrier really necessary?"

"If you think you are Ramona, you might do something rash. This is only for your protection." Sam released Con from his grasp and exited the room. After he departed, a silvery panel sealed the doorway that led into the interior of the mesa. Con was alone and yet not alone. There was only one body on the bed, but there were two people within it.

CON EXPERIENCED THE truth of the saying that life consists only of the present instant and memory. Her memories included a childhood that had been erased from history. Now, they also recalled a life that had ended. Both sets of recollections seemed equally real. Con was certain she had eaten two breakfasts this morning—a bland one in this room and another in a hotel restaurant. The latter breakfast of rich black coffee, an omelet with chorizo, and corn bread had been much tastier. The waiter who served it had been cute, and she had flirted with him and talked about her new job. It was her first since graduating from the university. She was excited about it.

At times, Con was fully aware of all that had happened to her, and at other times she was only Ramona. As Ramona, she was frightened and confused by the abrupt transformation of her world. In that persona, she approached the swirling colors between two columns and felt a searing jolt of pain. She fled weeping to the bed, then realized she was Con.

Slowly, in ways she did not understand, Con began to sort the memories of two lives. She became able to distinguish between them as one might recall separate vacations or the lies told to different friends. Eventually, she felt capable of looking at herself in the mirror. It was still a shock, and something within her felt that the face peering back was wrong. Con controlled that feeling as she compared her face with the one in Ramona's memory. They were remarkably alike. With the advent of the DNA-based Personal Identification Code, no one was identified by his or her appearance. Nevertheless, Con was relieved to see that she resembled Ramona. Ramona's hair was a darker brown and cut differently, but her skin was the same shade. Ramona considered her coloring exotic in a world where most of the population had blended to a light brown. Ramona's eyes were close in color to Con's hazel ones, but Con's lips were fuller, and her eyes were larger also. In the twenty-seventh century, Con would be considered pretty. She knew that in the same way she knew what clothes were in fashion, which cigarettes to smoke, what was sexy, and the lyrics to "My Bebe Makes Amor Todos Noche."

In the process of separating Ramona's recollections from her own, Con gained an understanding of the woman whose memories would guide her. Ramona was an orphan who had been on her own for seven years. She had slept with eleven different lovers, none of whom compared favorably to Rick. She was bright, hardworking, and ambitious, but Con could detect no signs of genius. *Maybe I don't know what to look for,* thought Con, *or perhaps, inspiration really comes as a bolt from the blue.* Con saw nothing in Ramona's memories that revealed why she would have a key role in history. If Sam had said Ramona's momentous discovery occurred later in her life, it would have been more understandable. Instead, he stated she died shortly before it took place. Ramona was a newly trained molecular assembler going to an entry-level job in a pharmaceutical corporation. It was hard to see how her death would change the world.

KAT ARRIVED AT dinnertime with food and the same device Sam had used to download Ramona's memories. She used it to ascertain that Con's personality had stabilized before removing the pain barrier and departing. After eating, Con wandered the beach before going to sleep. The next morning she awoke from dreams of unfamiliar people and places to find a set of garments laid out upon the bed. Along with them was a small handbag and a device that Ramona's memories told her was for removing body hair.

The clothes looked strange to Con but familiar to Ramona, who thought them too conservative. Con took the device into the bathroom and used it to vaporize the hair on her legs and armpits. Then she bathed and dressed herself. The underwear looked familiar, but without Ramona's memories, Con would not have known how to don the outer garments. These consisted of a separate top and bottom. Their fabric was woven from genetically engineered cotton that produced elastic, blue fibers. The lower half of the outfit was a pair of skintight shorts that reached Con's knees. A long triangle of cloth was sewn to the back of one of the legs. Con wrapped it around her waist to form a partial skirt. The upper portion of the ensemble resembled a narrow tube top with two, very long, four-inch-wide scarves sewn to the back. Guided by Ramona, Con wrapped these over her shoulders and around her midriff in a complicated crossing pattern. The "scarves" adhered to each other wherever they touched. Con stood before the mirror and carefully adjusted the placement of the wrapped portions of her apparel until she was satisfied. Then she stepped into her shoes. These looked like thick-soled slip-ons made from translucent blue plastic, though they did not feel like plastic on her feet.

The handbag contained no makeup, for in the twenty-seventh century, only men used cosmetics. The bag held a bracelet that kept track of Ramona's finances and could be used to make small purchases, a wristwatch, a package of cigarettes, and a lighter. Con looked at the cigarettes dubiously. She did not smoke, nor did she wish to. Ramona, however, was a smoker. Furthermore, she was going to work for a pharmaceutical corporation where it was both customary and smart to smoke the corporate product.

Kat arrived the moment Con was dressed. She looked at Con with approval. "You look perfect, except for your hair." She set down a box of food. "After you eat, I will take care of that."

"Maybe I'll fit in, but I still don't know what I'm supposed to do."

"You know everything Ramona does," replied Kat.

"That doesn't help," retorted Con. "What does your father expect me to do? It must be more than assembling molecules."

"I am certain he has it all planned."

"Does that mean you don't know either?"

"Father will explain it to you," said Kat, becoming flustered. "I am only here to cut your hair."

Con hurried through her breakfast. Then Kat cut her hair, employing a device similar to the one Con used to shave her legs. Afterward, Con appraised her hairstyle in the mirror. On one side, her hair had been cropped so it only covered half her ear. From that point back, Kat had trimmed Con's locks so they were progressively longer, until they touched her shoulder on the other side. Using Ramona's fashion experience, Con deemed it a satisfactory job.

As Con gazed into the mirror, Sam's reflection appeared next to hers. She turned and saw Sam looking her over. He smiled with approval. "Today is the big day. You must be nervous."

"I'd be less nervous if I knew what I was supposed to do."

"I have kept you ignorant for a purpose," said Sam. "At this point in Ramona Eberlade's life, she has no idea what the future holds for her. You cannot either. It would not be wise to let you anticipate events."

"You mean I'm supposed to do this blind?"

"You have Ramona's memories to assist you," said Sam, "and I will guide you at every critical juncture." As he studied Con's anxious face, his own expression became compassionate. "I realize it will be difficult for you, but this is for your loved ones. Soon, their suffering will be erased. Only you will remember their deaths, and it will make you cherish them even more."

"Can't you tell me anything about what will happen?"

"I can tell you this much," replied Sam. "Ramona was on her way to her first job when the 'accident' happened. I will leave you outside Finoporto, the town where it took place. Ramona's hotel will just have been destroyed. When you enter the town, you will need to contact the authorities. They will assist you. By nightfall, you will have assumed Ramona's place. Once her destiny is fulfilled, you will depart from the future."

"When will that be?"

"That is all you may know."

"Okay," said Con. "If that's the way it must be . . ."

"I am afraid it is."

Kat stood silent throughout the conversation and was staring away when Con looked in her direction. Only after Sam left the room did Kat give Con an impulsive hug. She was smiling, though her eyes seemed sad. "Good luck," she said.

CON'S TRIP UPWHEN was as unpleasant as her previous trips through time. When they arrived in the future, it was dusk. Con exited the craft alone. She was on a path surrounded by trees covered by weedy vines. As she looked around, the time machine's stairs retracted. Then, to her astonishment, the craft rose into the sky and disappeared. The machine Peter Green had stolen had been incapable of such a feat; it needed days of sunlight to store up enough energy for a return trip. Con had assumed Sam's time machine would remain as a hidden refuge while she accomplished her task. Its departure was totally unexpected.

While Con was recovering from that shock, a second one hit. A loud explosion resounded in the twilight, shaking the trees with its force. The horizon began to glow; then a brilliant fireball ascended into the sky, counterfeiting a sunrise. Con had to shield her eyes from the light's intensity. A stark realization came to her—the actual Ramona Eberlade had just been vaporized within that inferno. All that remained of her resided in Con's brain. *TAKE THE PATH IN THE DIRECTION OF THE FIRE-BALL*, said Sam's voice within Con's mind. Con complied and hiked through the woods, guided by the light of disaster and the memories of a ghost.

8

THREE DAYS LATER, CON WAS IN A BUILDING WITHIN
the sprawling Mergonic Pharmaceutical Corporation's complex, preparing to take a proficiency test. Part of her still felt
overwhelmed by the twenty-seventh century, while another
part—the part governed by Ramona's memories—was
comfortable in her new surroundings. Ramona's knowledge
had enabled her to enter a town in the grip of a major disaster and instantly blend in. She had presented herself to the
authorities, who confirmed her identity and gave her emer-
gency assistance. They had notified her employer of her sur-
vival, provided her with a hotel room, and even credited her
account for her destroyed possessions. As Ramona, Con
had bought a new wardrobe, smoked her first cigarette, and
rebooked transport to work. There, she had checked in and
found herself a small apartment within the corporate complex, which resembled a small, self-sufficient city. Finally,
on her first day at work, she was ready to prove her skills.
    Con waited with the other newly hired assemblers while
the large molecule assembly units, with their complicated
controls and banks of monitors, were readied. The test was
a competition where the best assemblers got first choice
among the open positions. It actually measured aptitude
more than proficiency, for constructing complex organic
molecules was as much an art as it was a science. Judgment
was required to interpret the images on the monitors. It also
came into play in assembling the molecules, for there was
no single way to do it. Experience played an important role
in the process, and the test takers were only expected to
demonstrate basic skills.

Con was set before an assembly machine, given the specifications for a moderately complex protein, and told to demonstrate her talent. As soon as the intricate displays appeared on the monitors, a profound sense of competence came to Con. Ramona had trained on similar machines for several years, but Con's sensation went beyond familiarity. She understood the entire process in all its nuances. The controls seemed extensions of her fingers. The monitors were additional sets of eyes. Con had the impression she had been handed a violin for the first time and played it like Paganini.

Half an hour later, a test proctor came up to Con. "You shouldn't give up so easily," he said. "You still have lots of time left."

"I haven't given up," replied Con. "I'm done."

An indulgent smile came to the proctor's face, but as he examined the monitors, it was replaced by an expression approaching amazement. "Your elapsed time was seventeen minutes!"

"It was only a protein," said Con.

"Still," said the proctor, trying to contain his surprise, "seventeen minutes is good, *very* good. I presume you'll want that position in the Tobacco Division."

For the first time since the explosion, Con heard Sam's voice in her head. *CHOOSE THE RESEARCH DIVISION.*

"Actually," replied Con, "I want the position in Research."

The proctor looked puzzled. "Research? Why waste your talent there? They haven't issued a bonus in years."

"Still, it's my first choice."

The proctor shrugged. "It's your future."

CON WAS ASSIGNED to do general assembly work at the Research Division's main facility. There, she quickly acquired a reputation for aloofness, speed on the assembler, and a voracious appetite. Assuming her stay would be brief, Con focused on her work and waited for a message from Sam. She relied on Ramona's experiences to such an extent she came to feel it was Ramona who actually lived her life.

In reality, her relationship with the woman whose memories guided her was more complex. Though Con wasn't entirely herself, she wasn't Ramona either. Ramona was naturally flirtatious, but Con suppressed those tendencies. She worked late, ate alone in the company cafeteria, and returned to an empty apartment. Ramona hated this existence, but Con didn't care. She was not there to have fun.

A few weeks after Con's arrival, a young man appeared at her workstation, "Senor Peters would like to see you," he said.

"Roberto Peters? The Research Division Manager?"

"The same."

"What does he want with me?"

"You'll find out soon enough. Follow me."

Con anxiously followed the young man, hopeful things were beginning to happen at last. As Ramona, she was also awestruck, for in the twenty-seventh century corporate management had assumed the role of nobility. Its privileges were hereditary and a division manager was like a duke, or even a prince. As Con approached Roberto Peters's office, Ramona's excitement came to dominate her psyche.

The Research Division Manager graciously rose when Con entered. He was elegantly dressed in tight, dark blue shorts with a scarlet codpiece. His shirt was the same shade of scarlet. A dark blue, sleeveless jacket that vaguely resembled a frock coat completed his outfit. Ramona considered him very handsome, though his scarlet lipstick and black eyeliner disconcerted Con. Those scarlet lips were smiling, as were the dark, intense eyes.

"Ramona," said Roberto, "please take a seat."

Con walked over to a chair, very aware of Roberto's gaze. She behaved as Ramona would have and sat in a manner that displayed her legs advantageously.

"I've been monitoring your work," began Roberto, "and have concluded your talents are wasted on general assembly work. I would like you to join my special research team. It will mean a pay increase and more challenging assignments."

"I'm honored, sir," replied Con.

"I'll tell you, right off, a lot of people consider this project a dead end," said Roberto. "They believe the future for Mergonic lies in tobacco or cosmetics. I think we should concentrate our efforts on drugs."

Con knew the maladies that afflicted earlier generations had been cured. The pharmaceutical industry had been a victim of its own success, and Mergonic was the sole remaining drug company. "You're designing new drugs, sir? For what diseases?"

"Actually, we're working on a delivery system."

"Oh," said Con.

"It's an old idea," said Roberto, "but one that might work, now that we can precisely assemble complex molecules. I propose to use viruses as delivery vectors."

"Viruses?"

"Si," said Roberto. "Viruses interact with the body at the cellular level. Usually, they alter a cell's chemistry to produce more viruses. But my idea is to create viruses that would introduce desirable changes in cells. If we succeed, whole populations could be treated by introducing a medically desirable virus. Health would spread like the plagues of olden times."

"That sounds like you'd be giving your drugs away. How could such viruses be profitable?"

Roberto smiled. "Profits are not your concern."

Roberto's answer struck Con as odd, but she did not question him about it. Instead, she changed the subject. "The work sounds very interesting."

"Then you want the position?" asked Roberto.

TAKE THE JOB, echoed Sam's voice in Con's brain.

"Si," said Con.

"Good. You'll be working under Gerald Sanchez," said Roberto. "Report to him, and he'll get you started. Good luck and congratulations."

"Thank you, sir."

Con left the division manager's office and asked the assistant outside where she could find Gerald Sanchez. She was directed to the special projects lab where a guard was positioned at the entrance. "You Eberlade?" he asked.

"Si," said Con. "I'm supposed to see Senor Sanchez."

"Before you enter or leave, I'll have to get a blood sample. It's only a finger prick."

"Is the blood sample because of the viruses?"

"You got it, sweetie," replied the guard. "We can't have you taking your work home. Now give me a finger."

The guard took Con's sample. Then he directed her to where she could be fitted into virus-proof work clothes, which resembled a lightweight space suit. After she was suited up, she was directed to the decontamination room. After decontamination, Con was led to the research lab, where she finally met her new boss. He was a balding, middle-aged man who was studying tissue analyses on a viewscreen when Con entered.

"Senor Sanchez?"

The man turned to regard Con. "Si?"

"I'm Ramona Eberlade, your new assembler."

"So, *you're* the one they call Speedy. Well, viruses are trickier than the stuff you're used to."

"I'll do my best, sir."

"See that you do. This is Peters's pet project, and he's turned up the heat. I hope you don't have a social life."

"Not much of one."

"Good, because you won't have any, now." He turned off the viewscreen. "You'll be working on receptor modifications. I'll get you the specifications."

"What changes are the viruses supposed to induce?"

"You don't need to know. Your job is assembling molecules. Period."

"Si, Senor Sanchez."

"Everything you do is a corporate secret. Do you understand?"

"Si, Senor Sanchez."

"Good." He walked over to a desk, grabbed a data tablet, and handed it to Con. "Here are your specs. Build them and replicate a thousand copies of each. Bring them to me when you're done."

Con took the data tablet over to her work area and studied it. As she looked at the diagrams and notations, she suddenly understood them as thoroughly as if she had studied viruses for decades. *Sam must have implanted this knowledge,* she thought. She quickly spotted errors in Sanchez's designs and knew none of them would succeed. *MODIFY ONE DESIGN SO IT WILL WORK,* said Sam's voice in her head.

Con knew precisely what to do. She rapidly reviewed the seven receptor designs and decided the one that was numbered 53 had the fewest flaws. She corrected them, then assembled and replicated the new design. Afterward, she assembled and replicated the other designs exactly as written. The work wasn't finished until late.

Lying in her bed that night, Con was too excited to sleep.

CON WAS TIRED when Gerald Sanchez dumped a stack of new receptor designs at her workstation the next morning and disappeared into the tissue lab. She stared at the pile of work before her and realized it would be a long day. Unlike yesterday, she had no special insight into the diagrams and notations on the data tablets. They were merely directions she must follow. Con thought her lack of understanding was due to her tiredness.

The next two days were easier because Con went to work rested. She worked efficiently, although her detailed understanding of viruses did not return. She had begun to question the significance of her temporary knowledge, when Gerald Sanchez appeared at her workstation, his face beaming with satisfaction.

"Throw that work away," he said. "It's no longer necessary. You work for a genius!"

"I do?"

"No question about it. It only took me fifty-three tries to get it right."

"You mean receptor number 53 works?" asked Con, trying to sound surprised.

"Perfectly. No need to tell you Peters is very pleased with me. I sniff the scent of a bonus in the air."

"A bonus!" said Con."

"A bonus for *me*," said Gerald. "After all, it was *my* design, but you may take the rest of the day off as a reward."

"Thanks. I could use a break."

"Enjoy it while you can," said her boss. "The next phase will be even harder than the first." Then he strode away.

Con went through the procedures to leave the lab and had just given her blood sample when Roberto Peters's assistant walked up to her. "Senor Peters would like to see you."

"Right now?"

"Si."

Con entered the division manager's office, keenly aware of his eyes on her body. Something about the man awoke Ramona's pent-up flirtatiousness. Surrendering to impulse, Con moved with a sultry grace that was all the more provocative for having been suppressed. Then she flashed Roberto a big smile. "You wanted to see me, sir?"

Roberto Peters tried to hide a grin. "Si," he replied. "I wanted to thank you personally for your contribution."

"I'm honored by your attention," replied Con.

"When you check your account, you'll notice an increase."

"You're giving me a bonus?"

"You may be only an assembler, but I think you deserve one. Just don't mention it to Sanchez."

"He is a little touchy," said Con with a sly smile.

"Si," said Roberto. " 'Touchy' is the word for it."

"Thank you, sir. I won't breathe a word about it."

"Good. Discretion's the best course."

"I'm glad you're pleased with me," said Con in a breathy voice.

"I am," said Roberto. "Very pleased indeed."

CON DECIDED TO spend her afternoon as far away from Mergonic as she could. She visited her apartment only long enough to pack a picnic and order a personal transport vehi-cle. A few minutes later, a small driverless car parked in front of her apartment. Con walked over to it and brushed her hand against its identity reader. The vehicle turned on, and its door opened. Con climbed in. "Take me to the lakeshore," she said. "Use the scenic route."

As the car drove, Con stared pensively out its window at the passing scenery. Her flirtation with Roberto disturbed her. At the time, the impulse had been compelling. Now that compulsion seemed inexplicable, and she felt guilty about it. *Was it Ramona's fault?* she wondered. She knew Ramona was flattered by the manager's attention. She could be acting out of desire, ambition, or both. Still, Con didn't think Ramona could force her to do anything. *She's only a set of memories,* she told herself. *Maybe Sam's behind this, instead.* That idea was ridiculous. *How could flirting change history?* There was another possible explanation—one that justified Con's guilt. *I did it because I haven't been with Rick for months.*

TWO HOURS AFTER Con left Roberto Peters's office, a man with a nervous demeanor entered it and closed the door. "Your boss doesn't know you're here?" asked Roberto.

"I've been careful, sir," said the man as he handed Roberto a data tablet.

When Roberto scanned the tablet, he broke into a grin. "I knew it! Women get that look, and men have recognized it long before blood tests."

"Then why risk testing?" asked the man. "If they find out . . ."

"They won't," assured Roberto. "And soon my friends in Accounting will fix your little problem."

"Thank you, sir."

"A smart manager thinks several moves ahead," said Roberto. "I could have asked her, but that would have betrayed my interest. Why give her that advantage?"

"I should be getting back," said the man.

"We're not done yet," said Roberto. "Now that I know she can conceive, I'll require more information—precise information. It shouldn't be hard, she has blood tests twice a day."

The man bit his lip nervously. "Sir, I'm not sure that's a good idea."

"*I'll* decide that," snapped Roberto, "Just give me what I want. You know how these things work. I'm a manager. She's an employee."

9

THE UNDULATING LANDSCAPE THAT HAD BEEN LAKE Michigan in Con's time was desolate and uninhabited. Its hollows were choked with strange weeds, while the higher areas bore grass already turning brown in the dry winds of Maio. The "scenic route" proved a long one, and it was late afternoon when Con reached what remained of the lake. She had the place to herself. When Con kicked off her shoes and walked to the shore, she discovered why. The air reeked of chemicals, and what appeared to be a sandy beach was actually an encrustation of minerals. As Con walked upon it, her soles began to burn. She retreated to the dry grass for her picnic, wistfully recalling the unspoiled landscapes of Montana. She wolfed down her food, returned to the car, and told it to take the most direct route back.

The return trip was uneventful until Con spotted a car that was behaving strangely. Personal transport vehicles were programmed to drive at prudent speeds, yet this particular car was racing down the highway. As Con watched it approach, she felt certain it was pursuing her. "Go faster," she shouted to her car.

"That is an improper directive," stated the voice from the dashboard.

Con's vehicle maintained a speed that seemed maddeningly slow as the other car drew ever nearer. Soon, she could see its passenger. To her surprise, it was a child so small it could barely peer over the dashboard. The pursuing vehicle braked to avoid a collision, and, for an instant, Con and the child stared at one another from only a few feet away. A floppy hat came halfway down the child's forehead, emphasizing the eyes. They bored into Con with chilling enmity.

Con's pursuer slowed down, and the distance between them increased. Then a green light flashed, and the hum of the motor in Con's vehicle ceased. Con turned around to see that all the displays on the dashboard were blank. "Give me vehicle status!" she shouted.

Con's directive was met by silence. Her car drifted from its lane and she watched in helpless terror as it moved into oncoming traffic. Several vehicles swerved out of her way before she left the road. When the car hit rough terrain, its interior filled with white foam that hardened almost instantly. Trapped in the substance's gentle but firm embrace, Con felt the car become airborne, slam to earth, and roll several times before it came to rest on its side. After about thirty seconds, the material that enveloped her softened until it was no more substantial than soapsuds. The billows of foam blinded Con as she wildly groped for the door handle. Eventually, she found it and pushed the door open.

Spotting two vehicles halted by the roadside, Con hid among the weeds. She was crawling away from the wreck when she heard the sound of running feet. Con whirled about, prepared to make a desperate defense.

A woman was hurrying toward her. She called out. "Are you all right? Can I help you?" As the woman spoke, Con saw one of the cars make a U-turn and speed away.

Con relaxed. "I'm okay," she answered. "Just shook-up."

"Can I take you somewhere?" asked the woman.

Con had lost one of her shoes in the crash, but she didn't dare look for it. Fearing she had just encountered one of Sam's adversaries, her only concern was getting back to her apartment. Then she recalled how a fireball had destroyed Ramona's hotel in Finoporto and decided to go someplace more protected.

"Could you drop me off at the Mergonic Research Center?" she asked.

"Sure," said the woman.

When Con was dropped off at the Research Center, she hurried to the Special Projects Lab. The night guard stared in puzzlement as Con, barefoot and covered with the foam's sticky residue, came running toward him. "Ramona, what the hell happened to you?"

"I was in an accident, Jose."

"Then what are you doing here?"

"I'm scared to go to my apartment."

"Why?"

"I can't say. Can I stay here?"

A leery expression came to Jose's face. "Stay here? For how long?"

"Please, Jose."

"We'll see," he said. "Why don't you get cleaned up?"

Con went to the ladies' room to wash. The foam's residue proved difficult to remove, and she was still a mess when she heard a knock and Roberto Peters's voice. "Ramona, may I come in?"

"Si, Senor Peters."

The door opened and the Division Manager walked in. He was casually dressed and without makeup. He looked amused. "You're a sight."

"I was in a wreck."

"That's what Jose told me. But why are you here? He said you were frightened of something."

Con hesitated as she tried to decide what to say. *If I'm to change history, I'll have to live long enough to do it.* "Someone attacked my vehicle," she said at last.

"You told Jose it was an accident."

"Si, but I'm telling you what really happened. Someone chased me and fired a beam or something that made me crash. That's why I'm afraid to go to my apartment. I don't think it's safe there. It sounds crazy—I know that—but it's the truth."

Roberto touched Con's sticky shoulder. "There's a special spray for removing that gunk. I'll have it brought to my office along with a change of clothes."

"So you believe me?"

"I'll have people look into it."

"Could they keep my name out of it?"

"What's going on, Ramona?"

"I don't know," said Con, "but I'm certain someone's trying to harm me."

"Who?"

"I have no idea," replied Con. Then she decided to reveal more of the truth. "I think it has something to do with your project."

Con watched Roberto's face, and when it turned grave, she saw that her tactic had worked. Roberto took her to his office, where he made some urgent calls. Within minutes, people brought up a robe and the special spray. "Use my private rest room," said Roberto. "It has a shower."

"Thank you, Senor Peters."

"We're not working now. Why don't you call me Roberto?"

Con responded as Ramona would. She lowered her voice to a sultry tone, and said, "Si, Roberto."

CON CLEANED HERSELF and dressed in the robe Roberto had provided. The aroma of food greeted her return. Upon a low table were several restaurant containers from which tantalizing smells issued. An open bottle and two glasses were there also.

Roberto filled a glass and handed it to Con. "I thought you might be hungry," he said with a smile. A call sounded in his inner office, and Roberto went to receive it, closing the door behind him. While he was gone, Con sipped her drink. The fragrant, straw-colored liquid seemed to be a kind of wine. She was peeking in the food containers when Roberto returned. He had a concerned look. "That was Security. They checked out your vehicle."

"And?"

"Something fused the power system. They've never seen anything like it. If the safety foam had failed also, you'd be spattered inside the canopy."

Con grew pale and lost her appetite. "So you believe me?"

"Si," said Roberto. "Tell me more about what happened."

Con precisely described the encounter, omitting only her speculations on the nature of her assailant. When she finished the story, Roberto shook his head in bewilderment. "I don't know what to think of it," he said. "To be honest, if it weren't for the evidence in your vehicle, I wouldn't believe you."

"So, you don't think I'm hysterical?"

"Not at all."

"I . . . I don't think I'm safe in my apartment. What am I going to do?"

"There's a room on the third floor with a cot and a bathroom. You could stay there," answered Roberto. "It's nothing fancy, but this building's secure. I've already fixed it so you can't be traced through the Personal Identity System."

"I didn't know that was possible."

"It is if you know the right people." Roberto refilled Con's glass and poured himself one. "You can relax now. You're safe, and you can remain here until we discover who was behind the attack. I'll have your things brought over."

"Thank you," said Con. She sipped her drink, and as she felt its effects, her appetite returned. "That food looked wonderful."

"It's all for you, I've already eaten."

"All for me? Have you been spying?"

"Spying?" asked Roberto innocently.

"Si. You've discovered my reputation." Con began to giggle. "Did you know people call me 'the Pit,' as in 'bottomless pit'?"

Roberto laughed. "Not until now."

"Well, they do. I don't think they like me."

"Don't worry," said Roberto. "I like you."

* * *

NOW THAT CON never left the building, Roberto's project completely dominated her existence. The initial stage of the project had involved the receptors that bonded the virus to the target cell, while the second phase concerned the DNA that would enter the cell and alter it. Although Sanchez did not enlighten Con as to what he was trying to accomplish, he was clearly having difficulty. The long strands of DNA Con fabricated involved hours of complicated assembly and, as evidenced by Sanchez's growing frustration, it was futile work.

Three weeks into the project's second phase, Con was working late when Sam's voice came to her. It simply said, *ASSEMBLE A NEW DESIGN.* As before, Con suddenly understood what she must do down to the smallest detail. She jettisoned Sanchez's half-finished design and began working on a new one. Her fingers sped over the controls, and sometime after midnight, she was done. Con replicated the virus and set the package on Sanchez's work area. Then she went wearily to her room.

Late the following afternoon, Gerald Sanchez appeared at Con's workstation. "Ramona, stop what you're doing." The coldness in his voice made Con look up quickly. Her boss glared at her with barely controlled rage. "Decontaminate yourself. We're going to see Senor Peters."

"What's the matter," asked Con.

"I think you know. Now, hurry up."

A few minutes later, Con and her boss were seated in front of Roberto Peters. "I want Ramona off the project," demanded Sanchez.

"Why?" asked Roberto.

"She's sabotaging my work."

Roberto shot Con a puzzled look before he asked Sanchez, "Do you have proof of this?"

"Si," replied Sanchez. He turned to face the viewscreens on Roberto's wall. "Display Sanchez design specifications for virus number 147." A complex molecular diagram appeared on the viewscreen. "Also display virus number 147 as assembled." A second diagram appeared. "Even at a glance," said Sanchez, "it's clear the virus

Ramona assembled is completely different from my specifications."

Roberto's face grew stern. "Ramona, did you change Senor Sanchez's specifications?"

"Si, Senor Peters. I . . . I had a hunch."

"A hunch!" exploded Sanchez. "She's a damned assembler! She's not fit to conduct research!"

"Ramona," said Roberto, "what do you have to say?"

Con reddened, then turned to face the viewscreen. "Display Sanchez design specifications for receptor number 53 and display receptor number 53 as assembled." She turned to Roberto. "As you can see, the two are different. Senor Sanchez claims his design proves he's a genius, but *I* designed and assembled the receptor that actually works."

Sanchez stared at the viewscreen intently while his face grew crimson. "It's some trick," he muttered. "She . . . she couldn't . . ."

"Tell me about your hunch, Ramona," said Roberto.

The clarity of mind Con had experienced the previous night returned to her, and the explanation came easily. "Senor Sanchez's designs are based on natural viruses, and that seems like the wrong approach."

"Why?"

"Because viruses are subject to natural selection. In the natural world, a virus thrives by altering a cell's chemistry to cause it to produce more viruses. That may kill the cell, but it spreads the virus. Yet you want a virus that will only change the cell's genetics and change it in ways that will be inherited by future generations. That's not the kind of thing a natural virus would do."

"So you've redesigned the whole damned thing?" asked Roberto.

"Si."

"On a *hunch*?"

"I've been working on viruses day in, day out," replied Con. "You get a feel for them."

"Display virus number 147 as assembled," said Roberto. Con's virus design reappeared on the viewscreen, and

Roberto studied it for several minutes. "What do you think, Sanchez?"

"She's a liar and a fraud!"

"Perhaps," said Roberto, "but I think I'll have Johnson do a tissue study."

"Sir?" exclaimed Sanchez, trying to control his exasperation.

"A test won't harm the project, and I'll reassign her if it fails," said Roberto. "Meanwhile, I'll get you a new assembler." He turned to Con. "Ramona, you're done for today. Until the test results are in, you'll do only routine replication. No more hunches. Understand?"

"Si, Senor Peters."

"You can both go now."

As Con walked to her room, her exultation grew. She was certain the virus she had assembled was Ramona Eberlade's great discovery, the bolt from the blue that would change history. She was unconcerned that the concept that had been so clear to her in Roberto's office was already beginning to fade from her mind. *It doesn't matter if I understand what I did,* she told herself, *it only matters that I did it.*

10

CON SAT IN HER ROOM EXPECTING TO HEAR SAM summon her to the time machine. *I'm done,* she thought, *I'm sure of it.* She could now see how Ramona had changed history, for her creation would affect countless lives. Yet, despite Con's conviction that she had completed her task, the summons did not come. After a while, she supposed that her sudden disappearance might jeopardize her accomplishment. It was a reasonable assumption, and it diminished her excitement. *How much longer until I see Rick and Joey?*

The following day, Con submitted to her blood test and suited up for work. There was no news about the tissue study, and her assignment was undemanding and tedious. The succeeding days followed the same pattern; Con performed make-work in the lab and spent her evenings in her room. Her mood alternated between boredom and anticipation. Dinner in the cafeteria became the high point of her day. Then, one evening, as dinnertime approached, Con heard a knock on her door. She answered it to find a man holding a huge vase of flowers. He handed them to Con, saying, "For you, Senorita." The arrangement was so large it blocked her view. When she set it down, the man was gone.

The flowers resembled calla lilies, but were larger and such a brilliant shade of blue Con first thought they were artificial. She was searching the arrangement for a note when she heard another knock on the door. This time, someone bore a bouquet of immense roses. Con barely had time to set them down when another arrangement was delivered, followed by a long procession of deliveries. Her little room became awash with flowers, and its air turned thick with their perfume. Finally, every surface was covered, even the cot, and it was nearly impossible to move about. Then the deliveries stopped. Con was wondering how to make space for sleeping when she heard one more knock.

The man outside her door handed her a single rosebud and an envelope. The note inside read:

Ramona—The results are in. My private vehicle will pick you up outside the building at seven.—Roberto

"At last!" said Con to herself. She assumed the flowers meant the news was good. As if to confirm her assumption, she heard Sam's voice for the first time since she created the virus. *GO TO HIM,* he said. Con did not need prompting, and Ramona, who had been quiescent of late, thrilled at the thought of seeing Roberto again. Soon, Con worked herself into a state of giddy excitement. She waded through the sea of blossoms to dress for the occasion. Guided by Ramona's tastes, she picked an outfit she had bought in Finoporto that was quite revealing. She had never dared wear it to work; yet tonight, it felt appropriate. After Con dressed, she waited impatiently for seven o'clock to come.

Roberto's car drove up precisely on time. Unlike the beige personal transports for public use, this vehicle was dark blue with a red interior. When it stopped in front of Con, its door opened. There was no one inside. She slid into the seat and closed the door. As the car drove away, Con nervously watched for a pursuer. Her nervousness departed only when the vehicle entered the gated area where the corporate managers resided.

Con had been born to wealth in the twenty-first century and was accustomed to stately homes. Tonight, however, she responded as Ramona to the residences. Thus, she was enthralled by what she saw. The sight of the big houses and their manicured grounds provoked a sense of wonder, envy, and excitement. Caught up in the moment, Con did not pause to consider her uncharacteristic reaction. Instead, she gazed about and tried to guess which home would be her destination. Finally, the vehicle pulled up the driveway of a large, three-story brick house with all its windows brightly lit. The architecture seemed more suited to the early twentieth century than the late twenty-seventh.

Roberto was waiting at the door. He was casually, but elegantly dressed in a pale blue robe that was open at the front; a pair of tight, dark blue shorts with a codpiece that matched the robe; and open-backed house slippers that were also pale blue. He was lightly made-up with silver blue lipstick and a touch of mascara. Roberto smiled at Con as she climbed the steps. "Ramona, it's good to see you."

"It's good to see you, Roberto," replied Con. "And you have news! What is it?"

Roberto's smile broadened into a grin. "Patience,

Ramona. Let me show you around first." He placed his hand on Con's back and gently guided her through the entrance. Roberto prolonged Con's suspense by showing off the opulent rooms of his home. After touring the first floor, he took her to the mansion's second level. There, the floors were carpeted in white, and Roberto asked Con to remove her shoes. The thick rug felt as soft as fur to her bare feet. They ended up in an intimate dining room with a table for two. The outer wall of the room featured a set of glass doors that opened onto a small balcony. Most of the luminescent ceiling was the same deep blue as the twilight sky outside. Only the illumination above the table was brighter. It bathed the tablecloth in a warm, soft glow reminiscent of candlelight. The table was heaped with delicacies. Roberto walked over to an ice bucket, removed a bottle, and popped its cork. *Imagine that,* thought Con, *they still make champagne.*

Roberto filled two glasses and handed one to Con. "Ramona, this is no ordinary news. The tissue study results are in. The virus is perfect in every way. The project is a success." He clinked her glass. "To your hunch—it will change everything."

Joy filled Con. *I've done it!* she thought. *Roberto says so himself. I've changed history!* She sipped her champagne, relishing its delicate taste and the success it celebrated. Soon, she had emptied her glass. Roberto promptly refilled it.

There were no chairs, and Con circled around the table to sample the delicacies. The food was elegantly and expertly prepared, abundant, and delicious. Yet, Con's excitement subdued her appetite. She moved about the table, sipping her champagne and only nibbling. As the wine went to her head, she began to enjoy how Roberto watched her. He ate nothing and seemed conscious only of her. Eventually, he set his glass down and boldly kissed Con's lips.

The kiss sent Con's heart pounding. Roberto had always made her feel and act differently, but the strength of her response surprised Con. The passion it aroused was unsettling. Also unsettling was her impression that she was somehow removed from the moment—that she was observing from a distance and not participating in it personally. Initially, the impression seemed absurd. It was her heart that was beating so rapidly, her face that was flushing red. *Why do I feel like this?* she wondered. Yet even as she asked herself that question, she also caressed Roberto's face with trembling fingertips. "What was that kiss for?" she asked in a low, seductive voice.

Roberto gazed into Con's eyes. "I've wanted to kiss you for a long time, Ramona."

"And I've wanted you . . ." Con's soulful gaze suddenly transformed to one of panic and confusion. She shrank back, grabbed a pastry, and stuffed her mouth before it could betray her. The pastry was rich and flaky, but its flavor was lost on Con. She was engaged in an inner battle. She felt the same as she had immediately after she received Ramona's memories—certain that two women occupied her body. She also sensed that Ramona had been waiting for this moment. Now it had arrived.

Roberto had not expected any hesitancy, and he looked puzzled. Then a confident smile returned to his face as he saw the reluctance depart from Con's. Her inner battle was over, and she met his eyes boldly and with invitation.

"Would you like to go out to the balcony?" asked Roberto.

Con swallowed, not even tasting the food. A different hunger possessed her. She picked up her glass and voluptuously walked toward Roberto. He held open the glass door and followed her slow, sensual movements with evident desire. Glass in hand, he joined her at the railing. Together, they gazed out over the darkening landscape. The sun had set, causing the empty, undulating hills to take on blue-gray tints.

"Long ago, this ridge was once the shore of a lake," said Roberto.

Con surveyed the vista, barely noticing it. "Lake Michigan."

Roberto smiled. "You surprise me, Ramona." He placed his hand upon hers.

"Because I know the name of an old lake?"

"Everything about you surprises me." Roberto turned his eyes from the landscape toward Con. He slipped an arm around her waist and gently pulled her to him. She pivoted as she moved, so her lips were but inches from his when their bodies pressed together.

Con's heart was racing. She knew she was responding as Ramona. That realization did nothing to quell the passion surging within her. Con was no longer in control. Ramona's emotions governed now. She saw Roberto as handsome, distinguished, and utterly desirable.

Their lips met in an inevitable kiss. Roberto pulled Con even closer, and she grasped his hand and guided it to her breast. Roberto briefly caressed her through the thin fabric, then slid his fingers beneath her clothes to fondle her with rough expertise. Roberto's other hand explored Con's body, rousing her to further heights. She grasped him and wordlessly assented to his desire.

Roberto undressed Con right on the balcony. She would have happily made love on the rug, but Roberto took her hand and led her into a nearby room. Con was oblivious to all her surroundings except the large bed against the wall. She lay back upon it, eagerly waiting for Roberto. He undressed quickly and joined her. Roberto kissed her as he groped between her legs. Con's own neglected sexuality merged with Ramona's, and she moaned.

Roberto rolled on top of her, spreading her legs with his. Con wished he would proceed slowly and tenderly, but instead, Roberto quickly pushed his way inside her. He began pumping rapidly and mechanically. Con looked at the flushed face above hers and Roberto's eyes seemed to stare far away. His lips drew back in a grimace. He thrust deep inside Con and stopped moving. Only his quivering tenseness betrayed his orgasm. He remained frozen in that position for a long moment, before relaxing and pinning her with his inert weight. Con lay beneath him, unsatisfied and disappointed. Finally, she felt forced to ask, "Are you done?"

Roberto rolled off her by way of response. Con started

to sit up, but he put his arm across her chest and pressed her back down. "Lie still awhile," he said. "I want you close to me."

Con acquiesced, though she was beginning to feel awkward. The wave of passion that had swept her away had broken, and it was receding as quickly as it had arisen. When Ramona's grip upon Con's psyche loosened, Roberto was transformed. Con saw him as he truly was—a stranger. And it was she, not Ramona, who lay naked in his arms.

11

CON LAY MOTIONLESS AND DISTRAUGHT NEXT TO Roberto until he dozed off. Then she left his bed and headed for the little dining room. It was hard to see, for the luminescent ceilings throughout the house had turned a midnight hue. Con stepped out onto the balcony. A half-moon lit the clear sky. By its light, Con collected the clothes that were strewn about, then went inside to dress in the dark dining room.

The aroma of the food roused her appetite. *No matter how miserable I am,* she mused, *I'm always hungry.* She was eating when the ceiling suddenly grew brighter. Roberto stood in a robe at the doorway, his smile surrounded by the smeared blue of his lipstick.

"I thought I'd find you here," he said.

"I didn't eat much before," replied Con, averting her eyes from his.

"I fancy a second helping, myself," said Roberto. "Hurry up and come to bed."

"I feel hungry, not sexy," said Con.

Con continued eating while Roberto watched. As she ate, Con anxiously considered what to do. One thing was certain—she would not have sex with Roberto again. The thought of it was unbearable, and her earlier attraction to him seemed totally incomprehensible. *It was Ramona, not I, who wanted him,* Con told herself. Yet, she was supposed to be Ramona. Eventually, Con could eat no more, and thus could not delay further. "Roberto, I think I should leave."

Roberto walked over to her. "Come on, Ramona, the night's still young." He reached out to caress Con's breast.

When Con pushed his hand away Roberto's face reflected surprise, then anger. "Don't," she said. Then she softened her tone. "Please, I want to go."

Roberto forced a smile. "Suit yourself."

"Thank you, Roberto," said Con, avoiding his eyes. "I don't want to seem . . . seem . . . ungrateful. It's just I'm not used to this."

"Who are you kidding?" asked Roberto.

"I'm . . . I'm ready to go now," said Con as calmly as possible.

Roberto's expression turned petulant. "Then wait outside. I'll send the car." With that, he strode out of the room.

Con hurried from the dark house, too upset to search for her shoes. The circular driveway outside was empty. As Con waited for the car, she tried not to cry. A whole range of emotions contributed to her misery. She felt ashamed, angry, and foolish. Furthermore, Con had the disturbing feeling she had been caught up in a game the rules of which she didn't understand. She was certain of only one thing—in trying to save Rick, she had also betrayed him. With that guilty thought, remorse overwhelmed her, and she began to sob.

Roberto's car was slow picking up Con, and it was early morning when she finally returned to her room. By then, all the flowers were gone. A few withered bits of foliage and a faint, lingering scent were all that remained of Roberto's extravagance.

* * *

ROBERTO HAD BREAKFAST in the little dining room. His servant had cleared last evening's delicacies and replaced them with coffee, eggs, and toast. As Roberto ate, he pondered if Ramona still fit into his plans. Her sudden change of heart was as irritating as it was unexpected. *It might not matter,* he told himself. *I'll know soon enough.*

He poured himself a second cup of coffee and went out on the balcony for a smoke. He was enjoying the tranquillity of the view when motion caught his eye. Three children wearing floppy hats scampered along the ledge below his balcony. There was something furtive about their movements.

"Hey!" he yelled. "What are you kids doing here?"

The three froze. One of them pointed an object at him, but a companion batted it down. The gesture reminded Roberto of Con's encounter on the highway, and he went inside to contact Security. After doing so, he peered out the window. The children were gone.

CON REPORTED TO the research lab dressed in the conservative clothes Kat had provided. She had already thrown away the outfit she had worn the previous evening. The change in wardrobe was part of her design to keep Ramona under control. So far, it had been easy, for Ramona had reverted to a passive set of memories. The forceful personality manifested the night before seemed to have dissipated. Regardless, Con was on her guard. She did not want to be surprised again.

The guard took a blood sample, and Con suited up for work. When she entered the lab, she found it nearly empty. A man noticed her entrance and rose. "Good morning, Ramona," he said. "I'm Pedro Johnson."

"You did the tissue study," replied Con.

"Si, and you'll be working for me from now on."

"Okay," said Con. "Where are the others?"

"Reassigned. Word came down after you left work."

"What happened?"

"Nothing happened," said Pedro. "The project's completed, thanks to you."

"So fast? But Roberto . . . uh . . . Senor Peters told me only last night that the virus works."

"So, he finally told you?"

"What do mean *finally*?"

"Everyone else has known for days, but we had to keep quiet."

"Why?" asked Con.

"Ask Senor Peters, it was his order," said Pedro. Then he added in a disdainful tone, "You know 'Roberto' much better than I do."

Pedro's remark made Con blush, and she tried to change the subject. "What will I be doing for you, Senor Johnson?"

"Not much," he replied.

"That will be a nice change. Senor Sanchez liked to work me late."

"Well, you needn't worry about Gerald," said Pedro. "He resigned."

"Resigned?" said Con. "I know he was jealous, but . . ."

"Jealousy had nothing to do with it," said Pedro. "He discovered he had principles. Maybe too late, but it makes him better than you or I."

"I don't understand."

"Ramona, stop playing games. I'm very pleased with my bonus, as I'm sure you are with yours."

"Senor Johnson . . ."

"It was a remarkable feat, Ramona. I'll grant you that. I didn't believe it was possible, but you proved me wrong. Now that it's done, it's too late to question the ethics of it."

"I did what I was supposed to," said Con. "That's all."

"As did I," replied Pedro. "Now, we'll have to live with the consequences."

CON HAD LITTLE to do, and Pedro told her not to come back after lunch. She spent the afternoon in her room. She tried to read, but nagging doubts about Sam spoiled her concentration. Until the previous night, she had thought she understood his goal. Now, not only was that goal less clear, it was also suspect. Pedro seemed remorseful for having worked on the virus, and that troubled her. He knew its purpose, while she—despite having created it—did not.

Equally disturbing, and even more bewildering, was Con's suspicion of Sam's involvement in her seduction. It was Sam who had provided her with Ramona's memories and mischaracterized them as passive. Con also realized those memories were curiously incomplete when it came to sexual matters, despite the fact Ramona had slept with eleven different lovers. Whatever knowledge Ramona had obtained from those encounters had been purged. All that remained were Ramona's urges. Yet Con's suspicions pointed to a conclusion that made no sense. *Why would Sam want me to have sex with Roberto?*

THE DAYS PASSED with excruciating slowness, and still Sam's voice did not beckon Con to the time machine. Her workload at the lab picked up, but it was only routine work. She spent her days monitoring production of the virus. It was virtually an automated process and required Con to do little more than watch the monitors. Over the entire time, she received no message from Roberto. She was not surprised by that. Her principal concern was, now that he was done with her, he would evict her from her room. She feared that would be a death sentence. Thus, when the guard told her at the end of work that Senor Peters wished to see her, Con became nervous.

Roberto smiled affably as Con entered his office. "Have a seat, Ramona."

"What do you want with me, Senor Peters?"

"Senor?" said Roberto. "After what's passed between us?"

"Si, Senor Peters."

"Don't look so glum. I have good news for you. You got what you wanted."

"And what is that?"

"Don't be coy with me, Ramona. Can't you guess?"

"No, I can't."

"Well, you're pregnant."

The blood drained from Con's face. "Pregnant? How could you possibly know that?"

"You get a blood test twice a day."

"That's for viruses."

"After our little get-together, I ordered an additional test."

"I . . . I can't be pregnant!"

"Save the dramatics, Ramona. One doesn't become fertile by accident. It's a conscious choice."

Roberto waited for Con to concede his point, and when she didn't, he addressed her in a businesslike tone. "Naturally, I choose not to marry outside my class. Thus, in lieu of a precoital agreement, I intend to take possession of the embryo."

"What do you mean? The child's in *my* womb!"

"I've already arranged for an extraction," said Roberto. "All I need is your agreement."

"An extraction?"

"I can force the issue, if necessary."

Con stared dumbly at Roberto, trying to make sense of what he was saying. "So you got me pregnant, and now you want to extract the embryo? Is this some kind of abortion?"

"Don't be absurd!"

"But where will the embryo go?" asked Con.

"To an artificial womb, like most babies" replied Roberto. "Why are you asking such stupid questions?"

"I'm just surprised, that's all," said Con.

"I find that hard to believe. Look, the time for playing games is over. I'll get you a position in management if you cooperate."

Con imagined returning to Rick bearing another man's child. "All right, I will."

"Good," said Roberto. His expression softened now that he had what he wanted. "You won't regret this. You'll retain some offspring rights. They'll be worth a lot; my son is going be a powerful man."

"Maybe the child will be a girl," said Con.

"I'll have a son, I'm certain of that."

Con almost retorted sarcastically, but thought better of it. "So how do I get this extraction?"

"I've already made an appointment. My car will take you to the clinic in half an hour."

"I guess you were confident of my reply."

"You're a smart woman, Ramona. I never doubted that."

AN HOUR LATER, Con was in a doctor's office wearing a hospital gown. The ill-fitting gown and the examination table with its raised stirrups reminded her that some things never change, even over centuries. She was glad when the doctor turned out to be a woman.

"Senorita Ramona Eberlade?" she said.

"Si, that's me."

"Hello, I'm Dr. Perez. I'll be doing your extraction. But first, I have some legal documents you'll need to authorize." She handed Con a data tablet with an identity reader affixed to it. "They're the extraction and possession agreements between you and Roberto Peters. I understand you've already discussed them."

"Si. What do I need to do?"

"Read them over, first," said the doctor. "If you agree, say so as you press the identity reader."

Con read the agreements. They struck her as very one-sided, but she was completely ignorant about this aspect of the twenty-seventh century—intentionally so, she suspected. She pressed the identity reader, and said, "I agree." Handing the documents back to Dr. Perez, she asked, "What's next?"

"Climb onto the table and put your feet in the stirrups. The extraction shouldn't take too long."

"Will it hurt?"

"You'll feel only minor discomfort."

Con climbed up on the table while Dr. Perez wheeled up a device that featured a monitor, a joystick-type control, and a long thin tube. Then Dr. Perez adjusted Con's position on the table and pulled up her gown. The procedure was virtually painless, but throughout it, Con felt violated. After it was over, she asked Dr. Perez, "When will you know if it's a boy or a girl?"

"It doesn't really matter."

"Why not?" asked Con.

"The child's sex can be adjusted at the Kynden Clinic."

Con froze. "Did you say the *Kynden* Clinic?"

"Si, that's where the embryo is going," answered Dr. Perez. "Dr. Kynden's clinic is new and very exclusive. Your child will benefit from the latest technology."

"Do they do genetic engineering?"

"They must. They guarantee perfect children."

CON WAS RIDING back to her room when she heard Sam's voice in her head. *GO TO FINOPORTO,* it said, *THE TIME MACHINE WILL BE WAITING FOR YOU.* The joy she expected to feel at that long-awaited summons was subdued by her recent experiences. Instead, her doubts about Sam made her apprehensive, and she had to suppress them to concentrate on planning her departure. *I'll leave tonight and arrive at Finoporto before dawn.* Con thought she could find her way in the dark; as she recalled, there was only one path through the woods. *By the time they miss me at work, I'll be long gone.*

Con waited until evening to order a personal transport vehicle. She had not bothered to pack, for she planned to leave this century with the clothes on her back and a handbag. Five minutes later, a car arrived. Con rushed out to the vehicle and brushed its identity reader. The car's door opened, and she entered. "Take me to the Mass Transport Terminal," Con said.

The terminal was nearly empty when Con arrived. She booked transportation to Finoporto and was told a module would arrive in twenty minutes at platform position 13. When the charge was deducted from her account, Con noted she would be leaving a sizable sum in the twenty-seventh century. Roberto had given her a generous bonus. It made her wonder who would receive it. *My son?* Even thinking the word felt strange.

Con waited on the platform, very aware her transactions could be used to trace her movements. The minutes dragged. The tension became almost unbearable as Con worried that Roberto might prevent her departure. Each time someone stepped onto the platform, she feared she might be apprehended. Though Con told herself she was free to leave, she was certain that if Roberto wanted her to stay, he had the means to enforce his wishes.

A transport module halted before Con at the appointed time. Its doors parted to reveal an empty compartment. Con hurried inside. When the module started to move, she slumped in her seat and tried to relax. Eventually, she fell into a fitful sleep.

CON AWOKE AS the module began to decelerate. Her mind was foggy with fatigue, yet edgy. There was one last hurdle to overcome before she left this century. The tension she had felt waiting on the platform returned, then rose to new heights. As soon as the module's doors opened, Con rushed through the station to the street beyond.

Finoporto's streetlights shone on deserted lanes. Con found a personal transport vehicle and brushed its identity reader to activate it. *This will be the last trace of me*, she thought. With pleasure, she envisioned Roberto's perplexity upon discovering her disappearance—first from work, then from the planet. She wondered how long he would search for her.

After a short ride, Con reached the broad lawn of the park on the outskirts of town. Beyond, lay the vine-covered woods where Sam waited. Con was halfway across the lawn when a police car approached. Her exhaustion forgotten, she sprinted into the thick undergrowth. From there, she watched a uniformed officer emerge from the vehicle and scan the woods with what looked like binoculars.

Con began running through the woods in the direction of the path. When she finally spied it, she stopped and approached it cautiously. Poking her head from the lush foliage, she peered up and down the trail's length. It appeared empty. She could run down the path in a dash for freedom or follow it more slowly while remaining hidden among the vines and trees. Con decided to place her faith in speed. She burst forth from hiding and ran as fast as she could. Con was looking for the time machine when the police officer stepped onto the pathway ahead.

"Senorita Eberlade!" shouted the officer. She was a middle-aged woman, and though her face was stern, it also contained a hint of sympathy. She aimed something at Con. "Stop or I'll stun you!"

Con halted and stood panting. "Why are you chasing me? I've done nothing wrong."

"Then you won't mind coming with me to answer a few questions."

"I do mind," said Con.

"I'm afraid that doesn't matter, Senorita. I'd prefer not to stun you, but I will if necessary."

Con looked the officer in the eye and saw she was earnest.

"Come on, Ramona, it's not pleasant being stunned and it won't help your case."

Con clasped her hands. "Please let me go, and you'll never see me again."

"This is not a matter that . . ." A loud "crack" resounded in the woods, and the woman's head and torso disintegrated into a red mist, leaving only her two legs. They remained upright for a moment before buckling and falling over. Con stood frozen in horror. A long moment passed before she realized she was covered with the woman's blood.

Con was wiping the gore from her face when Sam seemed to appear from nowhere. He was carrying a black cylindrical object. From her experiences in the Cretaceous, Con recognized it as a gun. Sam walked over to the two fallen legs, made adjustments to the settings on his weapon, and fired again. The severed limbs and a circle of ground around them were pulverized beyond recognition.

"Do not stand there," he said. "Come with me."

Without a word, Con hurried after Sam, who strode silently down the path. After a few minutes, Con detected the faint image of the camouflaged time machine against the trees. With each step, it grew more distinct. She followed Sam up its stairs into the cabin. "Sit down," said Sam as he positioned himself at the controls.

Con slumped into a seat. She was too shocked and exhausted to do anything else. The time machine rose into the sky. When it stopped ascending, the luminescent cylinder within its central column expanded into a writhing mass of ghostly worms. They consumed Con and sent her tumbling through the void that separated the centuries.

THE WORLD RETURNED to solidity, and the sensation of perpetual falling departed. Con's journey was over. She gazed at the viewscreen and saw mountains bathed in the dying light of day. *We're back in Montana!* she thought, as her apprehension dissolved into joy. *It'll be summer when we land, because Rick was killed in the summer. Only now, he's not dead. He's waiting for me.* Con looked down at her strange clothes and her dirty, bloodstained body. *I'm such a mess!* Yet, she knew Rick wouldn't care how she looked. He would hold her in his calm, loving way and tenderly listen as she recounted her ordeal. *He'll believe me, too. After all we've been through, it won't seem fantastic to him.*

The time machine descended farther, and the foothills came into view, inky green in the shadow of the mountains. Then a sight appeared that strangled Con's growing euphoria—the sea. The mountains she saw might very well be in Montana, but it would be millions of years before Rick walked among them. The time machine had not taken her home. It was flying over the Interior Seaway. As Con's vision blurred with tears, she saw the mesa of Montana Isle towering above the water's surface.

12

CON'S EXHAUSTION RENDERED HER NEARLY CATA-
tonic. After the time machine landed, she mutely stared at
Sam, incapable of deciding if he was her rescuer or tormentor. For the moment, it took all that remained of her
strength to keep from blubbering. Lacking the energy to
confront Sam, Con expressed her distrust through silence.
She staggered down the stairs and headed for her room.
Sam seemed aware of Con's state of mind as he followed
her, staying a few paces behind.

It was not a long walk to Con's room, but the effort
depleted her. When she arrived, she collapsed on the bed.
Kat was waiting and tended her after Sam departed. First,
she brought a soft flask to Con's lips and squeezed sweet,
aromatic liquid into her mouth. The liquid cleared Con's
head and gave her a little energy. She looked up at Kat and
saw the same look of compassion she recalled from their
first meeting.

"I am glad you have returned," said Kat.

Con sensed Kat was sincere. "So am I," she mumbled.

"Would you like me to bathe you?" asked Kat.

"I'll do it myself."

"Then I will get you some food and clean clothes while
you wash."

Con entered the bathroom and filled the tub with hot
water. The effort of scrubbing expended what little energy
Con had received from the aromatic liquid. She drifted off
to sleep and awoke only when the bathwater chilled. Con
climbed out of the tub, cursorily dried herself, and stumbled
back into the bedroom. A robe lay on the bed alongside a

box of food, but Con was too spent to eat or dress. She sprawled upon the bed, grateful that her fatigue made it impossible to think.

CON AWOKE WITH a start. A midday sun shone beyond the colonnade, and a second box of food lay on the bed. Con dressed and ate the contents of both boxes. As she satisfied her appetite, she pondered her situation. Con suspected Sam had deceived her, and that thought deeply troubled her. Yet expressing her suspicions seemed counterproductive. *I must find out what's going on,* she thought, *and I'll have a better chance if Sam's not on the defensive.*

As if on cue, Sam appeared as soon as Con finished eating. Con forced herself to smile. "Hi," she said.

"Are you rested from your journey?" asked Sam. "Yesterday, you appeared distraught."

"I thought I was returning to Rick, not here."

"I never said a single action would undo all the damage that has been done to history," replied Sam.

Con recalled Sam saying Ramona's murder had led to Rick's death and thought his reply disingenuous. Nevertheless, she said, "No, you didn't."

"You accomplished a great deal," said Sam. "It will take only a little more effort to complete your work. The difficult part is over."

"I'm glad," said Con, "but how will creating a virus prevent Rick's murder?"

"The chain of causality is a very complex one," said Sam. It would be tedious for me to explain and difficult for you to understand."

Con watched Sam closely as he spoke, but his expression was inscrutable. "So making the virus will eventually save Rick," said Con. "What about my son?"

"Your son?" said Sam. "He will not starve once your husband is saved."

"I don't mean Joey," said Con, "I mean the child I conceived in the twenty-seventh century."

"You conceived a child?" asked Sam in a tone of surprise Con found unconvincing.

"Yes," replied Con. "I thought you knew. After all, it seemed like something Ramona would do."

"Among my kind, sexual activity is predictable. I fear I failed to take your differing nature into account."

"So I wasn't supposed to get pregnant?"

"Of course not."

"Oh well," said Con, "When I see Rick again, he won't mind that I'm with child." Con hid her satisfaction at Sam's look of dismay.

"Are you still carrying the child?" he asked, struggling to disguise his agitation.

Con delayed answering to watch Sam squirm. "No," she replied at last.

"But you just said you were."

"Oh, the embryo was extracted," said Con as innocently as possible. "I only meant I wouldn't hide my pregnancy from Rick. I tell him everything."

"I see," said Sam, who briefly looked both relieved and angry before he regained his composure. "It is fortunate you will not have to raise two children under primitive conditions."

"Yes," said Con. "So, what happens next?"

"You will need to make one more trip upwhen."

"Where to?"

"The thirty-first century, I think," replied Sam. "I will need to confirm my calculations before I prepare for your journey."

"Will that take long?"

"Several days at least. You should relax and rest until then. You have been through a lot."

"I'd relax easier without Ramona's memories," said Con. "Can you get them out of my head?"

"Of course," said Sam. "My daughter will do that for you."

"Thanks."

"I must go to send probes to the thirty-first century,"

said Sam. "When my daughter has finished assisting me, I will send her to remove those memories."

Con watched Sam depart, knowing she had caught him in a lie. *Conceiving that child was one of the reasons I was sent to the future,* thought Con. *He nearly died when he thought the baby was still in my womb. I got him good. He knows it, too.* That last thought made Con worry what her ruse might cost her later. If she had exposed his deceit, she had also betrayed her suspicion.

KAT ARRIVED TWO hours after Sam departed, bearing the device that had originally transferred Ramona's memories to Con. "Lie down upon the bed," she said. "I will need to access your implant."

Kat used an instrument to remove the skin that covered the dot above Con's brow. That accomplished, she turned on the memory device and began making adjustments.

"Will I remember anything about Ramona?" asked Con.

"I will remove only the memories that were originally implanted," replied Kat. "When you interacted with Ramona, you formed new memories of your own. I will not remove those."

A frightening thought came to Con. "Do you mean it's possible to remove my memories as well?"

"Yes, or even alter them, but that is very complicated."

Con sat up. "I'm not sure I want this done after all."

"Do not be nervous, Constance," said Kat. "Your original desire was an appropriate one. Having the memories of another can result in strange behavior, and I believe Ramona behaves toward men in a manner that might cause you difficulty."

With a pang of guilt, Con recalled her night with Roberto. "Okay," she said, "do it."

The procedure took less than a minute, and this time, Con experienced no confusion when it was over. Everything Ramona knew was forgotten; she was a stranger again. Con tried to ascertain if Kat removed any memories besides Ramona's. Her recollections of the twenty-seventh century seemed complete. She remembered her dealings with Sam, and her suspicions remained intact. She felt unchanged. As far as Con could determine, Kat had been truthful with her.

Con sighed. "Now Ramona's truly dead."

"She did not have a happy life," said Kat.

"I don't recall that anymore," said Con. "All I know is she had poor taste in men."

AFTER KAT DEPARTED, Con wandered the island. She walked to its far end and found the rock where she and Rick had gone fishing the day before all hell broke loose. It was the day she began to fall in love with him. Con recalled Rick's shyness and how it contrasted with his courage in a way she had found endearing. Where water had once lapped against the rock, there was now sand. The sea was a quarter mile away and emptied of the exotic fish they had pulled from its depths. A geologist's hammer, not a fishhook, would be necessary to catch them in the future.

Con sat on the rock and thought how young she had been that day, though only a few years had passed. Life had changed her. Both she and Rick had been tempered by their adventures. They had survived the greatest catastrophe in the Earth's history, passing through earthquake, fire, flood, cold, and starvation; they had witnessed the death of friends; they had endured a humiliating captivity; and they had lived on the frontier and had a child together. Con wondered, if she met the girl who had fished on this rock, would she recognize her or even like her.

One of Con's traits from that vanished day had not changed—she was still stubborn. She was determined to get Rick back. Sam had made a promise, and she was resolved to make him keep it. She would not simply play his game and hope for the best. She would play a game of her own. In this contest, Con had only one advantage—Sam needed her to effect the changes he desired. She did not understand why this was so, but everything pointed to that conclusion. If Sam could have made the changes himself, Con was convinced he would have done so. Instead, he had made her his pawn. Her extraordinary skill at assembling molecules, her insight into viruses, and her susceptibility to Ramona's influence were all means he had used to direct her toward his ends. Only in the most superficial sense had Con acted on her own volition. She saw Sam's hand behind everything she did, and the thought infuriated her.

13

THE FOLLOWING MORNING, CON FOUND THREE BOXES of food on the corner of her bed. She considered it a sign that neither Sam nor Kat would make an appearance, and she was relieved there would be no need to hide her anger. Con spent the day outside, swimming, walking, and brooding. The hours dragged until even the seashore lost its charm. She returned at dusk to eat the same boring meal that had served as breakfast and lunch. The next two days were similar. On the fourth morning, there was no food on the bed when Con awoke. It was not quite dawn, and she went out to watch the sun rise over the water. She was nearing the beach when she saw the time machine ascend into the sky and disappear. When Con returned to her room, Kat was waiting there with breakfast and remained as Con ate.

"I saw the time machine leave this morning," said Con. "What's going on?"

"Father finished his calculations last night," replied Kat. "He went upwhen to get some things required for your final trip."

"Like what?"

"Clothes, an identity chip, and certain skills you will need to fit into the culture."

"I don't want another person's memories again," said Con.

"Father says this trip will be less complicated. You will not have to impersonate anyone."

"Do you know what I'll be doing?" asked Con.

"No," replied Kat, "but you will not return when you finish." She paused, then said, "I will never see you again."

The forlorn note in Kat's voice puzzled Con, and what Kat said next puzzled her even more. "I never got to know you this time."

Before Con responded to that cryptic remark, Kat asked, "Are you going swimming this morning?"

"Yes," said Con, "right after breakfast."

"May I join you?"

Con was surprised by the request. "That would be nice."

Kat looked pleased. "Thank you, Constance."

"I really prefer to be called Con."

"Oh, of course. I forget."

Con rose. "Shall we go?"

Kat bounded up like a child released to play. As they walked to the beach, she seemed a different person—relaxed, even buoyant. Con suspected that the sudden change was related to Sam's departure. When they reached the sand, Kat quickly shucked her clothes. She shouted, "Beat you to the water," and took off running. Con undressed and sped after her. With her head start, Kat was splashing waist high in the waves before Con even got her feet wet.

"That wasn't fair," Con called out. "You had a head start."

"You always fall for that trick," Kat yelled back.

That's a strange answer, thought Con. She started to ask Kat what she meant, but her companion had disappeared. A flicker of movement underwater caught Con's eye, then Kat broke the surface to spit a stream of water. She laughed and quickly submerged. Con laughed also and gave chase, caught up in Kat's playful mood.

As they frolicked in the waves, Con grew accustomed to Kat's body. It reminded Con of her own when she was on the verge of puberty. The tall *Homo perfectus* woman had girlish hips and only a hint of budding breasts. Her skin was virtually hairless, except for the fine down of childhood. Kat's appearance made Con feel she was the elder of the two, despite the fact Kat was probably twice her age. The two women jumped waves and swam until Con grew tired and retreated to the beach. Kat joined her on the warm sand.

"That was fun," said Con. "Too bad you didn't swim with me before."

A look of sadness crossed Kat's face. "Yes."

"Why didn't you?" asked Con. When Kat did not answer, Con said, "It's because of your father, isn't it?"

Kat simply nodded.

The anger Con felt toward Sam welled up. "Do you have any idea how lonely I am? I could have used some company."

The remark brought Kat to tears. "I wanted to, Constance. I truly did, but this time was different."

Con was so surprised by Kat's tears it took a moment before the implications of her reply sank in. When they did, she looked at Kat with a dumbfounded expression. "What did you mean when you said *'this time'?*" asked Con. "Have I been here other times? Times I no longer remember? Have you raced me to the water before? Is that what you meant when you said you always trick me?"

Kat grew pale and did not answer.

"Look, Kat, I've already figured out your father's lied to me. Have you been lying, too?"

Kat stared down at her sandy feet with a hurt look on her face. "I never lied," she said in a small voice.

"You just kept things from me."

"Constance . . ."

"That was my name last time, wasn't it? My name in a reality I no longer remember."

Kat stared out to sea with moist eyes. "Constance no longer exists. Why bother asking about her?"

"Don't you think I have a right to know what's been done to me?" asked Con.

"Your life is exactly as you remember."

"*This* version, maybe," retorted Con. "Your father has already told me my reality has been changed. Maybe I should take this up with him."

"No!" cried Kat. "You must not!"

"Why?"

"Father will get angry!"

Kat's alarm seemed infantile to Con. Looking at her decades older companion, Con thought, *You've never grown up. You're still "Daddy's Little Girl," afraid of his displeasure.* Con decided to exploit the situation. "If you won't answer my questions," she said, "I'll go to your father. I'm not entirely helpless in this matter. I can force him to talk."

"Constance, please . . ."

"I'm Con, remember. Tell me about Constance." She reached out and gently touched Kat's arm. "It'll be our secret. Your father will never know."

Kat looked at Con with a face reflecting turmoil. "Promise?" she said in almost a child's voice.

"I promise."

"Father made you different," said Kat.

"How?"

"He altered your existence to free you from the timestream."

"Why?"

"I am not really sure," said Kat, "but there have been several versions of you on this island, each different from the last. You were not always your own ancestor, and you didn't have a husband or a child until this time."

"Have there been other changes since you last saw me?" asked Con.

"I do not know. Father told me to stay away from you."

Con said softly, "We were friends weren't we? I can't remember, but I feel we were."

Kat had been sitting with her knees hugged close to her chest. Now, she rocked back and forth as she stared out to sea. "You were the only friend I ever had," she said.

"I'm still your friend."

"You have changed," said Kat.

"I *was* changed," said Con. "It isn't my fault. Your father did it."

"Father had his reasons," replied Kat.

"I'd like to know what they were. Was it so I could change history?"

"I am too stupid to understand Father's work," replied Kat.

"What makes you say that?"

"Because it is true."

"You do all his research," said Con. "You must have some idea what's going on. What was I doing in the twenty-seventh century?"

Kat mutely stared at her feet.

"I deserve to know what I did."

Kat hesitated.

"Please," said Con, "for Constance's sake."

"You will not tell Father?"

"I've already promised I wouldn't," said Con. "You researched the effects of my visit. What was the purpose of that virus I created?"

Kat wavered for a moment before answering. "It changed everyone's genetics."

"I suspected as much," said Con. "How?"

"Everyone born after 2693 must take a pill each day once they reach puberty."

"A pill that only the Mergonic Corporation makes," added Con. "So Roberto created the perfect product, something everybody needs."

"Yes," said Kat. "It made him a powerful man, and his son became even more powerful."

"You mean *my* son," said Con, "the one that went to the Kynden Clinic."

"Correct."

"He wasn't a *Homo sapiens,* was he?" said Con. "He was genetically engineered to be 'perfect.' Did they call him a *Homo perfectus* or a Kynden?"

"Neither term was used until the middle of the twenty-eighth century."

"By then, there were two human species, weren't there?"

"Yes," replied Kat.

Con shook her head in dismay. "What have I done, Kat? It certainly wasn't restoring history."

"I cannot say."

Can't say or won't say, wondered Con. At present, she sensed it was pointless to press Kat further.

The two women quietly watched the waves for a while, until Con broke the silence. "It feels awkward," she said, "to be remembered as someone who no longer exists. Am I very different from that person?"

"You were so carefree," said Kat wistfully.

The remark made Con strangely melancholy. She sighed. "I'd like to become friends again."

"There is no time," said Kat, pointing to the sky. "Father is returning."

CON AND KAT hurried to where they had left their clothes, put them on, and rushed back to the room. Kat quickly rinsed and dried her feet, then disappeared into the interior of the mesa. She seemed so anxious Con felt sorry for her. *What must her life be like?* she wondered. Con thought it could not be a happy one. Clearly, Kat's isolation made it easy for her father to dominate her.

As Con sat alone in her room, she attempted to envision the carefree version of herself who had become Kat's only friend. Con could not recall a time when she could be described as "carefree," even before she visited the Cretaceous. She wondered what alterations to history had brought about her current existence. The possibilities seemed endless. As Con tried to imagine them, a chilling thought came to her—*Sam could have murdered Rick!* It seemed likely. Yet, it would not explain why someone had attempted to kill her in the twenty-seventh century. *That wasn't Sam's doing. Perhaps, neither was Rick's death.*

Kat entered the room and interrupted Con's speculations. "I have come to prepare you for your journey," she said.

Kat had reverted to her reserved demeanor. She had the manner of someone being watched, and Con realized that manner was not new. She looked into Kat's eyes and was reassured by the warmth there. It gave Con the courage to continue pretending she was Sam's willing accomplice.

"What's next?" asked Con as casually as she could.

"I will implant your identity chip, first," said Kat. "You will need to be unconscious for the procedure."

"Identity chip? What's that?"

"A tiny device that goes inside your skull. It is used to identify you."

A chill went down Con's spine. "That sounds drastic," said Con. "What happened to the Personal Identity Code?"

"It is no longer used for your kind."

"My kind?" said Con, acting as if the conversation on the beach had not taken place.

"There are two species of humans in the thirty-first century, the Sapenes and the Kyndens."

Con feared undergoing another operation. "I already have an implant. Now, you're going to put another thing in my skull?"

"This device does not interact with your brain. You will not know it is there." Kat walked over to Con and gently squeezed her hand. "It will be all right. I promise."

"Okay," said Con, "get it over."

"Lie on the bed facedown," said Kat. She pressed an instrument to Con's neck and rendered her unconscious.

CON OPENED HER eyes and looked around the room. Kat was sitting close to her. She smiled. "How do you feel?"

"Okay." Con gingerly touched a tender spot at the back of her head. "Is the chip there?"

"Yes," said Kat. "Now, I will finish your preparations by cutting your hair."

Kat took a pair of scissors and trimmed Con's hair so it was a uniform length. Con looked at herself in the mirror. The short haircut was crude and unattractive. "Is this the height of fashion in the thirty-first century?"

"Appearance is not important in this time."

"Then people have really changed," said Con.

"They have," replied Kat. As if to reinforce that point, Kat produced the clothes Con was to wear. The worn footwear resembled cheap rubber flip-flops. They were mismatched in both size and color. Instead of panties, there was a plain white undergarment that looked like a loincloth. A short, baggy dress that lacked sleeves was the remaining garment. Its material seemed more like paper than cloth and featured a gaudy print. The dress was not even clean. Kat handed Con a clear plastic vial that had a cord attached to its threaded top. Inside were seven large, yellow pills. "Tie the cord around your waist," said Kat, "and hide the vial within your undergarment."

After Con put on the dress, Kat handed her a colorful, coarsely woven sash. "This is called a cordeya," she said. "Tie it around your waist."

Con tied the cordeya, then looked at her apparel with consternation. "How come I'm dressed like this?" she asked. "What's happened to people?"

"You will understand everything after Father downloads information into your implant," said Kat. She grasped Con's hand, and as she spoke, her eyes welled with tears. "Goodbye, Constance. Soon you will be with Rick and Joey."

Sam stepped into the room carrying the device he had used to download Ramona's memories. He spoke to Kat in the Kynden language, and his tone sounded harsh.

Kat immediately let go of Con's hand and quickly left the room, eyes downcast.

Sam smiled. "One more journey until you see Rick and Joey."

"No," said Con firmly.

"What did you say?"

"I said no," replied Con. "I'm not going anywhere until I see Rick and Joey."

"They are both dead," said Sam.

"Take your machine to the time before Rick was shot and bring them both here."

"That is impossible," replied Sam.

"I don't believe you," retorted Con.

"You are asking me to interfere with your existence."

"You've already done that, and we both know it," replied Con. "Besides, whatever you do won't affect me here, because I'm downwhen. You told me that yourself."

"You are asking me to alter history," said Sam. "I cannot do that."

"Oh, tell the truth for once! Ramona would never have discovered that virus. She didn't have the brains for it. That was your doing. I doubt she would have become pregnant, either. So don't tell me you're restoring history. I'm not buying that anymore."

Sam stared at Con, his face reddening.

"Look," said Con. "You said that to be effective, I must act of my own free will. Well, if I'm going to do that, I must see Rick and Joey first."

"Otherwise what?"

"Otherwise, you can go to hell."

"It is true I needed your cooperation . . ."

"And you still need it now," said Con. "So, ante up."

"You leave me little choice."

Con smiled. "I thought you'd see it my way."

She was still smiling when Sam withdrew an object from his pocket and pointed it at her. Con saw a flash of blue light, felt a jolt of pain, and everything dissolved into darkness.

14

CON OPENED HER EYES, AND THE WORLD CAME INTO focus. She was surrounded by green. She sat up. The color came from the long leaves of plants. She was sitting in the dirt between rows of green, woody stalks that were reminiscent of bamboo. *How long have I been out?* she wondered.

Her empty stomach provided a partial answer. *So, Sam's dumped me here. I guessed wrong. He didn't need my cooperation after all.*

Apparently, he still had some use for her, for Con had been provided with both knowledge and physical resources. *I'm in a field of perennial corn*, she thought. *It's near a town called Mergonita.* Con's hand went to her forehead. Skin covered her implant again. A bag lay next to her. She examined its contents. Thanks to the information Sam had provided, Con saw everything with the eyes of a native. There was a piece of embroidery, an exquisite rendering of leaves and flowers. *I can do this kind of embroidery*, Con realized. *This is a sample of my skill.* She recognized the different stitches and knew the names for every one. Her fingers recalled the motions required for each, as they had once known the controls of a molecule assembler.

Con had acquired only the basics for thirty-first-century life—how to speak the language, how to work, and the fundamentals of personal conduct. Unlike before, she had no knowledge of the era's technology, government, or economics. The events that had occurred since the twenty-seventh century were unknown to her. Although Con knew little about the workings of society, Sam had downloaded two crucial bits of information—the two human species lived apart and the yellow pills in the plastic vial were called "kana." At puberty, a tingling only kana could keep at bay marked the onset of a lifetime dependency. The pills meant life itself for everyone on the planet. Although Sam had provided no additional facts about the drug, Con knew kana was Roberto Peters's legacy, and his descendents were Kyndens.

Now that she was aware of the value of her pills, Con checked to ensure the vial was well hidden. People were known to kill for kana. That explained the three knives in the bag. Con knew the one with the broad, eight-inch blade was called a "cerdo," and the two smaller knives were "pajaroes." Each knife had a plastic sheath. The cerdo and one of the pajaroes attached to Con's cordeya, while the other pajaro was worn beneath her dress, strapped to her thigh. She took one of the pajaroes from its sheath. The stiletto-like, four-inch blade had a triangular cross section. Con balanced the knife in her hand, then, with a flick of the wrist, sent it flying into a cornstalk twelve feet away. Although the feat felt instinctive, it still surprised Con. *What strange new skills I have!*

Con emptied the bag of its remaining contents. There was a pale green bead necklace, a change of undergarments, and a money bracelet—a vestige of the twenty-seventh-century monetary system. The bracelet indicated Con had thirteen credits to her name. *Not much,* she thought.

Her inventory complete, Con put on the necklace and the bracelet, strapped the knives in place, and put her spare undergarment and the embroidery sample in the bag. Then she gazed about. The terrain undulated and the cornfield lay in a hollow between two gently sloping hills. Con headed up one of them. As she climbed, the ground became drier and the corn grew stunted. By the time she reached the crest of the hill, there was only brown, knee-high grass.

Con surveyed the landscape. She recognized it as the same one she had viewed from Roberto's balcony. The ridge upon which his house had stood was miles away and formed the distant horizon. The Mergonic Corporation's sprawling complex had shrunk and become a city of concrete-and-glass towers. High walls surrounded it, giving it a medieval aspect. The city was the abode of the Kyndens. It was not Mergonita. That place was also visible. Its buildings covered a hill beneath the walled city like a gray scar.

The hollows between her and Mergonita had crops within them, but the cultivated areas gave way to grass in the other directions. The land looked dry and empty. Con could spot no other signs of habitation. Scanning the desolate land gave Con a depressing awareness of her ignorance. She lacked the information any traveler needed to survive. Unknown territory lay in every direction. Only

Mergonita promised food, water, and shelter. It was the only place she could go, and she was certain Sam had planned it that way. "All right, Sam," said Con. "You win this round, but only this one. I'll go to Mergonita, but once I get my bearings, I'll leave."

Con took a dirt road that led toward the Sapene town. It wound around the hills, staying in the low areas. Despite the semiarid conditions, an abundance of crops lined the roadway. The plants were perennials that apparently needed little care. Nothing was ripe, for despite the heat, it was only spring.

After three parched hours, Con saw Mergonita again. The walled city had been visible for miles, but the hills had hidden Mergonita. For the first time, Con had a clear view of its ramshackle buildings. They encrusted a hill below the ridge, making it resemble a huge garbage heap. A sense of foreboding came over Con as she gazed at the town. The scant information Sam provided her and the clothes she wore had already caused her to expect a place of poverty. The actual sight of it was even starker than she had imagined.

Rows of corn flanked the roadway, and as of yet, Con had seen no one. Then, to her left, she heard the sounds of children at play. Con left the roadway and followed the voices. After pushing through fifty feet of cornstalks, she reached a clearing. In its center was a long, broad ditch, filled with muddy water. Over a dozen naked boys and girls were playing in the water or the mud around it. All had black hair, dark eyes, and coffee-colored skin. Some were toddlers, and the rest were not much older. The eldest was a girl about seven.

Con smiled at the sight of the children, for they seemed carefree. A rusty girder spanned the middle of the ditch, and the older children walked to its center. There, they tried to upset each other's balance until one, or both, tumbled into the water. They would disappear beneath its surface with a splash to emerge moments later, laughing and eager to repeat the contest. Con remained beyond the clearing's edge, unwilling to intrude and unable to break away.

Two girls had just tumbled from the girder when a muddy toddler, perhaps a year older than Joey, scampered out on its length. When he reached its center, he stood there momentarily. The girl whom Con thought was seven yelled, "Jonny!" The boy turned, lost his balance, and fell. The girl shrieked and rushed into the ditch. She was only a few feet from its bank when she was forced to swim. Other children joined her, but none rose to the surface with the missing toddler.

Con dropped her bag, kicked off her flip-flops, and dashed into the ditch. Pushing her way through the startled children, she dived beneath the muddy water. It was impossible to see, and Con groped about until she touched a tiny limb. She grabbed it, then swam to the surface bearing the toddler. Con held his head above water as he coughed and gasped for air. Then she swam with him to the shore of the ditch and staggered out, surrounded by grave, silent faces.

Con laid the toddler on the ground to give him mouth-to-mouth resuscitation, but he gave a cry and struggled to break away. Con drew back, and the boy shrank from her into the arms of the girl who had called his name.

The girl hugged the boy, then started yelling at him. "Jonny, you're so stupid! Why'd you do that? You know you can't swim! I should hit you."

While the girl shouted, the boy stared fearfully at Con. "Gabbry, why does she got strange eyes?"

Another small boy touched Con's arm, then jerked his hand away. A girl voiced what the boy apparently thought. "What's wrong with your skin?" she asked.

"I'm . . . I'm from the south," replied Con. "Lots of people there look like me."

The girl Jonny had called Gabbry gazed at Con fearlessly. "He's *my* brother. I would have saved him, you know."

"I thought you could use some help," said Con.

"Well, you were wrong. I've saved lots of kids."

"I wanna go home, Gabbry," whimpered Jonny.

The girl regarded her brother with a mixture of irritation and affection. "All right, but don't whine when you're hot."

She walked over to a pile of clothes and put on a soiled dress that appeared to have been made out of a larger garment. Jonny remained naked.

After she dressed, the girl spoke to Con as if correcting a playmate. "You take off your clothes when you go swimming."

"I was in a hurry," replied Con, smiling at the girl's bossiness.

"Well, it was still stupid," said the girl. "Now, you're wet and smelly."

Con looked down at her muddy, soaked garment. "Yes, but your brother's safe." She smiled at Jonny, who was peeking from behind his sister.

"Are you really from the south?" asked the girl.

"Yes, I just got here," said Con.

"What's your name?" asked the girl.

"Con Clements. And you must be Gabbry."

"*Gabriella*. My name is Gabriella. Only Jonny calls me Gabbry. He doesn't know better."

"Pleased to meet you Gabriella."

"Conclements is a silly name," pronounced Gabriella. "You should be Dusty Eye, because your eye looks like dirt."

Con smiled. "Maybe you could call me Dusty."

Gabriella considered the idea for a moment. "All right, Dusty, come on."

Con found herself obeying. "Where do you want to take me?" she asked as they entered the cornfield.

"To my house."

"Why?" asked Con.

"Do you have a place to stay?"

"No," said Con.

"Then maybe Mama will let you stay with us."

"Is your mama home?"

Gabriella gave Con a look that reflected her low opinion of Con's intelligence. "No, she's at work. All grown-ups work at daytime. 'Cept whores." She eyed Con knowingly.

Con blushed. "I'm not a whore, if that's what you're suggesting. I do embroidery." She pulled the sample from her bag as proof.

Gabriella stopped to look at it. "Oooh, that's pretty!" She wiped her hands on her soiled dress before delicately touching the needlework. "That's real good stitching. That's what I wanna do when I get the tingles."

Con knew Gabriella was referring to the sensations that marked the onset of kana dependency. The language the girl spoke included over a dozen terms for the varieties of tingles, tremors, and spasms that now afflicted humanity.

"Sometimes," said Gabriella, "if they do good, stitchers get an extra pill! That's what Mama says. A whole pill!"

"So that's a lot?"

Gabriella's look made Con feel stupid for asking. "Don't you know anything?"

Con said nothing. She put the sample away as Gabriella resumed the march through the cornfield.

The field ended at the edge of town, and Con got her first close view of Mergonita. She thought the jumble of dilapidated buildings that crowded the hill looked Neolithic. Only the inclusion of cast-off technology into the structures spoiled the impression. Weather-beaten car canopies served as windows. Bits of metal, hammered flat, patched roofs. Tattered plastic mended broken walls. The effect was chaotic and bespoke poverty and neglect.

Gabriella led Con into the town and turned up a street where the crumbling pavement gave way to dirt. Closer up, the buildings showed their antiquity. Con saw that they had originally been constructed from concrete, though generations of repairs and additions had drastically altered them. In the late afternoon, only a few children roamed the hot, dusty streets. Yet the air bore the smells of crowded living, mingled with the odors from communal latrines. "Where are the grown-ups?" asked Con.

"I told you," said Gabriella. "Work."

"Doing what?"

"Stuff for the fecs," said Gabriella.

Thinking "fec" came from *Homo perfectus,* Con asked, "You mean the Kyndens?"

"Si. Fecs." Gabriella pronounced the word as if it were a curse.

"So what do they do for the fecs?"

"Things fecs are too lazy to do themselves. That's what Mama says, and she knows—she's a maid. I'm never gonna do *that*. Don't want no fec telling *me* 'do this, do that.' It's better stitching."

"Then why doesn't your mama stitch?"

"She used to, but she got the tremblitos," said Gabriella, referring to the trembling fingers that came from insufficient kana. "So now she's a maid."

Gabriella left the street and turned up a shadowed alley-way where Con spotted an adult, the first she had seen since her arrival. A woman sat in the dirt with her back against one wall of the alley, which was so narrow her bare feet nearly touched the opposite wall. She was filthy and emaciated, but it was the quivering and twitching that drew Con's attention. The tremors animated the woman's entire frame. Con tried not to stare, but it was impossible. Gabriella, however, acted as though the woman was invisible. She walked up the alley holding Jonny's hand and stepped over the thin, shaking legs with no more concern than if they were branches lying on the ground.

After some hesitation, Con stepped over the legs also. She caught up with Gabriella, and asked in a low voice, "What's wrong with that woman?"

"She's a perdido," replied Gabriella in a matter-of-fact tone.

Sam had omitted any information about such people. Con risked seeming stupid by asking, "What's that?"

"No work. No kana. Perdido," replied Gabriella as if she were speaking to an infant.

Con nodded, then glanced over her shoulder at the woman, who had seemed oblivious of them. When she looked forward again, Gabriella had halted before a door and opened it. "Come on, Dusty, we're here."

Con passed through the doorway into a hall flanked with seven doors on either side. Gabriella opened one of the middle doors and Con followed her inside. The small, rectangular room was dim, with the only light coming from a dirty skylight and a small, unglazed window high on the far wall. Con looked about the room. While only nine feet by twelve feet, it was apparently the site of all the family's activities. In a corner was a short stack of foam pads that looked like sleeping mats. Clothing hung from nails along one wall. Beneath the clothes were a small, rectangular plastic tub, a plastic bucket, and a covered container. The stench of excrement emanating from the container explained its function. The opposite wall had shelves with food containers, a few bowls, a pot, and some spoons. Below the shelves was a small metal table that seemed to be where food was cooked. It was the only furniture in the room.

"Papa died last winter," said Gabriella. "So there's only Mama, me, Jonny, and Melena. We have lots of room." She paused, then added as casually as she could, "A space won't cost you much."

Con suddenly understood it was not gratitude that motivated Gabriella to invite her home. "I'll talk to your mama about it," replied Con. "When will she be home?"

"After dark."

"Then maybe I could wash my dress before she arrives."

"You can use our bucket," said Gabriella. "There's water in the courtyard. Just go down the hall."

Con followed the directions to a small square, paved with crumbling cement. It was surrounded on all four sides by walls, each with a door. There were no windows facing the courtyard, and the stench from the communal latrine explained why. The water faucet was outside the latrine. Con filled the bucket and returned to Gabriella's apartment to wash her muddy dress and loincloth. Afterward, she hung her undergarment on a nail to dry and put on the damp dress.

Gabriella and Jonny had stared at her throughout the process. Their fascination with her appearance made Con feel like a freak. The blending of humanity she had witnessed in the twenty-seventh century had culminated in a uniform population. Con's pale skin was an aberration. So were her hazel eyes and light brown hair. Con sensed this might pose a problem, but it was like all her problems now—it lacked a solution.

Con took the bucket and drained it in the courtyard. There, she removed a pill from her vial of kana and hid it in her hand before returning. "I think I'll walk about outside to dry my dress," she said.

Con entered the alleyway. The twitching woman was the only person there. With trepidation, Con approached her. Although it seemed incredible, the woman was young. The incessant tremors, rather than age, had withered the perdido's frame. Con squatted so she could look the woman in the eye. Her face was as dirty as her clothes, the only clean spot being where a stream of drool bathed her chin. "What happened to you?" asked Con.

The perdido's glazed eyes briefly cleared and met Con's. For an instant, they communicated hopeless despair. Then the effort was too great to sustain, and the woman's eyes lost their focus. Con took her pill and pushed it through the woman's quivering lips. At first, nothing happened, but gradually the tremors became less violent. The woman did not become completely still, and Con realized only one form of stillness would ever halt her suffering. Yet, a degree of calmness and lucidity came to the woman's face. She looked at Con with astonishment and gratitude. She whispered, "Bl . . . bleh . . . bless . . . bless . . . bless . . ."

Con felt she had contracted the perdido's affliction. Her hand's shook and her vision blurred with tears. *I did this*, she thought over and over again. *I made this possible. I should have died in the cabin. That would have been better than this.*

Con staggered to her feet, unable to face the misery she had wrought. She stumbled up the alleyway and did not see Gabriella until she was right in front of her.

"I saw what you did," the girl said with outrage. "How could you do such a thing? A pill to a perdido. A perdido!" She was shouting now. "My mama has tremblitos, and you throw your kana away. Stupid! Stupid! Stupid! Stupid!"

Con stood numb, barely aware that Gabriella was pummeling her.

15

CON BEGAN TO WEEP. HER SOBBING DISCONCERTED
Gabriella and quelled her anger. She stopping hitting Con,
and said, "Don't cry." The plea made Con bawl all the
louder, and Gabriella felt pangs of remorse. She grasped
Con's hand and gently pulled it. "Come on, Dusty. Come
on inside."

Con allowed herself to be led into the apartment. There,
she retreated to a corner of the concrete floor, slumped
down, and continued sobbing. Jonny watched her solemnly,
then asked his sister, "Why's she crying?"

"Because she's stupid," Gabriella answered.

"Oh," said Jonny. He sat down on the floor and sucked
his thumb as he watched Con.

The sight of Jonny made Con cry even harder, and it
was several minutes before she could bring her sobbing
under control. When Con was quiet, except for occasional
wrenching sighs, Gabriella cautiously approached her. "I'm
sorry I hit you," she said. "I guess you can't help being stupid."

The apology brought Con close to a fresh round of sobs.
"It's okay," she said. "I deserve to be hit. I should be the
perdido, not that poor woman."

"Don't say that!" said Gabriella. "A perdido can't help
Mama."

"It's too late for me to help anyone."

"Work and stay here," said Gabriella. "Mama needs the
money."

Con sighed. "All right."

Gabriella looked relieved. "Just sit," she said. She took

the bucket and left to return with water. She poured some into the plastic tub and washed the dried mud from her feet and legs. Then she cleaned her brother, warning him, "Don't tell Mama we were at the ditch." She turned to Con. "You don't tell either."

"I won't," promised Con.

After Gabriella washed, she busied herself with cooking. She poured dried beans and corn into the pot, added water, some salt, and a few dried peppers, then set the pot on a tripod atop the metal table. Gabriella placed a very tarnished, two-inch metallic cube beneath the pot and said, "On." The cube levitated in the air and began to glow feebly. It reminded Con of the cube Sam had used to heat her cabin. It was the first piece of advanced technology she had seen in the thirty-first century.

"What's that metal thing called?" asked Con.

"You mean the fiero?" asked the girl. "Don't you use them down south?"

"No."

"Ours is very old. It takes forever."

Con walked over to the pot, her stomach cramping with hunger. "This smells good already."

"It'll be done when Mama comes home. She's always tired and hungry."

Gabriella's remark brought Con close to tears, causing the girl to turn her attention quickly to her brother, who was beginning to droop. She pulled out a mat for him to nap upon. He lay down, thumb in mouth, and drifted off to sleep. Gabriella busied herself stirring the pot, glad Con had retreated back to the corner.

Con sat mutely in her damp dress, fighting the urge to lie next to Jonny and cradle him in her arms. *He wouldn't like it*, she thought. *He's not my child. Mine's dead.* Tears began to roll down her cheeks again. *Dead.* During her visit to the twenty-seventh century, she had refused to think that word. Joey was "waiting," not truly dead. Now Con realized his demise was irrevocable. The hope that had sustained her was completely gone. Her travails had merely ensured that she, Joey, and Rick would die apart.

And one more thing, she reminded herself, *I've ruined everyone's life in the process.*

GABRIELLA GAVE LITTLE indication whether she regretted having invited an erratic and moody stranger home. However, she did watch Con carefully, and she did not speak to her. Instead, she puttered aimlessly about the tiny apartment. The uncomfortable silence persisted as the daylight gradually faded outside the window. The illumination from the skylight remained constant, though it began to take on a yellow, artificial hue.

A siren sounded, and soon afterward, voices drifted through the thin walls. The workday was over, and the building was filling up. Somewhere, a man and woman were having a heated argument. Then the sound of crying children accompanied their yelling.

The door opened, and a tired woman entered. Her hair was streaked with gray, and her hands and arms were stained a dark purplish blue. Her dress bore a rainbow of spots and spatters, as did the tops of her feet. A large cerdo hung from her cordeya.

The woman paused inside the threshold and wrinkled her nose. "It stinks in here. Gabriella, empty the shit pot. Your mama should have taught you better." Then she noticed Con slumped in the corner for the first time. "Who's this?"

Gabriella halted on her way to dump the chamber pot. "She's Dusty. She'll be staying here if Mama says so."

The woman impassively regarded Con, then grunted to show it was none of her business. She dragged a mat from the pile and lay down with a sigh. When Gabriella returned, the woman said without sitting up, "Your mama should take the ride from the city. Then I wouldn't have to wait so long for supper."

"If you paid more," countered Gabriella, "maybe she could."

"I pay too much already."

Con assumed the woman was Melena, and Melena was not a relative. Her arrival reminded Con that having a place to stay was not assured; it was up to Gabriella's mama. She arrived about an hour later. In the dirt-filtered, yellow light it was hard to determine the woman's age. Her face was unlined, and her hair was solid black, but she did not move like a young woman. Con rose from where she sat.

"Who's this, Gabriella?" asked Mama sharply.

"It's Dusty, Mama. She needs a space."

Mama carefully scrutinized Con. "I don't know you."

"She's from the south, Mama. She stitches."

"From the south," said Mama to no one in particular. Then she looked at Con even more suspiciously. "A long journey? What did you sell along the way?"

"Not myself, if that's what you're asking. I saved up my kana for the journey."

"Do you have any left?"

"Do you want to rent me a space?" asked Con.

"Perhaps."

"Then why don't we speak outside?" said Con.

"There are few secrets in Mergonita," replied Mama, "but if you like, we'll discuss this elsewhere."

Gabriella rushed up and grabbed her mother's hand before she could head for the door. "Mama," she whispered, "I need to tell you something."

Mama bent down to listen, keeping an eye on Con as she did. After a moment, her expression became puzzled. Then she said, "Come, Dusty."

"Don't gab all night," said Melena. "I've waited long enough for supper."

The light that shone through the skylights did not find its way into the alleyway. "Come to the street," said Mama, "I want to see your face while we talk."

Con followed Mama out to the harshly lit street where the elder woman looked her over. "My daughter thinks you're stupid."

"I know."

"She can't understand why someone would give kana to a perdido. I can't either."

Despite herself, Con's eyes began to glisten. "She was suffering."

"We all suffer," said Mama.

Con glanced at the woman's trembling fingertips and nodded.

Mama studied Con's face as she made up her mind. "If you help Gabriella learn stitching, two pills a week—paid in advance—will buy a space and meals."

"All right," said Con. "I'll pay you when we get inside."

"Is your name really Dusty?"

"No, your daughter calls me that. My name is Con."

Mama got a hint of a smile. "Well, Con, you shouldn't let her boss you around, or she'll hog the sleeping mat."

"I think that's easier said than done."

Mama sighed. "She's become headstrong. We should go back, or Melena will bitch all night about waiting for supper. Talk to her about work. She dyes and visits all the stitching houses. She'll know who's hiring."

"Thank you, Mama," said Con.

"Call me Marianna. I have enough children."

When Marianna returned to the apartment, she said, "We'll need five bowls, Gabriella. Melena, this is Con. She'll be staying with us."

"Take my advice," said Melena, "and buy your own mat. You'll not get much sleep next to little wigglebottom."

"Well, you snore," countered Gabriella. "Mama, do I have to sleep with Dusty?"

"Si. And she's Con," said Marianna. "You should call her by her proper name."

"She told me it was Conclements."

"I have two names," said Con. "Con is mine and Clements is my husband's."

"You have a husband?" asked Marianna.

"He's dead," said Con. "So's my son."

"Is that why you cry so much?" asked Gabriella.

"Hush!" said Marianna.

"I'm happy Dusty's staying," announced Jonny. "She saved me from the water."

Marianna whirled and grabbed her daughter's arm. "Were you at the ditch?" When Gabriella did not answer, her mother slapped her. "I told you not to go there!"

Gabriella glared at her brother with watering eyes, but she did not cry. Mama hugged her daughter, and said gently, "Now go serve supper."

While supper was being served, Con gave Marianna her rent.

Gabriella saw the pills, and said, "Don't sell them, Mama. Use them for your tremblitos."

"We have an extra mouth now. Some of it must go for food. And you'll need thread if Con's to teach you stitching."

"I can get her thread," said Melena. "Marianna, take some of that kana for yourself. You're not getting enough."

Marianna gazed down at the quivering hand that enclosed the precious pills. "I might take a little."

Gabriella placed a worn straw mat on the floor and set bowls of stew and a loaf of bread upon it. Water was drunk from the bucket using a common ladle. The beans and corn had swollen as they cooked, and what had earlier appeared to be a meager supper was actually quite ample. After eating bland food cubes, Con relished the meal. It seemed food was not a problem in Mergonita, but a shortage of kana was. Con guessed that the yellow pills functioned like gold had in the nineteenth century, as the precious commodity upon which the monetary system was based. There were some major differences, however—no one ate gold, nor did they need it to live.

Everyone was hungry, and no one talked while they ate. After Con sopped up the last of her stew with a piece of bread, she spoke to Melena. "Marianna said you know who's hiring stitchers."

"I heard Clever Mari lost her top stitcher," said Melena.

"The tremblitos?" asked Marianna.

"Worse," replied Melena in a dramatic tone. "The woman disappeared."

"Disappeared?" said Gabriella.

"Si," replied Melena. "In the middle of the night. Her husband saw a light. It hurt, and he fainted. When he woke up, she was gone."

"Don't scare my children with such tales," said Marianna.

"It's no tale. A friend of mine knows the man. He's beside himself."

"The woman probably ran off," said Marianna.

"To where? And she has children. No mother leaves a child."

"What could have happened?" asked Gabriella.

"Fecs," stated Melena. "They say a fec took her."

"Why would they take a woman?" asked Marianna.

"Who knows?" said Melena. "No one can understand a fec." She glanced at Con. "But there's no running from them."

Con felt the blood drain from her face and was glad the light was dim. "Are there other places besides Clever Mari's?"

"Fat Rosa's hiring," said Melena, "but she's stingy."

"What's a fair wage?"

"A beginner gets eight pills. Rosa will give you that. Getting more is hard. You'd think you were asking for her teeth."

The light above the skylight extinguished, plunging the apartment into darkness.

"Clean up, Gabriella," said Marianna.

As Gabriella did her chores, the two older women removed their dresses and lay down on their mats. Con hung up her dress, but there was no room for the third mat until Gabriella finished up. Meanwhile, Jonny nestled with his mother.

Gabriella undressed, lay next to Con, and quickly fell asleep. She proved a fidgety sleeping companion with a tendency to sprawl. It was uncomfortable when her bare skin pressed against Con's in the hot, close apartment, yet Con did not push her away. She craved the nearness of a child more than physical comfort. Slowly, the girl took over most of the sleeping mat until Con lay awake at its very edge, listening to Jonny suck his thumb in his sleep, the whine of mosquitoes, Melena's snoring, and the muffled sounds of passion coming through thin walls.

16

MAZAFALAMA DID NOT VENTURE OUT TO HIS BALCONY until the lights of Mergonita were extinguished. He approved of the two-century-old edict that had expelled the sapes from the city, but he wondered why their town had been constructed within view. The sape habitations marred an otherwise pleasant landscape. Only at night, after curfew darkened the town, was it possible to ignore its blight.

He called to his guest. "The lights are out, Tavamanana. Come see the stars."

His friend, glass in hand, joined him at the balcony. Mazafalama spoke words in his singsong language, and the ceiling of the room behind them dimmed to afford a better view of the night sky. The metallic dots on the foreheads of the two Kynden men softly reflected the starlight as they appreciated the vista.

"It looks peaceful this time of day," said Tavamanana.

"Yes," agreed his host. "Romantic."

"Romantic?" said Tavamanana. His expression turned quizzical. "Where are your thoughts traveling?"

"Karinalalina is approaching her Ripening," said Mazafalama.

"Has it been a year already?"

"Nearly so," said Mazafalama.

"Ahhh, the fragrance of a ripe woman," said Tavamanana, breathing in deeply as he recalled the scent of pheromones. "Do you have any hope this time?"

"With luck, I might join her in seclusion."

"Then you'd be lucky indeed," said Tavamanana. "She's out of my league."

"You're too modest, my friend."

"Well, she's certainly beyond my means."

"She does have expensive tastes," said Mazafalama, "but I've had a profitable year."

"It makes you yearn for the good old days when women ripened and seized the first man available."

"I don't believe those days ever existed," replied Mazafalama. "I suspect women always took care about who they were with when their urges became irresistible."

"Well, they certainly do now," said Tavamanana with a laugh.

"I was hoping you might help me find a suitable mating offering. She likes embroidered robes, and your work takes you to sape town."

"If you're looking for a bargain, forget it. The kana laws are very strict," replied Tavamanana.

"I wouldn't dream of violating them," replied his friend. "I'll go through a licensed dealer, but I'm hoping you would act as my agent. Dealers often hold back the best goods. If I hope to be secluded with Karinalalina, I'll need something impressive."

"It will be expensive. The dealer may pay in kana, but he'll charge you a small fortune."

"That's the law of supply and demand," said Mazafalama. "How many times does a woman like Karinalalina ripen?"

Tavamanana grinned. "Not often enough."

"Then you'll help me?"

"I have contact with a sape called Clever Mari that runs an embroidery shop. Her sapes do good work. I'll look around for you."

"Thank you, my friend," said Mazafalama. "I appreciate this."

"I've always been a romantic," replied Tavamanana.

They gazed at the stars for a while before Mazafalama broke the silence. "So, how's your work going?"

"Terrible," replied Tavamanana. "Sometimes, I think it's hopeless."

"It can't be that bad."

"Oh, yes it can. All the records were sabotaged during the expulsion. There's nothing left."

"Dirty sapes!" cursed Mazafalama. "Vicious, devious, destructive animals."

"But thorough animals," said Tavamanana. "Our ignorance of our dependency prevents discovering its cure. We can only guess how many times viruses altered our genetics before disappearing—five, ten, maybe scores of times. They left a tangle no one can sort out."

"People created this problem, so they can solve it."

"I don't wish to sound pessimistic," said Tavamanana, "but the sciences have declined. We lack our ancestors' understanding."

"Oh well, we have kana. It's cheap and plentiful."

"That's true, but I think if we could cure our dependency, we might solve the sape problem also."

"I don't see the connection," said Mazafalama.

"Kana links us to the sapes. They'll do anything for it, so we use them, even though their presence enervates our race. They're filthy, yet they clean our homes and offices. They're lazy, yet we depend on them for labor. Their women are always ripe, and for a few pills . . ."

"Don't disgust me!"

"They're animals," said Tavamanana. "What do you expect? When we permit them in our midst, they spread their perversions."

"If you feel that way, how can you bear to go to sape town?" asked Mazafalama.

"It's a sacrifice I make for our species," replied his friend. "I hope to find a genetic throwback among the sapes, one that shows what the genome was like before the virus. I believe such a creature would point the way to a cure."

"Could such a sape exist?"

Tavamanana shrugged. "It's likely one does not. Still, it's worth the search. If our species no longer needed kana, perhaps we would stop making it."

A look of understanding came to Mazafalama's face. "That would mean . . ."

". . . that you could enjoy the view from your balcony in the daytime," said his friend.

CON WAS AWAKENED by the insistent sound of a siren. The lights above the skylight turned on, illuminating the room though the sky was still dark. Marianna and Melena stirred, but did not rise. Only Gabriella got up. She sleepily dished out three bowls of cold stew, got fresh water, and said, "Breakfast's ready." Con rose and dressed with the other women while Gabriella crawled beside her brother, who still slept on Marianna's mat. Before the three women had finished their meal, Gabriella was asleep again.

Melena scowled at the girl. "Marianna, you spoil that child. She's old enough to be working."

Marianna glanced at her daughter, and a sad look came to her face. "She'll feel the tingles soon enough. Then she'll have the rest of her life to work."

"She might earn two pills a week," said Melena. "Look at your fingers. You must think of yourself."

"She takes care of Jonny," said Marianna.

"She took him to the ditch yesterday," retorted Melena. "He'd be better off if he went with her to work. That girl's wild and irresponsible."

"I want her to have a little freedom, a little happiness."

"That's the way girls become perdidoes," replied Melena.

Marianna glared at Melena angrily before wearily rising for the long walk to the city. After Marianna departed, Melena said to Con, "No need to leave until the second siren." Then she went over to nudge Gabriella with her foot. When the girl looked up, Melena said, "Empty the shit pot before I get back."

Gabriella groaned, then rolled to face away.

Shaking her head, Melena looked toward Con. "I was younger than her when I went to the dyeworks."

The second siren sounded. Con strapped her pajaro to her thigh and followed Melena into streets that thronged with people. There, Con saw the first men since her arrival. All were unshaven, though many were too young for beards.

They wore short, sleeveless tunics that differed from the women's dresses principally in their drabness. The tunics were shades of tan or brown, with plain sashes from which knives hung.

No one in the crowd was elderly, though many were infirm. Con realized that Mergonita's entire adult population mobbed the streets, for when people ceased to work, they ceased to live. Swept along by this human flood, Con lost sight of Melena. She was released from the mob's grip only when the workers dispersed at the edge of town. There, someone pointed out Fat Rosa's shop. As Con walked in its direction she passed a number of small, open-front stalls. Men stood inside them scanning the faces of the people that passed. When Con made eye contact with one, he called out, "Have kana to sell?" Con shook her head and moved on.

THE COMPLEX OF workshops at the base of the ridge was a dilapidated and chaotic place of slipshod repairs and makeshift additions. The long, single-story building that housed Fat Rosa's shop was typical. Its cracked concrete walls were windowless. Its curved metal roof was rusty except where translucent sections served as skylights. Plastic sheeting fluttered where broken skylights had been repaired. There was a large, double door in the building's front. A few women, late for work, hurried through it. Many carried infants or tugged the hands of older children.

Con approached the open door. The long, crowded room reeked of sweat. Long tables, with only narrow aisles between them, filled the shop. Several hundred stitchers sat on small stools about them, busily decorating long robes. Almost all the stitchers were women, and most of them were young. *Too young to have the tremblitos,* Con thought. All the pastel-colored robes were ready-made from a satiny material and lacked only decoration. This was embroidered on them entirely by hand. Despite the lack of machinery, a dull roar echoed through the crowded shop. Hundreds of conversations mingled with the shouts of supervisors, the sounds of bored children, and the wail of hungry infants.

The din hurt Con's ears as she entered the building to find Fat Rosa.

After a shouted inquiry, Con was directed to a door at the far end of the shop. Behind it, a sharp-faced woman sat alone in the small, cluttered office. She wore a dress that featured elaborate embroidery, but was greasy about the neck and armholes. Although the woman was slightly plump, Con thought only in Mergonita would she be called fat. "Are you Fat Rosa?" she asked.

"Everyone knows me," replied the woman.

Con assumed the reply was "yes." "My name is Con. I've heard you're looking for a stitcher."

"I might be. Come here and hold out your hands." Con complied, and Rosa scrutinized them. "Your fingers are steady, do you know how to use them?"

"Here's some of my work."

Con produced the sample, which Rosa examined with an expressionless face before handing it back. "It's nice enough," she said. "Fancy. But we don't do fancy work here, and I can't pay fancy wages. I'll give you eight pills a week."

"I'm skilled," said Con. "I'm worth more than that."

Rosa glanced at the sample again. "I'll give you nine. Take it or leave it."

"I'll take it."

"All right, Con. You'll get a pill at the end of each day and the other two pills at the end of the week. Now let me give you some advice." Rosa extended both her arms. "Feel my hands."

Con touched them.

"I'm forty-one, an old woman, but my hands are steadier than many a girl half my age. That's because I take a pill every day, and you should, too. Pop it in your mouth as soon as you get it. Don't take it to the kana buyers. When you're young, you think you can do with less and maybe have a few nice things. So, you take half a pill and ignore the tingles. It's easy when you're young. But tingles become tremblitos, and tremblitos only get worse."

"Then why don't you pay your stitchers more?"

"Do you see a kana tree growing here?" retorted Rosa. "The fecs are stingy with their pills. If I paid some girls more, others would get less or maybe nothing. How many perdidoes do you want?"

Con had no reply, for she thought Rosa's answer was largely truthful. She was certain some people profited handsomely from the scarcity of kana, but she thought none of them lived in Mergonita.

TAVAMANANA PARKED HIS car in front of Clever Mari's workshop and steeled himself for the unpleasantness ahead. He hated visiting sape town. He hated its ugliness . . . its filth . . . its decay. And most of all, he hated its subhuman inhabitants. Their smell, their grotesque bodies, and their animal depravity rendered them disgusting, while their treachery made them dangerous. He took a stun gun from his pocket, clicked off the safety, and replaced it. Then, taking a deep breath, he exited his vehicle.

Clever Mari had been summoned as soon as Tavamanana's car arrived, and she waited to greet him at the workshop's entrance. She bowed deeply when he approached. "Perfected One, I am honored by your visit, but I fear I have no news."

"We can discuss that later," said Tavamanana. "First, I promised a friend I would select an embroidered robe for him."

"Please do not be offended, Perfected One, but I must obey the law. I may sell only to an authorized dealer."

Tavamanana regarded her, certain she would sell her children for a handful of kana. *That's why the kana laws must be so strict,* he thought. *A shortsighted and greedy man could easily undermine the drug's scarcity.* Tavamanana was not such a man; Mazafalama would get his robe, but through proper channels. "I only wish to select the robe," replied the Kynden. "Razalambadura will purchase it for me. You are licensed to sell to him, are you not?"

"Si, Perfected One."

"Good, then bring out only your finest wares. I am looking for something special, *very* special."

"Would you prefer to view the robes outside?" asked Mari. "The light would be better."

"Si," said Tavamanana, relieved he would avoid the stink of the workshop.

"It will only take a few minutes, Perfected One." Mari bowed, then hurried inside the workshop.

Ten minutes latter, Tavamanana was examining five different embroidered robes. Each was a unique and exquisite creation. For a while, he forgot their source as he marveled at their beauty and artistry. He tried to envision Karinalalina adorned in each, and each vision was a delight. Finally, he chose a soft blue robe that reminded him of starlight on the rolling hills. "This one will do," he said. "I will have Razalambadura pick it up tomorrow."

Clever Mari bowed. "You have a connoisseur's eye, Perfected One."

As the robe was wrapped up, Tavamanana said to Mari, "Come down to my vehicle. There is some more business we might do."

Mari dutifully followed the Kynden, who led her behind his vehicle where they could not be observed. "The last time I was here, I told you I was looking for someone," said Tavamanana. "Have you seen anyone fitting my description?"

"A strange-looking one?" said Mari. "I told you. I have no news."

"Strange is not a proper description. Long ago, your race had more variety. Some had golden skin; others were dark brown or even pink. Eyes came in different shades, and hair also. A person you might call 'strange' would have such traits."

"Sadly, Perfected One, I have not heard of such a person."

"You are a busy woman," said Tavamanana. "I think the reward I offered failed to reflect the value of your time. I have come to increase the amount." He pulled a half-liter jar from his robe. It was filled to the top with kana pills.

Mari could not have been more astounded if Tavamanana had produced the sun from his pocket. The brimming jar contained more than wealth, it held life itself.

"Hold out your hands," said Tavamanana as he unscrewed the top of the jar. When Mari did so, he poured pills into her outstretched palms. "Offer a larger reward for information. If you are successful, this entire jar—refilled to the top—will be yours. Tell Razalambadura you have been successful, and the word will get to me."

Clever Mari quickly closed her hands around the treasure. They were already shaking with excitement. She bowed low. "I will do everything in my power to aid you, Perfected One."

"I am pleased you understand me," replied Tavamanana. "I will await your news." Then he entered his vehicle and drove off.

CLEVER MARI WATCHED Tavamanana drive away. She was glad the fec knew so little about life in Mergonita. *Any kana buyer would scour the town for a fraction of what he gave me.* As usual, her obsequiousness had paid off. *He didn't even bother to count the pills.* Holding so much kana made her nervous. She glanced around, then hurried to her office. Once inside, she locked the door and spilled the pills on the table. She counted fifty-seven, over a year's worth of profits.

Heretofore, Clever Mari had disregarded Tavamanana's request, for she was not inclined to sell out her own. The riches before her had changed that. As Mari pondered how to ensure the kana would not slip through her grasp, she had no illusions the fec's intentions were benevolent. If the person he sought could be found, Mari did not care to imagine that person's fate. *I've had friends who've been murdered for a few pills,* she reflected. *Should I care about a stranger?* She readily answered that question, for the jar of kana had poisoned her compassion.

17

AFTER CON WAS HIRED, SHE WAS ESCORTED TO A workstation near the center of the room. "Emli," said the manager, "show the new girl what to do."

Emli looked up from her stitching. She was several years younger than Con, with a large, thin nose and crooked teeth. Emli had the same dark eyes, tan skin, and black hair as everyone around her. She looked at Con curiously.

"Hello," said Con, feeling self-conscious. "My name's Con."

Emli ignored Con's greeting and took a robe from the table. A pattern of leafy vines had been stenciled around the neck. "Stitch the vines," said Emli. "Two colors, like mine. Make sure you cover the lines." Then she turned to a girl with a large mole on her chin. "So, is Anna really interested in Manuel?"

Con began stitching. She was the subject of many surreptitious glances, but otherwise ignored. The talk that swirled around her was always directed elsewhere. Con kept her gaze on her embroidery, glad she could at least be busy. While Con worked, she eavesdropped. Mostly the talk was gossip about the romances of others. Who was "visiting the cornfield" was a topic of particular interest. Con's ears pricked up when the subject turned to the missing woman. She found that Melena's belief that a fec had taken her was the common one.

"What do you think he did with her?" asked the girl with the mole.

"Who knows?" said an older woman in a dark blue dress. "I have no wish to find out."

Later, it was the same woman who broke the ice with Con. She examined a robe Con had just finished. "You stitch fast," she said, "and well, also." She paused. "You're not from Mergonita."

"No, I'm from the south."

"Really? What's it like there?"

Con had already prepared an answer. "I don't know. I was attacked while traveling and woke up with a bump on my head. I remember almost nothing before then."

Con's reply provoked everyone's interest, and they were suddenly willing to talk to her. "Don't you remember anything?" asked Emli.

"I remember my name. I think I had a husband and a child, but I also think they're dead."

"You don't know for sure?" asked the girl with the mole.

"No," said Con. "Everything's fuzzy."

"That's sad!" said Emli.

"How did you manage to get here without any kana?" asked the woman in blue.

"It wasn't taken," said Con. "I hid it where they couldn't find it."

The woman in blue gave a ribald laugh. "I guess they had short fingers."

"Well, I heard," said Emli, "bandits cut people open looking for kana."

"Me too," said the girl with the mole. "You're lucky, Con."

"I guess I am," said Con. "But I wish I knew where I come from. Are there other towns nearby?"

"I've heard of some," said the woman in blue, "but I don't know where they are. I've never left Mergonita, and I don't know anyone who has."

Con quickly discovered this was true for everyone at the table. Their knowledge of the world did not extend beyond the farthest cornfield. "Isn't there someone I could ask? Surely, there must be a map somewhere."

"You should see the Padre," said Emli. "He has things like that."

"You'll need kana," warned the girl with the mole. "He'll want a contribution."

"Where can I find him?" asked Con.

"On a street near the top of the hill," said the woman in blue. "People can direct you."

"Do you think he could help me?" asked Con.

"Maybe," replied the woman. "He knows things most people have forgotten. Perhaps one of those things will answer your question."

CLEVER MARI SPENT a busy morning recruiting spies. She sought out persons who made deliveries to the workshops. They would cover the greatest ground and see the most people. Additionally, they would be cheap to deal with. A single pill would get their attention, and a dozen would be a handsome reward. She had already spoken to several individuals, when she spotted Melena laden with skeins of embroidery thread. "Melena," she called out, "this is a lucky meeting."

"The turquoise isn't ready yet," said Melena.

"That's not what I want to discuss," said Mari. "I need a favor."

"What?"

Clever Mari approached very close, and said in a low voice, "It's really not a favor, because I'll pay." As she spoke, she pressed a pill into Melena's hand.

Melena gazed down at the kana pill in her palm, then quickly closed her fingers around it. "What's that for?"

"To show my sincerity."

"What do you want me to do?"

"Keep your eyes open."

"And what do you hope they'll see?"

"I'm interested in finding a man or a woman who is different in some way. Perhaps their hair is an unusual shade, or their skin is lighter or darker, or their eyes . . ."

"Dusty-colored?"

"Have you seen such a person?" asked Mari quickly.

"Perhaps," replied Melena.

"Well, if you have, I've a dozen pills for you."

Melena's eyes narrowed. "Why do you seek this person? Are fecs involved?"

"Kana's involved," answered Mari. "Twelve pills."

"I must hold them in my hand," said Melena, "before we speak more of this."

CON WORKED UNTIL a siren sounded at dusk. Leaving took a while, for each worker was paid at the end of the day. Con joined the slow-moving line to receive her pill. Some workers swallowed their wage immediately, but more than a few made only a show of putting the pill in their mouths. They palmed their kana, as did Con. She realized that not needing kana gave her a financial advantage. Her coworkers must consume their daily pill or, at least, most of it. Con could use hers as she pleased. She visited the kana buyer's stalls and, after haggling, turned her pill into 110 credits. Beyond the stalls of the kana buyers, vendors of various goods sat by the road or in stalls. They had not been there in the morning, but now that the workers had been paid, they were eager to sell to those who had converted their kana into credits.

With the sale of the pill, Con's money bracelet was worth 123 credits. The bracelet was a carryover from the days when people had financial accounts maintained in a central file. Now, such accounts resided only in the bracelets themselves. Still, Con's credits were safe, because the bracelet was linked to the identity chip in her skull. A money bracelet functioned solely for its owner. So far, this was the only use Con had encountered for the identity chip, though she suspected there were others. The Kyndens implanted the chips in all newborn Sapenes, and Con assumed the chips benefited the implanters more than the implanted.

The first thing Con bought was a loaf of bread, which she ate on the spot. With her hunger dulled, she went shopping for an additional dress. The garments for sale seemed little better than gaudy sacks. Even so, Con quickly discovered she could not afford a new one. She found a stall that sold used clothing and started rummaging among its wares.

Appearance was no longer a criterion, only serviceability. Nothing she saw was completely intact, and though everything had been washed, the garments were still stained and soiled. After rejecting dresses that were little more than tattered rags, Con found one that at least met the requirements of modesty. It was worse than the garment she wore—frayed at the hem and stained to boot. The busy pattern featured ghastly shades of pink, chartreuse, and lavender. Even after much haggling, it cost the entire amount on her bracelet. Con looked at her pathetic purchase and realized that, to an untrained stitcher who swallowed her daily pill, it represented a week's wages.

The streets were emptying as Con inquired where the Padre lived. After a few wrong turns, she found his apartment building. Knowing the Padre would ask for kana, Con looked for a private place to remove a pill from her vial. A short way up the road was a narrow gap between two buildings. Con walked over to it and peered down its dark length. It was empty. She quickly stepped inside. Hastily, Con fished the vial from her undergarment and took out a pill. Only when she was done did she notice the sticky puddle beneath her feet. It was a pool of clotted blood.

AFTER HER DISCOVERY in the alley, it took several minutes before Con had the composure to knock on the Padre's door. A man in his early twenties opened it.

"I need to speak to the Padre," said Con.

The young man regarded her suspiciously, but let her in.

The room Con entered was only slightly larger than Marianna's apartment and differed from it in only two ways—its shelves were laden with documents, and it contained an ancient-looking table and chair. A man in his forties was seated at the table and talking to two women. "Here's your agreement," he said, displaying a scrap of paper, "properly written and witnessed." He handed it to the women, who examined it with satisfaction, although they held it upside down.

"Thank you, Padre," said the women. They turned to leave.

Con started to approach the Padre when the young man touched her arm. He held out a shallow metal dish by its rim. In its center were yellow chips of kana. Con dropped her pill into the dish. Everyone in the room reacted to the clink of the pill hitting the metal as if it were the crash of a cymbal. The young man stared at the pill, then at Con with surprise before quickly ushering the two women out.

The Padre rose. "I thought I recognized everyone in Mergonita, but your face is new to me. I'm Padre Luis."

"I'm Con. I live with Marianna, mother of Gabriella and Jonny, but I'm not from here. That's why I've come to see you."

"You must have an extraordinary request," said the Padre, eyeing the collection dish. "That's a great deal of kana for some writing."

"I'm looking for a map. One that shows towns where Sapenes live."

"Why do you want such a thing?"

"I don't feel safe in Mergonita."

"Then you should return to wherever you came from."

"I was hit on the head," said Con, "and it's affected my memory. I no longer know the way. I thought a map might help."

"Perhaps I can find one of use," said the Padre.

Con looked at the shelves with interest. "You don't use data tablets?"

"Those are books, my child, a venerable invention. Unlike data tablets, they're unchangeable. People started making them when they discovered the fecs were rewriting history. Not so long ago, owning a book brought trouble. Now, the fecs don't care. When everyone's worried about getting their next pill, history doesn't matter."

"No," said Con, "I guess it doesn't."

"But you're here for a map," said the Padre. "Let's see if I can find one."

The Padre sifted through a pile of dog-eared papers, then pulled one out. He gingerly unfolded it on the table. Despite his care, the paper cracked along the lines of the folds. "This is a map of the mass transport system. Sapenes can't use it, but you can follow the tracks." He studied it for a minute. "It has only the names of the fec cities. Here we are," he said, pointing to a spot some distance from a small lake, "outside Mergona."

Con walked around the table to examine the map. "The cities are so far apart!" she exclaimed. "Napolis seems the closest. Do Sapenes live there?"

"We live wherever there are fecs."

"Then I'll for head Napolis," said Con. "Could I have this map?"

"I cannot part with it," replied Padre Luis, "but Tomas, my acolyte, could make you a copy tomorrow. His hands are steadier."

"What will it cost me?"

"You have already paid for it," replied the Padre. He looked at Con and sighed. "Yet, I worry this map will lead to your destruction. Travel is dangerous. There are bandits."

"Don't worry about me," replied Con.

"I worry over everyone, my child," said Padre Luis. "I'm more than a keeper of books, a writer of contracts. I'm here to testify that every life is precious, and a greater power determines our destiny."

"But Padre," Con said, "what if that power favors the fecs?"

18

IT WAS NIGHT WHEN CON LEFT THE PADRE'S AND hurried through Mergonita. After the harshly lit streets, the shadowed alley leading to Marianna's apartment seemed very dark. Con nearly tripped over the perdido's legs before she saw them. They were not trembling. As Con's eyes adjusted to the darkness, the woman's pale form became more visible. Someone had stolen her dress, but the woman would not miss it. *No work. No kana. Perdido.* Con realized after "perdido" came "death." She stepped over the motion-less legs, wondering where her newly purchased dress had come from.

Everyone was eating when Con entered. Gabriella rose to get another bowl. "I told you, Melena," she said. "Dusty's only late."

"I stopped to buy a dress," said Con, holding up the shabby garment.

Melena said nothing, but regarded Con in a way that made her uneasy. Con sat down at the straw mat, and Gabriella handed her a bowl of stew. "Melena said we'd never see you again," said Gabriella. "But that's stupid, because you just paid Mama."

Con looked at Melena. "Why would you say that?"

"You're not from here," replied the woman, "I doubt Mergonita is what you expected. There are too many fecs."

"I've yet to see one," said Con.

"You should hope you don't."

* * *

THE FOLLOWING DAY, Con stitched while the map was being copied. It would be her last day at Fat Rosa's. Con intended to use the day's wage with her remaining pills to purchase provisions for her escape. A water container was essential, and she planned to buy as much food as she could bundle in her spare dress. Con hoped to purchase better footwear, but would do with what she had if necessary, for she was unwilling to remain any longer. Con was gripped by a foreboding that Sam's unseen hand was still pushing her toward his ends. That concerned her more than the danger of her journey, and she felt that if her death thwarted Sam, it would not be in vain. As Con stitched, her thoughts turned to another journey, 65 million years in the past. It had been even more desperate than the one she contemplated now. *But I had Rick with me then. This time, I'll be alone.*

Con sighed, and as she did, the workshop grew deathly silent. She looked up, and her gaze was directed by the other eyes in the room toward six Kynden men who were advancing between the tables. Each held something in his hand that Con assumed was a weapon. Con had the impulse to run, or at least hide beneath the table, but she thought that would only draw attention. She needn't have worried. Her brown hair and light complexion had already given her away. Con soon realized that. Again, she considered fleeing. She scanned the packed workshop and saw the futility of flight. All the weapons pointed at her, and the fecs were closing in.

"You!" shouted the closest fec. "The one with brown hair. Stand up!"

Con hesitated.

The fec advanced, aiming something at her head. It had a trigger. "Up!"

Con rose, her eyes fixed on the object pointing at her face. She winced when the fec pulled the trigger.

Nothing happened, except that the Kynden looked at the top of the device in his hand. "Your identity implant is not registered. Come with us."

"Why?"

"You must be registered. We can do it in my vehicle. You will be back to work in minutes." Con noticed the fec had put the first device away, and now pointed an object identical to those his companions held. "Hurry up," he said. "Let us be done with this."

Despite the Kynden's assurances, Con felt she was being taken prisoner. The expressions of her coworkers did nothing to change that impression. She slowly marched out of the workshop, frantically thinking how she might escape. By the time she had room to run, the fecs had surrounded her. There were two vehicles parked outside the shop entrance. The door of one was open.

"Sit in the backseat," said the Kynden who had checked her implant. "This will only take a moment."

The other Kyndens were talking among themselves in their own singsong language. Con had no idea what they were saying, but by their expressions, she assumed the topic was humorous. Con slid into the seat of the car. The fec peered inside. "See that flat gray thing with the cord? Hold it against your head." After Con complied, he said, "You can put it down. You are registered now."

"Can I go?" asked Con.

"Just one more thing," replied the fec. He grinned and raised his weapon. Con saw a flash of blue, felt a jolt of pain, and blacked out.

TAVAMANANA PEERED AT the viewscreen in his office. The female sape was regaining consciousness. He turned to his assistant. "You prepared it as I directed?"

"Cleaned it up, drew blood, and left a bucket so it wouldn't soil the floor."

"You kept its old garments?"

"They're at the Domestics Processing Center."

"Look," said Tavamanana with amusement, "it's discovered it has clean clothes."

His assistant chuckled. "That must be a shock."

The two Kyndens watched Con methodically explore

the locked room, looking for a means to escape. She discovered the lens in the ceiling and started shouting.

"I wish we had audio," said Tavamanana.

"It's a storeroom, sir. Shall I find someplace better?"

"I want to see the blood tests, first. They'll tell me if the sape's worth keeping. Go see if they're done."

Tavamanana's assistant departed, leaving him alone to view his captive. *It certainly is an unusual specimen,* he thought.

Tavamanana's observations were interrupted by the arrival of his superior. He looked extremely vexed. "What's this about a sape in the lab?" he demanded.

"It's the throwback, sir. I found it!"

His boss glanced at the viewscreen. "It has brown hair. So what? I can't believe your gullibility. Someone sends you a crackpot theory, and you embark on a pointless quest. Genetics aren't revealed by superficial traits."

"Sir . . ."

"I want that dirty thing out of here! Now! Then have the room cleaned."

In the midst of Tavamanana's upbraiding, his assistant rushed in excitedly. "Sir," he said, "there's no kana in the sape's blood!"

"None?"

"Not the smallest trace."

Tavamanana turned to his superior with the look of a vindicated man. "Sir, does that sape look ill to you?"

"It's young . . ." hedged his boss.

"Even so, it should be trembling. To have a zero reading, it couldn't have consumed kana for days."

Tavamanana's superior's look of derision transmuted into one of respect as he recognized the significance of the find. "That sape must have the baseline genotype!"

"There can be no doubt," replied Tavamanana.

"What will you do next?"

"Since the specimen is a female, I'll extract ova," said Tavamanana, in a voice that reflected newfound confidence. "Sape females ovulate frequently, and there are drugs that stimulate egg production."

"Why not use regular body tissue?" asked Tavamanana's boss.

"I'll take some of that, too. But the virus infected the germ cells, so I'm particularly interested in them. With tissue culture, we'll soon have ample material for our experiments."

"Tavamanana, I misjudged you. I believed the throwback theory was only wishful thinking. I'm glad you thought otherwise. A discovery like this could change the world."

"I'm sure it will, sir."

CON WAS MOVED to another windowless room soon after she regained consciousness. The Kyndens who escorted her would not answer questions, though they did bring food. The new room was only marginally better than the first. It had a sleeping mat on the floor, a toilet, and a lens on the ceiling. Otherwise, the room was featureless.

Con had no idea what would happen to her, and the few clues were disturbing. Con discovered the first of these when she woke up. She had been washed, and her skin bore the lingering scent of disinfectant. Her clothing had been replaced by a single garment. It was a light green, sleeveless robe. Slit in the back and fastened behind at the neck, it bore a disconcerting resemblance to a hospital gown. Later, Con's impression that she was undergoing some medical study was increased when a Kynden drew blood and gave her injections. Her cooperation was obtained at weapon point.

Con endured the worst form of solitary confinement. No one spoke to her, except to bark orders when they drew blood and gave her shots. Although she was adequately fed, the bowl of bland gruel was slid through an opening at the bottom of the door. Her situation, whatever it was, seemed hopeless. She was utterly powerless, and she feared her captors needed her only as a specimen. If that were the case, there was no way to thwart them—they already had what they needed.

No dimming of the lighted ceiling marked the days. Two

meals, plus the daily blood test and injections were the only events in Con's existence. Sensory deprivation loosened her grip on reality. She had already lost track of the days when she began to see others in the room. Melena peered from a corner. Rick made appearances, staring dumbly at the bloody exit wound in his chest. Roberto Peters lunged at her, naked and eager. However, the most frequent visitor was Sam, who came to gloat over his victory.

After each visitation, Con would be shaken and fearful she was going mad. *It's only in my head,* she would tell herself. Yet, it was increasingly difficult to distinguish reality from hallucination. When she tried to be objective about it, "reality" seemed equally fantastic. *Have I really traveled through time? Is the world's misery truly my fault?* Her vanishing visitors seemed less bizarre than those notions. *Perhaps I'm in a mental institution.*

The numbing routine ended with the appearance of guards who escorted Con through the corridors of a laboratory into an operating room. Three Kyndens were standing around its table, which had a pair of raised stirrups at one end. Con panicked and made a dash for the door. Fear gave her speed, and she made three bounding steps before she felt a jolt of pain and descended into darkness.

WHEN CON AWOKE, she lay on the floor of a vast room. She was naked. A Sapene woman with an officious air stood over her, holding a bundle. "I have your things," she said, handing them to Con.

Con quickly dressed in the clothes she had been wearing when she was captured.

"You'll get back your knives and kana beyond that door," said the woman, nodding in its direction.

Con looked about the room. It reminded her of a locker room, except the clothes were hung on hooks that dangled from lines. There were benches for dressing, and banks of open showers lined the walls. "Where am I?" she asked.

"Domestics Processing Center."

"What's that?"

"Everyone who works in the city goes through here," answered the woman in a bored voice.

Con thought of Marianna. "You mean maids?"

"Si. Look, you can't stay here." The woman handed Con a piece of plastic with numbers on it. "Here's your claim token. Just go out that door."

Con took the token and walked over to the door, which slid open as she approached. It revealed a large, window-less room. Con entered. The door behind her closed, and, a moment later, a second door opened to reveal the land-scape beyond the city. Con claimed her knives and her vial of kana. It contained seven pills, three more than it had originally. Apparently, they were intended to compensate for her ordeal.

19

CON COULD THINK OF NOTHING TO DO EXCEPT WAIT BY the gate for Marianna, though she had no idea how the woman would greet her. As she waited, ancient vehicles pulling wagons parked nearby. *These must offer the ride Melena mentioned,* thought Con. Soon afterward, hordes of men and women began to pour out the gate. Some climbed aboard the wagons. Most trudged toward Mergonita. Con scanned the faces of the latter and eventually spotted Mari-anna. She halted when she saw Con approach. "Con?" she said, as if unable to believe her eyes. "The fecs took you three weeks ago!"

"They turned me loose today. How are Gabriella and Jonny?"

"They were upset when you were taken. Me, too. What did they do to you?"

"I . . . I don't know," Con replied. Her lip started quivering as she fought back tears.

Marianna regarded Con with motherly sympathy. "Come home with me," she said gently.

Con wiped her eyes. "Thank you, Marianna," she said. "You'll be safe. The fecs got whatever they wanted."

GABRIELLA WAS AS surprised as her mother when she saw Con, but she expressed her curiosity more directly. "Dusty! How'd you get here? You run away? I *told* Melena you'd be back. I'm glad she doesn't stay here now. Were the fecs mean? Did they . . ."

"Gabriella!" admonished Marianna. "Give Con some peace."

"It's all right," said Con. "It's good to see her again."

"Was it terrible?" asked the girl.

"I was lonely and scared," admitted Con.

"But you're happy now," said Gabriella. "Aren't you?"

Jonny ran over to Con and hugged her. "Be happy, Dusty!"

A wan smile came to Con's face.

"Gabriella," said Marianna, "pour some more water in the stew and add some cornmeal."

"Marianna," said Con, "while there's still light, would you look for marks upon my body?"

"Do you think the fecs did something to you?"

"I'm certain of it, but I have no idea what."

"I'll look."

Con removed her clothes, and Marianna examined her skin for marks while Jonny watched curiously and Gabriella tended the stew. No one noticed the fly that alighted on the ceiling. For a split second, it transformed into a tiny, translucent sphere before it changed again into a fleck of paint.

IN THE GRIP of a dream, Gabriella tossed about the sleeping mat, but it was not the girl's stirring that kept Con awake—it was her own restless mind. She pondered the future, trying to decide what to do. Con thought there was no point in leaving Mergonita now. *Sam's won. He got what he wanted. I was doomed the moment I walked into town.* Con was certain he would never return. *I'm no more use to him. I'm stuck here for the rest of my life.*

Con was considering that dismal prospect when the door of the apartment opened. Only moonlight filtered through the dirty skylight, and the three figures that entered were little more than shadows. Their short stature made Con think they were children engaged in some prank until one began to shine a pale violet beam about the room. When the beam passed over the ceiling, an object the size of a pea began to glow. The beam fixed on the tiny sphere, which shone ever brighter until it illuminated the entire room.

Con could see the intruders clearly now. They resembled children, but there was an adult aspect to their faces, and their foreheads bore metallic dots. However, it was not the strangeness of their faces that sent chills down Con's spine, but rather the familiarity of one of them. She recognized him as the driver who had fired at her car in the twenty-seventh century.

The light woke Marianna and Gabriella. Marianna started to speak, but a flash of blue light cut her short. Marianna uttered a short cry and collapsed. The light flashed twice more, rendering Gabriella and Jonny unconscious. Meanwhile, the glowing object on the ceiling flared out, and the room was plunged into darkness. One of the intruders shined a light into Con's face, blinding her to everything but its glare. "Who are you?" asked Con, trying to conceal her terror.

A high-pitched voice replied. "Be still!"

Con froze and heard someone advance. The beam illuminated a small hand that held a small rod-shaped object. A voice said, "This won't hurt." Still, Con flinched when the object touched her forehead. After it was withdrawn, Con felt her brow and discovered that her implant had been exposed.

"Be still!" commanded the voice. A different rod touched Con's implant. After it was withdrawn, Con heard voices speaking in a strange, melodic language. The rod was pressed against Con's implant again. A minute later, the high-pitched voice spoke again, this time in perfect English. "Your implant was set to destroy you. We have neutralized it, yet it also means we have found you too late."

"Too late for what?" asked Con.

"We think you know. Why don't you tell us?"

"Is this some kind of trial?" asked Con. "If so, the woman and the children are innocent. Promise me you won't harm them."

"It is only your deeds that concern us," said a deeper voice. "We want a full confession."

"As a nicety before my execution?" asked Con, who felt strangely calm now that her life seemed about to end. "I know you tried to kill me once before."

"We were trying to prevent the eradication of billions," replied a voice.

"Today, you caused the Purification—the extermination of your own species," added the deeper voice. "You're hardly one to accuse *us* of murder."

"I didn't do anything today," retorted Con.

"You must have done something. Samazatarmaku would not destroy you unless you had accomplished your task."

"Samaz-who?"

"The individual who sent you to this time."

"You mean Sam?"

"If he's your master, then I mean Sam."

"He's not my master," replied Con.

"Did you think he was your friend?" asked a voice in a derisive tone.

"Yes," said Con. "I'm ashamed to admit it, but I once thought he was. What I did with the virus, I did out of ignorance. He told me I was setting things right. I know differently now, but at the time . . ." Con hung her head. "I guess it doesn't matter. If you're here to punish me, I deserve it. But I didn't cause the Purification. I know that for a fact."

"Why do you say that?" asked a voice.

"Because, before I met Sam, the Purification had already happened. The people from the future who rescued me 65 million years ago said *Homo sapiens* were extinct. They even referred to the Purification by name. They sent me to the nineteenth century so the future would remain unchanged."

Con's reply set off a heated discussion among the intruders in their own tongue while she sat blinded by the light, certain her fate was being decided. Finally, a voice spoke in English. "You stated the Purification already happened. Such an absurd assertion demonstrates your ignorance."

"Perhaps she didn't wreak havoc intentionally," said another voice.

"I didn't" said Con. "I'll do anything to fix the harm I've caused."

"I doubt that's possible," said a voice.

"She could try," said another.

"Yes, let me try," said Con.

The light that had shone in Con's face transformed into a soft glow, and she could see her interrogators again. They were the size of ten-year-olds, though more muscular. They had soft-featured faces with the same olive skin, dark eyes, and black hair as the Kyndens and the Sapenes. Their clothes were shades of faded green or muted earth tones and consisted of loose-fitting pants that ended midcalf, a roomy short-sleeved shirt, and sturdy sandals. Two were women. It was the man who had attacked her vehicle.

Con, who was only partly dressed, felt self-conscious in their gaze. "May I put on my dress?" she asked.

"Of course," answered one of the women.

Con slipped on her dress, but not her cordeya with its knives. Then she sat down in front of the intruders.

The man said, "We are Gaians, *Homo gaia*. Our species no longer exists. You took care of that on your first visit to the future."

"Well, Oak, *that* was blunt," said one of the women. "You certainly know how to put someone at ease." She turned to Con and smiled. "Hello, I'm Violet and this is Fern." She nodded toward the other Gaian woman.

"I'm Con Clements."

"Fern and I left the thirty-seventh century to gather plants and returned to find reality altered. Oak is from the thirty-eighth century, when tact is less in fashion."

"The girl should know she destroyed our world," retorted Oak.

"I . . . I'm sorry," said Con.

"There, Oak," said Violet. "Con's apologized. Now, do you feel better?"

Con blushed, feeling stupid, and Violet detected her embarrassment. "Con, Samazatarmaku had all the advantages. You didn't stand a chance."

"Who really is this person I called Sam?" asked Con.

"A genius," replied Violet. "One with contempt for anyone different from himself. History is full of such bigots, people who believe there's a master race. Yet, only Samazatarmaku eliminated all but his own kind."

Con hung her head. "And I helped him do it."

"Samazatarmaku distorted your existence, just as he distorted history. I don't blame you, and Oak shouldn't either. You don't even understand what you are."

"What I am? What do you mean by that?"

"You'll confuse her if you try to explain," said Oak to Violet.

"Perhaps not," said Violet. She paused to collect her thoughts. "Con, you must understand the timestream is a continuum. All of history exists simultaneously. That is why time travel is possible. The past, present, and future are relative to your location on that continuum."

"That seems simple enough," said Con.

"Your existence stretches through time and throughout its length there is a person who calls herself Con. At some points, she is young. At others, she is old. Each correctly believes she is living in the present, for there are an infinite number of presents. Now, does it still seem simple?"

Con thought a moment. "No," she replied, "but I guess it makes sense."

"Good," said Violet. "Now, let's talk about the timestream itself. There is only one, and it has a shape that we call 'history.' That shape is not static, although it appears that way to us. Since there is only one timestream, if it changes, we perceive the new version of history as having always been that way."

"That can't be true," said Con. "You know reality was once different. You just accused me of changing it."

"That's because time travel permits us to observe some of those changes. For people trapped within the timestream, the past seems fixed. The inhabitants of Mergonita may regret what happened in the past, but they believe it is impossible to change. They think change is only possible in the present."

"But there are an infinite number of presents," said Con.

"You catch on quickly," said Violet. "That's why it's possible to change time. I speak of a 'timestream' because time acts very much like a river flowing through a landscape."

"Does that explain why only the past can affect the future?" asked Con.

"Precisely," replied Violet. "Entropy causes the timestream to have a current. The past flows toward the future."

"If time flows, is it possible for the timestream to change on its own?" asked Con.

"Yes, but only in very limited ways" said Violet, "There are powerful forces that constrain the degree of variation. A river does not change its course easily."

"It takes an extremely powerful phenomenon to alter the course of time," said Oak.

"Stick your hand in a river, and you disturb it," said Violet. "Water is displaced. Ripples form. Yet a few feet downstream, nothing is different. Throw a boulder in the current and the changes are greater, yet the river doesn't veer in another direction. Time is the same way; it's not easy to alter. The upwhen from a change, history resumes it natural course, like water closing around a hand."

"History follows the optimal course," said Oak. "It will always return to it whenever possible."

"If you want to change the shape of a river, a hand or a boulder won't do," said Violet. "You need a dam. Something totally unnatural."

Con shook her head in confusion.

"Samazatarmaku created an entity that is largely unaffected by the forces that keep the timestream on its natural course," said Oak. "That entity is you."

"Me?" said Con. "You talk as if I were a phenomenon, not a person."

"In the twenty-seventh century, you destroyed my species," said Oak. "I couldn't even destroy your car."

"In ways we don't fully understand," said Violet, "your actions have a vastly greater effect on the timestream than those of other individuals."

"And I have this ability because I'm my own ancestor?"

Violet looked at her companions, clearly surprised by this information. "*That* would explain a lot."

"I think it goes even deeper," said Oak. "Con, you said you were rescued by people from the future, people for whom the Purification was already history."

"Yes, they sent me back to the nineteenth century, where I became my own ancestor."

Oak's face lit up with understanding and drudging respect. "What elegance," he exclaimed. "What a masterpiece of paradox!"

Con stared at him blankly.

"You are able to change history," said Oak, "because you are your own ancestor and you are your own ancestor because you changed history."

As Con's confusion grew, Violet recognized her perplexity. "Time travel makes it difficult to understand chronology," she said. "Before time travel, one's perception of the sequence of events perfectly matched the flow of the timestream. Yet, time travel allows people to jump about the timestream. We think you did something today that changed history. Yet once that change was made, everything upwhen was affected. What seems like the present to you is the distant past to the people who got in their time machine and visited you 65 million years ago."

Con nodded her head. It seemed logical until she thought about it. "I'm not sure I can make sense of what you said."

"Time travel results in illogical situations," said Violet. "Logic is an inadequate tool to understand the universe."

"Since changes in the past only affect the future," said Oak, "the timestream is now riddled with inconsistencies—relics from realities that no longer exist."

"I was told my childhood no longer exists," said Con.

"It doesn't," said Oak. "We looked for it."

The remark had disturbing implications. "So, you've been following me."

"Unfortunately, yes," said Oak.

"Why do you say unfortunately?" asked Con.

"Since there's only one timestream," said Violet, "only one present can exist at any given instant. That prevents us from returning to any time we visited before."

"Unless reality is changed," added Fern, "so that we no longer exist in that time frame."

"You mean you can't visit me in Finoporto and warn me not to make the virus?" asked Con.

"No," said Oak, "because we were already there, searching for you."

"The same is true in this century," said Violet, "and you no longer exist in the twenty-first."

"You could visit me in the Cretaceous, before I was rescued," said Con.

That remark precipitated a vigorous discussion among the Gaians in their own language. Oak seemed to be arguing with both Fern and Violet. As Con watched them, she realized too late they needed only to kill her in the Cretaceous to undo all the harm she had caused.

Finally, Violet spoke in English. "If Samazatarmaku was about to destroy you, it means he fears you can still affect his plans. You are a potent force, and we should try to take advantage of your power."

"I want to help you, but I don't know what I did today to change history."

"You must find out," said Oak. "When you do, this should prove useful." He took out a metal sphere the size of a baseball. "This is a fusion grenade from World War IV. Samazatarmaku used one in Finoporto. This one is not as powerful, but it could destroy part of a building."

Con thought a minute, trying to determine the consequences of altering history once again. "If I undo whatever I've done, won't I prevent people from visiting the Cretaceous to rescue me?"

"That event took place before the change we're proposing," said Violet.

"But their time journey starts in the future."

"Their departure will no longer exist," said Oak, "but what they did in the past will remain unaltered."

"Don't worry," said Violet, "you'll be safe."

"I wasn't thinking of me," said Con. "I wasn't the only one rescued. Rick, my husband, was saved with me. If I reverse this change, he'll be stranded." The idea of such a death made Con's eyes well with tears, and she fought to keep her composure. "I . . . I don't care what happens to me, but I won't let Rick die like that."

"Weren't you listening?" said Oak. "Changing the future cannot affect the past."

"What you say doesn't make sense," said Con.

"Then take it on faith," replied Violet.

"Doing things without understanding them got me in this mess," retorted Con. "I won't risk Rick's life solely on your word."

"He's one person," said Oak. "This involves the fate of humanity."

An inspiration came to Con. "You can bring him here! Take your time machine and bring him to me!"

"That's absurd," said Oak. "It would complicate everything. Besides, Samazatarmaku would find out."

"Then I won't help you," replied Con.

Oak looked at Con menacingly. "We could go back to the Cretaceous and stop you there."

"You mean kill me? Go ahead. Just kill us both. It would be kinder that way."

Con's demands sparked another vigorous and unintelligible debate among the three Gaians. This one lasted longer than the first. Eventually, Violet said, "Tell us all you know about this person, so we may find him."

"And be quick about it," said Oak. "We disabled Samazatarmaku's miniprobe so he won't know about our visit. Still, we're safe only briefly. Being here puts us in jeopardy."

"You're also in danger," said Violet. "When Samazatarmaku finds out you're still alive, he'll seek to kill you."

"You should leave this dwelling tonight and prepare for this Rick person's arrival," said Fern.

"We'll monitor history for the precise time of the fusion explosion and arrive just after it occurs," said Violet. "If you meet us, we will take you both downwhen to safety."

"Bringing this person here is all we can do," warned Oak. "Keeping him safe is your responsibility."

Con nodded her agreement, but her thoughts were already elsewhere. She was imagining watching a sunset in Montana with Rick's arms clasped around her.

THE REMAINING BUSINESS between Con and the three Gaians was concluded hastily. Con answered all their questions about Rick and agreed to rendezvous the following evening. Afterward, Fern downloaded some information into Con's implant before using a device to cover it with skin. "Now you can understand and speak the Kynden language," she said. Then the Gaians departed. Their sense of urgency had infected Con, and she no longer felt safe in the apartment. She hurried about the dark room, anxious to leave.

Marianna, Gabriella, and Jonny were still unconscious, and Con worried what they would think of her disappearance. *They'll be frightened,* she thought. *The blue flashes will remind them of the woman who was taken.* Con pondered how she could leave a message. She wanted to reassure them, and also prevent them from spreading a story about her disappearance. *I can't write them a note. I'll have to leave something else.* Eventually, Con decided to use her necklace as a sign. She placed it on the table, spread it to form a circle, and put a kana pill in the circle's center.

Con was gathering her belongings when her bare foot stepped on something that was small and very warm. She bent down and located it by feel. It was a black sphere about the size of a pea. Con slipped it in her pocket before she fled.

The streets of Mergonita were dangerous at night. Unlit and flanked by shadowy alleyways, they were ideal sites for ambushes. A lone woman was especially vulnerable, and Con held her cerdo unsheathed. Despite the danger, she could barely contain her growing euphoria. She felt truly happy for first time since Rick's murder.

20

CON WAITED FOR THE DAWN IN A CORNFIELD, HER mind in a giddy whirl. It was impossible to sleep. There were many difficulties ahead—she had no place to stay, no job, and no idea what she had done to change history or how to undo the damage. Yet as pressing as these problems were, she found it difficult to dwell upon them. Seeing Rick was foremost in her mind. She joyfully imagined their reunion in countless variations.

When the siren pierced the predawn darkness, Con stirred into action. She had to sell her kana to eat and to buy clothing for Rick. Contemplating the business ahead made her finally confront the problems she postponed considering. Her abduction by the fecs was common knowledge;

surely, her reappearance was also. Con feared the gossip
would alert Sam. If he were not to track her down, she would
need a refuge. Con pondered her options. She couldn't return
to Marianna's. Hiding in the cornfields wasn't practical. She
doubted her former coworkers would be helpful, and she was
leery about approaching strangers. There seemed to be only
one possibility.

PADRE LUIS WAS surprised to hear a knock on his door, for
he seldom had visitors during working hours. He rose to
answer it. Tomas had to earn his kana elsewhere, for lately,
contributions had been meager. *The day's drawing near
when Mergonita will no longer support a Padre,* mused
Luis. His trembling fingers were proof it wasn't fully supporting one now. He opened the door and recognized the
girl who had asked for the map. She looked ill at ease.

"May I came in, Padre?" she asked.

"Of course, my child."

Con entered, and Luis closed the door.

"I'm Con. Do you remember me?"

"Si," said the Padre, "though I never expected to see you
again. Have you come for your map?"

"It's useless now."

"Then why are you here?"

"I've nowhere else to turn," said Con.

"What of Marianna?"

"I'm afraid of drawing trouble to her."

"But not of drawing it to me?" A wry smile came to Padre
Luis's face. "You must suppose I'm a man of courage."

"I'm not here for shelter, just advice."

"Then how may I advise you?"

"I must stay in Mergonita," said Con, "but I have no
idea where it's safe."

"There are places that will rent spaces," replied the
Padre. "They're crowded, but cheap. Ordinarily, they're
safe enough. Whether they'd be safe for you is another
matter. You'll need to tell me more if I'm to give you good
advice."

Con hesitated. She looked at the Padre, trying to determine what sort of man he was. He was inquisitive, but he also seemed kindly and unlikely to betray her. *I'll have to confide in someone,* she realized. *I can't hope to do this on my own.* Con decided to tell some of the truth and wondered what she might say. *I can't mention time travel.* Then an idea came to her. "Padre, I don't need kana."

"What?"

"I never take it. It's unnecessary."

"How can that be?" said Luis. "Even the fecs need it."

"I was born this way."

"To live without kana," said the Padre in a wistful voice. "No wonder the fecs wanted you. What did they do to you?"

"I don't know for sure," said Con. "They kept me locked up, then did something to my body while I was unconscious."

"How do you know that?" asked the Padre. "Do you have a mark or a wound?"

"No, but I found blood on my undergarment."

The Padre's face reflected his outrage. "No wonder you wanted to flee!"

"Yet now, I believe I came to Mergonita for a purpose, and it's important to find out what it was."

"If you're going to stay, why don't you stay with me?"

"I couldn't do that. It could be dangerous for you."

"Should I send this danger to someone else?" asked the Padre. "I'm an old man with tremblitos. I've little to lose."

"People visit you all the time. News would spread I was here."

"I didn't always keep my books in the open," replied the Padre. "I have a place where you can hide."

"It . . . it wouldn't be just me," said Con. "I have a husband."

"I thought you were alone," said the Padre.

"We've . . . we've been apart for many months, but now he's joining me."

"Well, two can fit in my hideaway as easily as one," replied the Padre. "However, hiding won't solve your mystery."

"I know. I'll have to find a way into the city," said Con. "I'm sure the answer lies there."

"Then your quest is hopeless. You'll learn nothing from the fecs. They're impossible to understand."

"Perhaps if one knew their language . . ."

"But no one does," replied Luis.

"I do," said Con.

"Where did you learn such a thing?"

"I . . . I don't remember," replied Con, who was made uneasy by the Padre's questions.

"Assuming you succeed in discovering what you seek, what will you do?"

"That will depend on what I find," replied Con.

Padre Luis was unsure whether he was in the presence of a heroine or a lunatic. Either way, Con piqued his curiosity. "I'll help you if I can. When will I meet your husband?"

"He's arriving tonight."

"Does he have a name?"

"It's Rick," said Con in a dreamy voice. "Rick Clements."

Padre Luis moved his sleeping mat away from the wall and pushed the side of one of the concrete blocks on the floor. It teetered. Grabbing the edge of the block, he pulled it away to reveal a hole that passed under the wall. "This is the entrance to my former library," he said. "Would you like to see your accommodations?"

Con wiggled through the hole to the other side of the wall. There, she found a long, narrow room about three feet wide. A small skylight provided illumination. One wall was lined with empty shelves. Con slid back out into the main room.

"It became hard for me to get my books," said Padre Luis, "so I moved them in here." He smiled. "Perhaps I became bolder, though I think lazier is closer to the truth."

"The room's perfect," said Con.

"That's not a word I would choose," said Padre Luis, "but I'm glad you're satisfied. I hope your husband is as easily pleased." He saw the way Con's eyes shone, and added, "I think he would be pleased to be anywhere you are."

Con smiled.

"So that solves one problem," said Padre Luis. "You can get into the city as a maid."

"A maid! Isn't there some other way?"

"It's impossible to sneak in," said Luis. "Your identity chip prevents that. The fecs would know the instant you crossed the wall."

Con sighed. "So, how do I become a maid?"

"I think Marianna could best tell you that. I'll have Tomas arrange a meeting."

Con thought a moment. "Be sure he's careful what he says," said Con. "The fecs have means for listening."

"They do?"

Con withdrew the blackened miniprobe from her pocket and handed it to Luis. "They use devices like these."

The Padre examined it. "It looks like a pebble to me," he said, thinking it was proof Con was delusional.

Con saw doubt clouding the Padre's face. *It was a mistake to show him the miniprobe,* she thought. "It looked different before," she said. "It glowed."

The Padre set the blackened probe down on his table. "So what will you do today?"

"I'll have to buy my husband some clothes when the stalls open." Again, Con saw a questioning look in the Padre's eyes, and she tried to explain. "We dress differently where I come from. He'll need them to fit in here."

"I see," replied the Padre, trying to keep his expression veiled. "If you remember how you dressed, you must remember other things about the place you came from."

Con felt flustered. "Bits and pieces, that's all."

"Well, doubtlessly, your husband can tell me all about it."

Con began to regret her decision to confide in Padre Luis, but she realized there was no turning back. "Padre, I know I must sound crazy."

"You have suffered, my child. I am certain of that. To be frank, I don't know what else to think. But I said I would help you, and I will keep my word."

Con put the only pill she hadn't sold into the collection dish. "Thank you," she said in a quiet voice.

"You're too generous," said the Padre. "I've done nothing to deserve this."

"I told you," said Con, "I don't need kana."

The Padre eyed the pill, as his conscience fought with his need. *Perhaps, she only imagines she doesn't need it.* He picked the kana up with fingers shaking with tremblitos. "I'll set this aside," he said, "in case you want it later."

CON HID IN the former library while she waited for the end of the workday. The hours passed with agonizing slowness. She napped fitfully and borrowed one of the Padre's books, but was too preoccupied to read it. Her impending reunion with a man whose corpse she had washed and buried seemed miraculous, though she knew he lived in several different stretches of the timestream. *The Gaians will simply take him from one of those.*

When the siren sounded to mark the end of the workday, Con rushed to the stalls of the clothes vendors. She bought everything without haggling. A tan tunic, a brown sash, two loincloths, and a pair of rubber flip-flops reduced her credits to forty-three. She could not afford a cerdo for Rick, so she decided she would give him hers—a man should not walk about Mergonita unarmed.

Once her purchases were made, Con hurried to the rendezvous point. It was a long walk down the same dirt road that had first brought her to Mergonita. By the time she reached the hollow that contained the farthest cornfield, it was late at night. Con clutched Rick's garments to her breast and gazed skyward, swaying happily.

THE TIME MACHINE was nearly invisible against the night sky, and, until it landed, Con thought she might be imagining it. It was completely black and more spherical in shape than Sam's machine. A section of its underside lowered and transformed into a silvery stairway. Dim light spilled onto the road and the rows of corn. It illuminated Violet as she descended the stairs, followed by Oak and Fern. The latter two were carrying Rick's still, pale form.

After Fern and Oak lowered Rick's naked body to the ground, Con embraced it and wept for joy. Oak had to shake her roughly to get her attention. "We must leave immediately. So, listen carefully."

"You shaved his beard and cut his hair. He looks so . . ."

"Pay attention!" snapped Oak. "Here's the fusion grenade. You must know how to use it."

Impatiently, Con listened to Oak's instructions and repeated them to show she understood. Then she asked, "From what time did you take him?"

"The one that would cause the least disruption," said Violet.

"Which one was that?" asked Con.

"We don't have time for this!" said Oak. "Samazatarmaku surely knows we're here."

"We must leave now," said Violet. She headed for the time machine. The others had already entered it.

"But why . . ."

"We've tipped our hand to Samazatarmaku, and now we're vulnerable," said Violet in response to Con's unfinished question. Violet entered the time machine, and the stairway sealed the entrance. The craft rose and disappeared into the night sky, leaving Con alone with Rick.

Con tenderly stroked Rick's face and chest, evoking memories with every touch. She kissed his still lips and gazed at him with loving, tear-filled eyes as she waited for him to rejoin her life.

21

RICK OPENED HIS EYES TO FIND THE NIGHT SKY, WHICH had been cloudy above Missoula, Montana, was clear and starry. Then came a cascade of discoveries, none of which made the least bit of sense. The frigid air had turned warm. The snowy university town had transformed into a leafy cornfield. There was a strange girl who babbled words that sounded vaguely Spanish. Tears flowed down her cheeks, and she kept repeating his name. She seemed about to kiss him. Rick jerked upright and, with shock and embarrassment, realized he was naked.

It's a dream, he told himself.

The girl pressed her mouth against his. He felt her tongue on his clenched teeth. Her hands moved over his body. *This can't be real!* Yet, it seemed real. He pushed the girl away. She gazed at him, looking surprised and hurt, then babbled some more. Rick covered himself with his hands. The dream would not go away.

The girl approached him again, and Rick cried out, "Who are you? Where am I?"

The girl replied in English. "It's me. Con. Your wife."

"I don't have a wife. I've never seen you before. What have you done to me?"

The girl looked stunned, then asked a nonsensical question. "What day is this?"

"Monday"

"No, what date. What day and year?"

"February 16, 2059."

His response sent the girl into a fit. "Shit!" she shouted. "Those idiots! Why did they do that? Why? Why?"

Rick watched her nervously, convinced he had fallen into the clutches of a lunatic. He noted her knives and suspected his life depended on remaining levelheaded. "What did they do?" he asked.

"Took you from a time before we met."

"Yeah, that must be it."

The girl glared at him. "Don't humor me!" Then she broke down crying. It took a while before she could speak again. "Oh, Rick! I've waited so long. You can't imagine what I've gone through to bring you back. And now . . ." She began to sob again.

Rick rose, hoping to dash for safety while the girl was distracted, but she rose also. "I brought you clothes," she said, and held out a bundle.

Rick took it. There was a pair of rubber flip-flops on top of what appeared to be a bag made from clothlike paper. The "bag" turned out to be a garment rolled around two loincloths and a sash. Rick quickly put on a loincloth, wishing the girl would look away. She did not. After he had covered himself, he examined the larger garment. "This is a dress!" he said.

"It's called a togla here," said the girl. "It's what men wear. Tie the sash around your waist."

Rick slipped on the garment, feeling ridiculous. "And where is 'here'? You've obviously taken me down south."

"I haven't taken you anywhere," replied the girl. "They brought you to me."

"So, where am I?" asked Rick.

"Have you met Peter Green yet?" asked the girl.

Rick sighed, despairing of ever getting a straight answer. The girl was clearly unbalanced. Nevertheless, he answered her. "Never heard of him."

"Has anyone contacted you about a job?"

"No, why should they?"

The girl looked puzzled. "Someone should have hired you to be a guide at a resort called Montana Isle. You'll get there via time machine because it's in the Cretaceous Period."

Rick replied so as not to provoke the girl. "I didn't know time travel's possible."

"It is. I didn't believe it either, at first. It wasn't invented in the twenty-first century. Peter Green stole the machine."

"Oh," said Rick, still playing along. "So when was it invented?"

"I'm not sure. Certainly not in the twenty-seventh. They don't have it here, but everything's screwed up. The timestream has been . . . Oh God!"

"What?" asked Rick.

"I don't exist!" said Con. "I mean, I don't exist in the twenty-first century. Maybe they don't need a guide. That's why you didn't get that job offer."

"So that explains it."

"You don't believe me," accused the girl.

"No, no, I do."

"I know you, Richard Clements. I'm your wife. Remember? You never could fool me."

"Don't get mad," said Rick as calmly as possible. "This takes getting used to."

"I know it sounds fantastic," said the girl, "but tomorrow I'll show you proof."

"Great," said Rick, trying to keep his expression neutral. "I'd like some proof."

"You'll get it," assured Con. "Tonight, you'll just have to take my word. We met at the resort and discovered it was really an observatory for the K-T event."

"You've heard about the meteor impact?" said Rick. "Most people haven't."

"I've not only heard about it, I lived through it. We both did. We were rescued by people from the future. They were a different species that called themselves *Homo perfectus*. They live in this time, too. They took us to the nineteenth century, where we got married. We had a child, Rick. A beautiful boy named Joey."

"So this is the nineteenth century?"

"No. You got shot, then Joey starved. A guy from the future, a *Homo perfectus* I called Sam, said you and Joey would return to life if I helped him change history. I did, but he lied to me, Rick. I screwed up the timestream, and he dumped me here."

"Where's here?"

"You mean 'when's here.' We're in the thirty-first century."

"Men wear dresses and flip-flops in the thirty-first century?"

"This place is really messed up," said the girl, "and I've got to set it straight."

"How are you going to do that?" asked Rick.

"I don't . . ." She glared at him irritably. "Oh, what's the point? You don't believe a word I'm saying. I can see it in your face."

"Look . . . uh . . . What's your name again?"

"Con. Con *Clements.*"

"Look, Con, I was walking back to my dorm after working late in the prep lab. I felt a pain, and everything went dark. Now I'm here, and I'm more than a little confused."

A tender look came to the girl's face. "Of course you are." In the moonlight, Rick could see her eyes filling with tears again. "You're still my Rick. We'll just start over. You can't help but love me, you're destined to." She suddenly looked shy. "Would you kiss me, Rick? I've waited so long."

"Sure . . . Con. Just remember, for me, it's our first kiss."

"I recall how shy you were," said the girl with a smile. "On the beach, I had to ask you to kiss me back."

"I'll try to do better this time," said Rick. He walked over to Con and gently placed both his hands on her shoulders. "Close your eyes," he said.

Con closed her eyes, lifted her chin, and puckered her lips. Then, with all his strength, Rick pushed her away. She slammed into the cornstalks and fell over backward. Before Con even hit the ground, Rick dashed into the rows of corn and disappeared.

RICK RAN WITH the heedless speed of desperation. The cornstalks were as hard as wood, bruising him every time he slammed into one. He ignored the pain, convinced he was running for his life. He ran a zigzag route through the hollow, staying in the densest growth. Every once in a while, he paused and listened. He could hear the girl pursuing him, calling his name. He didn't stop running until her voice sounded far away.

Rick slowed to a walk, treading noiselessly until he found a weedy thicket. He crawled inside to hide and rest. As odd as it seemed, the girl was apparently alone. Only her cries broke the stillness of the night. Over and over, she called, "Rick! Rick! Don't leave me!" The despair in those cries was heartrending to hear, but also chilling. *She's clearly schizophrenic,* Rick thought, marveling at the extent of her delusions. *I wonder how she kidnapped me.* Remembering the pain before he blacked out, he felt his head for the lump from a blow. Rick detected none and theorized a dart had stunned him. *And how did she get me here? I must be in Mexico or South America.*

As Rick pondered these mysteries, drowsiness crept over him. He was in good shape, and though he had run long and hard, Rick couldn't understand why he was so utterly exhausted. He was also extremely hungry. *There's no cure for that until tomorrow morning,* he told himself. Rick couldn't keep his eyes open, and neither did he try. The last sound he heard as he drifted off to sleep was distant sobbing.

PADRE LUIS SLEPT poorly, for he was concerned about Con. Though he suspected her ordeal had unhinged her mind, he hoped she would prove him wrong. As the night wore on, the slightest sounds wakened him. Each time, he thought it marked the arrival of Con and her mysterious husband. It wasn't until dawn that the Padre abandoned hope. *She's probably wandering about, searching for an illusion.* He grew dispirited at the thought. There were many ways to become a perdido, but madness was the surest.

After people went to work, Padre Luis had some breakfast. He was halfway through his meal when he heard a knock on his door. He opened it to find Con standing alone in the hallway. She had clearly been through a hard night. Her dress was torn; her unnaturally pale skin was darkened by dirt and covered with scratches; and her face was drawn

with fatigue. Yet it was her eyes that disturbed the Padre
most. The light that had shone in them was extinguished.
Puffy from crying, they were dull with grief. Though Luis
was familiar with the faces of tragedy, Con's was particularly painful to see.

"Come in, Con. Where's your husband?"

Con entered slowly, and at first, Luis wasn't sure she
had heard his question. After a long silence, Con finally
answered. "I found him," she said in a flat voice.

In the heavy silence, Luis feared she had discovered him
dead. He refrained from further questions and patiently
waited for Con to explain in her own time. Watching her, he
sensed Con was teetering on the edge of an abyss, and she
might easily tumble into utter despair.

For a while, Con stood still, as if her mind were elsewhere. Finally, in a very faint voice, she said, "I'm so tired."

"You should rest," said Padre Luis. "Please, use my
mat. Are you hungry also?"

"I'm always hungry," mumbled Con.

Luis took her willingness to eat as an encouraging sign.
He hurried about making some porridge, while Con slumped
down on the mat. When Luis glanced her way, he saw silent
tears had washed pink lines down her dusty face. After the
porridge was done, he brought over a brimming bowl and sat
on the floor beside the mat. Con ate ravenously.

"Can you sleep?" asked Padre Luis, when she was finished. "You look exhausted."

"I was up all night trying to find him."

"Your husband? I thought you said you had found him."

"He ran away," said Con.

"Why?"

"He doesn't know me. He doesn't know where he is."

"That doesn't make sense."

"Nothing makes sense, Padre. Nothing at all."

"Perhaps if you slept awhile, it would."

"I doubt it. Besides, I have to find him."

"Then you must build your strength first." Luis gently
pushed Con down on the mat. She didn't resist. "Just a little
rest," he said in a lulling voice. "Rest will help."

Con's eyelids slowly closed as her fatigue took hold. As she drifted off to sleep, she mumbled, "He doesn't know me, we've never met."

Padre Luis regarded the young woman who slept before him. Though the thought shamed him, he briefly regretted offering to help her. Then that shame strengthened his resolve to keep his word. *How many times have I said we lose our humanity when we ignore the unfortunate?* mused the Padre. *Now, it is my turn to be tested.* He was painfully aware of how meager were his resources. Everyone in Mergonita lived on the edge, especially him. *I have little to offer this poor, mad child. Only words and compassion. Those will not stave off the tremblitos.* He rose and took the kana pill from the collection plate. With his finger, he pushed it between Con's lips, convinced he was giving her a few more days of life.

THE EXHAUSTION RESULTING from time travel ensured that Rick slept late. When he opened his eyes, it was mid-morning. For an instant, he thought he would be in his dorm room, waking from a nightmare. The sight of the tangled thicket dashed that hope, and he listened warily for his pursuer. He heard only the rustle of leaves and the call of a distant bird. It seemed unnaturally quiet. There were no sounds of traffic, nor voices of any kind. Regardless, he was cautious when he emerged from the thicket.

His first concern, once he determined he was alone, was to figure out where he was. *Someplace where it's hot in February,* he thought. *That eliminates Montana.* He peered about. By the light of day, the cornfield struck him as very odd. Rick had taken botany, and he began to use that knowledge to analyze his surroundings. Without the immature ears, the plants more closely resembled bamboo than corn. There was also evidence they were mature perennials, while all cultivated corn varieties were annuals. After several minutes of examination, he concluded the plants were genetically engineered. *I must be at an agricultural research station,* thought Rick. He looked about for tags or other markers that would confirm his hypothesis, but found none.

Rick decided to investigate further. He was in a hollow, and he headed uphill in hopes of gaining a better view of the locale. He ascended stealthily, keeping a wary eye for his kidnapper or her henchmen. When he reached the summit, he was perplexed by what he saw.

The empty landscape surrounding him and the strange walled city on the distant ridge were totally unrecognizable. All the mundane details of civilization were missing—power lines, highways, and aircraft. The buildings of the city were not outlandish; tall, glass-and-concrete towers were common enough. However, the city's walls seemed completely anachronistic. Moreover, Rick thought he would have heard of a modern walled city, despite his general disinterest in geography.

Rick quickly recognized that the hill upon which he stood was part of a dried lake bed. He had spent a great deal of time around such places, albeit, ones that were millions of years old. He was much better informed about geology than geography, and it puzzled him he could not place this formation. Clearly, the lake had once been huge, and it had dried up mere centuries ago, an instant in geological time. He could think of no feature on the planet that conformed to what he saw. *She certainly dragged me to someplace exotic.*

Rick's conjectures turned to his kidnapper. She was as puzzling as the landscape. *She's crazy, that's for sure. She seemed obsessed with me.* Rick had a hard time picturing himself as the object of obsession. Absorbed in his own interests, he tended to be shy around women. He couldn't imagine how he had attracted her attention. If he had no answer as to why she had kidnapped him, how she had managed to do it was even more mysterious. Although the mechanics were simple enough to imagine—a tranquilizing dart, a waiting car, and a plane trip south—it was hard to envision the girl pulling it off. She seemed to lack the resources. *She looked like a beggar in those shabby clothes,* thought Rick. *Even her flip-flops were mismatched.*

A second hypothesis came to Rick. *Perhaps, she's actually a rich girl acting out some fantasy.* That image didn't fit either. Then, Rick imagined a wealthy father humoring the madness of his daughter. That idea explained the girl's pathetic earnestness. *Maybe, the poor thing actually believes I'm her husband. She certainly was upset when I escaped.* That possibility seemed the most plausible.

Rick decided it was dangerous to remain where he could be spotted. *I must make my way to that city and contact the authorities.* He hurried back into the cornfield, planning to avoid the road while making his way to safety as quickly as possible.

CON OPENED HER eyes to see Padre Luis seated near her, reading a book. She grimaced. "Ugh, what's that taste in my mouth?"

"I gave you a pill while you slept."

"Then you didn't believe me when I said I don't need kana," replied Con. She sighed. "Why should you believe me? If I were in your place, I probably wouldn't either. I'm just sorry you wasted a pill." She rose wearily from the mat and slipped her feet into her flip-flops. "Can I borrow something to carry water? It's dry in those cornfields, and Rick's bound to be thirsty."

Padre Luis was both encouraged and disappointed by Con's behavior. The rest seemed to have improved her spirits, but not cured her delusions. "This morning, you said things about your husband I don't understand. That he ran away. That he doesn't know you."

"He was brought here unconscious," said Con. "He doesn't understand where he is."

"Even if that were possible," said Padre Luis, "I'd think he would recognize his own wife."

"A lot has happened," replied Con. "He's very confused."

"How could a man become so confused?"

"I don't expect you to believe me," said Con. "Only please, *please,* lend me a water container. I promise to bring it back. It's really important."

Padre Luis scanned his shelves for something that could hold water. As he did so, he reflected he was acting as if Con's quest were a rational one. "You shouldn't worry," he said. "When you husband arrives in town, he can get a drink."

"He won't know how to ask," said Con. "He doesn't speak your language. God knows where he thinks he is."

"How can that be?"

"He's from far away—Montana." Then Con answered the Padre's uncomprehending stare by speaking to him in English. "Dear, sweet man, you couldn't possibly understand what's happened to me. I know you think I'm crazy. If I stay here long enough, I'll begin to think so myself." Then she switched back to the speech of Mergonita. "That's the way he talks."

Padre Luis searched Con's face for signs of madness. Though he found anxiety and grief, what impressed him most was the resolution he saw. *Where will this resolution take her?* he wondered. He imagined Con wandering in the empty cornfields vainly searching for an imaginary man. *Can I stand by and let this happen?* He was certain he could not dissuade Con from her search, nor could he forcibly restrain her. *Perhaps, I could accompany her and hope she recovers from this delusion.* All this went through his mind before he spoke again. "To be honest, little of what you've said makes sense. Yet, I believe there are things you know with your head and things you know with your heart. My heart says you are sincere."

"Then you believe me?" asked Con in a voice that reflected surprise.

"I believe you should not search alone. I know this place and its people. Will you let me help you?"

Con looked as though a great burden had been lifted from her shoulders. "Thank you," she said, as her eyes welled with tears. "It's been hard doing everything myself."

"Would you tell me what you said in that strange tongue?"

"I said you couldn't possibly understand me," replied Con. "I see now I was mistaken."

22

WHEN RICK SAW MERGONITA CLOSE-UP, IT WAS NOT A welcome sight. The town's emptiness and poverty disturbed him. Moreover, the place seemed wrong. It appeared incomplete, with everything familiar and commonplace missing. The absence was so total Rick could only think of the most prominent gaps—vehicles, sounds, and even signs. It was as if civilization had been reduced to crumbling concrete, rusty metal, and tattered plastic. Only Rick's thirst drove him to enter the town.

As he ventured up a deserted lane, the main evidence that people lived there was the smell of sewage. There was no sign of water, and Rick quickly became discouraged about finding any. He was turning to leave when a pack of children emerged from an alley. Although the oldest looked only five, no adult accompanied them. They matched the poverty of their surroundings; the oldest dressed in ill-fitting rags, and the youngest were naked.

The children froze to stare at him in wary amazement, as if he were some sort of freak. Rick halted also. "I'm very thirsty," he said. "Do you know where I could get water?"

The children looked puzzled and remained mute. Then Rick recalled the girl who called herself "Con" had first spoken something that sounded like Spanish. Rick tried to recall his high school Spanish vocabulary. *"Agua?"* he said. The children did not respond. He hung his tongue out, and said, *"Sed! Sed!"* as he stepped in their direction.

The children rushed back into the alley, screaming. Rick stood alone again, frustrated and also worried that the terrified youngsters might provoke an outcry. He hastily left the town for the city on the hill.

AS PADRE LUIS accompanied Con through the streets of Mergonita, he pondered how he might ensure she stayed close. To gain her confidence, he did not challenge her statements, no matter how outlandish. When Con said her husband had blue eyes and yellow hair, Luis acted unfazed. He also tried to behave as if he shared Con's urgency.

"You said you last saw him in the cornfields north of town?" he asked.

"Si," Con replied, "in the farthest hollow."

"What provisions did he have?"

"Only the clothes I gave him."

"Then he must come here," said Luis, hoping to avoid wandering about the parched fields.

"He'll probably head for the fecs' city instead," said Con. "It would look more familiar to him."

"Then we should go there," Luis said. "A friend sells rides to the workers. He'll take us to the city without charge."

"What would happen if Rick tries to enter there?" asked Con.

"They will stop him at the gate, register his identity chip, and send him away."

"He doesn't have one," said Con.

"No identity chip?" exclaimed Luis, declining to ask how such a thing was possible.

"What will the fecs do if they find out?"

By the alarm on Con's face, Padre Luis saw she had already guessed the answer. "Let's not think about it," he said. "Let's find him instead."

AS A SCIENTIST, Rick preferred to base his hypotheses on observation. He believed facts, when objectively considered, pointed to the truth. That belief had been severely tested that day, for everything he observed only increased his confusion. The children he encountered were not

African or Asian, but the topography was not South American. The crops showed highly sophisticated genetic engineering, while the town lacked the most rudimentary technology. As Rick hiked up to the modern city, it seemed his only hope for solving these mysteries.

On the final turn of the switchback road, Rick got his first close view of his destination. While there was nothing extraordinary about the buildings, the wall was peculiar. It stood forty feet high and was constructed of poured concrete. Weathered into the wall's surface were cracks that a determined man could use to scale it, yet the large metal gate at the roadway's end indicated that the barrier was still functional. The closed gate made Rick feel unwelcome, and intuition cautioned him not to approach it.

While Rick considered what to do, he observed the treeless plain around him. The only man-made structure was a series of tall poles that supported a foot-wide metallic tube. The poles extended to the horizon, and Rick assumed they supported some form of power line. Then he spied a line of large cylindrical objects traveling above the "power line" at high speed. He watched them approach with amazement. They moved so rapidly, he caught only a glimpse of them before they vanished over the wall. The objects seemed a form of transport that levitated above the metallic tube. Of all the day's discoveries, this was the most unsettling—a thing that clearly did not belong to the twenty-first century. *But it must belong,* thought Rick. *The alternative is too fantastic.*

Rick was still pondering what he had seen, when a strange vehicle drove up pulling a wagon. It stopped a hundred feet away. A middle-aged man was sitting in the wagon, accompanied by the crazy girl. She stepped out onto the road, holding up a plastic bottle. "Don't run, Rick," she shouted. "I won't get close." She advanced to within fifty feet and halted. Rick noted that her knives were gone.

"What do you want?"

"You were eleven when you found your first fossil. It was an ammonite," she called out. "That was after your parents died, and you were living with your brother, Tom. You slept with that fossil every night. Tom called it your stone teddy bear. You gave it to him when he got his doctorate."

"How do you know that?"

"Tom owns a hunting knife you coveted as a child. There's a pocket on its leather sheath that holds a whetstone."

"Who told you about the knife?"

"I've seen it, Rick. Tom gave it to you the night before you left for Montana Isle. You cherished that knife."

"Is this about that time travel crap?" shouted Rick.

"You're a scientist, Rick. If you have enough time, you'll figure it out yourself. But you don't have time. This is a dangerous place."

"Yeah, filled with girls who carry knives."

"I brought a knife for you. It's back at the wagon," shouted Con. "You'll need one here. I've got water, too. Would you at least drink?"

"How do I know the water isn't drugged?"

Con took a long drink from the bottle. "Satisfied?"

"I want those guys to back off."

Con shouted, and the vehicle moved away.

"What language did you speak?" asked Rick. "Portuguese?"

"This isn't Brazil."

"Then where are we?"

"North America. On the site of Lake Michigan."

"You're nuts."

"And you'll go nuts trying to figure things out. Don't risk your life doing it."

"Why would I do that?"

"I know you. I lived with you almost two years."

"I'd think I'd remember."

"I've already explained why you don't," shouted Con.

"Your explanation doesn't make sense."

"If you haven't traveled through time, how do you explain what you've seen? The crops? The lake bed? This city? There's no place like this in the twenty-first century.

And if I hadn't been your wife, how would I know about your childhood? That you're still a virgin?"

Rick blushed. "You scare me."

"I understand," said Con. "Look, I'm sorry about last night. I wasn't prepared." She set the bottle on the road and backed far away. Rick advanced to drink as Con, on the verge of tears, watched him intently.

Rick began to feel foolish. For the second time that afternoon, he relied on his intuition. "You needn't keep your distance," he said. "I've decided you won't bite."

A look of relief came over Con's face, and she started to approach him. Rick suspected she would fling her arms around him, and he wanted to avoid that. "Don't push things, though," he added quickly. "I don't know you."

Con gazed into Rick's eyes and saw wariness, confusion, and curiosity, but nothing else. There was no love to be found. As familiar as those blue eyes seemed, they peered at her as a stranger's might. She suddenly felt awkward. "You . . . you must be hungry," she said.

"I'm starved," said Rick.

"We can get food in town," said Con. "It'll be safer there. The man in the wagon is Padre Luis. He'll hide us."

"Why do I have to hide?" asked Rick. "What kind of a place is this?"

"A perilous one," replied Con. "A place I hope we'll leave soon."

"For where?"

Con realized she didn't have an answer to that question. For an instant, she thought of saying she didn't know, but she told him "home" instead.

THE PADRE'S FRIEND stayed to wait for passengers, while he, Con, and Rick returned to Mergonita on foot. As they walked down the twisting road, Con did her best to tell Rick everything that had happened. Despite condensing her story, it was a lengthy one. She related how they met and recounted their adventures in the Cretaceous and the nineteenth century. She described Rick's murder and Joey's death. She talked about Sam and what she did for him, though she omitted mentioning the child she had conceived with Roberto. She concluded with Mergonita and her encounter with the Gaians.

Rick listened to Con intently, though he gave no indication whether he believed her or not. Afterward, he plied her with questions. Those on the nature of the timestream surprised Con, while the inquiries about prehistoric life were more expected. Rick grew animated when she spoke of dinosaurs. Then Con briefly saw the Rick she remembered.

Throughout the discussion, Padre Luis walked beside Rick and Con, baffled by their strange language. Although he was excluded from their conversation, he paid close attention to it, reading gestures and expressions. Having spent a lifetime discerning hidden meanings, he learned a great deal. Luis now believed Con's story was essentially true, though he suspected there was more to it than she revealed. The confused and wary man was indeed her beloved—a single glance at her face told him that. Luis pitied Con when he observed Rick did not return her devotion. The Padre saw a man perplexed by everything about him, and most of all, by the woman who claimed to be his wife.

THE WORKDAY ENDED before the three arrived at Mergonita, dashing Con's hopes to pass unobserved. The streets were still full when they entered the town and, as she feared, Rick's appearance caused a stir. Resigned to being observed, Con stopped to buy some bread. Rick watched with interest and afterward asked why no coins were used. "I used my money bracelet," Con explained. "It works with an identity chip inside my skull."

"Inside your skull?" exclaimed Rick. "That sounds drastic."

"The chips really benefit the fecs. They use them to monitor us."

"The fecs?"

"*Homo perfectus.* It's good you didn't try to enter their city. Anyone without an identity chip is eliminated."

Rick realized how close he had come to dying. "I take it our kind's the bottom rung here."

"We are."

Rick looked about the bleak street and the misery that filled it. "And this is all your doing?"

"Yes," said Con in a tiny voice.

Rick shook his head. "It hardly seems possible."

"I wish it wasn't."

IT TOOK A while before Padre Luis was able to sneak Con and Rick into his apartment. There, he found Tomas waiting and concerned. "Padre, I see the rumors are true."

"There are too many wagging tongues," said the Padre. "Don't add yours to their number."

"What's going on?" asked Tomas.

"I'm not sure," replied the Padre, "but I'm certain it's important."

Thomas bowed his head. "You are my mentor. Tell me how I may help."

"These two will stay in the hidden room. This must remain secret. Get word to Marianna that Con needs work as a maid. She will visit her tomorrow morning."

"Is there anything else?"

"If you can find a sleeping mat, that would be good."

"I'll try," said Tomas. Then he departed to speak with Marianna before the curfew.

Padre Luis turned to Con. "You and your husband should hide," he said. "With rumors about, I'm sure to have visitors."

As if to reinforce that statement, someone began knocking on the door. Con and Rick hastily retreated to the secret room, taking bread and water with them. Padre Luis slid the stone back in place and thought up a story for whoever was outside the door.

RICK RAVENOUSLY ATTACKED the bread. Con, as hungry as always, ate with equal voraciousness. She was glad the meal kept them occupied, and they had an excuse not to talk. Rick was eyeing her as he ate, and Con dreaded what he saw. She had not peered into a mirror since Kat had chopped her hair and could only imagine what it looked like now, unwashed and uncombed. What she could see filled her with dismay. Her shoddy clothes were soiled and tattered. Her legs and arms were scratched, bruised, and filthy. Each toenail was tipped with a black crescent. Her body odor permeated their close quarters. *What must he think of me?* she wondered.

Con recalled herself on Montana Isle, the privileged daughter of a wealthy man. She had been clean, well dressed, and respectable. Imagining her former self plunged Con into despair and sapped her confidence. For the first time, she realized Rick might not love her again. They were starting over, and all of her advantages had been erased. She imagined herself as Rick must see her—unlovely and unstable—and it occurred to her that this was her punishment for altering history.

23

MARIANNA EXPECTED A KNOCK ON HER DOOR, BUT NOT so early. The morning siren had just sounded, and Gabriella was still setting up breakfast. Marianna rose and dressed, feeling cheated out of the last rest she would have until evening. She opened the door to find Con standing outside, looking like she had barely slept. "Come in," said Marianna.

"I don't think I should."

Marianna shrugged. "All right. What do you want?"

"Didn't Tomas tell you?" asked Con. "I need to find work in the city."

"He told me," said Marianna, "but I thought he was mistaken. Why would you want to work for the fecs?"

"I have my reasons."

"The head boss will cheat you, and the fecs will treat you worse. It's hard work, too. Your fingers are still good; go back to Fat Rosa's."

"I thought you'd help me."

"I *am* helping you."

"Please, Marianna."

Marianna sighed. "If you insist, I'll take you to my head boss. I guess my daughter was right about you."

"Thank you."

"You won't thank me later."

Con hid in the shadows until the older woman emerged from the building. As they began the long trudge toward the city, Marianna told Con what to expect. "There's a processing center inside the gate. That's where the hiring's done. The head bosses are Sapenes, but they might as well be fecs. Don't expect fair treatment. They charge you for everything—watching your things, your shower, uniform rental, lunch. By the time they're finished, they've taken back half your pay."

"Is your head boss like that?" asked Con.

"Salana? She's no worse than the others. No better either."

"Will she hire me?"

"With your steady hands, you'll have no problem."

"What will I end up doing?"

"That depends on the crew boss. He or she decides what you do."

"What about the fecs?"

"Be careful around them," said Marianna. "Address them as 'Perfected One' if they speak to you. Be submissive. Never look them in the eye. Show any spirit, and you'll lose your job. People become perdidoes that way."

"I'll remember that."

"Most of the time, they'll ignore you and gab in their language you can't understand. Still, it's safest to stay out of their way whenever possible."

"I will," said Con.

The two women walked silently up the road, as the sky grew lighter. After a while, Con noticed Marianna was looking at her suspiciously. It unnerved her. "What are you thinking?" she asked.

"You're young, and your breasts are not large."

"So?"

"Women like you are sometimes tempted . . ." her voice trailed off as if she expected Con to understand the rest.

"What are you implying?"

"You know," replied Marianna. "It's a very bad idea."

"I don't know what you're talking about."

"Fec women fuck only once a year," said Marianna. "So, some fec men look elsewhere. They can be very free with their kana."

"Is *that* why you think I'm seeking work? So I can be a whore?"

"A woman who does it with a fec is worse than a whore."

Con glared at Marianna with a mixture of outrage and humiliation. "I thought you were my friend!"

"I'm just warning you."

Too insulted to reply, Con lapsed into offended silence. She felt wronged, yet unable to defend herself, for she had to admit Marianna's assumption was natural, even logical. Working as a domestic seemed a foolish choice for someone with Con's skills. Jobs in the city were jobs of last resort.

For the rest of the journey, Con attempted to put Marianna's suspicions from her mind. That led to brooding over her previous night with Rick. It had not gone well. Con hadn't been so nervous around a guy since middle school, and she had blabbed too much about her life in the twenty-first century. *I no longer exist there,* she thought. *I could have told him anything. Why admit I was a billionaire's daughter?* Her succeeding revelations had put further distance between them. *The worst was when I told him I was souped.* Con recalled Rick's cool response. *Was he really that judgmental on Montana Isle? Did I just forget?* It seemed to her all they had in common had vanished, leaving only what made them different.

Their first disagreement occurred over the sleeping mat Tomas brought. It filled over half the narrow room, but Rick had insisted Con have it to herself. At first, Con thought he was being chivalrous. When she realized he would rather sleep on a stone floor than lie next to her, she had exploded. *Did I really tell him to go to hell?* Con recalled Rick crawling sheepishly to the opposite end of the room. He had gone to sleep soon afterward, while she had lain awake, feeling both angry and guilty. Rick had been asleep, or feigning to be, when Con had left for Marianna's.

THE GATE TO the city was open, and men and women poured into it. For most, this was routine, and the crowd moved into the Domestics Processing Center in an orderly manner. Knives were checked in the antechamber, and everyone was screened before passing into the vast room beyond. Con had never seen a cattle lot, yet she imagined it would look like the sight before her—dispirited and docile creatures herded to meet others' needs.

Those who did not already work for a head boss negotiated their employment on the floor. Marianna led Con to Salana, who hired her for fourteen pills a week—"less expenses." Salana handed Con a small packet of body and hair cleanser and told her to shower, get in uniform, and report to her crew boss, a man named Tani.

There was no privacy. Both men and women undressed and showered within sight of one another, then lined up naked to receive their uniforms. These were plain gray, sleeveless robes that reached the ankles. Made of a papery material, they were baggy and worn without a sash or any undergarments. Each one bore a serial number printed in four-inch-high numerals on the front and back. Along with her robe, Con received a food cube that would be her lunch. No footwear was issued or allowed.

Con's crew boss was a sharp-faced man in his twenties with cold eyes that regarded Con disdainfully. "You're young for this work," he said. "Let's see your hands." Tani gazed at Con's steady fingertips. A thin, knowing smile came to his lips. "Hope to earn extra kana?" he said in a low voice. "I get my cut."

Con blushed and shook her head.

"All right," said Tani, "then you'll scrub pots."

Over the next twenty minutes, Tani's crew assembled. All were older than Con and showed symptoms of kana deficiency. Con's reception was chilly, for her coworkers apparently shared Marianna's assumption. A gate opened, and Tani led them out into the city.

As Con walked, she took in the sights. At first, the city seemed wonderfully modern. Everything was well maintained, and technology was evident in the vehicles and architecture. Only after her initial impression wore off did Con note how little progress had occurred. Things looked different, but no more advanced from what she had seen in 2693. Con suspected the aristocratic Kyndens, by suppressing the rest of humanity, had stagnated. Their city also appeared largely empty. The roads the Sapene work crews swept bore little traffic and many of the windows Con passed peered into vacant rooms. The emptiness quickly became oppressive. Mergona was the opposite of Mergonita in almost every way, but its clean, well-maintained streets and buildings shared the same air of desolation. Centuries ago, this had been a huge and thriving place, but it had diminished into something sterile and dreary.

Tani left Con at a huge commercial kitchen. There, Con was set to work washing very large pots. They had sat unwashed overnight, and the crusted food inside had dried and hardened. Cleaning each pot was a major effort, and Con was still at it when the activity in the kitchen picked up and the room grew hot and steamy. Soon, new pots were added to her pile, which grew as the kitchen began to bustle. Busy scrubbing, Con had few opportunities to observe her workplace. When she did, she was surprised to see most of the people there were Sapenes, though a few Kyndens directed them.

The parade of dirty pots never let up, and Con was

exhausted by the day's end. Worse, she realized her drudgery had been pointless. She had learned nothing about what had happened to her when she was captured. There seemed little prospect she ever would. She might as well have spent the day stitching for Fat Rosa.

When Tani finally escorted Con to the processing center, she discovered the showers worked only in the morning. She turned in her damp, greasy uniform; put on her own clothes; picked up her pay, which had been reduced by expenses to a single pill; got her knives back; and began the trudge to Mergonita. She had gone through the motions of swallowing her pill, but was still concerned someone might try to rob her. Thus, as she trudged back to town, Con was watchful and kept a hand on the hilt of her pajaro. She stopped at the cornfield outside of town to bathe in the ditch, wishing to be more presentable when she saw Rick again. That prospect made her nervous, and she took her time selling her kana and buying bread.

Tomas was waiting outside the Padre's apartment to usher her in when it was safe. Padre Luis greeted her inside. "Did you find work in the city?"

"Si," replied Con in a listless voice. "How's Rick been?"

"He was out most of the day," said Luis. "He returned only recently himself."

Con frowned, then crawled inside the hideaway. She found Rick seated on the floor, staring at his feet. He looked agitated. "Luis said you were out today," said Con. "I'm not sure that's a good idea."

"I don't like cages," snapped Rick. "I'm not cut out for them."

"I was only thinking of your safety."

"Yeah."

Con cringed inwardly at Rick's bitter tone, and she tried to steer their talk to a more neutral topic. "So, what did you do today?"

"Wandered about, thinking."

"About what?"

"About time travel. I've been figuring things out. The rules are simple, but the consequences aren't."

"I know," replied Con.

"You say we met on a trip to the Cretaceous."

"I know it sounds strange, but . . ."

"You've already explained it, and I believe you."

"You do?"

"Yeah. Hear me out. I know nothing about that trip, and it's not only because your buddies snatched me before it took place."

"They're *not* my buddies!"

"Well, they kidnapped me at your request."

Con cringed inwardly again. "So, what are you getting at?" she asked.

"Here's where that rule about only the past affecting the future has bizarre consequences. My kidnapping did not erase our jaunt to the Cretaceous, because I was snatched upwhen from that trip, right?"

Con thought his statement over. "Right," she said.

"And we still get rescued and sent to the nineteenth century."

"Yes," said Con. "I think that's why they took you from the twenty-first century. Sam would be less likely to notice your disappearance."

"So this Sam guy still shoots me. Am I right?"

"Rick . . ."

"Look, don't get teary-eyed. It happened to some other version of Rick, not me. And you know what? Because I got shot in 1880, reality gets changed, so now, I never go on that trip."

"I don't understand."

"Well, you should have. You said I was your great-great-great-grandfather. When I died, my descendents disappeared from history. That means you disappeared from the twenty-first century also."

"I already told you that," said Con.

"And me getting shot in 1880 wouldn't affect what happened in the Cretaceous because that's downwhen, and it didn't affect me in 2059 because that murder takes place in another reality. All of *my* past exists in the twenty-first century, and it's unaffected."

"I think that's right," said Con. "All this jumping around in time confuses me."

"So, you see, once you didn't exist in 2059, no one had any reason to offer me that guide job. What would be the point? They snatched me the night before you claimed we left, and yet no one ever spoke to me about time travel. Can't you see what you've done?"

"I just wanted to save you."

"From what? The Rick you knew still gets murdered, and the Rick I am gets . . ." Rick waved his arm at the cramped hideaway. ". . . gets this . . . this hellhole." He paused as anger colored his face. "Goddamnit! I was happy. I was doing what I loved, and you stole me from it. I've lost everything and everyone I care about."

"Once I make things right here, we'll go back . . ."

"Are you so sure? I'm not."

Con stared down at her dirty feet. "I . . . I'm not sure about anything anymore."

"Why am I not surprised?"

Con struggled to maintain her composure. "I'm sorry, Rick. I . . . I wasn't thinking."

"Well, you should have," retorted Rick. "The man who ran the stop sign and killed my parents said the same damned thing. 'I wasn't thinking.' Do you know how lame—how empty—that sounds?" In his rage and anguish, Rick ignored Con's weeping. "You weren't thinking when you twisted history into this dreary version of hell! You weren't thinking when you brought me here!"

"I . . . I did it out . . . out of love," said Con between sobs.

"Love? Love for whom? I don't even know you. For me, that stuff you talk about never happened. It can never happen."

"It did, Rick. You've got to believe me."

"It's not a question of belief," replied Rick. "History's different now. What you recall has nothing to do with me."

"If only . . ." said Con, ". . . if only they had taken you just before you were shot . . ."

"But they didn't."

Con seemed to crumple. She buried her face in her

hands and wept bitterly. Rick watched her, convinced he had the right to speak so bluntly. Yet he felt uncomfortable all the same. Part of him found justice in her tears, while another part regretted them. When his anger cooled, the latter emotion became the stronger. Still, he was hesitant to comfort her, for he worried she might get the wrong idea.

24

THE MORNING SIREN WOKE RICK. THROUGH HALF-shut eyes, he saw Con stir. She had slept in her dress, so she simply slipped into her mismatched flip-flops and crawled through the passageway under the wall. Once she was gone, Rick stretched his stiff body and went over to snooze on the vacant sleeping mat. It was still warm, and Rick found it impossible not to think of the woman who had lain there, sobbing softly while he pretended to sleep. *This situation is impossible!* he thought, feeling he should have handled it better. After some introspection, Rick crawled through the passageway, resolved on apologizing. Padre Luis was the only person in the outer room. He smiled at Rick sleepily. "Con?" Rick said, hoping his inflection carried the meaning of his question. The Padre answered by making walking motions with his fingers. Rick hurried into the predawn streets, but Con was gone.

CON'S SECOND WORKDAY in the city was a repetition of her first. She returned to Mergonita, tired and discouraged, with only a pill to show for her labors. She did not bother to bathe in the ditch, but bought some bread, then headed for the Padre's apartment.

"Did Rick go out today?" Con asked the Padre.

"No, he stayed with me and tried to learn our language," replied Luis.

"How'd it go?"

"I think you'd be a better teacher. He's in the secret room with one of my books."

Con found Rick seated on the sleeping mat, a closed book beside him. "I see you've been reading," she said.

"Maybe one word out of fifty. Look, Con, about last night . . ."

"You made yourself clear."

"I'm sorry," said Rick.

"No, I'm the one who should apologize. I wrecked your life."

"You didn't mean to."

"But you were right, Rick. That's no excuse."

"Let's not dwell on it. I'd rather help you get us out of here."

Con slumped to the floor, a picture of discouragement. "I don't know how you can. I don't even understand what I did to change history."

"It probably involves your captivity," said Rick. "What did the fecs do to you?"

"I'm not sure. They kept me prisoner for days, giving me shots and taking blood. Then they whisked me into an operating room and let me go afterward."

"What could they have wanted?" wondered Rick aloud. "Something that would have a big impact. Something like that virus. That changed history because it changed humanity's genetics."

"Yes, so . . ."

"Suppose the virus got out of hand, or suppose they fiddled with the genome too much."

"What does that have to do with me?"

"Your genes are different from everyone's here. They're previrus."

"That doesn't explain why they kept me prisoner."

"It would if they wanted oocytes."

"Oocytes?"

"Unfertilized egg cells. They'd have to stimulate your ovulation before they could take them. They'd need to give you shots for that."

"How would you know about that kind of thing?"

"Paleontologists need to know biology."

"But wouldn't taking eggs leave a mark?"

"The needle's inserted through the vaginal wall," replied Rick.

"That would explain the stirrups on the table and my bleeding."

"So we have a working hypothesis," said Rick. "The question is how would taking your oocytes change history?"

"I don't know," said Con, "but I do know what will happen. *Homo sapiens* become extinct in something called the Purification. I have no idea what that has to do with genetics."

Rick thought a minute. "Suppose your oocytes showed the fecs how to kick their kana habit."

"How would that make people extinct?"

"I don't know squat about history, but the Clements are Irish, and I know about the Great Famine. The British landlords exported food while millions starved. They didn't think the peasants were worth feeding. If the fecs stopped making kana, how long would people last?"

"Not long."

"But now, we reach a dead end," said Rick. "How can we stop such a thing?"

"I have a bomb," said Con. "A big one, too—a fusion grenade."

Rick grinned. "Well, *that* certainly changes matters. Your oocytes are probably still sitting in some lab. All we have to do is find out which one. Then, boom! No Purification."

CON AND RICK shared another dinner of bread and water, a meal made nutritious, if not savory, because grain had been genetically altered centuries before. Con ate the coarse

bread quietly, but tonight her silence was not due to discomfort. Relaxed by exhaustion, she did not feel tense
around Rick. *He's forgiven me,* she thought. *He was always
easygoing.* Con had begun to think of Rick in the past tense
because she had come to see him as two separate people.
The person in the room had never saved her life. Neither
had she saved his. This Rick had never suffered with her,
made love to her, or cherished their child. He was the Rick
she had met when she was eighteen, but she was no longer
eighteen. She had changed, and she loved the man who had
changed with her. That was not the man who sat so close
and yet so far away. He was only a facsimile.

Rick noticed Con's melancholy expression. "What are
you thinking about?" he asked.

"Only how tired I am," lied Con. "I can't stay awake."

Rick moved off the mat to let Con sleep alone.

THE FOLLOWING MORNING, Con arrived at the Domestics
Processing Center early to speak with Tani. "I can't earn
extra kana scrubbing pots," she said to him in a low voice.

"So?" replied the crew boss.

"I want to work around fec men," said Con.

A subtle smile came to Tani's face. "I thought you
might. I get half. Understand?"

Con nodded.

"Then today you'll use those steady hands to pour
drinks." Tani added in a whisper, "It's not my problem if you
get caught."

"I won't."

CON WAS SENT to work in a hall that served a banquet
each noon. It featured chairs that allowed the diners to
recline while they ate food selected from a buffet. Over the
course of the morning, a long table was piled high with
fare that could be eaten with fingers. Con's stomach growled
as she brought out the savory-smelling dishes, but having
been forbidden to sample any, she dared not.

When the diners began to arrive, Con couldn't help but envy them. The beautifully groomed women wore exquisitely embroidered robes, not papery sacks. The men were also elegantly dressed in soft, shimmering robes that reached their calves. Con had lived in Mergonita long enough that she felt no irony in her awe that all the Kyndens were clean and wore shoes. Tall, robust, and graceful, they moved in a manner that exuded superiority. Soon, the dining hall echoed with the rapid singsong tones of the Kynden language.

Once the meal commenced, Con's job was to refill the diners' glasses whenever they signaled her. It soon became clear to her why Tani had given her this job—it provided ample opportunities to encounter Kynden men. As she had hoped, it also presented the ideal opportunity for spying. The fecs generally ignored her, and they assumed she couldn't understand their language. Con had become the proverbial fly on the wall.

Kynden men and women behaved differently than Con expected. She thought they would mingle as equals, since sexual attraction between them was only periodic. Instead, the sexes tended to segregate themselves. Con was also surprised to discover the women's once-yearly occurrence of desire—the Ripening—featured prominently in the conversations of both sexes. This was not immediately obvious among the women, for they tended to speak of it indirectly. The men spoke more bluntly. Ripe women and the competition for them were discussed as if in a locker room. Con got the impression that, while women were circumspect about their potential partners, at a certain point their emotions overwhelmed their judgment. It made her understand their concern over this event, and she sympathized.

Sexual matters were not the only topics of conversations. Business was discussed. Politics came up occasionally. Gossip abounded, though talk about children and family was conspicuously absent. The "sape problem" was a frequent subject, and, once, Con filled the glass of a man while he advocated her extermination. It took all of her self-control not to react.

The beverage Con served was intoxicating, and, as time wore on, the diners' tongues loosened. Con discovered that not all the men favored exterminating her kind. Some had different ideas. She was walking by a group of the latter when one held up his glass. She hurried over to fill it.

"Now take this one, for example," he said in the Kynden tongue. "She's not too lumpy."

"I'd give her four pills," said a companion with a smirk.

"I'd give her eight, if she'd shave between her legs," said another. "That hair's disgusting."

"They never shave," said the first. "They're afraid the other sapes would find out."

"I'd think it'd be a badge of distinction," said another man with a laugh.

The conversation so agitated Con she missed the glass she was supposed to fill.

"You stupid, clumsy sape!" yelled the man holding the glass. "It's lucky for you my robe's not stained!"

Con bowed very low. "I beg your pardon, Perfected One. I'll clean this up right away."

After cleaning the spill, Con tried to avoid the men's groups. The meal was winding down as she stood near two Kynden women.

"It was a surprise to all of us," she overheard one say, "but especially to Mazafalama." She laughed.

"But why did she choose him?" asked her friend.

"Haven't you heard?" replied her companion. "Tavamanana made a big discovery. He's an important man now."

Con's ears perked up at the word "discovery."

"What did he discover that would make *him* a catch?" asked the other woman.

Her companion seemed amused. "Some freakish sape from what I've heard. All I know is that he's the director of the genetics project now. It was quite a promotion."

"Did she keep the robe Mazafalama presented her? I heard it was extraordinary."

"It was an offering," replied her friend with a knowing look. "What do *you* think?"

The other woman sighed. "I should be so lucky. My

time is only two months away, and I don't want to repeat last year." She raised her finger, and Con rushed over to refill her glass. "Men can be such sapes at times."

"Isn't that the truth," said her friend.

If the women had bothered to notice, they would have thought Con had the tremblitos, for her hands shook with excitement. She was certain she had overheard something significant—the first clue that could lead to finding the lab. *Tava . . . Tavama . . . Tavamanaza? Tavamanama? Damn those long fec names! What was it?* Con eavesdropped on the two women until she was called to serve other diners, but their conversation had drifted away from the man and his discovery.

The dining room emptied, and Con helped with the cleanup. The untouched food on the buffet table was strictly off-limits, but Con noticed her fellow workers ate what was left on the plates. They did so slyly, when the fecs in charge weren't looking. Con did the same, relishing the stolen scraps. As she continued cleaning, most of the women on the crew wandered off until it was largely men who cleared the dining hall. The women did not return until near the end of the day, when Tani and the other crew bosses arrived to pick up their workers.

As Tani escorted Con back to the processing center, he said, "Well?"

"Well, what?" replied Con.

"Don't play games. I want my half."

"There's nothing to split."

Tani looked at Con sharply. "We need to talk outside the gate."

"All right," said Con. "I'll wait for you."

"You'd better."

CON TURNED IN her uniform, dressed, received her pill, claimed her knives, and exited the city. She waited nervously outside the gate for Tani, who took his time arriving. When he finally showed up, he was clearly angry. "What happened today?" he asked. "Where's my kana?"

"I . . . I didn't get any," said Con. "No one . . . no one asked to do it."

"You're either stupid or lying."

"Then I must be stupid. I don't understand why you're so mad."

"The fecs don't approach you," said Tani. "You have to approach them."

"I do? What should I say?"

"Ask them if they need any cleaning done. If they're interested, they'll say something about a messy apartment and offer you some kana. No one ever mentions sex."

Con grew pale as she realized where her ploy had led her. "But, won't the fecs who run the dining hall object?"

"You really *are* dumb. Didn't you keep your eyes open? How many girls did you see after the meal?"

"I didn't realize . . ."

"Now you do," said Tani. "I expect some kana tomorrow, or cleaning pots will be the least of your worries. Is that understood? That dining hall's a prime spot. I don't waste it on lazy sluts."

Con started to reply, but Tani punched her in the stomach. The blow was as hard as it was unexpected, and Con doubled over in pain, gasping for breath. Tani struck her several times, in places that wouldn't show, until she crumpled to the ground. "Maybe you're as dumb as you claim," said Tani, "so I'm giving you a break. But don't think you can play games with me. It's dangerous." Then he strode away.

CON WAS MORE shaken by Tani's beating than injured, and offsetting her trauma was her thrill over the clue about the lab. As Con walked to Mergonita and the pain of the blows faded, she grew eager to share the news of her discovery with Rick. The ploy she had used to get into the dining hall and her problems with Tani were things she would keep to herself. Tomorrow, she could give Tani the kana she had saved. *That will buy me some time,* she thought, though she realized it was only a stopgap solution.

When Con sneaked into the Padre's apartment, she discovered Rick was not there. "He left in the morning with the water container," said Padre Luis. "I haven't seen him since."

"Oh, no," said Con. "Not again."

"Is this man truly your husband?" asked the Padre.

"He was," said Con, "but he's forgotten."

"Yet you remember," said Luis, in a sympathetic tone. "It must be hard." He waited for Con to open up to him, but she simply nodded. When he realized Con would not discuss it, he said, "You're both outsiders. You try to hide your strangeness, but he does not. Everything about him declares he comes from far away."

"It's because he looks different and doesn't speak the language."

"Si," said the Padre, "yet those are small things compared to something far more important—he's not ashamed to be a Sapene."

"That never occurred to me," said Con, "but you're right, he's not."

"I would like to be from such a place," said Luis.

The door opened, and Rick entered. There were scrapes on his legs and he was dusty and sweaty.

"Where have you been?" asked Con, looking both concerned and cross.

"I was up at the city, checking out the wall," replied Rick. "I found a place to climb it."

"Climb it?" exclaimed Con.

"Did you think you could waltz through the gate with that bomb?" retorted Rick.

"I hadn't thought that far ahead," replied Con. She turned to Luis and said in his language, "Rick says he was out walking."

"For what purpose?" asked the Padre.

"Just for something to do," replied Con.

"What did you just tell him?' asked Rick.

"I told him you were out for a walk."

"Why don't you tell him the truth?" said Rick. "He's already hiding us, so he knows we're up to something.

Besides, we're going to need a rope. We shouldn't count on walking out the front gate."

Con looked at Padre Luis and tried to decide what to do. She suspected he had been patiently waiting for her to reveal their plans. Gazing at the man whose fingers shook from the tremblitos, Con chose to trust him.

"Rick thinks I should tell you the truth," said Con quietly.

Padre Luis glanced at Rick and smiled. "I would like that," he said.

"It will be hard to believe," said Con.

"Then I will accept it on faith," replied the Padre.

Con thought it was possible to reveal the truth without mentioning time travel. "I come from far away," she said. "From a place where no one needs kana, and the Sapenes live as well as the fecs. I was sent here to change things. Now Rick has come to help me."

"I see," said Luis.

"Little has gone as planned, but there's still hope. The change we hope to make will not improve life here, but it will prevent it from becoming much worse."

"How can I help?"

"Our plan is dangerous," said Con, "and may fail. It could be dangerous for you, too."

"I understand," said Luis. "It doesn't matter."

Con turned to Rick. "I told him, and he wants to help. What kind of rope do you need?"

As Con translated for Rick, the risk ahead became more real, and all the difficulties in planting the bomb began to oppress her. Suddenly, the whole idea seemed foolhardy and doomed to failure. *What other choices do I have?* Con asked herself. *Wait for Sam to track me down?* She could think of no other option except to proceed.

As Luis listened and realized they intended to strike at the fecs, his eyes grew wide with both amazement and enthusiasm. "You will have the rope tomorrow," he said. "Tonight, I will cook for you." He set at once about the task with an exuberance Con had never witnessed before. He began to make a stew that promised to be a welcome change from bread and water. While the Padre cooked, Con told

Rick what she had learned that day. "But I only have part of a name," she concluded, saying the part she remembered. To Rick, it sounded like she was singing the opening notes of a nonsense tune.

"Call directory assistance," he suggested, "just like you would in our time. I imagine they still have phones or something like them."

"It couldn't be that easy," said Con.

"Why not?" replied Rick. "The fecs assume none of us can speak their language, so they have no reason to secure their communications."

"Just call?"

"Sure. Not everything has to be hard."

25

THE DINNER WAS FESTIVE, THOUGH CONSPIRACY dominated the conversation. The three talked, with Con serving as translator, until the light went out and it was time for sleep. Con was lying on the mat when Rick entered the secret room. "It's silly," she said, "for you to sleep on the floor."

"It's all right."

Con slid over. "There's room for two."

After some hesitation, Rick crawled beside her in the darkness. He turned his back to her. "Thanks," he whispered. "Good night."

Con turned away also, but the space was too narrow to avoid contact. Although she had thought it would be comforting to have Rick close, she resented how quickly he dropped off to sleep, while she lay awake and struggled with her feelings.

* * *

WHILE CON POURED drinks the next day, she was keenly aware of the subtle negotiations taking place and pitied the Sapene women who made such arrangements. When they drifted from the room after the meal, Con left also. By then, her heart was pounding with anxiety. She had looked for communication devices and observed Kyndens speaking into small, dark panels set into the walls. How the panels functioned was not entirely clear to her. They seemed voice-activated, but Con had no idea if there were charges involved or whether the receiving party could identify her. What had seemed so simple the previous evening now did not seem simple at all.

Below the dining hall was a colonnaded area where vehicles picked up and dropped off passengers. Con arrived there as a willowy girl, whose forlorn face held not even a pretext of desire, climbed into a car with a Kynden man. Con waited until they drove off before rushing over to one of the communication panels. She spoke to activate it. "Hello," she said. "I require assistance in locating the director of the genetics project." For an anxious moment, Con feared an alarm would bring fecs to seize her.

"Do you mean Tavamanana, the Director for Kana Genetics?"

"Yes, that's him."

"I'll connect you."

Before Con could respond, she heard a voice say, "Director's office, how may I help you?"

"I'm looking for directions to the lab working with the sape genes."

"The Research Institute's located on grid 17 Zedda. You can't miss it—it's the second tallest building in the city. The genetics lab is on the ninth floor."

"Thank you," said Con. She rushed back to the dining hall, her heart pounding. It was a half hour before she finally calmed down. *That was easy*, she thought.

It was the last thing that would be.

* * *

PADRE LUIS HAD an easy time borrowing a thick rope. He set it in a corner of his empty apartment and sat in his chair to rest. The rope had been heavy, and he was no longer young. Upon the table, he spotted the tiny black sphere that Con had told him fecs used to spy on her. For the first time, he examined it closely and noted the perfection of its form. *It's clearly not a pebble,* he thought. He took out his cerdo and scraped its surface. A bit of black coating flaked away. The material beneath was translucent. Curious, Padre Luis scraped away the rest of the coating. He held the sphere close to his eye. Its interior was filled with an intricate pattern of shifting shapes. Luis watched them, mesmerized by their changes.

The sphere suddenly glowed with such brightness, it startled Luis. He let go of the thing, and it bounced on the table. It bounced only once. Then, to the Padre's astonishment, the tiny ball remained suspended in air. With a trembling finger, he reached to touch it, but the light winked out as the sphere disappeared. He looked around the tabletop and on the floor, convinced his eyes were playing tricks on him. "It must be here," he said to the empty room. "Where could it go?"

RICK STOOD BEFORE the city's steeply slanted wall and surveyed the long crack that ran to its top. It appeared to be an expansion crack that had weathered until it was two to three inches wide and several inches deep. As a seasoned climber, Rick considered the ascent only moderately difficult. He kicked off his flip-flops and removed his togla. Then, taking a deep breath, he inserted a hand into the crack and made a fist to wedge it against the crack's sides. Using this technique, called "crack jamming," Rick ascended the wall like a four-legged spider. Although he appeared to move effortlessly, the ascent was strenuous and hurt his hands. By the time Rick pulled himself over the edge of the wall, he was shaking from the exertion.

Behind the wall was a concrete walkway with a metal railing. Rick quickly dropped to its pitted surface. He rested while he nervously scanned about for signs he had been detected. The top of the wall was well monitored, but as Padre Luis had stated, the sensors embedded there detected only identity chips. Lacking one, Rick was invisible to them. He was also fortunate that few windows faced the bleak wall and a small, tree-filled park hid him from the sight of the rare pedestrians.

Once Rick became confident he hadn't been seen, he began to search for a means down into the city. About twenty yards from where he ascended, he found a rusty metal ladder. He memorized the landmarks so he could give Con good directions, then retreated to the crack. There, he massaged his hands before beginning his descent.

As Rick kneaded his sore hands, his thoughts turned to Con. She had been correct in assuming he had forgiven her for his abduction. He could see Con was not at fault for the time travelers' unfortunate choice. *She expected a happy reunion,* he thought. *Instead, she got me.* Rick felt miscast in a melodrama. *I can't play the long-lost lover and fake emotions I don't have.* Rick's only solution was to escape the place and Con also.

AS TANI ESCORTED Con to the Domestics Processing Center, she handed him two pills. "Here's your half," she whispered.

Tani answered loud enough for the crew to hear. "So the fec gave you only four pills?" He seemed amused when Con grew red.

"Did you have to make an announcement?" she whispered.

"Did you expect to keep this secret?" asked Tani. "It doesn't matter what they think. It's me you have to worry about, and I'm not happy. You should be getting more than four pills for your services."

Con had just given Tani all the kana she had, and she knew the pill she earned today would not satisfy him tomorrow. Circumstances were forcing her to act, and she only had three options. She could flee and abandon any hope of changing history or escaping this century; she could sell herself for kana; or she could put Rick's and her plan into action. Con hesitated for only an instant before replying. "If you help me, I can do much better tomorrow."

"Help you? How?"

"There's a fec that wants to dress up like a Sapene domestic. You know, in one of the robes you issue us. He'll pay well for it."

"How well?" asked Tani.

"Ten pills, if I bring a robe tomorrow."

Tani grinned. "That's more like it. I get half . . . *and* an extra pill for the robe. Six pills in all."

Con agreed to Tani's terms, knowing she could not come up with the pills. The robe was necessary for Rick and her plan. Now that she knew the lab's location, proceeding with the plan was possible. Her agreement with Tani made it imperative.

On the way to Mergonita, Con retrieved the fusion grenade from its hiding place. If all went well, by the time Tani came looking for his kana, she would be gone. If things didn't go well, Tani would be the least of her worries.

EVEN AS CON walked back to Mergonita, she began to worry that her haste had doomed her. It took only a little thought to realize how unprepared she was. All she knew was the location of the lab. She imagined Rick plying her with questions for which she had no answers: *Is the building guarded? What's the layout? How do you reach the ninth floor?* By the time Con reached the apartment, she dreaded to reveal her rashness to Rick. *After all,* she thought, *I've committed him, too.* Yet, when Con told Rick what she had done, his response surprised her. "Good," he said. "The waiting was killing me."

"I was afraid you'd be mad."

"Why?" said Rick. "You've done your part. I've scouted

a way up the wall. The Padre got us a rope. We're as ready as we're ever going to be."

"Rick, I've been thinking. Maybe I should plant the grenade."

"We've already agreed that I should. I see no reason to change that."

"It doesn't seem right," said Con. "This mess is my fault, I should fix it."

"It's not a question of fault," said Rick, "it's a question of practicality. I'm less likely to be detected."

"We don't know that for sure," said Con.

"What *do* we know for sure?" retorted Rick. "At least, it worked today."

"I still don't feel right about it," said Con. "It's bad enough I had you brought here."

"Your taking an unnecessary risk won't change that," replied Rick. "You don't even need to go near the building."

"What if a crew boss stops you?" said Con. "You don't know the language."

"I'll improvise."

"That's ridiculous. I'm going with you."

"You've taken all the chances so far," said Rick.

"What about your climb today?" retorted Con. "There's no use arguing, Rick, you're not doing this alone."

Rick sighed, signifying his surrender. "Are you always this stubborn?"

The question made Con smile.

"What's so amusing?" asked Rick.

"You've asked me that before," said Con.

"In my other life, I suppose."

LONG AFTER CON and Rick had gone to sleep, Sam's time machine settled on the plain south of Mergona. Sam had calculated the temporal coordinates hastily and was vexed to discover he had arrived close to dawn. Despite his anxiousness to settle matters, he knew he must sleep to recover from his journey. Even a minimal rest would mean he would arrive at the city in the afternoon.

Sam's agitation fought with his exhaustion. "She should be dead," he said aloud. Yet, despite his meticulous planning, he feared Con was not. Sam realized he had grown careless after his success. He should have taken notice when the miniprobe failed to return. When the second miniprobe found no trace of Con, he should not have assumed she was dead. Because his daughter was unaware of his plans, she had been incapable of pointing out these oversights. Only happenstance had saved him. If the damaged probe had not returned, Sam might not have discovered that others still threatened to undo his work.

Sam sat in one of the time machine's chairs and adjusted it to the reclining position. Then he performed a mental recitation to calm himself in preparation for sleep. *She does not understand her power. There are means to track her down. She may be dead already. If not, she soon will be.*

26

CON DREAMED SHE WAS BACK IN THE CABIN. SNOW drifted over her face, but it did not feel cold. Instead, it was as soft and pleasant as a blanket. Then it became a blanket, and Con nestled beneath its folds. She felt safe and at peace. *Sam can't get me now*, she thought, *I'm with Rick and Joey.*

Con awoke, feeling that the dream foretold her death. She did not find it frightening. On the contrary, the vision of her dissolution left her peaceful. When she thought of the day ahead, her goal dwindled merely to completing the upcoming task. She had little hope for a happy ending. An end to suffering would suffice. Thus, she arose with the calmness of one resigned to suicide.

During her last meal in Mergonita, Con did not know if Padre Luis guessed the source of her tranquillity. There was a sadness in his gaze that made her suspect he did. Saying good-bye to him was particularly difficult. When it was time to depart, she grasped his trembling hands. "I won't see you again," she said.

"Yours has been a hard journey," he replied. "I hope it ends well."

"Well or not, it will end this afternoon," said Con. "If we succeed, there'll be a sign in the city."

"I will look for it."

"Good-bye, Padre," said Con as she embraced him.

"Good luck, my child."

Con turned to Rick. "I'll see you at the wall."

As Con hurried to the city, she focused on the task ahead, and her calmness was replaced with anxious energy. Resignation could come later. Action was required now. Though the day might end with her death, Con resolved it would not also end in failure. Having done great harm, she desperately wanted to make amends. Her chief regret was that Rick had become involved. He was likely to share her fate, and she suspected he knew. It was the ultimate irony. Because of her and the paradoxes of time travel, he could die twice—first in the nineteenth century, and now in the thirty-first.

Con walked without her pajaroes, for she had given them to Rick to sneak into the city with the grenade. Being unarmed on the road made her feel vulnerable, and she was relieved when she reached the gate. Con undressed, showered, put on a domestic's robe, and reported to Tani.

"Six pills," he said, handing her a gray bundle.

Con nodded.

The morning passed slowly for Con, while pouring at the meal was a blur of anxiety. Finally, the diners departed. As the Sapene women drifted from the dining hall to their assignations, Con slipped out the door. She lingered in the colonnaded area until all the other women departed. Then, clutching the extra robe, she began walking down the street.

At Security headquarters, Con's departure was noted.

The identity chip of every Sapene within the city appeared as a glowing dot on a large map. The establishment where Con worked was notorious, and the cynical Kynden security officers were familiar with the routine. After the midday meal, dots would disperse from that location and return near the close of the workday. While some of the officers disapproved of the activity this pattern reflected, most shrugged it off. Women were seldom ripe. If some men used sapes for satisfaction, it wasn't anyone's business.

MERGONA WAS HOT and still as Con walked its streets alone for the first time. The early-afternoon sun beat down from a cloudless sky, and the pavement burned her bare feet. No one watched her from the sidewalks, for the heat had driven the city's inhabitants inside. The streets were nearly as empty as the sidewalks, and the passengers inside the sporadic vehicles paid no attention to Con. Nevertheless, she feared someone might question her about her business. Con was trying to invent a convincing story when she spied some street-cleaning equipment standing unattended by the roadside. There was a trash barrel with wheels and a handle so it could be moved about. Its side held several push brooms. Con rushed over to the trash barrel and wheeled it way.

In the guise of a street sweeper, Con eventually found the park. It was overgrown and empty. She located the ladder Rick described; then hid in the bushes to wait for him. The shaded earth felt good against her scorched soles, but she was too tense to relax, and every sound startled her. When the sunlight filtering through the leaves had the low angle of late afternoon, Con heard the soft sound of bare feet rapidly descending the ladder. Then Rick was on the ground, wearing a loincloth and carrying a small bundle. Con rushed from her hiding place and gave him an impulsive hug, which he stiffly returned.

Con went to the trash barrel and retrieved the gray robe. While Rick slipped into it, she hiked up her own robe and strapped the two pajaroes to her thighs. Then she hid the fusion grenade in the barrel and handed Rick a broom. They left the park, cleaning the street as they went. When they turned a corner, the tall Research Institute building was prominent in the skyline. It looked at least a mile away. Con pointed it out, and Rick gazed at the structure. "It's not very impressive," he said, "but then, I never imagined they'd have street sweepers in the thirty-first century."

Con did not reply, for she was lost in thought. She did not speak until they had swept several blocks. "I'm worried something's wrong with our plan," she said at last.

"We can still turn back."

"It's too late for that," said Con. "I've burned my bridges."

"Probably just as well," said Rick. "This won't get easier."

"I'm tired of it all," said Con. "I want it over."

"Yeah," agreed Rick. "When do you think I can enter the building?"

"Soon, I hope. I wish I had a watch."

"That would be nice," said Rick. He chuckled humorlessly. "A thousand years in the future, and we can't even tell what time it is."

WHILE CON AND Rick approached the Institute, Sam arrived at the city. He went to the gate reserved for the Kyndens, where a guard admitted him immediately.

"I'm late for an appointment," said Sam, "and require a communicator."

The guard directed him to a small plastic panel on the wall that looked primitive to Sam's eyes. He regarded it with annoyance. Sam was fully aware his manipulations distorted societies, for altering history meant pushing it from the optimal course. This version of the thirty-first century was particularly dysfunctional, and he disliked visiting it. He considered its technology wholly inadequate, an opinion that was quickly reinforced when he attempted to contact Tavamanana.

"The director has left for the day," said a voice over the communicator. "Would you care to leave a message?"

"I need to speak to him now."

"That's impossible, but he should be home shortly. I'll arrange to . . ."

"Just give me his address," barked Sam. "I'll meet him there."

Sam got the information and strode into the street. The vehicles in the city, like those in the twenty-seventh century, were for public use. Sam found a vacant one and aimed a device that overrode the car's identification protocols and activated it. He climbed inside and was driven away. As he sped to Tavamanana's residence, Sam reassured himself. *She cannot do any harm unless she's in the city.* He thought that unlikely. *If she's here, it will be easy to track her down.* Sam pulled out his weapon and checked its settings. They were still those used when he blasted the policewoman. He adjusted the power level and blast width upward. *No need for precision here,* he thought. Sam imagined the effect of a discharge at the higher settings, and for a moment, he almost hoped Con was in the city.

WHILE SAM TRAVELED through Mergona, Rick and Con watched the Research Institute empty out. The Kynden workday was shorter than that of the Sapenes, and the people leaving the building did not find it unusual that street cleaners were still at work.

"How much longer should I wait?" asked Rick.

"Oh God, I don't know," said Con in an agony of indecision. "There might be people still in the building, but I'm expected back at the dining hall."

"What happens when you're missed?"

"I'm not sure, but I know Sapenes aren't allowed in the city after work hours." A group of Kynden women exited the building. Con watched them enter vehicles and drive away. "Let's give it a few more minutes," she said.

TAVAMANANA OPENED HIS door to find an imposing stranger. "Hello," he said, "I'm Samazatarmaku. I sent you the theory about genetic throwbacks among the Sapes."

"Samazatarmaku! I've been meaning to contact you," said Tavamanana, forcing a smile on his face. "I found a female sape that was just such a throwback."

"So I heard," said Sam. "I also hear that you are on the verge of great things."

"Yes, I'm sure of it, even though we're only in the initial stages."

"I presume you have destroyed the sape that provided the specimen."

"No," replied Tavamanana. "We might need it again."

"Didn't you get my second communication?" asked Sam, feigning puzzlement.

"No, I didn't."

"Surely you recognize the threat of it breeding," said Sam. "Where is it now?"

"Sape town, I suppose," said Tavamanana.

"You don't know for sure?" asked Sam.

"It's easy enough to find out."

"I strongly recommend you do."

"I'd need the sape's identity chip code for that. It's at the office."

"Then we must go to your office immediately," said Sam.

"Look here," said Tavamanana, "I'm a program director. You can't barge in, giving orders."

"Pardon my urgency, but I fear your work is about to be sabotaged."

"Sabotaged?"

"Yes," said Sam. "Do you have tissue cultures at more than one site?"

"No."

"Then it is imperative we locate the sape that provided the specimen. There's no time to lose. We can talk on the way."

Tavamanana's confidence dissipated before Sam's commanding presence, and he meekly followed him to the waiting vehicle.

* * *

CON WENT THROUGH the motions of sweeping the street while she anxiously waited for Rick to return. He had been gone only a few minutes, yet over that time, Con's feeling that their plan was flawed intensified. *I know Rick says it's safer for him to plant the grenade*, she thought, *but it's my genetic material in there. Shouldn't that mean something? Rick says it doesn't make any difference, that only practicality matters.* His argument seemed to make sense. *After all, he got inside. There's been no alarm. He may pull it off.*

Then, with a flash of insight, Con saw what was wrong. *Rick thinks pulling off our plan means planting the grenade. That's not really what we're trying to do. We're trying to change history.* Con quickly saw the reason why Sam had brought her to the thirty-first century when billions of others had previrus genes also. *My actions affect the timestream in ways those of others can't. I'm different. I was specially created to alter history.* Con became absolutely certain that only she could effectively place the bomb. She had altered the timestream, and only she had the power to change it back. Without her, the fusion grenade was insufficient. She dropped the broom and rushed into the building.

Con's identity chip was detected the instant she stepped into the Research Institute. Its code was automatically checked for authorization, and when none was found, an alert appeared on the security officer's screen. The building had a single guard, for trespassers were easily detected, making such transgressions rare. The guard used the violator's identity code to call up an image. When the face of a young female appeared, he smirked as he surmised the purpose of her visit. A second screen showed the trespasser scrambling up a stairwell. *No point in chasing after her,* thought the officer, *I'll wait until she gets off at a floor.* When Con exited the stairwell on the ninth floor, the guard took out his stunner and headed for the elevators.

27

OUT OF BREATH FROM RACING UP THE STAIRS, CON studied the floor directory, looking for the genetics lab, until she realized the futility of it. *Rick can't read this. He could be anywhere.* She had the sinking feeling her insight had come too late. Now, she had to find Rick before she could attempt to plant the grenade. She surveyed the array of doorways and tried to guess which one Rick had chosen. Before she made her choice, she heard the elevator doors open.

"Don't move!" commanded a voice. "I have a stunner."

Con froze.

"Now turn around slowly."

Con turned to face the Kynden security officer. "Why are you here?" he asked.

By the way the guard leered at her, Con guessed he anticipated her answer. Inspired by that leer, she hung her head to look ashamed. "He told me to come, Perfected One. He said . . . that . . . that he'd give me kana."

"Who?" asked the guard, now grinning.

"I don't know his name. I don't know any of your names."

"Then how can you prove you're not lying," said the officer. "Perhaps you're here to steal something."

"He . . . He makes me shave between my legs," said Con as she slowly reached for the hem of her robe and just as slowly began pulling it upward. "He says it makes me look like a ripe woman."

The guard said nothing, but stared as Con's robe traveled up her legs. When it approached her thighs, Con's right hand briefly disappeared beneath the rising folds and emerged with a flicking motion. A pajaro flashed through the air and struck the guard's eye, penetrating to the hilt. He fired one wild shot before dropping to the floor in convulsions. Con dashed over to the writhing man and squatted next to him. Memories of her degrading captivity welled up, and terror transformed into rage. With her second pajaro, she slit the fec's throat.

Con wiped and sheathed her knives before picking up the stunner. Then she turned to choose what door to enter. It was unnecessary. Rick stood immobilized at one of them, staring at the dying man and the growing pool of blood. He was so pale Con thought he might become sick.

"Take me to the grenade," she barked.

Color returned to Rick's face. "This way," he mumbled. Then he hurried through the open doorway. They ran down the hall until Rick halted at a door. "It's in here," he said. "What's going on?"

"I must plant the grenade," replied Con. "There's no time to explain."

Rick retrieved the baseball-sized metal sphere and handed it to Con. Seizing it, she dashed down the hall. Rick raced after her until, once more, they confronted the guard. He had stopped twitching. Rick looked away from the gruesome sight while Con glanced at the directory. Then he followed as she ran to a small room.

The grenade had been set to detonate in an hour, but the dead security officer had changed circumstances. Con reset the timer and pulled open a drawer. Inside were liquid-filled jars, in which fetuses floated. Con placed the grenade in the back corner of the drawer and pushed the jars around it. "In fifteen minutes, it's all over," she said. "Let's get out of here."

AS RICK AND Con ran down the stairwell, Tavamanana rode the elevator with Sam to his tenth-floor office. Tavamanana was disturbed by what he had been told on the trip over. He had no idea sapes were capable of understanding his project, much less resisting it. The idea still struck him as far-fetched, but Samazatarmaku was not a person who was easily brushed aside. Tavamanana had readily agreed to track down the female sape.

It was after work hours, and the building was empty. Tavamanana ushered Sam into his office and switched on the datastation. "Call up the identity chip for the Sapene female with the baseline genome."

The machine complied, and the code appeared on its screen beneath Con's image.

"Is this subject still employed stitching robes?" asked Tavamanana.

"The subject is currently registered for work within Mergona," responded the datastation.

"Where?"

"The Thousand Flowers Banquet Room."

Tavamanana frowned. He knew of that banquet room and its reputation. "Is the sape there now?"

"The subject left that location three hours and forty-two minutes ago," responded the datastation.

"Pinpoint the subject's current location on a map," said Sam.

A map appeared on the screen with a blinking dot showing Con's position. Tavamanana gasped. "It's only a few blocks away!"

"Retrace its movements," said Sam.

The two Kyndens watched as the dot entered the research building. They followed Con's movements through the ninth floor before Sam said to his shaken host, "We'd better check the lab."

They took the elevator to the floor below and discovered the security officer lying in a crimson puddle. "Now you see the sape's true nature," said Sam.

"And to think I let it live," said Tavamanana in a faint voice.

"Go search the room it visited last," said Sam. "Be thorough. Then check the other room." Sam headed for the elevator.

"Where are you going?" asked Tavamanana.

"I'm going to track the creature down," said Sam, "and exterminate it."

RICK WALKED DOWN the street alone, gazing about nervously and pushing the trash barrel. "Do you see anything?" asked Con from inside the barrel.

Rick glanced over his shoulder. "Somebody just left the building. They're getting in a car."

"Slow down," said Con in a hushed voice. "Look normal." Rick stopped pushing the barrel, took out a broom, and started sweeping. The car sped by. He had just breathed a sigh of relief when the car screeched to a stop and started to turn around.

TANI DELIVERED HIS crew to the Domestics Processing Center, then went to Salana. "I need the hand-held tracer," he said.

His boss regarded him with a knowing look. "Your new girl go missing?"

Tani scowled and nodded.

"It's near the end of the workday. Be smart and report her to the fecs."

"I want to find her myself. I think she's pulling some trick."

"The trace will cost you two pills," said Salana. "Sure it's worth it?"

Tani punched his palm. "It's worth it." He struck his palm again. "The lying, thieving slut!"

Salana laughed. "If I'd known you were so angry I'd have charged more." She handed Tani a small, flat, rectangular device and warned, "Don't get caught with this."

"Don't worry." Tani entered Con's identity code into the tracer and the tracer's top illuminated. An arrow pointed to Con's location. Beneath the arrow was a number. It indicated Con was not too distant. Tani smiled. "There's still time to catch her."

Tani dashed from the processing center and jogged down the street, pausing occasionally to check the tracer. He had guessed Con would head for the wall and the tracer bore him out. *She thinks she can toss the kana over and pick it up later,* he thought. He halted to glance at the number below the arrow. He was close now. *If that bitch thinks she can cheat me and get away with it, she's in for a surprise.*

SEARCHING THE SPECIMEN room, Tavamanana puzzled over Con's actions. *What could it possibly want here?* he wondered. The murdered guard was proof of the creature's savagery, but he saw no purpose in that savagery. *Perhaps I'm giving the sape too much credit in looking for a reason.* He envisioned the thing killing without conscience and, afterward, wandering about aimlessly, looking at things as a bored child might. It was an idea that conformed to his prejudices, so it made sense to him. Nevertheless, Tavamanana conducted a thorough examination of the room because Sam had been adamant that he do so. He did it, however, without urgency.

Tavamanana had nearly concluded nothing had been disturbed when he opened the last drawer in a cabinet. The formerly neat rows of jars within had been disturbed. *Perhaps it took one of the fetuses,* he thought. *That seems something a sape would do.* He pulled the drawer out farther and spotted a metal sphere in its corner. He picked up the thing and looked at it curiously. Tavamanana had never seen anything like it. *No sape could have made such a thing.* There was writing on the sphere, but he couldn't make out the language. There were also some simple controls. Tavamanana touched one and a series of numbers appeared on a tiny screen that had been blank before. *Is this an instrument?* he wondered. Tavamanana peered at the screen. The numbers were changing. 00:00:08 . . . 00:00:07 . . . 00:00:06 . . . 00:00:05 . . . 00:00:04 . . . 00:00:03 . . .

* * *

LOOKING FOR CON, Sam had given the male street cleaner only a cursory glance. It took him a moment before he recognized that something was wrong. *His coloring is not from this time period.* Sam ordered his vehicle to stop immediately. The brakes jarred the speeding vehicle to a halt. Sam's weapon slid off the seat and bounced onto the floor. As he bent over to pick up his gun, the interior of the car suddenly filled with light. Sam looked up. Through squinting eyes, he saw an expanding fireball envelop the upper floors of the Research Institute. It illuminated the city like a second sun, and Sam could feel its heat on his face. He shut his eyes so as not to be blinded. He could still see light through his closed eyelids, and when it began to fade, he opened them again.

The top three floors of the building had disappeared. Molten concrete dripped down the blackened remains of the structure, giving it the appearance of a candle. Its top glowed dull red, and a fireball was ascending into the sky at the head of a billowing column of black smoke.

Sam peered down the road and saw the street sweeper lying on the pavement. Even as he watched, the man rose and appeared to be looking for something. The trash barrel he had been wheeling was overturned, and Sam spied someone crawling out from it. He recognized Con immediately. Retrieving his gun from the vehicle's floor, he turned it on and switched off the safety. "Proceed slowly," he instructed the vehicle.

RICK'S EARS RANG and his head throbbed from the concussion of the explosion. The force of it had tossed him on the street like a doll. An elbow and both knees were raw, and he ached all over. None of that mattered. He had dropped the stunner, and finding it was paramount. He spotted the weapon ten feet away and limped over to it. As he picked it up, he saw Sam's vehicle approaching. He aimed at the figure inside and fired. The man slumped over, and his vehicle took him slowly down the street, which was beginning to fill with people.

Rick set the trash barrel upright and lifted Con from where she huddled, dazed and oddly passive. "I'm going to wheel you out of here," he said. He gently lowered her into the barrel. Then Rick ignored his injuries and began to push Con as fast as he could through the growing chaos.

TANI WAS SHIELDED from the sight of the explosion, but not from its sound. Its roar shattered windows and vibrated his bones. He had never experienced anything remotely like it. When he caught sight of the rising column of smoke, he found it incomprehensible. The Kyndens had kept him ignorant and ensured his life revolved around kana. He knew no more about explosives than the ancient wars that produced them. The streets were filling with panicked, injured people, but tragedies visited upon fecs were no concern of his. He focused solely on getting his kana. He glanced at the tracer. Its arrow pointed to the girl with the pills that should be his. The wall loomed ahead, and his quarry was close. Tani began to sprint.

RICK LIFTED CON from the barrel. "We're here," he said.

"I can't believe we made it."

"Up the ladder, down the rope, and we're out of here," said Rick. "You go first."

Con started to climb and was halfway up the ladder when Tani appeared, yelling as he ran. "Thieving bitch! What do you think you're doing?"

When Con froze momentarily, Rick shouted, "Keep climbing." Then, he blocked the way of the man who was screaming at Con. Though Rick could not understand Tani's insults, the fury in his face was clear. When Tani tried to get on the ladder, Rick shoved him aside and began to climb. Tani scrambled up after him. Close to the walkway, he seized Rick's leg and attempted to pull him off. Rick hung on the rungs tightly and kicked free from Tani's grasp. Tani fell backward, slamming on the ground and breaking a leg. Rick finished his ascent, then peered at the man moaning below. "Who's that guy?" he asked Con.

"My pimp," she replied.

Rick stared at her, uncertain how to respond.

"He sold girls to the fecs for kana," said Con.

"Did he sell you?"

"He thought he did. Come on. The fecs will find him soon enough. It'll serve him right."

With one last glance at Tani, Rick climbed down the rope after Con. Once on the ground, he quickly changed into his clothes from Mergonita. Con changed into her spare dress and wished she had not left her flip-flops behind. The ridge was close by, and they made their way down its steep slope, avoiding the road. The explosion had diverted the fecs, and there were no pursuers. Con was withdrawn and quiet as she scrambled through the hill-side's scrubby vegetation. Rick ascribed her silence to shock and exhaustion. The sun was close to setting when they finally reached the dry lake bed. As they entered the first of the cornfields that surrounded the town, Con spoke at last. "I have water hidden here."

"Great!" said Rick, "I could use a nice long drink."

"Me, too." said Con. "But don't drink too much, we'll have to make it last."

"Why? Your friends will have lots of water, won't they?"

"They will . . ." Con paused. ". . . when we see them."

"And that's tonight. Right?"

"In a way."

Rick looked at Con sharply. "What do you mean by that?"

"Let's drink first," replied Con. She led Rick to the place she had hidden the water. When they both had drunk, she said. "Let's head out. We should avoid the road until dark."

"Okay," said Rick. "What did you mean earlier when you said 'in a way'? Is there some catch I don't know about?"

"The Gaians will be at the rendezvous point," said Con. "They will have arrived just after the explosion."

"You had me worried for a moment."

"They told me they would be there because they'll be able to pinpoint the time of the detonation. They said the research shouldn't be too hard."

"That's good," said Rick.

"But they won't do that research today. They might do it years or even decades from now."

Rick stopped walking and shot Con a puzzled look. "What are you getting at?"

"There's only one timestream, Rick. When history gets changed, it seems things were always that way. You don't remember the old version, because it no longer exists. We'll walk to the rendezvous point, and the time machine will be waiting. We'll never know what happened the time when it wasn't there."

"What you're saying is that there *will* be a time when it's not there. Your friends don't yet know the grenade's exploded. They may not find out for years."

"But they will eventually," said Con, "and then . . ."

"They'll get in their time machine and arrive in the nick of time."

"Yeah."

"But that's only one version of the future. There'll be two. Right?"

"I think so," said Con.

"This is way too weird!"

"But it makes sense when you think about it."

"Oh, it makes sense, all right. That doesn't mean I like it." Con said nothing.

"When did this occur to you?" asked Rick.

"A couple of days ago."

"And you waited until now to tell me? Thanks."

Con started sobbing softly.

Rick walked silently beside her awhile; then with a sigh, he put his arm around her shoulder. "I'm sorry," he said. "I shouldn't have snapped at you."

"I've ruined your life."

Rick smiled ruefully. "Yeah, but you meant well. Come on, maybe this is the version where we live happily ever after."

Con wiped the tears from her eyes. "Yeah, maybe."

AFTER SUNSET, RICK and Con stopped struggling through the cornstalks and began to travel on the empty road. A thin moon lit their way, and on the horizon, the burning Research Institute glowed against the starlit sky. Padre Luis viewed it from Mergonita, violating the curfew with most of the other townsfolk. He saw it as the sign Con had foretold and also as a beacon of hope. He thought he would record her story so it could inspire future generations.

Samazatarmaku saw the same sight from inside the city when he recovered from being stunned. No one had come to his aid while he lay slumped in the vehicle for hours. For him, the burning building was a token of defeat and a warning he still had adversaries. They were faceless at present—all except one. Now that his anger had cooled, he thought it was fortunate he had not destroyed Con. She could still be useful. He briefly considered tracking her down, but felt too vulnerable. He needed to retreat down-when, where it was safe. There, he could plan anew. He wondered if the vehicle he was in could make it all the way to his time machine and decided to find out.

THE ROAD CON and Rick traveled meandered between rolling hills, and the hollow that was to be the rendezvous point remained hidden as they approached the last bend. It was shortly before midnight. Both their hearts were pounding with apprehension.

"Remember, Rick," said Con, "this moment always exists, but it isn't always the same."

When they rounded the curve, their hearts sank. The hollow was empty.

Rick sighed. "So there'll be a time machine here," he said, "just not now."

Con nodded, as her eyes filled with tears.

"Maybe we should wait," said Rick.

"There's no point, it'll be years before they find out about the explosion."

"So, now what?" asked Rick.

"I don't know," said Con. Rick thought her voice sounded tiny and lost.

"Well, I'm not going back to that wretched town," said Rick. "I'll take my chances heading north."

"Rick, can I . . . can I come with you?"

"Con, I have a snowball's chance in hell."

"It doesn't matter," said Con, "as long as I'm with you."

"You're souped, and there won't be much food, if any. Hell, there may not be any water."

"I know that."

"You're not being rational."

"No, I'm not."

Rick looked at Con. Her tear-filled eyes glistened in the pale moonlight and pleaded silently. Despite his reservations, he realized it would be heartless to abandon her. Rick reached out and wiped away a tear with his dirty finger, leaving a smudge. He forced himself to smile, and an echo of his smile crept onto Con's face. "I guess we're stuck together," he said.

Con sighed and grew peaceful. "This reminds me of another time," she said, "and another reality. I thought we were doomed then, also."

"What did you do?"

"I kissed you."

Rick saw that Con wanted to kiss him now, but was holding back. She looked almost shy, yet the events of the day fought with that impression. *She slit a man's throat,* Rick remembered. *She had a pimp.* Rick could not reconcile those facts with the seeming innocence before him, and it made him wary. Yet he knew he had to do something, and Con was waiting for him to do it. Rick leaned over and kissed her forehead. "I guess there's no point in hanging around here," he said. "Let's go."

28

THE ROAD MEANDERED AMONG THE DARK HILLS, hiding the way ahead. "Remember, Rick," said Con, "this moment always exists, but it isn't always the same."

When they rounded the curve, they spied a large black ovoid in the center of the hollow. It stood on three legs, a shadow against the gray of the moonlit corn.

"Is that the time machine?" asked Rick.

"Yep. Right where they said it'd be."

"That's a relief," said Rick. "All your talk about alternate futures had me going. You almost had me convinced we wouldn't be rescued."

Con said nothing, not caring to defend an idea that seemed far-fetched when faced with the reality in the hollow. She wondered only briefly what happened in the future that no longer existed.

A panel on the underside of the craft lowered and transformed into a silvery stairway. A child-sized figure descended the stairs and called out in English. "Con! Rick! Hurry!"

Rick and Con ran as rapidly as their tired limbs allowed and entered the time machine. Once they were inside, the stairway lifted up and merged seamlessly with the floor. That portion of the floor was the only uncluttered area in the cabin. The hemispherical space was piled with exotic equipment, potted plants, and other items.

"Find a seat," urged Violet, "and be quick."

As in Sam's time machine, all the seats, with the exception of the pilot's, faced toward a transparent central column containing an immaterial cylinder that was difficult to gaze upon. Con did not even try, but Rick stared, blinking and curious, at its shifting colors until Violet guided him to a seat. It was too small for him, and he squeezed in with difficulty. Its sides grasped his waist as the time machine began to rise.

High-resolution viewscreens covered the interior walls of the craft, making them seem virtually nonexistent. Only the seams of the various hatches and the technical displays in front of the pilot's console spoiled the effect. As the craft rose into the sky, the perspective on the viewscreens changed to show the ground below, producing the illusion that the Earth was above them. Later, the view shifted again, and a starry sky with a crescent moon covered the walls.

When they stopped rising, Con leaned over and touched Rick's arm. "We're going to start time travel soon," she said. "It feels like falling, only worse."

"How long will the trip take?" asked Rick.

"It's impossible to say," replied Con. "I don't think time exists while we're traveling."

A foggy, shimmering arch emerged from the central column, like a groping tentacle. Everything it touched turned immaterial. It was quickly joined by other writhing entities that removed everything they contacted from reality. Rick couldn't help but shrink back into his seat as they advanced. One quick glance at Con showed she was doing the same. The emanations from the central column engulfed Rick, and he sank, without form or duration, into timeless chaos.

Then it was over. A full moon lit the night sky. It was huge and different-looking. The view shifted, and again, Rick had the sensation the Earth was above him. The time machine was so high up he could see the planet's curvature. An archipelago of immense islands spread across the sea. Nothing about them looked remotely familiar. Then, the view changed to include luminous lines that delineated all the geographic features as on a topographic map. A series of concentric circles surrounded a point on the coast of a huge island. As the time machine descended, it became evident the point marked their landing site.

Rick was intensely curious about the time machine and their destination, but he was also overwhelmingly fatigued. Despite the marvels around him and his myriad questions, he struggled to keep his eyes open. Con, who could recall several journeys through time, had never experienced this degree of exhaustion before. "Why am I so tired?" she asked.

"We just traveled 520 million years downwhen," replied Violet, with a yawn. Con was so sleepy, Violet's answer barely registered. She slumped down in her seat and was already asleep by the time her chin hit her chest.

RICK AWOKE ON the floor of the time machine, not knowing how he got there. He sat up and peered around. The viewscreens on the wall showed a rocky landscape with the sun low in the sky. He didn't know if it was morning or late afternoon. The stairway was extended, and the people from the future were gone. Con, however, lay nearby. She was still sound asleep. Curled up on the floor in her tattered and garish secondhand dress, she looked like a homeless person, though her face bore a peaceful expression.

Gazing at Con's face made Rick think about her idea that they had lived—if that was the correct tense—in a future different from the one unfolding at the moment. He briefly wondered what that future would have been like. *Did we part ways?* He doubted it. Whether he liked it or not, they seemed bound together. *I'll never know what happened.* In a way, he was glad he didn't, for he suspected it did not end well. *We probably starved or died of thirst.* That raised a further question. *In the end, did I resent her or come to care for her?* He felt either was possible.

Rick's empty stomach quickly turned him from his musings. The viewscreens showed the Gaians outside, eating in an open structure that resembled a metallic tent. Spurred by the prospect of food, Rick left the time machine to join them. He was nervous, for the hurried departure and his subsequent exhaustion had delayed any real introductions. All he knew about them was their names and the little

Con had told him. Moreover, the Gaians were not simply strangers from the future, but a different human species as well.

When Rick exited the time machine, the strange landscape made him momentarily forget his hunger and the Gaians. He appeared to be in a moist desert. Nearby, water cascaded over a low rocky cliff to fill a broad, clear stream that flowed noisily to the nearby sea. A recent rain had dampened the clay beneath his feet, and puddles lingered in the low places. Yet, despite the abundance of water, Rick had never seen such a barren place. The land looked more Martian than Earthly. Rock, clay, and sand comprised its features. Only when he peered at the rocks more closely, did he note a covering of lichens. Once he recognized them, he realized most of the weathered rocks were tinted by their hues. This symbiotic combination of algae and fungus was the sole terrestrial plant life. Lichens were already an ancient life-form here, though it would be over 100 million years before the first vascular plants invaded the land and turned it truly green.

The warm air had the oxygen level of a high mountain-top, and Rick had to breathe deeply as he walked about. *That woman said we've traveled 520 million years into the past,* he recalled. *That puts us in the Cambrian Period.* He thought happily of the wonders in the nearby sea—organisms formed in a burst of evolutionary exuberance termed the "Cambrian explosion." There would be trilobites and far more bizarre creatures.

"Are you hungry?" called out Fern from the silvery tent.

Rick grinned and ambled over to the Gaians. "I'm starving," he said.

Fern switched on a boxy device. "I'll make you some food squares. Would a fruit favor be satisfactory?"

"If it's edible, I'll eat it," said Rick.

He sat on a boulder, while Fern made some adjustments to the machine. "It'll take only a few minutes," she said.

Rick glanced at the faces of his hosts and saw they were friendly. Their features appeared partly childlike, and Rick found it hard to conceive that the Gaians were older than he, perhaps much older. The most exotic aspect of their appearance was the silvery dot on their foreheads. Con had explained the dot's purpose, so Rick did not confuse it for an ornament. He soon relaxed out of habit, for he always got along well with children. A love of dinosaurs was something they had in common. He smiled at Fern. "I can't recall when I've been so hungry."

"You slept nearly fifteen hours," said Fern.

"Hunger and exhaustion are aftereffects of all time travel," said Violet, "and we just traveled over half a billion years downwhen."

"Why so far back?" asked Rick.

"It's safe here," said Oak.

"Safe?" said Rick.

"This camp once held five parties of time travelers," said Violet. "All the others have been lost upwhen."

"Samazatarmaku picked them off, one by one," said Oak.

"You mean the guy Con calls Sam?" asked Rick.

"The same," replied Oak.

"How?"

"By tampering with history," replied Oak. "It takes only a minor change to wipe out a time traveler. They are always the first to go."

Violet added, "Whenever the timestream is altered, forces act to return it to the optimal course. Anomalous elements upwhen from the change, such as time machines and their passengers, tend to vanish from the new reality."

"Couldn't the same thing happen here?" asked Rick.

"Changes in the human era pose the greatest danger to time travelers," explained Violet.

"So that's why you were so anxious to leave the thirty-first century," said Rick.

"We must survive," said Violet. "We are the last hope of a vibrant world."

"Vibrant? Then you're from a very different future than the one I visited," said Rick.

"Yes, and you saw firsthand why the timestream should not be altered," said Violet. "The reality you were in was an unnatural, distorted place."

"And the whole mess resulted from the virus Con created?" asked Rick.

"Con's son was also a major factor," said Oak.

Rick shot Oak a surprised look. "Her *son*? What son are you talking about?"

"I think we should have this discussion in Con's presence," injected Violet, giving Oak an irritated look.

"Why do you need her approval to tell me the truth?" retorted Rick. "When did she get the right to run my life?"

Oak regarded Violet smugly. "I told you getting him was a bad idea."

"I agree," said Rick.

"Con forced us to do it," said Oak to Rick.

"Oak! The girl can't defend herself," said Violet. "Rick would feel very differently if we had taken him from the nineteenth century."

"We probably wouldn't be here if we had tried," retorted Oak.

"Then we should have warned her about our plans," said Fern.

"She got what she asked for," said Oak.

"Did she?" retorted Violet. "I doubt she'd agree."

"That didn't bother you earlier," said Oak. "It was your idea to have her work with us. You know what *I* wanted to do."

"You tried that in the twenty-seventh century," said Violet, "and it didn't work."

The arguing made Rick uncomfortable. Moreover, he wanted to introduce the topic foremost on his mind. "Now that we agree my kidnapping was a bad idea," he said, "why don't you take me back to my own time? I doubt even Con would object."

"It's not that simple," said Violet.

"And we have other priorities," added Oak.

Several pink squares emerged from the boxy machine, and Fern quickly handed Rick one. "Here, have something to eat," she said.

Despite his hunger, Rick refused to be put off. "What's going to happen to me?"

"We'll have to discuss it," said Violet, "and Con will have to be part of that discussion."

A frown clouded Rick's face, but he kept his thoughts to himself and started to eat. The square had the texture of firm tofu, and its exotic flavor was reminiscent of berries and peaches. Rick also detected a faintly putrid aftertaste that the fruit flavor only partly masked. In his hunger, he did his best to ignore it. "This isn't bad," he said for the sake of politeness. "What's the flavor?"

"It resembles a fruit not yet created in your time," said Fern.

"Something genetically engineered?" asked Rick.

"Yes," answered Fern.

"Like yourselves," said Rick.

"Yes, like ourselves."

"I hope you don't mind me asking, but . . . well, evolution is a major interest of mine . . . and I was wondering . . ."

". . . why?" said Fern, anticipating his question. "You want to know why we exist."

"Well, yes."

"As a scientist, you're aware that civilization halted human evolution by preventing natural selection," said Fern.

"So people created new humans from scratch?" asked Rick.

"Not truly from scratch. People made improvements, and sometimes the improvements created genetic barriers," said Fern.

"You mean interbreeding became impossible," said Rick.

"Exactly. That's the definition of speciation."

"And how were these improvements accomplished?"

"Dramatic changes can be achieved by modifying the genes that affect growth rates. Those genes have always been the engines of evolution."

"I understand about neoteny," said Rick. "It played a part in the evolution of *Homo sapiens*. It's why baby chimps look more human than adult chimps. I guess that's why you look like children to me."

"Our size is intentional," said Oak. "It makes us more

robust, and we require fewer resources. Before Samazatarmaku altered history, Mars was populated almost exclu-
sively by Gaians."

"So, how many species are there?"

"Three," said Fern.

"And do they get along?" asked Rick.

"Yes," answered Fern.

"Even with the fecs?" asked Rick.

"We don't use such derogatory terms," said Violet.
"People in our reality lived in harmony. Then, one day,
Fern and I returned upwhen from gathering plants to discover reality had been completely altered. *Homo perfec-
tuses* were the only species, and their world was entirely
different from the one we knew."

"We retreated to the past," said Fern. "Eventually other
time travelers—Sapenes from the fortieth century—
contacted us and brought us here. Every time traveler who
survived the change was here also. After many months and
at great risk, we were able to discover what happened."

"But Con said she altered history just a few days ago,"
said Rick.

"That's a meaningless distinction where time travel is
involved," said Oak. "Those 'few days' take place over half
a billion years from now."

Rick shook his head. "It still doesn't seem logical."

"The entire timestream exists simultaneously. Your sub-
jective sense of chronology is irrelevant," said Oak.

"If you say so," said Rick.

Con emerged from the time machine looking sleepy-
eyed. As she headed toward them, Rick said to Fern,
"You'd better crank up your food machine. Con's souped,
you know."

"Souped?"

"Genetically enhanced. It's something done to rich kids
in our century. Her slim figure's due to a hyperactive
metabolism, so she's always hungry."

"You sound like you don't approve," said Oak.

"It has its drawbacks," said Rick in a low voice.

Con entered the shelter. "Good morning," she said.

"Actually, it's late afternoon," said Violet.

"Did I really sleep that long?"

"The Earth spins faster this far in the past, so the days are shorter," said Violet.

"Fern's making you something to eat," said Rick.

"That sounds great, I'm ravenous."

"So we've heard," said Oak.

"We were discussing what happens next," said Rick quickly. "I guess you have a big say in that."

"I do?" said Con, looking at the three Gaians with a curious expression.

"Con," said Violet, "we don't have many resources left. You're our greatest asset."

"Do you want me to undo what I did in the twenty-seventh century?"

"The root of the problem doesn't lie there," said Violet. "It lies with Samazatarmaku. As long as he exists, the timestream will never be safe."

"So, you want me to go after Sam?" A grin slowly crept over Con's face. "When do I start?"

29

RICK FELT LIKE A MERE SPECTATOR DURING THE strategy session.

"I know Sam's armed," Con said. "We had similar guns in the Cretaceous, and I've seen what they can do. They shoot a kind of metal powder. Depending on the settings, they can blast a boulder to dust or neatly slice it in two."

"Particle guns," said Oak, "an invention of my century."

"Do you have anything that can face that?" asked Con.

"You needn't confront Sam," said Violet. "You can do

to him what he did to our companions—alter time to erase him from history." Then, she explained to Con, as she had to Rick, how changes to history affected time travelers upwhen from them. "The trick," Violet said, "is to make the change only a short interval downwhen from your intended target."

"But how will we find him?" asked Con.

"We still possess two miniprobes," said Oak. "Now that you have told us of Samazatarmaku's base on Montana Isle, we can pinpoint the moment he abandons it. We have a device that can track a time machine if it's employed right after the craft's departure."

"I get it," said Con, grinning. "We find out where he goes; arrive a bit downwhen from his destination; I do my thing and—poof!—no more Sam."

"That's putting it crudely," said Oak, "but that's basically our plan."

"But he has a daughter!" said Con, remembering Kat. "Will she disappear, too?"

"If she's with him, yes."

"But she's not like him," said Con.

"Perhaps not," said Oak, "but she helped cause billions to vanish—Sapenes, Gaians, and Kyndens, too. You must think of them."

Con sighed, her enthusiasm departed. "I guess you're right," she said.

"Then are we agreed to this plan?" asked Oak.

"Yes," said Violet and Fern together.

"Sure," said Con.

"I assume my opinion doesn't count," said Rick. When no one answered, he said, "I thought not."

"You don't have to go with us," said Oak.

"Yeah," said Rick, "and if something goes wrong, I'm marooned here." He stood up. "I'm going for a walk."

RICK FOLLOWED THE stream until he caught sight of the seashore. The view made him pause in enchantment, for this was his first encounter with the sea. In his era, seawalls had replaced beaches as the oceans had risen. Thus, Rick gazed at a sight none of his contemporaries could enjoy— waves breaking on pristine sand.

The rarefied atmosphere made it impossible to hurry, and once Rick reached the sand, he had no desire to rush. The moon was closer to the Earth in this period, and the tides left their mark far up the beach. Rick approached the irregular line of dried seaweed and spotted a cephalon, or head segment, of a trilobite. He picked it up. Only an inch across, the soft parts had rotted away, leaving the delicate exoskeleton. It felt like papery plastic. Rick gazed at compound eyes of crystalline calcite, which were unique in all the animal kingdom. He thrilled at the thought that such eyes still peered about the sea before him.

Rick soon discarded the cephalon for a more intact trilobite. It was both familiar and exotic. He had seen countless trilobite fossils, having devoted his twelfth summer to collecting them. Holding the dried shellfish invoked that early fascination, though the object in his palm was light, not stony. There were details no rock could preserve. Minute sensory spines projected from the shell—short hairs, golden in the sunlight. A few delicate legs, sprouting flat, feathery gills, still dangled from some of the segments. Rick carefully cupped the shell in his hand, then rose to seek one on a living creature.

Rick was wading in the surf when he heard Con ask, "What are you looking for?"

He turned to see Con holding a clear bag stuffed with tidal deposits.

"A trilobite," he answered.

"Any luck?"

"Not yet," said Rick. "What's the bag for?"

"Input for the food-square maker."

Rick made a face, "So that's what we were eating."

"Yeah. It's okay."

"But then, you'd eat anything."

Con shot Rick a hurt look, then silently watched the waves while Rick resumed his search. After a few minutes, she asked, "Do you think it's safe to swim here?"

"We're giants in this world," said Rick, "The biggest predator they've ever found couldn't even take on your toe."

Con waded a short way into the water. It was pleasantly warm, and she was tempted to go swimming. The idea of undressing in front of Rick quickly quelled that impulse. She looked at him sadly, recalling how differently she had once felt about his viewing her body.

Rick caught the look without understanding it. "What are you thinking about?"

"How you loved the ocean," lied Con.

"You talk as if I were dead," said Rick.

"In a way, you are," replied Con.

"I don't need to hear this."

"I'm sorry."

Rick looked away and kept his gaze on the horizon while he spoke. "I want to go back to my life as it was before. The Gaians will listen to you."

"We have to take care of Sam first."

"We? There's no 'we' in any of this. The Gaians dragged me away only to please you."

"We've gone through this before," said Con. "I'm sorry. What else can I tell you?"

"The truth, for starters. If you pined for me so much, how come you had a child in the twenty-seventh century?"

Con splashed over to Rick and grabbed his shoulder, forcing him to look her in the eye. He saw a mixture of pain and anger. "Who told you that?" she asked.

"Oak let it slip. I guess I wasn't supposed to know."

"It's not what you think," said Con, "and I didn't really have the baby. They have artificial wombs in the twenty-seventh century."

"So that makes it different?" retorted Rick.

"I'd think you'd be more interested in your own son."

"I'm not that child's father. It was a different reality."

"It certainly was!" said Con, striding back to the shore. "And the Rick Clements I loved was a different man. And you know what? He was a hell of a lot better man than you!"

Con grabbed the bag and ran up the beach, slowing

down only when the thin air left her gasping for breath. Rick watched her go. He resumed his search for a trilobite, but thoughts of Con's accusation distracted him. He waded about fruitlessly until he noticed that the sun was setting very rapidly. Rick knew a day in this period was less than twenty-two hours long, but he was still surprised to see that fact demonstrated so dramatically. He turned and headed back. By the time he reached the stream, the sun had disappeared into the sea. He paused to view the waves reflecting the day's dying colors. Their ceaseless motion reminded him of his own turmoil, and he did not look forward to the evening.

Rick made it back as the sky turned dark. A three-inch sphere levitated in the air, casting a soft glow over the camp. Con and the Gaians were seated outside around a platter piled with food squares of varying colors.

"So you've come back," said Con in a cool tone.

"Yeah," replied Rick.

"There's food here," said Fern.

"I'm not hungry," said Rick.

"You should eat anyway, then sleep in preparation for our journey," said Violet.

"The miniprobe returned while you were gone," said Con. "Oak's already calculated the temporal coordinates. We're leaving tomorrow morning."

"I was hoping to catch a trilobite," said Rick.

"Don't feel disappointed," said Violet. "Even if you caught one, we couldn't allow you to take it home."

"Home?" said Rick.

"Yes," said Con. "As soon as we deal with Sam, the Gaians said they'd take you home."

"That's great!" said Rick, suspecting he had Con to thank for this. His regret over their fight on the beach increased. Not wishing to seem ungrateful, he awkwardly asked, "And you? What are your plans?"

"There are some major loose ends to tie up and then . . . well . . . I don't know."

"Maybe you could hook up with the other version of me," said Rick. "The one more to your liking."

"That would be very problematic," injected Oak.

Con stared down at her bare feet. "I'll be okay," she said. "We'll figure something out."

Rick realized when Con said "we" she meant her and the Gaians. "Sure, of course you will," he said.

"Our destination lies 455 million years upwhen," said Oak. "I strongly recommend getting plenty of rest. This journey will be almost as exhausting as the last one."

Rick forced himself to eat, and afterward asked if there was something he could sleep upon. After a little searching, Violet produced a Sapene-sized sleeping roll. Although only a millimeter thick, it was incredibly soft. "How does this thing work?" he asked.

"Don't ask me, it's fortieth-century technology," said Violet. "Normally, time travelers from different centuries strictly avoid each other."

"But Oak's not from your century," said Rick.

"Circumstances are far from normal," said Violet. "When the surviving travelers joined together, Oak left his party to pilot our time machine. Fern and I have very limited navigation skills. We only know how to travel between linked coordinates."

"It was a sacrifice on Oak's part," said Fern. "His life partner and her brother were on his craft. They went upwhen and they . . . they never . . ." She hung her head and sobbed softly.

As Violet rubbed her weeping friend's back, she turned to Rick. "They disappeared only recently. She hasn't recovered from the shock."

Rick thought he heard Fern murmur a name as she wept, but it was in her language, and he couldn't be sure. When he tried to imagine how it must feel to have one's world erased and replaced by something twisted, his own complaints seemed petty. "I'm sorry," he said.

"Fern," said Violet, "we really must sleep."

"You're right," said her friend, wiping her eyes. She rose and Violet, Oak, and Con followed her into the time machine.

Rick rolled out his sleeping mat. The night was clear

and warm, and the planet was pest-free. The only sounds
were rushing water, the crash of distant breakers, and the
melodic tones of the Gaians talking in their own tongue.
Soon, the talk died out. Rick gazed alone at strange con-
stellations, brilliant against the black void. A glow on the
horizon announced the coming moonrise. By the time it
spilled silver over the sky's edge, Rick was dreaming of
Missoula, Montana.

30

THE MORNING BROUGHT A SENSE OF URGENCY TO
everyone, though there was no need to rush. They could
have dawdled for weeks, yet arrive at the same moment
upwhen. The urgency was solely internal, and each had
reasons for haste. Rick thought of his brother and his work
awaiting him once this was over. The Gaians had a whole
world to recover. Even Con, who would gain nothing and
no one, wanted revenge and a chance for redemption.

When they arrived upwhen, Rick looked at the viewscreens and saw that the planet had changed. Below was
a continent with mountains at its edges and a sea project-
ing into its interior. The time machine descended, and a
speck in the sea grew larger until Rick could see that
it was an island formed by the eroding core of an ancient
volcano.

"That's Montana Isle," said Con.

Rick knew about the island, but it felt strange to see the
actual site of the adventures Con had related. It gave them
substance they had previously lacked. Below lay the sea
where they had encountered the mosasaur; the sheer cliff
they had climbed together; the beach where they had fallen

in love; and the stone rooms in which they had been imprisoned.

For Con, the island had acquired additional memories. Seeing it again made her realize how thoroughly her life had been shattered by Sam. The death of Joey became achingly immediate, and the mockery of Rick's return seemed especially cruel. She burst out into sobs that surprised both her and her companions by their intensity. Rick looked away uncomfortably and was relieved when Con ceased crying.

As soon as the time machine landed, Oak hurried off with an instrument. "He can't take a reading close to our machine," said Violet. "He'll be gone for a while. Con, would you show us around?"

Con was bone tired, but the idea of moving about was appealing. "Sure," she said. "I'll show you where Sam worked."

"I'd rather explore the island," said Rick.

While Rick headed down the beach, Con led Fern and Violet to the stone rooms. "Con," said Violet, "why were you weeping?"

"Coming back here made me think . . ." Con paused to rub tears from her eyes before she continued. ". . . think how Sam said Joey was not supposed to die and Rick was not supposed to be murdered. I had . . . had such hopes . . ."

"It's terrible to lose a child," said Violet. "I know, three of my own vanished when reality changed."

"Then you . . . you must hate me," said Con fighting back sobs.

"I still hope to see my children again," replied Violet. "Now that I know you, I don't blame you for what happened."

"Sam told me I was restoring history to its proper course."

"And so you shall," said Violet.

"How old are your children?" asked Con.

"Fifty-two, forty-seven, and forty-one."

Con stared at Violet in disbelief, and for a moment, she thought the woman was joking. Violet smiled at her expression. "I know I look like a child to you."

"I knew you weren't," said Con, "but I had no idea that . . . that you're . . . How old *are* you, anyway?"

"Ninety-seven. But Fern's still a youngster. She's only forty-two."

"Do you have any children, Fern?"

For some reason, the question caused Fern to blush. "Not yet," she replied.

"Con," said Violet, "you asked me if I hated you. I don't, but when we first met, I was unsympathetic and a little vindictive."

"I can understand why," said Con in a small voice.

"Still, we shouldn't have done what we did, and I apologize."

"Done what?"

"Even though we understood the consequences, we took Rick from the time that was safest for us to do so. We brought you a stranger, not your husband. It was a callous thing to do."

Con simply looked down, not answering.

"Don't blame him for your disappointment," said Violet. "Blame us."

"At first, I thought, somehow, it wouldn't make any difference," said Con, "that he'd still . . . Oh, what's the use? The whole thing's impossible."

"Samazatarmaku played with your life," said Violet. "I feel we've behaved little better."

"You didn't shoot Rick so Joey and I would starve," said Con.

The three arrived at the stone rooms to discover that the lights no longer worked. Violet and Con stayed at the room, while Fern went to get some lights. Con slumped wearily on the bed. Violet investigated the outermost rooms. As Con watched Violet poke around as energetically as a youngster, she smiled, and said, "You're pretty spry for an old lady."

"I'm only middle-aged," replied Violet in all seriousness.

Just then, Oak appeared outside, walking back to the time machine. Violet called to him. "Did you get a trace?"

Oak ambled over. "He's gone downwhen."

"Downwhen?" replied Violet, concern evident in her voice.

"About 84 million years downwhen," replied Oak. "Too far back to be a threat to us."

"Why would he do that?" asked Con.

"He's probably setting up a new operation, unaware we can trace him," said Oak. "I'm using fortieth-century technology. He may not know it exists."

"Let's hope so," said Violet.

"I'll use our last probe to pinpoint his landing site," said Oak.

"But how can I change history back then?" asked Con. "There's no history to change."

"History is just another name for the timestream," said Violet. "You can still cause an alteration downwhen from Sam sufficient to erase his existence."

"An ecological disruption should do the job," said Oak, "the kind caused by a fusion grenade."

"To be certain it does," said Violet, "we'll have to detonate it only a few days downwhen from his arrival in the time period."

"I'm going to ready the probe now," said Oak.

Oak departed as Fern arrived with three luminescent spheres. These served as flashlights when the women headed for the central room carved into the mesa. On their way, they passed the chamber that had contained all the utility equipment. It was evident Sam had discharged the particle gun into it, for most of the room's contents had been blasted to dust. Only a few fragments remained, parts outside the cone of fire. When they entered the central room, they found it devastated also. Even less remained.

"I'd say Samazatarmaku knew we were coming," said Violet. The remark filled Con with apprehension.

Once the Gaians discovered that Sam had destroyed all

his equipment, they lost interest in the facility. Violet and Fern headed back to assist Oak. Con was accompanying them, when she glimpsed into one of the side rooms. There, laid out upon the bed, were the clothes that Kat had given her. "You go on ahead," she told the Gaians. "I think I'll poke around a little more."

When the Gaians were gone, Con entered the room. She was sure it had been Kat's room, though little remained except Con's garments upon the bed. The short robe of satiny blue material was spread out unfolded and without a wrinkle. The matching panties lay on top, positioned with similar care. The arrangement bore an eerie resemblance to a memorial.

Shedding her shabby clothes from Mergonita, Con gladly replaced them with the garments on the bed. Then she explored further. The next three rooms were mostly empty. A few bulky items of furniture remained, but that was all. A fifth room contained trash. There was a broken chair, pieces of disassembled equipment, the garments Con wore in the twenty-seventh century, and other odd items. Con was about to leave when something caught her eye. It was one of Rick's sneakers. She approached it in amazement. *This is from when we were imprisoned here!* she thought, recalling that their *Homo perfectus* captors had sent Rick to the nineteenth century barefoot. Con picked up the filthy shoe, knowing it had lain there for over a century. Then she spotted a real treasure. It was the hunting knife and sheath that Rick's brother had given him on their last night together, the same knife Rick had carried throughout their adventures in the Cretaceous. Its cavelike resting place had left it well preserved; the leather sheath was only a little stiff. Simply touching it conjured up images from those times—visions of Rick striking sparks from the blade to make a fire; the sight of him butchering dinosaur meat; the desperate struggle with the nightstalker. Clasping the knife with trembling hands, Con was glad she had found it when she was alone.

*   *   *

RICK WAS EXHAUSTED from time travel, and only adrenaline kept him going. Believing their stopover would prove a short one, he was determined to make the most of it. Rick was particularly interested in how the Earth was recovering from the extinction event. He had made a methodical examination of the plant life, even though paleobotany was only a side interest of his. Now, he was investigating the shore life, trying to finish before sundown. Rick was so preoccupied that Con surprised him when she called out his name. Thinking she was about to cut short his exploration, he answered curtly.

"What?"

"I brought a peace offering," said Con.

Rick turned and saw Con was dressed differently. She held a hand behind her back, and her face bore a faint smile that puzzled him. Then, like a magician performing a trick, she produced the knife with a flourish. Rick stared at the knife in the weathered leather sheath without immediately recognizing its significance.

"It's the knife your brother gave you," said Con.

"Tom's knife?"

Con placed it in his hands. "It's been through a lot," she said, "and it lay in one of the rooms here for a very long time."

Rick examined the leather sheath with its pocket for a whetstone. His hand began to tremble when he saw the initials "THC" embossed there. "Tom Harrison Clements," he said, his voice sounding distant.

"I know what that knife means to you," said Con. "Just don't tell the Gaians about it. They might not let you take it home."

"But Tom never gave me this," said Rick, still trying to reconcile that knowledge with the fact of the knife in his hand.

"When you return, maybe you'll each have one. That should be interesting to explain."

Rick pulled the knife from its sheath. He knew it immediately, despite the blade being worse for wear. It felt strange to hold it and think how he had held it in a different existence. "Thank you," he said softly.

"I shouldn't have said those things to you," said Con. "It wasn't fair of me. When this is over, I'd like us to part as friends."

"We will," said Rick. "I'm sorry I was so snotty."

"It's been a hard time for us both."

"Yeah," agreed Rick, thinking how much harder it had been for Con.

Con followed Rick down the beach, but she let him conduct his research in peace. She watched him study every shell he picked up, displaying the curiosity that was so familiar to her. When Rick noticed how intently she was watching him, he became self-conscious. "I'm pooped," he said. "I think I'll head back."

As they returned to the time machine, Con said, "Oak says Sam went 84 million years downwhen."

Rick did some mental math. "That's 149 million years before our era. Upper Jurassic. There'll be dinosaurs." His face brightened. "Will we be staying long?"

"I don't know. Probably not. All I have to do is set off another fusion grenade."

"And blow up Sam?"

"No, just change the timestream so he'll disappear. He'll never see it coming."

"And his daughter, too? The one who was nice?"

"It can't be helped," Con replied.

"Then, afterward, it's back to the twenty-first century for me," said Rick, suddenly less enthusiastic about the prospect now that dinosaurs were involved.

"Yeah," said Con. "You'd better hide that knife before the Gaians see it."

Rick and Con returned to the landing site to find the Gaians inside the time machine. "The miniprobe just returned," said Violet. "We're about to extract its data." In her palm, she cradled a tiny sphere that glowed weakly. When the light faded entirely, Violet placed the miniprobe in a receptacle on the pilot's console. The screen in front of

the console had been displaying a view of the landscape
outside, but now a rectangular image replaced a portion of
the rocky coastline. It showed a view of the Earth from
beyond the stratosphere. A continent lay below.

"Where's that place?" asked Con. "It looks completely
strange to me."

"That's North America in the Late Jurassic," said Rick.
"There's the Pacific Ocean."

Con pointed to the coast. "So that's California?"

"No," said Rick. "Nevada and Idaho had the beachfront
property then. That arm extending inland from the Pacific
was called the Sundance Sea. It covered most of Montana
and North Dakota."

"So that's where Montana Isle is?" asked Con.

"The Sundance Sea and the Cretaceous Interior Seaway
were entirely different bodies of water, tens of millions
years apart."

"You seem very knowledgeable about the geography,"
said Violet.

"I've spent a lot of time there," replied Rick. "The land
south of the sea became the Morrison Formation. It's
prime fossil territory, famous throughout the world."

"I've never heard of it," said Con.

"That's because you're not a paleontologist, or a nine-
year-old boy," replied Rick.

The miniprobe had descended after materializing downwhen, and the views it recorded changed. While the Pacific
Ocean was no longer visible, the Sundance Sea still occupied the top of the screen. A mountain range of Andean
proportions lay to the west. The probe descended farther.
Only the seacoast and the foothills of the mountains were
green; the large plain south of the sea was colored in
shades of dun and beige.

"Dry season," said Rick.

As the land grew still closer, dried lake beds could be discerned. The image on the screen showed the probe's progress
over the parched landscape to the coastal forests and the
seashore in the north. A cluster of five islands appeared on
the screen. They seemed close to the coast. Several of them

were low and covered with greenery, but two were rockier, with steep cliffs rising over stony beaches. The probe headed for one of the latter. Eventually, it hovered only a hundred feet in the air. Sam's time machine rested on a flat shelf of rock. A large rectangular opening had been blasted into the face of the nearby cliff.

"I'd say Samazatarmaku has a fondness for island hideaways," said Violet.

"By making that cave," said Oak, "he's made our job easier."

"How so?" asked Rick.

"That artificial feature does not belong in the landscape," replied Oak. "Any shift in the timestream will eliminate that cave and its creator."

The screen went blank as the miniprobe departed for its return trip. "That's it," said Oak. "We know where to go and when to arrive."

"Would you mind replaying that data?" asked Rick, his voice sounding almost dreamy. "I'd love to see it again. I spent three summers working in the Morrison Formation."

"When we're done," said Con, "do you think Rick could get a little tour before he goes home?"

Con's question made Rick's face light up immediately, but Oak and Violet seemed to have a different reaction. Con was certain she caught Violet giving Oak a strongly cautionary glance. Oak immediately clammed up, and Violet replied, "Why not? It would be fun." Violet's glance made Con suspect that getting Rick home might not be as simple as she imagined.

31

THE GAIANS GATHERED FERN FRONDS FOR THEIR food-making machine and produced squares without a putrid aftertaste. Con ate heartily. Afterward, she found a flat area close to the time machine and unrolled a sleeping mat. The warm, humid air had cooled after dusk, and it was pleasant to be outside. Rick chose to sleep outside also, but not nearby. Con started to imagine what might have been, but forced herself to think of other things. *Tomorrow I'll avenge Joey's death.* Con wished she could drop the grenade directly on Sam, so he might know that she had won; yet, she realized a direct attack would be foolhardy. Stealth ensured their plan's success. *There's a whole world to think about,* Con told herself. *It would be stupid to risk it for revenge.*

THE JOURNEY TO the Late Jurassic began after a quick breakfast and a few last-minute preparations. Fern made some extra food squares before packing away the machine. Con strapped the two pajaroes to her waist, arming symbolically for the task ahead. Oak activated the actual weapon that Con would use—a fusion grenade. They would view its detonation from a safe position, then make a short jump upwhen to verify Sam's elimination.

Compared to Sam's elaborate machinations, Con thought their plan was simplicity itself. Of course, its goal was merely to remove one man from the timestream. Con would worry about restoring history later. That would be more involved. Yet, without Sam and the threat of countermeasures, she felt it would be easy. After all, her very existence had been transformed so that she could alter time.

It was still morning when the time machine departed. When it arrived downwhen high above the Earth, its viewscreens displayed a different and more ancient world. The same image recorded by the miniprobe now covered the walls of the cabin, though in greater detail. Rick gazed at it with fascination. He could now discern that many of the snowcapped mountains had volcanic craters. To the north, the mountain range extended into the mouth of the Sundance Sea to become a chain of islands. Great alluvial fans of eroded gravel and earth, created by a network of streams, spread from the highlands into the plain to the east.

The time machine began to descend, and as it did, topographic lines were superimposed over the landscape. Their flight path over the vast arid plain was marked, as was their destination in the Sundance Sea to the north. As the craft sped over the land, it lost altitude. By the time it approached the sea, the trees of the coastal forests were only a thousand feet below. The sea spread out before them, and the cluster of islands where they would land came into view.

Rick was peering at those islands when the explosion occurred. The images on the cabin walls flickered, then faded into darkness. The only light came from a large, jagged hole in the side of the cabin. Rick stared at it in shock as he was pushed deeper into his seat by the time machine's rapid acceleration. He realized they were rising, not plummeting to Earth. In the dim cabin, Rick could see illuminated instrument displays on the wall in front of the pilot's console, and he assumed Oak still had some control over the craft.

"What happened?" cried Con.

"We've been hit by a particle gun," shouted Oak over the sound of rushing wind.

A second explosion ripped another hole in the cabin, close to the first one. The time machine continued to rise, but it no longer accelerated. The cabin turned icy cold, and Rick had to gasp for air. *I'm going to die,* he thought.

The craft's upward momentum slowed until it hung motionless for an instant. Then it began to fall. The view through the two gaping holes showed only blue sky, and it was impossible to tell how high they were. The time machine began to spin slowly on an off-center axis as it headed earthward. The spinning became more rapid, and the cabin's contents tumbled about with ever-increasing violence. Soon, things were bouncing everywhere and flying out the holes. Rick tried to protect his head with his arms and hands.

"Are you still flying this thing?" he called to Oak.

"As best I can."

"Steer for the mountains," Rick yelled.

Oak didn't respond, and Rick had no idea if his advice was heeded. The time machine now spun around like an amusement park ride. Rick's stomach churned as it had when, as a kid, he rode the "Crack the Whip." Just when he was certain his destruction was imminent, the spinning slowed. Rick caught a glimpse of brown through the gaps in the walls as Oak shouted, "We're going to crash!"

An instant later, Rick was jolted as the cabin shuddered. If his seat had not been grasping him, he would have been smashed against the wall. Afterward, everything seemed to happen in slow motion. Rick felt the machine bounce upward. It became airborne again before slamming to Earth and bouncing a second time. When the time machine bounced a third time, Rick envisioned the craft skipping like a stone thrown across the surface of a pond.

A dry hillside was visible through the gaps in the cabin wall a second before a fourth jolt. It was the final and the most violent one. The impact sent dirt and stones flying through the openings. The cabin filled with dust as its remaining contents slammed against the crumpled wall to form a jumbled heap. The stillness and silence that followed seemed eerie. The only sounds were those of coughing and of Con retching. Rick's seat released him. He sat, stunned, for a moment before he made an anxious self-examination for wounds and broken bones. Rick felt nauseous, and his head throbbed. When he touched a sore spot on his scalp, his fingers came back bloody, though he did not recall being struck.

"Is everyone all right?" asked Violet in a shaky voice.

Slowly, voices answered affirmatively, but without conviction.

The floor of the time machine now slanted steeply, and as Rick stood up, he grabbed his seat to steady himself. He was dizzy, and it was hard to see, for little light entered the cabin. One of the holes in the wall seemed buried into a hillside. Some daylight spilled around the edges of the other gap, but a pile of jumbled supplies filled much of the opening. The only other source of light was the immaterial cylinder within the transparent column. Initially, it was not particularly luminous, but as Rick watched, the cylinder grew brighter and began to expand. A brilliant tendril, no thicker than a thread, emerged from the central column. Rick instinctively shrank from it.

"Oak," Rick called out, "what's happening with the column? Should it be doing . . ."

"Everyone out!" shouted Oak. "Now! Hurry!"

The urgency in Oak's voice spurred everyone into action, and they rushed for the opening in the cabin wall. Meanwhile, the glowing tendril brushed along the ceiling and left a path of destruction in its wake. Any object it touched disintegrated in a burst of energy. The effect was dramatic and terrifying.

Rick reached the opening first. He seized a large box that blocked the exit and hefted it aside. Sensing this would be their only opportunity to get provisions, he shouted, "Don't leave empty-handed. Grab something as you go."

Fern scrambled out the opening, wrenching a bag from the pile as she exited. Con slipped on her vomit and slammed into the jumble of specimens and supplies. As she tried to regain her footing, a section of the time machine's ceiling crashed to the floor, looking as if it had been cut with a blowtorch. Rick helped Con to her feet, then pushed her outside.

She grabbed something from the pile as she left. Violet departed next, pulling a tarp.

"Run!" Oak shouted at her. "Run far away!"

A second glowing tendril joined the first one, and both ranged more widely about the cabin. Everything they encountered was destroyed. As Rick desperately searched for something useful in the chaotic pile, Oak shook his shoulder. "No time! Get out!"

Rick grabbed something at random and bolted through the opening. Oak let out a surprised cry as he followed after him. Once outside the ruined craft, Rick spotted Violet, Con, and Fern scrambling up the hillside.

"Hurry!" yelled Oak.

Rick needed no encouragement, for the tendrils had thickened and increased in number and were reaching beyond the time machine. Rick feared they would not halt with the craft's annihilation. He dashed halfway up the hill before he dared look back. The time machine was gone. In its place was a large, perfectly circular crater that glowed with iridescent colors. It contained a luminous haze that seethed furiously. Even as Rick watched, the crater steadily ate into the hillside. Rocks and earth tumbled toward the growing cavity to vaporize instantly when they slid past its edge.

Rick looked up and saw Con and the two Gaian women gazing down from the hillcrest in shocked amazement. Oak called out to them. "Don't stop! Keep going!" The three took off and disappeared behind the hill. Rick and Oak hurried to join them. Rick ran, focused solely on escape as the hillside disappeared into the voracious crater. *Perhaps it will swallow everything,* he thought.

Despite his smaller size, Oak had no difficulty keeping up with Rick. They reached the hilltop together and headed down the slope on the other side. The three women were running toward an irregular line of trees that marked the center of the valley three hundred yards away. The trees constituted most of the greenery in an otherwise brown landscape. Once Con, Violet, and Fern reached them, they halted in their shade and waited for Rick and Oak to catch up. They did so shortly. While Rick and Con were sweating and panting, the Gaians seemed scarcely out of breath.

"Do you think we're far enough back?" Violet asked Oak.

"We should be," said Oak.

The hilltop's profile began to change as the crater expanded, and a crescent of sky appeared where earth had been but a moment before. The crescent grew, but it grew slowly.

"I think it's almost over," said Oak.

"What's over?" asked Con. "What happened?"

"A temporal discontinuity."

"A what?" said Con.

"The column in a time machine contains an entity similar to a wormhole," replied Oak. "When we crashed, that containment was breached. The destruction was a form of uncontrolled time travel."

"If that had happened while we were in flight," said Rick, "we'd be toast."

"I'm certain that was Samazatarmaku's intent," replied Oak.

"He was expecting us," said Violet.

"But he's supposed to be upwhen," said Con.

"Obviously, he wasn't," said Rick, "We flew into an ambush, plain and simple." He peered upward and saw something shiny in the sky. "Speak of the devil, that's probably him now."

Rick pointed out a silvery speck to the others. They nervously watched as the speck grew, knowing they were defenseless. Sam's time machine descended until it was only a few hundred feet above them. Then, it halted briefly before rising again and heading north.

"Whew!" said Con. "He didn't see us. He must think we're dead."

"I think he spotted us," said Oak, "and knows we're doomed."

The lifeless quality of Oak's voice made Con think he was in shock. "Come on," she said, "you shouldn't . . . Oh my God! Oak! What happened to your arm?" She stared aghast at Oak's right arm. It was neatly severed midway below the elbow. The limb ended in a stump that was bloodless and gray.

Oak stared at his arm stupidly; as if he had absentmindedly misplaced his hand and had only just realized it. "Oh. A little disintegration," he said in a faint voice. "I didn't get out fast enough."

"Oh God!" said Con, her voice trembling.

"It doesn't hurt," Oak said. He gazed at his stump, and his face grew sorrowful. "Besides, what's a hand?"

Con felt incapable of responding.

As the immediate terror of the crash and its aftermath subsided, the extremity of the situation hit the five time travelers. Fern, in particular, seemed overwhelmed. She turned pale and began to shake. Violet hugged her and pulled her away for a whispered conversation. Oak watched them dolefully, then buried his face in his remaining hand. "We're doomed," he said. "Samazatarmaku's won. He's marooned us."

"Then he's a fool," said Con, "for underestimating us."

Oak laughed bitterly.

"He has," asserted Con.

"He's left us to be devoured."

"That shows you how much he knows. We'll be invisible."

"Invisible?" said Oak with a voice that verged on derision.

"Yes," said Con. "We don't belong here, so the animals will ignore us. That's the same as being invisible. Since predators stick to known prey, we'll be safe from them."

"And where did you come by that bit of wisdom?" asked Oak.

"Rick told me," replied Con. "He said that when Darwin visited the Galapagos Islands, he was able to pluck birds off their perches."

"He was only theorizing," said Oak.

"No, he wasn't," retorted Con. "Rick's a proven guide. He's faced Tyrannosaurs and worse. Compared to the K-T event, this place is a picnic."

Rick shook his head. "Con . . ."

"You did, Rick," asserted Con. "And with no more experience than you have now."

"But . . ."

"What's our choice, Rick?" asked Con. "Give up? If we fell for Sam's surprise attack, maybe he'll fall for ours."

"*Our* surprise attack?" asked Rick.

"We'll steal Sam's time machine and maroon him," said Con. "I'm betting he can't quickly undo what we did in the thirty-first century. He's moved his base here, and I think he'll still be there when we reach it."

"Are you crazy?" asked Oak. "What you're proposing . . ."

"Is our only chance to stop Samazatarmaku," injected Violet.

"Then it's no chance at all," retorted Oak.

"We *have* to try," said Violet.

"Besides," said Con, "it's our only ticket out of here."

"How can we live long enough to reach the sea?" said Oak.

"Ask Rick," urged Con. "He'll guide us."

Rick suddenly felt everyone's eyes on him. The Gaians appeared both dubious and hopeful at once. Con seemed oddly triumphant. He searched for the confidence she seemed to expect from him and detected none. Nevertheless, he answered with counterfeit assurance. "Sure," he said. "We could make it."

32

WITHOUT BEING ASKED, RICK BECAME THE GUIDE. Though he felt inadequate for the job, he tried to be methodical and outwardly calm. "We should inventory what we saved from the wreck," Rick said. He pulled out his own contribution—a small, handled bag made out of fabric. Inside, he found a collection of two-inch plastic disks. "What are these?" he asked.

"You would call them movies," said Fern. She took the disk from Rick's hand and translated the writing upon it. *"Along the River,"* she said. "One of my favorites. Very romantic." She let the disk fall to the ground.

Rick dumped out the other disks. "Oh well, the bag will come in handy." Then he remembered the knife he had tucked in the waistband of his undergarment and withdrew it from its hiding place. "This will be more useful."

"Where did you get that?" asked Violet.

"Con found it yesterday."

"It's from Rick's first visit to Montana Isle," said Con.

Violet looked at Con sharply. "And you gave it to him? Do you have any idea what would have happened if he took it back to the twenty-first century?"

"It won't make any difference now," said Oak. "Forget about it."

"Fern, what did you rescue?" asked Rick.

Fern produced a bag containing three large plastic jars filled with the preserved remains of tiny mammals.

Rick grabbed a jar and regarded its contents with fascination. "Where did you get these?"

"The Paleocene," replied Fern. "They were for a colleague."

Con smiled. "Rick, I think the jars are more important than the rats inside."

"If they're from the Paleocene, they couldn't be rats," said Rick. He eagerly unscrewed the top of the jar. Then he remembered their situation. Almost mournfully, he poured the specimens onto the ground next to the useless disks. "These will make good water containers," he said.

Con produced a dark gray plastic cylinder she hoped was a weapon. It turned out to be a piece of broken tubing. Her pajaroes proved her real contribution. The green tarp Violet had seized was a valuable addition to their meager stores. Eight feet square, it was strong, lightweight, and waterproof. The item Oak had grabbed had been lost with his hand.

The clothes on their backs completed their inventory of resources. The Gaians' apparel would serve them well in the hot climate. Fern, however, had lost one of her sandals in her escape. If they couldn't find it, it would mean two of the party would have to hike barefoot.

With the inventory completed, Rick turned to his first priority. "We have to find water," he said. The hot afternoon was so dry his perspiration had already evaporated. Rick knew dehydration came quickly in such conditions. The greenery about him indicated he was standing on one of the moistest spots in the valley. Nevertheless, the ground was dry. *Any water here,* he thought, *is deep underground.*

"Find a shady spot to rest," Rick said. "I'm going to climb the hill. From there, maybe I can spot some water."

"I'll join you," said Violet.

"You should stay here," said Rick. "It'll conserve body fluids."

Violet did not reply, but to Rick's exasperation, headed for the hilltop. He followed her, but not before telling the others to remain behind. Violet slowed her pace, and Rick caught up. "If you want to be the guide," said Rick, not bothering to hide his irritation, "be my guest. This wasn't my idea."

"I don't want to guide anyone," said Violet.

"Or listen to anyone either."

"Con places a lot of faith in you," said Violet. "Is that wise?"

"Probably not."

Violet smiled. "That's a promising answer. Humility's always a good sign."

"I'm glad you approve."

"Plus, you've done this before."

"In a different reality, remember. *I* wasn't there."

"The reason it's so difficult to change history is because there are forces that work to return it to the optimal path," said Violet.

"What does that have to do with anything?"

"I think you are meant to guide us."

"Meant to? Don't get mystical on me," said Rick. "Are you trying to tell me that it's my fate?"

"Con believes so, and she should know."

"Well, I believe I'm in way over my head."

"Then start swimming."

"Boy, you're just full of good advice. While you're at it, could you tell me where to find water?"

"You're the guide, Rick. You know more about this period than we do, and I think Con's right about your potential. You're our best hope. It means more than our lives. Samazatarmaku must not be permitted to change history."

"So this is my pep talk?"

"I guess it is," said Violet. "But there's another reason I needed to talk to you. There's something you should know."

"What?"

"Fern's pregnant."

AS RICK AND Violet talked, Con rested in the shade of a tree. She wasn't knowledgeable about plants, but she knew the tree was some kind of conifer. All the green trees in the valley were. There were other trees, but they were both leafless and strangely shaped. *I'll have to ask Rick what they are,* she thought. She recognized the cycads from her visit to the Cretaceous. Although they were presently leafless, their squat trunks were distinctive. Their pattern of leaf scars made them resemble giant pineapples. Other plants she recalled from the Cretaceous, such as palms and hardwoods, were missing. Indeed, the entire landscape had a curiously half-finished look, lacking grass or any flowering plants. To Con, it seemed piney and primitive. In addition, the landscape was extremely dry. Even the greenery in the shade, which appeared to be some kind of fern, looked on the verge of shriveling up. The scene about her thoroughly contradicted the image of the age of the dinosaurs as a place of lush jungles.

These thoughts were interrupted by Fern's frightened whisper. "Something's coming." Con followed Fern's gaze. Three animals were slowly walking up the valley. Their roughly textured hides bore a mottled pattern of green and tan that blended with their surroundings, making them difficult to see. Though medium-sized for dinosaurs, they were still large animals. They walked on two powerful, birdlike legs, and their twelve-foot bodies pivoted at their hips, so the torso leaned far forward and counterbalanced a long, rigid tail. Their necks were relatively short, and their blunt heads seemed large. Despite their leaning posture, the creatures stood taller than a man. *The Gaians,* Con thought, *must think they're huge.*

"Meat eaters," whispered Fern. The terror in her voice raised goose bumps on Con. As the animals came closer, Fern grasped Con's arm with trembling hands. Meanwhile, the creatures continued their leisurely advance until they could be observed more closely. The five-fingered hands on their short arms bore stubby claws, and their squared-off snouts ended with bony beaks. The lead dinosaur halted only a dozen yards away and pivoted downward to nip some leaves with its beak.

"It's all right," said Con. "You're not the kind of Fern those animals eat."

The dinosaurs turned their heads at the sound of Con's voice, but, otherwise, they did not react. Con stood up after Fern released her arm and slowly approached the browsing animals. The three dinosaurs eyed her incuriously as they ate. Even when Con walked within ten feet of the nearest one, it was unperturbed.

If the creature could have read Con's thoughts, it would have been more nervous. Con recalled similar dinosaurs from the Cretaceous had made good eating. She was already very hungry, and the idea of meat made her mouth water, even if it was still on the hoof. She considered trying to bring the animal down with her pajaroes, but decided it wouldn't work. She would have to find something else to eat. Con was fully aware how quickly her accelerated metabolism could bring her to starvation. It had nearly killed her twice before. As Con returned to her companions, her stomach growled as she felt the first, all-too-familiar pangs of hunger.

* * *

RICK STOOD ON the hilltop with Violet and surveyed the surrounding countryside. High mountains rose to the west, their peaks covered with snow even at this time of year. Erosion from the mountains had formed a series of ridges and valleys that sloped toward a flat plain that had once been the floor of an ancient sea. Through the slow work of time and weather, the mountains were dwindling into sediments that covered the plain. Less than an inch accumulated every thousand years. Layered like the pages of a book and turned to stone, these sediments recorded the life of the land. They preserved the bones of its creatures and their tracks. They spoke of dry seasons and monsoon rains. They bore evidence of still, alkaline lakes and raging flash floods. Rick had studied those sediments. Now, if his dust was not to be mingled with them, he would have to apply what he had learned.

Rick knew the best chance to find water lay westward. Snowmelt and moisture caught by the high mountains would feed streams that ran year-round. He looked for evidence of such a stream—a valley with greenery and water-cut slopes. A likely prospect lay miles distant. The rippling heat from the baked hills in between made the valley waver like a mirage. Rick pointed it out to Violet. "That's where we'll head," he said.

As Rick and Violet walked back, they retraced Fern's flight, looking for her missing sandal. Their search began at the edge of the crater left by the time machine's destruction. Over three hundred yards in diameter, its walls were perfectly smooth and symmetrical. It more resembled the product of meticulous craftsmanship than the work of a destructive force. Rick noted that its sides were the same whitish gray as Oak's stump.

RICK AND VIOLET returned without Fern's sandal. Con was nearly dozing when they arrived. "Did you see those dinosaurs?" she asked in a sleepy voice.

"Yeah," replied Rick in a distracted tone.

Con realized the seriousness of their situation as soon as Rick ignored the dinosaurs.

"Did you find water?" asked Oak.

"I saw a likely spot," replied Rick.

"Then we'll wait here until you're sure," said Oak.

"Rick's our guide," said Violet. "We must stick with him." Then she said something in the Gaian tongue, and Oak rose reluctantly.

Rick stowed the three plastic jars in the bag and led the way up the hill with the crater. They would have to cross two broad, dry valleys and climb the hills that surrounded them before they reached their destination. Rick's hopes that it contained a stream or river were based solely on the valley's steep sides and a tiny glimpse of green near its head. If he had guessed wrong, he suspected they would be in serious trouble by the following afternoon.

Although he was anxious to reach the valley, Rick set a moderate pace and tried to pick a trail that would be easy on Fern's bare feet. Con's soles had toughened in Mergonita, and he was less worried about hers. Feet were not trivial concerns; there could be dire consequences if someone went lame. As the guide, such matters had become Rick's province. He also watched everyone for signs of heat exhaustion. He glanced at Oak's stump to see if it had started bleeding. He kept his eyes peeled for anything edible. *Was it only a week ago that I was sweating over a stratigraphy exam?* he wondered. It didn't seem possible.

The first valley they had to cross was gravelly and shallow, with a floor cut by numerous dry streambeds. The brown vegetation they encountered was unfamiliar. The most common plant had long thorns covering its dried stems. Rick led the way, but Con walked beside him. "Did you get a look at the dinosaurs?" she asked.

"Yes," said Rick. "They looked like *Dryosauruses.*"

"I saw something like them on my first trip downwhen," said Con.

"The one to the Late Cretaceous?"

"Yeah. You called them hypso-somethings."

"Hypsilophodontids," corrected Rick. "That family first appeared in the Middle Jurassic. Scientists think they were the antelopes of their time—quick, small-to-medium herbivores. The one you saw in the Cretaceous was probably a *Thescelosaurus."*

"Well, I remember they tasted pretty good, whatever you call them."

Rick couldn't help but smile. "Are you making a menu suggestion?"

"All I'm saying is they weren't bad."

"Didn't you have guns on that trip?"

"Yeah," said Con, "particle guns."

"It'd be a little different going after one with a knife."

"Maybe we could make spears," said Con. "I'm not afraid to hunt."

"I'm sure you're not," said Rick, thinking of the guard.

"I'll admit I need more food than most people. I just want you to know I'll pull my weight."

"I'm not worried about that," said Rick. "I'm worried about finding water."

The party walked steadily until they reached a boulder on the far side of the valley. Rick called for a rest in its shade. Con slumped against the rock and licked her parched lips. Fern massaged her sore feet.

"What a desolate place," said Oak.

"Dry season's a hard time," said Rick. "It's even worse on the plain."

"How could it be any worse than this?" said Oak. "We're stuck in a wasteland."

"Don't judge this region by one place," said Rick. "This valley's soil doesn't hold moisture, but other valleys should be wetter."

As Rick leaned against the boulder, perspiration flowed down his brow and stung his eyes. He had hunted for fossils in places equally harsh, but always with a canteen handy. The cardinal rule in the badlands was to drink plenty of water. That rule was impossible to follow here, and Rick was beginning to feel the consequences. His mouth was gummy, and he felt a little light-headed. The Gaians appeared to be faring better, but Con had the drawn look of someone approaching her limit.

The lengthening shadow cast by the boulder soon reminded Rick they were racing the sunset. He rose wearily to his feet and said, "We should head out." Everyone silently stood up and, just as silently, followed him up the hill. When they reached its crest, Rick got his first close view of the valley beyond. It was wider than he had anticipated, and its broad floor had been formed by a debris flow. A mixture of mud, gravel, and jagged rock had baked into a stark gray landscape, softened only by the brown remains of thorny plants. Rick sensed everyone's disappointment at the sight, though no one said anything.

The low sun still packed a wallop, and the way was more rugged than before. The stony ground was particularly hard on Fern's feet. After a few miles, she was hobbling. Rick halted. "Fern, I want to look at your soles."

"They're all right," Fern replied.

"Then you won't mind showing them."

Fern reluctantly sat on the dusty ground. Rick knelt down and discovered, as he had feared, that her soles were cracked and bleeding. *That didn't take long,* he thought. Rick handed his knife and the bag to Violet. "Would you take these for me? I'm going to carry Fern."

"You are not!" protested Fern.

"Look, if I'm to be the guide, you must respect my judgment," said Rick, in his best authoritarian voice. "Your feet could become a problem for us all."

Violet said something in the Gaian language, and Fern rose meekly. "All right," she said.

Rick bent at the waist, and Fern jumped up to wrap her arms around his neck and her legs around his waist. Rick slipped his forearms beneath Fern's knees and shifted her weight slightly, then headed out again. Despite Fern's child-sized proportions, Rick soon ached from carrying her. The way through the valley was long and arduous, and by the time he reached the crest on its far side, he was panting from exertion.

The valley beyond the crest fanned out to form a broad

green delta that extended into the distant plain. There, the greenery diminished and contracted until it became a meandering line across the parched land. Rick was certain the line of trees marked the banks of a river, although they hid it from sight. The ridge upon which they stood was near the valley's head, where the fan of greenery came to a point. The sides of the ridge were rocky, steep, and mostly bare. The first trees grew a hundred feet below.

Fern slid off Rick's back, limped over to a rock, and sat down. "Thank you," she said in a quiet voice. Her glistening eyes expressed her gratitude more eloquently than any words, and its depth embarrassed Rick.

"Don't waste water on tears," he said. "You weren't that heavy."

Con, Violet, and Oak straggled up before Fern could reply. "Are we resting here?" asked Con.

"I think we'll do more than that," said Rick. "I'd like you to set up camp while Violet and I get water."

Setting up camp meant little more than laying out the tarp. If Con weren't so exhausted and thirsty, she would have complained of being coddled. As it was, she nodded and mumbled, "Okay."

Rick saw how low the sun was in the sky and decided he didn't have time to rest. "Violet, are you ready to head out?"

Violet nodded, and the two set off. She waited until they were out of earshot of the others before saying, "I don't mind getting water, but if we camped in the valley, we wouldn't have to lug it up the hill."

"I know," said Rick, "but it's barren on the ridge, so we're less likely to be bothered by animals."

"I thought animals weren't supposed to be a problem, that we'd be invisible."

"Con was quoting the other version of Rick, not me."

"Do you disagree with the statement?"

"I think it's a valid generalization, but it was made by someone with a particle gun to deal with the exceptions."

"The exceptions?"

"We're talking about living creatures," said Rick, "and nothing alive is completely predictable."

33

THE SUN HAD SUNK BEHIND THE WESTERN MOUNTAINS
by the time Violet and Rick reached the valley floor. The
trees before them were engulfed in shadow. The diminished light brought forth insects and the pterosaurs that
pursued them. The bird-sized reptiles were furry, yet their
sickle-shaped wings did not resemble those of bats. A single, elongated finger supported the stiffened membrane
that stretched to their legs. The creatures had large heads
with long, toothy snouts and whiplike tails that ended with
a trapezoidal fin. They flew so gracefully, Violet and Rick
paused to watch them before entering the forest.

After the long hike through two dry valleys, stepping
into the forest felt like entering a different world. Conifers,
some familiar and many not, formed a canopy that reduced
the already dim light. Interspersed within the sparse, ferny
undergrowth were tall, roughly textured, earthen columns.
Violet pointed to one that loomed like a huge, grotesque
tombstone. "What's that?" she asked.

"A termite mound," replied Rick. "Some of them got
over a hundred feet tall."

Violet ran her hand over the mound's irregular surface.
"Is this just dirt?"

"Dirt and saliva."

The woods were quiet, but occasionally the silence was
broken by the sounds of small animals moving in the
undergrowth or the raspy cries of some unseen creatures.
After they traveled about fifty yards, Rick and Violet
detected the welcome sound of running water. They has-
tened in its direction and found a stream cascading over

stones. Rick and Violet pushed their way through the lush ferns and horsetails surrounding its bank, scaring a tiny dinosaur in the process. Rick only glimpsed its whiplike tail as it disappeared into the undergrowth.

Violet paid no attention to the animal. She got on her hands and knees to drink deeply. Rick did the same. The water was cold and had a clean, mineral taste. Rick set his knife on the bank and waded out into the water to lie back and let it flow over him until he felt cold. Violet, meanwhile, began to rinse out the plastic jars, mindful they had been filled with preservative. She was still at this task when Rick left the water, pleasantly chilled. Violet smiled at him. "You're going to make the others jealous, coming back wet and cool."

"In this weather, I'll be dry by the time we reach the ridgetop."

Violet sniffed each jar to assure herself no taint of the preservative remained before filling them. When that was done, she removed her shirt and thoroughly soaked it in the stream. Rick blushed and quickly looked away. "Tell me when you're dressed," he said.

"My shirt's going in the bag, Rick. I plan to use it to wash Fern's feet."

"Oh," said Rick, still looking away.

"Rick, I'm a Gaian, not a Sapene. I don't have breasts, so you needn't start acting strangely."

Rick forced himself to turn around. Violet gazed at him, bare-chested and amused. Rick thought her torso looked boyish, but not entirely.

"I've never understood the Sapene obsession with mammary glands," said Violet.

"There's an evolutionary reason for it," replied Rick.

"And I'm sure you'd explain it in detail if I were the least bit interested, which I'm not." Violet stuffed her dripping shirt into the bag, then placed the water jars there also. "Shall we head out?"

"I'll carry some of that water," said Rick.

"You carried Fern," replied Violet. "That's enough for one day."

* * *

IT WAS DUSK when Rick and Violet returned to the ridge, where they found their companions sitting listlessly on the tarp. The water was very welcome, but everyone's hunger redoubled once his or her thirst was satisfied. The falling darkness made searching for food impossible, even if any of them had the energy to do so. Only sleep could stave off hunger, and all embraced it.

Violet was the last to lie down. While there was still light to see, she used her wet shirt to clean the blood and dirt from the cracks in Fern's feet. After ministering to her friend, she donned the damp, soiled garment and curled up next to her. Though it was hot, they all slept crowded together on the tarp. No one wished to sleep in the dirt, no matter how cool. The thin layer of fabric was one of the last vestiges of civilization, and, as such, they found it comforting.

HUNGER PANGS WOKE Con when dawn was only a growing light in the eastern sky. She was exhausted, but the cramps in her stomach would not let her rest. Rick snored on one side, and the Gaians huddled on the other. She got up carefully, so as not to disturb anyone, and drank some water. There wasn't much left in the jars, and it was warm. Con drank as much to fool her empty stomach as to satisfy her thirst. The only edible things she had seen the previous day had been the twelve-foot dinosaurs. *There must be smaller things to hunt,* she thought. *I should practice with my pajaroes.* She looked around for a target. A leafless cycad stood nearby, and she decided to use that. She imagined one of the leaf scars was a bull's-eye and threw a pajaro at it. The knife's four-inch blade pierced the center of her target. Con had never thrown a knife before Sam sent her to the thirty-first century, and she was both pleased and amazed by her accuracy. This talent, like that with embroidery, had been downloaded into her implant while she was unconscious. *Sam probably killed someone to get* *these skills,* she thought, *just like he killed Ramona.* Con imagined that another leaf scar was the silvery dot on Sam's forehead and threw her second knife. The pajaro pierced it with such force that the blade was buried to the hilt.

"Hunting cycads?" asked a sleepy voice behind her.

Con turned to see Rick rubbing his eyes. "Did I wake you?" asked Con.

"It's all right. This is the coolest part of the day. I thought I'd refill the water jars. If you'd like, you could come and join me for breakfast."

"Breakfast!" exclaimed Con. "Are you teasing me?"

"No," said Rick. "I found some nutritious food, and there's all you can eat."

"Where?"

"Down in the forest. It's on the way to the stream."

"There's a catch, isn't there?" said Con. "Just what exactly *is* this breakfast?"

"Termites."

"Bugs! You want to serve me bugs?"

"You'd have to serve yourself. We'd be dining buffet style."

"Yuck!"

"People in Africa ate termites; they probably still do."

Con shook her head as a wry grin crept onto her face. "God help me, I'll do it. I'd eat anything right now."

Rick grabbed the water jars, then led Con down the ridge and to the stream. Along the way, he picked up a flat, pointed rock. They visited the stream first, where they drank and refilled the water jars. Afterward, Rick went to an eight-foot mound that rose near the edge of the forest. He found a small fern frond and stripped it of its leaves, leaving only the central rib, which was no thicker than a blade of grass. Then, he used the rock to open a hole in the side of the mound. Rick stuck the rib in the hole and withdrew it. A dozen pale brown insects, a little longer than a grain of rice, were clamped to the rib. "Soldier termites," he said. "Defending the nest." He plucked one from the rib and crushed it between his teeth.

"How does it taste?" asked Con.

"Sort of like a cashew nut, only soft."

Con stripped a fern frond and soon had her own cluster of termites. She ate one tentatively. "Not bad," she said. She ran her fingers along the rib to strip all the insects into her open mouth. "Ack!" she yelled. Con spit out the termites, then crushed one clinging to her tongue. "One of those bastards bit me!"

"Turnabout's fair play," said Rick.

"So I got to eat them one by one? This will take all morning!"

"Did you have other plans?"

Con sighed. "No."

Rick plucked a few more termites off his rib. "More protein than steak. I'm hoping you'll set a good example for the Gaians."

"Good luck with Fern. She even throws up food squares."

"I was meaning to ask you about that."

"Why ask me? I'm no expert on Gaians."

"Yeah, but you've been pregnant."

"What are you saying? Are you telling me Fern's going to have a baby?"

"In a way."

"Well, you're either pregnant or you're not. Anyway, you should talk to Violet, she's had three kids."

"Yeah, but she was never pregnant for more than a few weeks."

"So she had her embryos extracted, like I did in the twenty-seventh century?"

"All Gaian women do," said Rick. "They have to. Their newborns are the same size as ours. There's no way they'd fit through the pelvis."

Con grew pale as she realized the implications of what Rick said. "Oh God!"

"Fern doesn't know what to expect," said Rick. "Neither do Violet and I. All we know is that it looks bad, real bad."

"She'll die, Rick, and she'll die horribly." Con shuddered.

"I can't believe her species is engineered to be like that. What were they thinking?"

"It's not a problem in the future."

"Well, it's sure as hell one here!"

"I know. Getting to Sam's time machine is her only hope. If it's still here."

"A baby in that little body," mused Con.

"She's a mature adult," said Rick. "We assume things will proceed normally at first. Until . . . well, you know."

"I really don't know, Rick. I had our child in a log cabin. You were my midwife. All my medical knowledge was picked up in high school health class."

"You have practical knowledge."

"Well, at least now I know why she's puking." Con fished some more termites from the nest. This time, she plucked and ate them individually. "God, I'd hate to barf *these* up."

RICK HEADED UP the ridge while Con remained at the termite mound, trying to satisfy her hunger. Rick was leery about leaving her alone, but he realized his presence provided little protection. If the predators ignored her, she would be safe. If not, his hunting knife would not save her. The reality was stark. This world was now their home, and they were at its mercy.

By the time Rick reached the ridge, the sun had awakened the Gaians. Its rays were already fierce. "I brought cold water," said Rick as cheerfully as possible.

"Where's Con?" asked Violet.

"She's down in the valley, having breakfast," replied Rick.

"You found food?" said Violet.

"Termites," replied Rick.

"Oh, dandy," said Oak. "I'll pass."

"If we're to survive," said Fern, "we can't be picky."

"So you're going to eat bugs?" asked Oak.

"I'm going to try," replied Fern, looking queasy already.

"Let's break camp," said Rick. "We'll relocate in the valley."

"Fern," said Violet. "Wear my sandals."

Soon, everyone joined Con, who demonstrated how to catch the termites. All the Gaians ate the insects, but Fern became sick after a few minutes. Con stopped eating and went over to where Fern was wiping her mouth with a leaf.

"It's normal to have morning sickness," said Con. "I had it, too, when I was pregnant. It stops after a while."

Fern flushed and looked at Violet accusingly. "You told!"

"It's not something you should keep secret," answered her friend, "especially here."

Fern's face took on a wretched expression, and she began to sob softly. Con gently hugged Fern, as she recalled her own hopelessness during her final days in Montana. The child-sized woman was very different from Con, and the circumstances and the nature of her tribulations were different also. Nevertheless, Con identified with Fern's despair. "I'll help you get through this," she whispered. "I'll do everything I can."

Con half expected Fern to argue that her situation was hopeless, but she did not. Instead, she grew calmer and said, "I know you will."

Con coaxed Fern to try to eat again. Meanwhile, Violet assisted Oak, who was having difficulty eating with only one hand. The grayish end of his stump had darkened overnight, but the bizarre wound did not seem to pain him physically. As Rick watched him pluck insects off the rib that Violet held, he hoped two hands were not required to pilot a time machine. Rick devoured several more batches of termites before calling it quits. Although his hunger was only dulled, he was anxious to find a suitable campsite.

"While you guys eat," said Rick, "I'm going to look for a more permanent campsite."

"How permanent?" asked Violet.

"Just someplace where we can adjust before hiking to the sea," replied Rick. "We'll need to find food sources, and I'd like to make some spears."

"Spears?" said Fern.

Rick could tell she was envisioning fighting off dinosaurs with sharpened sticks. "Yeah," he said. "For hunting."

Rick left and followed the stream up the valley. As he

walked, the way grew steeper and rockier. As the soil turned thinner, the trees grew shorter. Their branches hung low to the ground, screening the view. Many of the trees and scrubs had the flat, pointed needles characteristic of yews. Ferns and horsetails, some of which grew twelve feet tall, crowded the damper areas. The denseness of the vegetation made Rick uneasy. He continued exploring, looking for a campsite that was open, yet still sheltered from the sun, and near water, but not on it. Animals would come to the stream to drink, and Rick did not want to camp in their path. Steep terrain was desirable also, for it would discourage the larger dinosaurs.

After a fair hike, Rick discovered a likely spot. It was near the valley's end, close to where the stream cascaded over a short cliff. There, a different sort of tree grew. One day, they would be cultivated in Victorian gardens and called "monkey puzzle trees." Tall, cylindrical trunks with scaly bark terminated in a dense, flattened canopy. Their shape was that of a piney toadstool. The rocky soil beneath them was mostly bare, except for a serpentine tangle of roots. When Rick found a place that was smooth and flat enough for the tarp, he was satisfied.

The spot he had chosen was elevated and open enough to gaze down the length of the valley. A dust storm on the plain beyond made the view hazy. He knew the green oasis before him was a refuge in the dry season. The giant sauropods that roamed the open plains in the lush, rainy times would be drawn here. Rick had not seen any yet, but he was certain they were around, along with the huge carnivores that stalked them.

34

RICK SOUGHT THINGS TO EAT AS HE RETURNED. HE scarely bothered looking for vegetable food. Flowering plants, with their sweet fruits, nutritious seeds, and starchy tubers were not due for another 20 million years. The Jurassic's slower-growing plants had tough foliage with low food value. Thus, nothing edible grew along the stream bank. *When the rains come,* he thought, *the ferns will uncoil new fronds and we'll have fiddleheads.* He had no idea when that would be, and when Rick searched the ferns, he was looking for creatures that lived among them.

He found frogs in abundance. They were colored differently than any modern frog Rick had seen, but otherwise, they resembled their modern descendents. Rick caught the eight-inch creatures and skewered them on a sharpened stick. They looked as unappetizing as the termites. Rick hoped when the legs were skinned and roasted, they would be more tempting. He wondered how many frogs it would take to feed them. The Gaians seemed to have modest needs, just as Oak had said. Con, on the other hand, was an eating machine. It seemed unfair that she would consume the lion's share of every catch.

By the time Rick returned to the termite mound, over two dozen frogs dangled from his stick, attracting a swarm of flies. Con and the Gaians were seated a short distance from the mound, and when Rick approached, Con stood up. She grinned triumphantly and held up a dead animal by its tail. Even from a distance, Rick recognized it as a *Compsognathus.* The delicate-looking dinosaur was only three feet long, mostly a slender tail and a long neck.

"I bagged us a green chicken!" said Con.

"How'd you do that?"

"It came looking for termites and got within throwing range." Con held out her catch, which had a chest a little larger than a pigeon's.

"Can I look at it?" asked Rick.

"As long as you remember it's lunch," said Con.

Food was the last thing on Rick's mind as he excitedly examined the creature. It was bipedal, with long hind legs that were thin and birdlike. The short forelimbs ended with two-fingered hands tipped with sharp, curved claws. A narrow head lay at the end of the flexible neck. Its long snout was filled with tiny sharp teeth. A hunter, it looked fast. Rick was amazed Con could hit it.

"Let's hope it tastes better than nightstalker," said Con.

"Than what?" asked Rick.

"Never mind," she said. "Different life."

"I found a camp," announced Rick. "It's about two miles upstream."

THEY ARRIVED AT the campsite an hour later. As soon as the tarp was spread out, Fern kicked off Violet's sandals, which she had bloodied by wearing. Violet soaked her shirt in the stream and began to clean her friend's bleeding feet. Meanwhile, Con pestered Rick for a fire. "Nobody's eaten that much," she argued. "We should cook this food."

Rick would rather have explored some more, but only he knew how to light a fire. Con's awareness of his skill puzzled him until he realized it was something he would have done in the Cretaceous. Once he agreed to make a fire, Con gathered firewood and tinder. She had obviously done it before, for she brought back the perfect combination of materials and skillfully assembled them. Rick took out the flintlike whetstone from its pocket on the knife's sheath. He remembered the grayish white stone as perfectly smooth, yet the edges of this one had been chipped from striking the blade. Seeing the worn stone gave Rick the same eerie feeling he had when Con first showed him the knife.

Rick struck the back of his knife blade with the whetstone. After several tries, he got a spark to fall into some dry, papery leaves next to a pile of twigs. He blew on them gently. The leaves glowed orange, then a tiny flame appeared. Rick continued to blow, and the flame spread to the twigs. Soon, a fire blazed. Con appeared satisfied, but not surprised, by Rick's achievement.

"We should clean our catch away from the camp," said Rick, "so the remains won't draw scavengers to us." Con went with him to help, but her pajaroes were weapons, not cutting tools. The cerdo had disappeared with the time machine, and only Rick's hunting knife proved up to the task. Con made herself useful by roasting the frog legs over the fire while Rick cleaned the Compsognathus. As hungry as he was, it bothered him to butcher a creature that so fascinated him. *In a few weeks these will seem as ordinary as squirrels,* he told himself. After he was done, he carried the gutted carcass over to the fire. Con was there, with tiny legs skewered on a stick. The Gaians were seated a distance away.

"Frog leg?" asked Con, "These look done."

"How are they?" asked Rick.

"You'll have to ask the Gaians," replied Con. "I haven't tried one yet."

Rick bit into the morsel of meat that surrounded a bone not much bigger than a matchstick. It was rubbery and fairly tasteless. "Garlic and butter would help," he said.

"I'll whip up a Hollandaise sauce next time," said Con. Even saying the words made her mouth water, and she regretted her quip.

"I'll cook the next batch," said Rick. "You eat."

Con pulled a frog leg from the stick and bit into it. "Not much meat for all that work."

"No," said Rick. Then he added in a low voice, "Why are the Gaians eating over there?"

"Violet and I thought that Fern might keep her food down if she didn't see it cooked."

Rick noticed that Violet blocked Fern's view of the fire. "Is it working?"

"So far, so good."

Rick spread out the embers with a stick and threw the Compsognathus directly upon them. "Why didn't you skin it?" asked Con.

"The meat should char less this way," replied Rick.

"I guess you skinned the nightstalkers because they had feathers."

"That's the second time you mentioned them," said Rick. "What were they?"

"A small carnivore. You said their name meant birdlike reptile."

"A *saurornithoidid?*" said Rick.

"Yeah, that's it. They had big eyes and hunted mammals. Later on, they hunted us."

"They sound nasty."

"They were, but you named them after me. *Noctecorreptus greightonae.*"

"You were still Con Greighton then?"

"Yeah," said Con. She felt it necessary to add, "You did it as a compliment."

Rick grinned. "I must have been a romantic cuss."

"Yeah, you were."

Con grew wistful and did not pursue the conversation further. Rick became silent also. After ten minutes, the dinosaur was entirely blackened. Grabbing the tail, Rick pulled it from the embers and set it on a rock. When it cooled, he peeled back the charred skin. The dark meat underneath was less burnt, and Rick cut off a drumstick that looked fairly palatable. "Why don't you take that over to Fern while I finish cutting up the rest."

When Con returned, Rick handed her the other drumstick. "To the huntress go the spoils," he said. "How is it?"

"Try some yourself."

Rick bit into a scrap of meat. It was tough and definitely did not taste like chicken. The strongest flavor came from the firewood, giving it a piney aftertaste. As he chewed, he heard Fern retching.

"Pregnancy can be a bitch," said Con.

Rick finished cutting up the Compsognathus, dividing the meat into five tiny piles. Unlike a bird, there was no extensive breast musculature. The two drumsticks and thighs were the meatiest parts of the animal.

"By the way," said Con, "the Gaians say they're full."

Rick looked down at the sooty scraps of meat on the rock. "You mean all this bounty is for us?"

"Yeah," said Con without enthusiasm.

"If you're hungry afterward, I found some of these," said Rick, handing Con a pinecone.

Con cast him an irritated look. "Don't joke with me when food's involved."

"I'm not. Haven't you ever heard of pine nuts?" Rick picked up a cone and spread some of its scales. Seeds that resembled brown flattened corn kernels fell out. He put one in his mouth and cracked its hull with his teeth. "You can eat them like sunflower seeds."

Con tried one.

"They're rich in proteins, carbohydrates, and fats," said Rick. "What more could you want?"

Con regarded the tiny pine nuts. "How about quantity? Why don't we go hunting instead?"

"We need to eat a balanced diet."

"I promise to eat my vegetables," said Con, "if we get some more meat, first."

"All right," said Rick. "We can't tackle a dinosaur, but we might find something."

A TWO-HOUR WALK downstream took Rick and Con far past the spot where they had first entered the forest. By then, other streams had joined with the one they followed to produce a small, shallow river. The land, also, had changed. It was now flat, and the newly formed waterway flowed sluggishly, though Rick found signs that floods regularly scoured the area. Many trees lay toppled, their roots under-cut, and others still had waterborne debris tangled in their lower branches. With fewer trees to shade them out and

year-round moisture, shrubby plants grew luxuriantly. They
screened the view, so at most places, Con and Rick could
see but a few yards beyond the bank, and the only clear line
of sight lay along the river. They moved warily along the
riverbank, the strangeness of the land and its potential dan-
gers discouraging conversation. Occasionally, they heard
the sounds of some large creature moving through the
greenery that blocked their view. Once, one came so close
they could hear its breathing as it snapped branches and
rustled leaves. They both froze, and the idea they would be
"invisible" was too abstract to offer any assurance.

On their search for larger game, they ignored the frogs
they encountered. These became less abundant as the river
grew broader. The first large animal they encountered was
a small crocodile about four feet long. Knife in hand, Rick
charged the reptile, but it escaped into the river. The crocodile was the first of many, all equally elusive.

Con had taken the lead and was rounding a bend in the
river when she suddenly halted. "Turtles," she whispered.
"I'll toss, you stab." She dropped on her hands and knees
to slink along the riverbank as a cat might. Rick dropped
also and crawled until he could see their quarry. A half-
submerged log lay close to the bank. Upon it, turtles sunned
themselves, piled on top of each other like stacks of pan-
cakes. Many of the greenish black shells were over a foot
across. Con crept toward them with patience and stealth—
the perfect predator.

In a sudden burst, she sprang into the water. The reptiles
scattered, but some were not quick enough. Con seized
them and threw them on the bank, where Rick sliced off
their heads. By the time the last panicked turtle disappeared into the water, five of its brethren lay decapitated on
the bank. Con looked at Rick with a grin of primal exultation.

Rick gazed at her thinking, *She's happy. She's truly
happy*. He found the idea both appealing and intimidating.
He was accustomed to more reserved women. He couldn't
imagine any of them celebrating the slaughter of turtles,
much less yearning to devour them. Yet, the latter was

clearly on Con's mind. "We'll cook them in their shells," she said, "so they stew in their own juices."

"Sounds like a good idea," said Rick. He picked up a turtle head and examined it before tossing it into the river. He threw the others away; then looked for rocks to prop up the turtles and drain their blood. Seeing none, he walked downstream to find some. Con trailed behind. Rick turned a bend and froze, staring at the muddy bank ahead. Con stopped also and followed Rick's gaze to a series of broad depressions in the mud. "What are you looking at?" she asked.

"Don't you see?"

"See what? Those puddles?"

"They're not puddles, take a closer look."

Con walked over to one of the depressions. It was nearly three feet wide and as deep as a small basin. She stepped inside the cavity and her bare toes sank into the mud. Then she noted another set of toe prints impressed on the border of the "puddle"—four broad, blunt ones and a fifth, apart from the others, made by a claw the size of a large banana. "Oh my God! It's a footprint!" She glanced around and recognized a pattern to the depressions. She was standing amidst the tracks of a huge animal that had crossed the river. The size of the footprints had prevented her from recognizing them, for though she had seen living dinosaurs, she could not picture one gigantic enough to make these tracks. She stepped out of the muddy cavity, leaving her own footprints within the larger one like dimples on a face.

The discovery disquieted Con, but it had the opposite effect on Rick. He poked about excitedly before wading into the river to follow the beast.

"We should head back," Con said.

"Those are sauropod tracks," said Rick, giving Con the impression he hadn't heard her.

"In case you've forgotten, you're our guide. You can't just wander off."

Con's irritated tone caught Rick's attention, and he reluctantly left the river. He found some rocks and took them back to prop up the turtles. While their blood stained the river's bank, Rick surveyed the scene around him. Brilliantly colored dragonflies darted over the water, just as they had 100 million years before the dinosaurs arrived. A small crocodile floated lazily with the current, a more recent arrival in the parade of Earth's creatures. A world he had spent much of his life trying to imagine lay before him, as real as himself.

"I swear, Rick, you've already fallen in love with this place."

"No, not at all. It's just . . ."

Con snorted. "Don't try, Rick. Don't even try. You may be different, but you're not *that* different."

CON AND RICK departed, leaving only footprints and turtle blood to mark their visit. A dragonfly caught an insect drawn to the blood and ate it on the wing. A pterosaur swooped down and snapped up the dragonfly. Within the river, turtles found the severed heads and devoured them. Afterward, they slowly returned to the log only to be frightened away once more when the *Allosaurus* arrived. A female, she was forty feet of muscle, bone, and hunger. She walked on two legs that were birdlike in form and elephantine in their mass and strength. Stepping into the sauropod track, her huge, clawed foot obliterated Con's footprints, which were tiny in comparison. The scent of blood made her pause. Despite her forward-leaning posture, her massive head scanned the countryside from a height twice that of a man's. She saw nothing of interest, for only prey interested her. She waded into the river and crossed it.

The female's pack followed after her, six individuals in all. Four were adults, and two were juveniles. The smaller of the youngsters came last. Three years old, it was already ten feet long. Like the others, it halted at the smell of blood. Yet, unlike them, it followed the scent to the dark stains on the riverbank. The pack's smallest member got only scraps, and it was always hungry. As it sniffed the ground, it detected a smell it had never encountered before. The adults had detected it also, but ignored it as they dismissed the scent of pines and other inedible things. The youngster, however, was still forming its impressions of the world. On this occasion, it forged a link between two sensations—the aroma of blood and the scent of humans.

35

THE STILL, HOT AIR WAS STULTIFYING. CON SLUMPED as she carried the heavy turtles back to camp, one under each arm. It was late afternoon before she and Rick trod wearily into camp. After Con set her turtles down, she went over to the tarp. Fern dozed there. Con lay down and joined her.

Someone had tended the fire, and there was a large pile of firewood. Rick left to gather some cooking implements, and when he returned, Violet was adding to the woodpile. He dropped his load of water-smoothed pebbles. "I see you've been busy," he said.

Violet eyed the turtles. "You've been busy also."

"Con caught these," said Rick. "I just helped."

Violet noted how Rick's gaze went to Con and lingered there. "What are the pebbles for?" she asked.

"They're cooking stones," said Rick. "You heat the stones in the embers, then drop them in containers to cook things. I'll place them in the turtles' shells. That way, the meat won't char."

Oak emerged from the woods with his partial arm wrapped around a collection of branches. When he dropped them on the woodpile, he wrinkled his nose at the turtles. "Dinner? How will Fern keep that down?"

"She's not squeamish," said Violet. "Con says she has morning sickness."

"What's that?" asked Oak.

"It's a result of pregnancy," replied Violet. "Con knows about such things. She bore a child naturally. Sapenes can do that."

"So I've heard," said Oak. "No one does, of course. It's uncivilized. Well, enough chitchat, I'm going to get more wood."

"We have plenty," said Rick. "You should take a rest."

"I'm not pregnant," replied Oak as he walked away.

Rick watched him disappear into the woods. "What was that about?"

"Oak's a proud man, and he needs to feel useful," said Violet. After a pause, she added. "He's grieving, too."

"Of course," said Rick. "Losing that hand must have been devastating."

"The hand was nothing. Unlike you Sapenes, we Gaians bond for life. Samazatarmaku eradicated Oak's partner. 'Yuvenor' is our word for his condition—'sorrowful emptiness.' It's often permanent."

"Permanent?" said Rick. "You're predisposed to perpetual mourning? How is that adaptive?"

"Is Con's accelerated metabolism adaptive?" countered Violet.

"Perhaps where food is abundant and thinness is desirable."

"I would think fidelity would be even more desirable," said Violet. "Every desirable thing has its price."

"Still," said Rick, "I'd think it'd be something you'd change."

"I wouldn't change my nature," said Violet. "Neither would Fern, though it may cost her her life."

RICK AND VIOLET cooked the turtles together. Violet built up the fire and heated the stones while Rick cleaned the reptiles. He removed the bony plastron that covered the belly and took out the lungs, gut, and gallbladder. Then he placed the hot pebbles in the shell along with the severed limbs and a little water. The plastron served as a lid while the shell's contents simmered.

Dinner was served as the mountain's shadow crept over the camp. The turtles provided a palatable meal, and to everyone's relief, Fern kept her food down. Even Con had her fill. The meat reminded her of veal, and the liver was particularly good. After dinner, they kept the fire burning. Gazing into its flames, Con recalled other campfires and was comforted. She did not find it strange that she preferred this place to Mergonita. This world was more dangerous, but at least she was not the cause of its perils.

WHEN CON ROSE the next morning, Rick was already up. She wandered over to where he sat, eating leftover turtle. "You're up early," she said.

"Morning's the best time for walking."

"Walking to where?" asked Con as she began to eat also.

"You know, hunting. It was tiring to lug those turtles in the afternoon heat."

"Yeah it was," said Con. "This is a good idea." Something about Rick's face made her ask, "We're going together, aren't we?"

"Sure. Of course," replied Rick. "We're a good team."

Sensing Rick was in a hurry, Con ate quickly. They left just as the Gaians were rising. On the trail, Rick set a pace better suited for covering distance than hunting. He was still walking briskly ahead when they reached the turtle log. By the time Con saw it, the reptiles had plunged into the water. "Crap," she said, "you scared them."

Rick seemed unperturbed. "They'll come back," he said. "We'll look downstream while they do. Come on."

They passed the sauropod tracks and discovered that other footprints had obliterated most of them. Rick readily identified the new prints, but kept his conclusions to himself. Farther downstream, the vegetation hemming the banks became more ragged, opening the view. Something had been eating the plants. They stopped before a large stand of yews that had lost much of their foliage. The stouter branches were still intact, but their leaves and twigs had been stripped away. Rick walked over to examine the plants more closely. Con was puzzling over what could have done this when Rick motioned to her. She joined him, and he pointed through a gap between two half-eaten trees. Five huge creatures stood in the distance. Their long necks and tails immediately identified them as sauropods. Con gasped in astonishment.

"Come on," said Rick, hurrying in their direction.

"Rick! What are you doing?"

Rick did not answer, but continued walking. Con hesitated, then ran after him. "Are you crazy?"

"Yeah, maybe. You can stay behind if you like."

Con continued to follow Rick, caught up by his enthusiasm. "Is this safe?"

"I think so."

"What are they?"

"Apatosaurus."

Approaching the creatures was similar to approaching mountains—they were so large they seemed closer than they actually were. What Con had assumed were bushes were actually small trees. Up close, the breathtaking immensity of the creatures was fully evident. The backs of the largest animals rose three times higher than a man. Con guessed the Apatosauruses were seventy feet long, but mere dimensions only vaguely conveyed the creatures' overpowering presence. They possessed a grace and power that denied all the ponderous stereotypes Con held about them. Their long tails did not drag limply. From massive bases, they projected horizontally, drooping only as they approached their whiplike ends. They were constantly in motion, as were the long, massive necks. Con was also surprised to see that the dinosaurs had a row of tall, flat spines, similar to those of an iguana, running from the top of the neck to the whiplike portion of the tail. Their hides were khaki marked with dark green rosettes, a pattern more pronounced on the two smaller Apatosauruses.

The dinosaurs ate continuously. Although their sheeplike heads were larger than a horse's, they seemed ridiculously small on such large bodies. The two large nostrils close to their eyes added to their outlandish appearance. The heads moved constantly, using teeth to rake foliage off plants. When the pouch beneath the jaws filled, its contents disappeared down the long throat. Con could see muscles ripple as the vegetation traveled to the massive gut.

"Don't they chew their food?" asked Con.

"They grind it up in their gizzards using stones they swallow," answered Rick.

When one of the dinosaurs emitted a long sonorous tone from its rear, Con laughed. "Was that sound what I think it was? Did that dinosaur just fart?"

"Their guts are giant fermentation vats," said Rick, "regular methane factories."

The huge creatures totally ignored them. Rick approached one closer, keeping a watchful eye on its swishing tail. Con remained rooted, but she was considering joining Rick when the dinosaurs suddenly began behaving differently. They filled the air with deep wavering bellows. At first, Con thought they were reacting to Rick's presence. He must have thought the same, for he started backing away. The Apatosaurus closest to him rose slightly on his rear legs, and with a smooth grace that Con would have thought impossible for so large a creature, pivoted so its hindquarters turned toward Rick. Rick dropped to the ground, and Con imitated him. As soon as the animal's forefeet touched the ground, it swung its tail. Tons of muscle, bone, and tendons whistled through the air two feet over Con's head showering her with leaves and twigs from the plants it mowed down. It took little imagination for her to envision what would have happened if it had struck her; a speeding car would accomplish no worse. The end of the swing was marked by a sound like the cracking of a whip.

Con looked up and saw with terror that the huge tail was making another pass. She hugged the ground as it whistled over her, closer than before. When she dared to raise her

cheek from the dirt, she saw Rick crawling toward her on
his belly. Two of the other Apatosauruses reared on their
hind legs and waved their forefeet, each with its large inner
claw. Con thought they would shake the Earth when they
lowered themselves, but the animals were so perfectly balanced she felt only a slight thump when they settled to the
ground. Once the distraction of the rearing dinosaurs was
over, Con glanced at Rick. He had ceased crawling. He
stared at something behind her, and the look in his wide
eyes increased her own terror.

Con turned her head and saw a sight as frightening as
the provoked Apatosauruses. Seven Allosauruses, striped
like tigers in shades of tan and brown, stood just outside
the arch of the swinging tail. They reminded Con of the
Tyrannosaurs she had seen in the Cretaceous, though they
were slightly smaller. The largest member of the pack
stood closest to her. Its tail counterbalanced the forward-
leaning torso, so the body that pivoted on the two legs was
nearly horizontal. A slight S-curve of the neck caused the
massive head to be held higher. The forearms were larger
than those of a Tyrannosaur, and Con's eyes were briefly
drawn to the great claws that tipped the three fingers. Yet it
was the three-foot head, with it mouth full of long, curved
teeth that captured Con's attention. A single bite would sever
her in two. Short, flat horns that projected above and in front
of each eye gave the creature a demonic look.

"Crawl toward me," urged Rick.

Con hesitated, convinced she was choosing between
two deaths. Then, the Apatosaurus retreated, and the carnivore advanced an equal amount. The sight of the huge,
taloned feet stepping in her direction caused Con to make
up her mind. She half slithered and half crawled toward
Rick.

"We'll escape through the herd," he said.

"Are you crazy? They'll squash us like bugs."

"Not on purpose. Those Allosauruses may charge, and
we can't be caught in the rush." Rick started crawling
toward the Apatosaurus, obviously expecting Con to follow
him. As he got closer to the animal, the arch of its swinging

tail passed higher above the ground. He was able to crawl on his hands and knees, then stand fully erect. "Come on!" he shouted.

"Oh shit!" said Con as she moved toward him. Soon, she was standing also. This close, the dinosaurs seemed more like animated landmarks than animals. Moving among the shifting limbs and tails was as frightening and confusing as stepping into freeway traffic. Too much was happening, and the great animals were as oblivious to Con and Rick as they were to the shrubbery they trampled underfoot. Con feared that, at any moment, a massive foot she hadn't even seen would reduce her to Jurassic roadkill.

Rick tugged Con's hand as he darted among the tree-sized legs. When they had passed to the other side of the herd, they started running. The five Apatosauruses were moving in the same direction. Although their huge bodies and stout limbs were not built for speed, their stride allowed them to move reasonably fast. Thus, Rick and Con were not that far from the herd when the attack came.

The largest Allosaurus had timed its rush and seized one of the smaller sauropods by the middle of its tail. This had the effect of immobilizing the weapon. The Apatosaurus, though only fifty feet long, was still many times more massive that its attacker, and it nearly wrenched its tail free. Yet, the Allosaurus held on. The sauropod reared upward, but it was unable to reach its tormentor. Then, three others from the pack charged, their jaws the principal weapon. The huge size of the quarry provided it with some protection, for much of the dinosaur's body was too large to bite easily. The Apatosaurus reared up, and the carnivores were temporarily held at bay. Then one of the attackers lunged and bit into a hind leg. Digging its feet into the ground, it pulled out a ragged chunk of muscle the size of a beach ball. The sauropod bellowed in pain, dropped to all fours, and the attack was renewed.

The remaining Apatosauruses, meanwhile, had slowed their flight and resumed eating as they walked. They were safe, and they knew it. The great dinosaurs lumbered off, leaving only Con and Rick to witness the final moments of their former herd member.

A fifth Allosaurus joined the fray. It helped the original attacker mangle the sauropod's tail, which now hung limply. The prey's wounded rear leg was shaking from the effort of supporting the massive body. A sixth Allosaurus, smaller than the others, joined the attack. It darted in to rip meat from the wound. The other predators were trying to seize the sauropod's neck. Their quarry swung its head, in an attempt to elude the snapping jaws. The neck, though not as massive as the tail, was still a dangerous target. It served as a club. In a desperate and risky defense, the sauropod tried to bludgeon its attackers while avoiding their snapping jaws. It bowled two of the Allosauruses over before a third succeeded in gripping its neck. The sauropod's panicked shrieks died out as its windpipe was crushed. The long neck writhed like a thick snake, shaking the predator that clamped it. The curved teeth held fast. Their serrated edges sliced deeper as the prey struggled. Blood spurted from the wound, marking each beat of the great heart.

The Apatosaurus's rear leg buckled, and the dinosaur collapsed. It still kicked feebly even as the pack tore open its belly and buried their heads in the soft entrails. The great animal died, and feeding began in earnest. As they ate, the carnivores were almost as dangerous to one another as they were to their prey. There was a pecking order within the pack, and it was enforced by tooth and claw. The creatures snarled and snapped at one another as they dined. The smallest Allosaurus was only ten feet long, and it had joined the attack only in its final moments. It did not dare approach the choicer portions of the carcass and tugged on the tough, bony tail while the others gorged.

As Con watched the bloody feasting, a wave of nausea passed through her empty stomach. She coughed and, though it was surprising with all the snarling going on, the cough caught the attention of the young Allosaurus. It gazed directly at her, the tail still hanging limply in its jaws. Con felt its awareness. She had been hunted before and recognized the look. The carnivore let the tail drop from its mouth.

"Don't move," said Rick in a low, tense voice. "Stay perfectly still."

The Allosaurus took a step forward, and Con felt the warmth of her urine on her trembling leg.

"Be still. Be still," Rick whispered.

A second Allosaurus passed in front of the small one, dragging a length of intestines thicker than a fire hose. It dropped them to return to the body cavity for a more desirable morsel. The small Allosaurus resumed moving toward Rick and Con. When it reached the uncoiled organ on the ground, it chomped off a length and withdrew to devour its prize.

Con and Rick retreated slowly, keeping a wary eye on the feeding carnivores. Once they were beyond the sight of them, they turned and ran. The way back to the river was long and circuitous, but Con's terror lent speed to her steps. She soon outpaced Rick and left him behind, halting only when she reached the riverbank. There, she waited for Rick to catch up. When he arrived, he was grinning broadly, and the sight of his grin made Con explode.

"You asshole!" she shouted. "What were you thinking? You almost got us killed!"

The grin vanished from Rick's face. "We're all right," he said. "I got you through it, didn't I?"

"Yeah, some hero. You got me in that mess in the first place." The words came fast to her, and she vented them without thinking. "Some fucking guide! We're supposed to be getting food, not playing chicken. When did you become such an idiot? You weren't like this before."

Rick stood silent and red-faced. For once, Con couldn't read him, and she was unable to tell if his crimson shade was due to shame or anger. At the moment, she didn't care. She turned and strode upstream. "Come on," she barked. "We still have to catch something to eat."

36

SUCCESSFUL HUNTERS CONCENTRATE ON THE HUNT, and Con and Rick's meager catch was a measure of their distraction. When they returned to camp in the afternoon, they had only a few dozen frogs to show for their efforts. Con threw her catch down and immediately stalked off to search for a termite mound.

Violet sauntered over to where Rick was cleaning the frogs. She eyed the catch, but declined to comment on its size. "I thought I detected some tension."

Rick kept his eyes on the frog he was skinning. "Yeah, you might say that."

"What happened?"

"Con keeps confusing me with someone else."

Violet studied Rick's face until he became uneasy. "Con will figure things out." With those words, Violet wandered into the woods.

Con arrived just as Rick was cleaning the final frog. She sat on the ground nearby and watched him work without saying anything. Rick remained quiet also, as if skinning the frog were an all-consuming task. When he rose, Con rose also. "I get grumpy when I'm hungry," she said. "I'm sorry."

"So that's what happened today? You got grumpy?"

"Rick . . ."

"I need to apologize to you, not the other way around."

"You don't need to do that."

"I feel I do. I'm sorry, Con. I'm sorry I don't measure up. Now, if you'll excuse me, I'm going to wash away these frog guts." Rick walked at a brisk pace to the waterfall. Con just watched him go.

* * *

THE AFTERNOON RICK and Con returned from the hunt
nearly empty-handed marked more than the occasion of a
meager dinner. A change had occurred, and everyone knew
it. In a society of five people, tension is impossible to hide
and difficult to bear. Daily tasks provided the only relief.
Game was hunted. Pine nuts and firewood were gathered.
Making spears became a priority for Rick, though finding
suitable materials proved difficult. After days of effort, he
had produced only two spears. By then, the weather was
even hotter, and the cloudless sky was often beige with
dust. Mornings were the coolest time, and everyone rose
early to work before the heat became oppressive.

The camp was empty by sunrise on the day Rick
searched for a tree to make his third spear. Con waited in
ambush for Compsognathuses. Oak was gathering his first
bundle of wood for the day. Violet and Fern were headed
downstream, looking for turtles and conversing in their
melodious tongue.

"How are your feet?" asked Violet.

"They're fine," replied Fern. She sighed. "It's good to
be away from camp, just the two of us."

"You'll miss Con if we catch turtles. They're heavy."

"I won't miss her moping. It gets on my nerves."

"It will pass. Give it time."

"How much time?" asked Fern. "It's been too long
already."

"Matters will come to a head. Soon, I think," replied her
friend. "Tonight, watch how each sneaks glances at the
other. There's an attraction."

"Then why do they pretend it isn't there? Why don't
they do something about it?"

"Like you did?"

"That was different!" said Fern. "We believed we were
doomed. It turned out we were right."

"You're alive. If we succeed, you'll have his child."

"What are the chances of that?" asked Fern.

Violet didn't answer.

"Well, I think they're both acting stupid," said Fern. "Sapenes! I swear I'll never understand them."

"They're not that different from us," said Violet.

"Do you know what happened between them?"

"Whatever it was, it's our fault. We created an impossible situation for them both."

"So what should we do?"

"I don't think there's much we can do," said Violet. "They'll have to work it out themselves."

"I guess so."

"Perhaps it would be better if they didn't," said Violet. "If we overcome Samazatarmaku, you know what must happen."

Fern sighed. "I do."

CON SAT PERFECTLY motionless, pajaro in hand, twelve feet from a pile of offal. The torrid air was still, and the only sound was the buzzing of flies about the entrails. Sweat darkened her blue robe as she strained for the sounds of little footsteps. She was hungry, hot, and thoroughly miserable. This kind of hunting was the worst, for it allowed too much time to think.

As usual, her thoughts were on Rick. She no longer dwelled on his slights, real or imagined. Con had become numb to their sting. She had also abandoned hope Rick would ever care for her. *I blew that chance,* she thought, *the day he saved me from the dinosaurs. I should have kissed him, not belittled him.* Instead, Con was convinced she had done everything wrong. Irrevocably wrong. It was a depressing thought, but an even darker one gripped her. She had become convinced Rick was planning something reckless. *That's why he's obsessed with making spears. He's going to do something that will get himself killed.* She imagined him facing an Allosaurus with only a sharpened stick. *Somehow, I've got to stop him. Otherwise, it'll be my fault when he dies.*

* * *

THE TREE RICK sought wasn't common, and small specimens with straight trunks were even rarer. It was past noon before he found likely spear material. By then, his togla was soaked with sweat. As he crawled through low-hanging branches to reach the tree's trunk, his baggy garment snagged on one of them. Rick's irritated errors to extract himself only made matters worse. By the time he was free, there was a long tear in the cheap material.

Rick took off the garment to examine it. Then, in a fit of anger, he tore it further. It was not something he was prone to do, for he was normally even-tempered. Yet Rick had not felt normal for days, and Con was the cause. Her mere presence made him uncomfortable, and the situation was getting worse, not better. She roused such contradictory feelings, avoiding her provided the sole relief, but only some. He could not get her disdain out of his mind. His scientific intellect was no help in solving this problem. He wasn't even sure there was a solution. Lately, he was unsure about everything, himself in particular.

RICK ARRIVED AT sunset. He wore only his loincloth and flip-flops, using the rags of his togla to cushion his shoulder from the partly trimmed tree trunk. Fern was cooking with Con and saw how Con's eyes fixed on Rick, only to turn away when he gazed in her direction. *So it begins anew,* thought Fern wearily. Throughout dinner, Fern watched Con's gaze dart in Rick's direction and retreat, like a hungry bird stealing food from a cat. Fern was certain she detected more than a little desire in those glances.

CON WAITED ALL day to make the proposal she hoped would preclude Rick's doing something foolhardy. After dinner, while everyone lingered around the campfire, she spoke up. "I think it's time to leave. Violet, what do you think?"

Violet considered the idea. "Now that Fern's feet have toughened, I think speedy action would be best. Oak, how far have we crashed from Samazatarmaku's base?"

"It's impossible to say," replied Oak. "After we were hit, I was only concerned with escaping."

"But you must have some idea," said Violet. "Give me a rough estimate."

"Two, maybe three hundred kilometers."

Violet turned to Rick. "How long will it take us to cover that distance?"

"We'll have to get food on the way, and that will slow us down."

"What if we just don't eat?" said Violet.

"Then starvation would slow us down," said Rick, "particularly some of us."

"You mean me," said Con.

"All right," said Violet, trying to keep things calm. "We'll gather food along the way. What kind of pace could we set?"

Rick shrugged. "Maybe twenty kilometers on a good day."

"So it's about two weeks to Samazatarmaku's base," said Violet.

"That's if we go in a straight line," said Rick. "The island lies somewhere northeast of here, but I wouldn't attempt a direct route without a compass. The plains are flat as a pancake. Without landmarks to guide us, we'd be walking in circles in no time."

"So what do you propose?" asked Oak.

"We head north, keeping the mountains in sight. When we reach the Sundance Sea, we follow the coast until we spot the island. It's longer, but safer."

"Then what?" asked Oak. "Swim?"

"Hardly," said Rick. "There are some nasty creatures in that sea. Like pliosaurs."

"What are they?" asked Fern.

"A type of plesiosaur," answered Rick.

"I've seen those," said Con. "They have four flippers and long necks. They eat fish."

"This kind has a short neck and a long head," said Rick. "They're major predators. One called *Kronosaurus* had a head nearly eight feet long, and most of it was teeth."

"So we'd build a boat?" asked Con.

"We'll have to," said Rick.

"How?" asked Oak.

"With difficulty," injected Violet. "But somehow, we'll do it because we have to. Samazatarmaku must not prevail."

"I'm ready to start," said Fern.

"I think we should wait until the rains begin," said Rick.

"Why walk in the rain?" said Con. "We should go now."

Rick shot Con an annoyed look, but his voice remained calm and reasonable. "The dry season is a risky time to be on the plain. There's little water or game. It's best to wait."

"But you don't know when it's going to rain," argued Con. "We could be stuck here for months. Hell, you don't even know if it does rain here."

"Con," said Violet, "that's enough. Rick's our guide. We'll wait for rain and hope it comes soon."

Con thought, *You'd better hope Rick's still here when it comes.*

THE FOLLOWING MORNING, Rick did not work on a spear. Instead, he handed Violet his knife. "I won't need this today, and you probably will," he said. "I'm going to scout a route to the plains."

Con worried that Rick was actually going dinosaur watching. Despite her trepidation, she blurted out, "I should go, too."

"That's not a good idea," said Rick, further confirming her suspicions.

"Why not?"

"It's unnecessary."

"I think it'd be better if two people knew the route," said Con. "Don't you agree, Violet?"

"That seems sensible," said Violet. "Fern and I can catch dinner."

"I'm leaving now," said Rick, knowing Con hadn't eaten.

Con rose from where she sat. "Fine. I'm ready."

Rick grabbed one of the two spears and brusquely tossed Con the other. "Come on."

Rick kept a brisk pace as he led Con along the riverbank. Although he said nothing, his silence and body language communicated clearly enough. Con felt that he was
acting put-upon, as if she were no more than a pest intent
on spoiling his fun. *He was planning something stupid,* she
thought. *That's why he's mad.* The idea of Rick's irritation
ignited Con's own as she became convinced she was in for
a miserable day. As they continued along the trail, her
anger grew, fueled in part by her growing hunger. Soon,
she was thinking of ways to vent it.

"You used to be modest," she said. "Now you prance
about half-naked." She was pleased when she saw his neck
flush red.

"I always hated that togla," retorted Rick. "It was like a
goddamn dress. Wearing it here was just plain stupid."

"I know why you're wearing that loincloth, and I'm not
interested."

"Don't kid yourself," said Rick.

"Don't kid *your*self."

Goaded, Rick whirled around to glare at Con. "Look,"
he said. "In case you haven't noticed, it's hot as hell here,
too hot for a damn dress. So get used to it."

Con glared back. "You're right, Rick. It *is* too hot for a
dress." She pulled off her robe and tossed it on the path.
Rick's discomfort was exactly the reaction she expected,
and it pleased her. "So get used it," she said, throwing his
words back at him. When Rick did not reply, she added,
"Now that we're both comfortable, we should head out."

Rick turned and resumed hiking down the path. Con
followed after him, clad only in her panties. At first, she
was tickled by how Rick walked at a subdued pace and
took care to keep his eyes ahead of him. Yet, before long,
she wished she could run back and don her dress again.
Only her stubbornness prevented her from doing so.

As they hiked in the torrid morning, together yet
apart, two things became clear to Con. The first was that
Rick was right about the comfort of going bare-chested.
The second was that embarrassed silence was not truly the
reaction she desired from Rick. His response—or more

precisely, his lack of one—was humiliating. At last, she could take it no longer. "Maybe I should head back," she said in a quiet voice.

Rick stopped and looked at her for the first time since she had taken off her robe. She saw he was embarrassed, but she also sensed he didn't want her to go. "It was your idea to come in the first place," he said.

"I'll stay, or I'll go, whatever you want," said Con.

The question seemed to create a struggle within Rick He looked down. "You should probably go."

Con's eyes began to fill with tears. "Why are you like this?"

"Like what?"

"You're so distant."

"I don't know. I'm jealous, I guess."

"Jealous?"

"Yeah. That's it. Jealous of my own damned self. Jealous of the Rick Clements who saved your life. The one who fathered Joey. The guy who married you, then got himself killed. I don't measure up to him, and it's pointless to try."

Con suddenly understood what she needed to say. "Yes, it is pointless" she said in a voice scarcely above a whisper. Moving closer, she reached out and caressed his bearded cheek. "It's pointless because he's not dead. He's you."

"But you said . . ."

"Forget what I said. I haven't been thinking straight."

Rick lifted his eyes from the ground until they met hers. "Con," he said with the tenderness she yearned to hear, "I've never met anyone like you."

"I forgot that for a while," said Con. "Please let me start over." She leaned forward and softly kissed his mouth, just as she had on the day she thought the world was about to end.

A smile crept onto Rick's face. Con's eyes glistened as she returned that smile. They drew closer, and there was an inevitability to the gentle collision of their bodies. This time, his lips sought hers. Soon, the world around them faded until it consisted only of the touch, the taste, the smell, and the thought of one another.

37

FERN EASILY SPOTTED CON'S ROBE LYING ON THE PATH,
the only bit of blue in the landscape. She picked it up. It
was still damp from Con's perspiration. She showed it to
Violet. "I wonder what's going on."

"Well, they're certainly not exploring the plains."

"Not today," said Fern, returning her friend's knowing
smile. "I'm surprised it's taken her this long." She looked
down the path that hugged the stream. "Should we turn
back?"

"I don't think that's necessary. Besides, they're bound
to be hungry this evening."

AS VIOLET AND Fern marched down the path to slaughter
turtles, they crossed a small stream. It ran clear and lively
through a thick growth of horsetails, and the rushing water
had already erased Con's and Rick's footprints from the
sandy bottom. Fifty yards upstream, the two lay naked on a
verdant bed of moss. Rick was still overwhelmed by a discovery that seemed as wondrous as time travel. The woman
whose warm, moist skin touched his and whose eyes gazed
upon him in triumphant adoration filled him with astonishment. He could hardly believe such bliss was possible, nor
imagine why he had ever been reluctant to embrace it. Con
had captured his heart with a totality only fate could explain.

Con moved languorously to press her mouth lightly
against Rick's warm, salty chest and begin a winding trail
of kisses up to his lips. She moved so her breasts brushed
over him. The feel of his body against hers seemed both

familiar and new. Con felt unable to decide if they had made love for the first time or enjoyed the comfortable ecstasy of married partners.

Yet as happy as Con was, there was also a shadow in the quiet glade. She had been this happy before and lost it all. That knowledge haunted her even as Rick wrapped his arms around her. Con rolled on top of him, and he brushed the moss off her back and buttocks in a gentle way that was also a caress. She felt his ardor renew.

"What are you thinking?" he asked.

"I wish this moment would go on forever," said Con.

Rick kissed her long and deeply. Then he grinned. "Do you want to know what I'm thinking?"

Con sensuously moved her hips against Rick's. "Mister Clements," she said with a gleam in her eye, "I know exactly what you're thinking."

CON AND RICK did not venture from the glade all day. They drank from the stream and bathed in it, made love, and talked. Through the alchemy of love, Rick transformed before Con's eyes. He wanted to know everything about Joey, and he held her as she tearfully described their child. Rick wept also for the son he'd never seen. When a low sun turned the moss golden green, they reluctantly dressed and departed.

On the way back to camp, Con found her robe neatly hung on a branch. She slipped it on, though it felt unpleasantly sticky against her skin. "I may go native like you."

"What would the Gaians think?"

"That I was being sensible. They find tits as erotic as pimples."

"I can't say the same."

"You'd get used to it."

"I never want to get used to you."

Con threw her arms around Rick's neck and kissed him. "Don't even try."

*　　*　　*

RICK FELT SOMEWHAT shy as they approached the waiting Gaians, and he blushed when Con kissed him. Violet and Fern did not mention their assumptions, but the carefully hung robe made that unnecessary. The two Gaian women smiled and presented the couple with frog legs roasted in anticipation of their return. Con fed one to Rick, then kissed him again to show she had her husband back.

The meal that evening had a celebratory air, as the Gaians were caught up in the couple's happiness. Con had been Rick's partner before, and she slipped into that role with the ease born of familiarity. It took a little longer for Rick. Yet, when he gazed at Con and saw the contentment and love in her eyes, he felt that the dinner was their wedding feast.

Later, Rick took Con to the waterfall. They snuggled together and watched the stars come out. Rick gazed at the sky contentedly, but when he looked at Con, he saw silent tears streaming down her face. "What's the matter?" he asked.

"I'm happy and scared at once," replied Con. "Sometimes I think Oak was right—Sam knows we're here, and he's toying with us."

"If he'd seen us, we'd be dead," said Rick.

"Sam doesn't work that way. He manipulates things so people do what he wants. Even in Mergonita, I played right into his hands."

"Not when you planted that bomb," said Rick with a smile. "It'll be the same when we steal his time machine."

Rick hugged Con close. "Going to the island's a risk," admitted Rick, "a big one. But it's Fern's only chance to live and our chance for a life together."

"Yes," said Con. "I'll try to think of only that."

RICK AND CON awoke the next morning to a world that felt different but still made the same demands. Food had to be caught. Spears remained a pressing need. The journey to the sea required preparations. However much Con wished to spend the day as they had the previous one, she knew they couldn't.

Instead, Con hunted alone, using a spear for the first time. It enabled her to kill a six-foot crocodile. Unable to butcher it without Rick's knife, she was forced to carry it back to camp. Before she hefted the bloody carcass upon her shoulder, she removed her robe so as not to stain it. Rick was at camp when she arrived. He looked up from smoothing a spear shaft and watched her with frank appreciation. Con flashed him a smile. She dropped the crocodile, then went over to the tarp. Violet and Fern sat there beside a small pile of bark strips. Violet was rubbing them between her hands until they shredded into fibers.

"What are you doing?" Con asked.

"We're trying to make rope," said Fern.

"How's it working out?"

Fern held up a length of twisted fibers. It resembled twine. "We've made this so far, but I think we'll need to braid it for strength."

Violet said something in Gaian to Fern, who smiled.

"What did you just say, Violet?" asked Con.

"I said Rick seems to have lost interest in spear making."

Con turned to see Rick approaching. "Do you know you have blood on your back?" he said.

"Yes," replied Con, tossing her robe down on the tarp. "I was about to wash it off."

"I could help," said Rick.

Con smiled. "That would be nice."

As the two walked to the waterfall, Violet said in Gaian, "See what I mean about the mammary glands?"

LIFE IN THE camp settled into a pattern. Con hunted each day, and crocodile became a staple. She became so successful at catching them, they had surplus meat to smoke for the journey. Rick finished making spears for everyone and also fashioned bone knives from crocodile femurs. Along with firewood, Oak gathered bark every day. This was twisted and braided by Violet and Fern into lengths of rope for use in constructing the raft they would need to reach Sam's island.

This comforting routine was shattered for Con when

Rick decided he should scout the route to the plain. "I'm going with you," she said after he announced his plans.

"I'd feel better if you stayed here," said Rick.

"If there's danger, we'll face it together."

"Con . . ."

"I've made up my mind, Rick. I won't lose you twice."

Rick saw Con's stubborn look and knew he wouldn't win this argument. "Okay, we'll go tomorrow morning. Eat a big breakfast because we'll spend the night on the plain."

The next morning, Rick and Con headed out. Each had a wooden spear. Rick carried the bag with water jars and strips of dried crocodile tail. Their clothing and their steel knives comprised the remainder of their equipment. Con's pajaroes were attached to the band of the loincloth she had fashioned from her robe. As she predicted, Rick had grown accustomed to seeing her bare-breasted.

Yet, while Con was comfortable in her new apparel, it underscored how reduced her resources had become. It seemed absurd to attack someone like Sam, a man able to shoot down aircraft and travel through time. Yet she knew this scouting trip was preparation for a journey that, if successful, would end in that very confrontation. She therefore resolved to find whatever happiness she could before that moment arrived.

The weather was hotter than ever, but a change had occurred. The air was no longer dry. Instead, it was heavy with humidity. Clouds occasionally made afternoon appearances in the southern sky, but as yet, no rain had fallen. The stream and the river were less deep, and Rick and Con often walked on newly exposed banks.

By late morning they reached the grazing grounds of the sauropods. The impact of the immense herbivores upon the landscape was plain to see. Large portions of trees were denuded of foliage. Great swathes of lower-growing plants were stripped beyond recovery, leaving bare patches of baked earth. Some of the creatures that had created the damage were visible a half mile away. Rick paused to gaze at them. Con forced herself to say, "Want to take a closer look?"

"Do you really mean that?"

Con wanted to flee the giant creatures, yet she understood Rick's need to see them. She felt that it was not only important for him to do so, but for her to accompany him. "I won't pretend I'm not nervous," said Con, "but you'll keep me safe." The look on Rick's face convinced her that she had said the right thing.

They advanced cautiously toward the Apatosauruses. "They're not eating," said Rick after they got closer. "None of them are."

"I don't think there's anything to eat," said Con. "The place looks barren except for those mounds."

"Let's take a closer look."

There were over two dozen animals in an area that was approximately a hundred yards across. No vegetation grew there, and the dry ground was packed hard by trampling feet. All the dinosaurs were adults, and they stood nearly motionless among the mounds, some of which were little more than eroded piles of dirt. Other, less-weathered mounds, seemed to have bowl-shaped centers. A few were capped with dried vegetation. These appeared to be the newest.

"It's a nesting area," said Rick, his voice low with excitement.

He dropped his spear and began to walk slowly toward the closest mound. A sixty-five-foot Apatosaurus stood nearby. Con wanted to drag Rick back, but she restrained herself. Instead, she watched fearfully as he advanced. Rick assumed, since the guardian had never seen a creature remotely like him, he would be safe, while Con feared mere movement would spur the animal to attack.

When Rick was a few yards from the nest, the sauropod moved, and Con was convinced it had been provoked. Rick froze, and the creature settled down. Rick sank to his knees and crawled the rest of the way. By then, Con was paralyzed by anxiety. Rick stuck an arm beneath the nest's cap of dry vegetation and retrieved a tan object. Cradling it in one hand, he snatched another. Then Rick slowly retreated, warily watching the Apatosaurus until he reached Con. He beamed triumphantly.

"I'll carry one," said Con.

Rick handed her an egg. It was a slightly flattened sphere, eight inches in diameter. The shell was hard, with a nodular surface.

"Is this dinner?" asked Con.

Rick sighed. "Eating these will feel like using Rembrandts for doormats, but yes, we'll eat them."

"I'm flattered by your extravagance. Are we done here?"

"Yeah," said Rick. Noticing the relief on Con's face, he added, "And thanks."

"For what?"

"You know."

They returned to the river, and as they continued downstream, the landscape became more barren. The stress the Apatosauruses put on the vegetation was partly responsible, but the seasonal drought was the main factor. The greenery followed the river, though occasional clumps of green trees or bushes marked the few remaining moist spots. The baked earth between was flat and red.

"It's beginning to look like a desert," said Con.

"It will green up when the rains come."

"When will that be?"

"I'm hoping these eggs will provide a clue. If the embryos are close to term, it means the rainy season's near. The babies can't feed like the adults; they'll need insects and tender shoots to live."

"Embryos! I thought we'd be having omelets."

"Yeah, with croissants and coffee."

"Please don't talk about food."

"If you're hungry, there's a termite mound over there."

Con sighed. "I'll wait for the eggs."

As they left the valley behind, the animals changed as well as the landscape. They saw no more sauropods or Compsognathuses, but they spotted Dryosauruses for the first time since they crashed. They saw several small groups of them grazing the sparse vegetation. By late afternoon, the valley was a hazy patch of green against the distant foothills. The river had begun to meander as it grew more

shallow, leading Rick to conclude it did not reach the sea.
Still, Rick and Con continued to follow it into the dusty
plain and had just rounded a bend when a full-grown *Ceratosaurus* headed toward them. A solitary hunter, at twenty
feet it was both smaller and more agile than an *Allosaurus*.
It resembled the larger carnivore except for the flattened
horn at the end of its snout and the four-clawed fingers on
its hands. Con and Rick put down the eggs to grip their
spears with both hands. Fortunately, they did not have to
test their weapons against the beast, which ignored them. It
drank from the river, then sprang upon a seven-foot crocodile swimming in it. Holding the struggling reptile cross-
wise in its mouth, the carnosaur waded to the opposite
bank. Once on dry land, it closed its jaws further. With a
ghastly crunch, the crocodile was severed into three parts.
The dinosaur bolted down the middle portion, then bent to
eat the two remaining pieces. Con and Rick slipped away as
it did.

Sunset arrived as they reached the place the river terminated in an alkaline lake. They found a grove of leafless
ginkgo trees for their camp. It made them feel less exposed.
Rick made a campfire, then cracked open the eggs. The tiny
dinosaurs inside moved feebly until Rick killed them. They
looked fully formed and their yolk sacs had been completely
absorbed. "The rains will come soon," he said.

They roasted the two infants, and their flesh was particularly tender. It reminded Con of duck, except it wasn't fatty.
As the fire died down and light faded from the sky, Con
gazed at the darkening land. The rains would make it seem
more hospitable. They would bring greenery, water, and
game. Yet Con feared that those good things would be
accompanied by death.

38

CON BECAME AWARE OF SOMETHING MOVING IN THE dark. The moon had set, and as she peered about the starlit grove she was looking for a shadow within shadows. Rick dozed peacefully beside her, so close she needed but move a hand to waken him. For some reason, she felt it was important to let him sleep.

Movement caught her eye. A black, man-sized shape approached. It halted a few feet away. A hood fell back to reveal Sam's face. In the dim light, it looked pale and nebulous. Yet his dark eyes were sharp as they gazed upon her.

"Unfinished business," he said in a low voice.

Starlight reflected off the silvery barrel of a nineteenth-century rifle. Con watched it slowly rise and point toward Rick.

"Some people forget they're dead," murmured Sam.

Con heard the sharp, metallic click of the rifle being cocked. She tried to scream, but something pressed on her chest, driving the air from her lungs. Con's limbs turned leaden, and she was unable even to lift her hand. *This is the weight of time,* she thought. Only when the muzzle flashed and the shot echoed across the dark plain was she able to scream. By then, it was too late.

Someone shook her, gently at first, then more vigorously. She heard a voice over her sobbing. "Con! Con! What's the matter?" Rick was leaning over her. She grabbed him and hugged him close, expecting to feel his warm blood spurt on her chest.

"Oh, Rick!"

"You're trembling." As Rick held Con with one arm, he

groped for his spear with the other. "Is there something in the grove?"

Con looked around to confirm that Sam had been only a nightmare. Then she gripped Rick all the tighter. "I thought Sam shot you," she said.

"It was only a dream," said Rick. "You're awake now."

Con continued shaking. "When they brought your body to the cabin, I kept waiting to wake up, but I never did. It seemed as wrong for you to be dead then as it does now."

"I'm not dead," said Rick, kissing Con to prove it.

Con let out a deep, wrenching sigh. "No, you're not."

"Can you get back to sleep?"

"If you hold me."

Con lay down on the dusty ground, and Rick wrapped an arm around her. Soon, he was snoring. Sleep came less easily to Con. Rick's arm, solid and slightly sweaty, did not bring the comfort she hoped it might. She did not doubt its reality, but she had come to doubt reality itself. She had witnessed it turn fickle and transform as the world transformed. The solidity about her had a conditional quality that, once having been experienced, deprived it of the power to reassure.

WHEN RICK AND Con returned late the following day, Rick said they should move camp to a place that could shelter them from the upcoming rains. He, Violet, and Con searched for one the next morning. They found a suitable spot at the end of the valley, where the top of a cliff overhung its base by a dozen feet. Violet looked at the site's rocky floor with dismay. "This will make an uncomfortable bed," she said.

"We could soften it with tree boughs," said Rick.

"I thought we were leaving once the rains came," said Con.

"We'll have to wait for the plain to turn green," said Rick.

A part of Con was pleased with that answer, but it also raised a concern. "Violet," she said, "how long has Fern been pregnant?"

"Twelve weeks."

"Well, it's hard to tell with her baggy shirt," said Con, "but she looks further along than that. A lot further. My belly didn't show until my sixth month."

"We're a different species," said Violet.

"That could be a problem," said Rick. "Your babies are genetically engineered for artificial wombs, and their growth rates may be different. When are they usually extracted from the mother?"

"The fourth week," said Violet.

"And what do they look like?" asked Rick.

"Like a baby," replied Violet, "only very small."

"With a recognizable face?"

"Yes. Why?"

"A fetus of a *Homo sapiens* takes three months to reach that phase," said Rick.

"Our babies still take nine months to grow," said Violet.

"That's irrelevant," said Rick. "A baby's size triggers the birthing process."

"So what you're saying," said Con, "is that Fern doesn't have nine months before . . . before . . ."

"How much time can the child stay in her womb?" asked Violet.

"I don't know," said Rick. "Less than nine months. Maybe a lot less."

THEY MOVED CAMP that day. Rick and Con went into the forest afterward to cut boughs for the sleeping area. They found a grove of soft-needled yews, and Rick began cutting boughs from the trees. After a pile had accumulated, Con pulled off her loincloth and flopped down upon the boughs. "Let's try it out," she said.

Rick gazed upon her nude body with desire. Yet he said, "I know this is a little late, but shouldn't we be worrying about pregnancy?"

"We'll get to Sam's island soon, so it won't matter."

"What if he's gone? Imagine raising children in this world."

"What if we don't make it? What if Sam kills us when we arrive?"

Rick knelt next to Con and kissed her. "Those are pretty grim arguments for making love."

"Don't you want to?"

Rick laughed. "Do you have any doubt? I just don't want to hurt you in any way."

"Well, it's safe today."

"Are you sure?"

"Absolutely positive," lied Con. She nuzzled Rick's shoulder as she pulled at his loincloth. "Time to test the mattress."

THE FIRST RAIN came three days later. The air felt thick with moisture all morning, and by early afternoon, the sky was dark with clouds. Con, Fern, and Violet were lugging turtles back to the new camp when the downpour hit. A few drops provided the only warning before the air filled with warm, falling water. The three woman were instantly drenched. The raindrops filled the forest with a soft roar, and soon the baked ground was covered with a dimpled, watery blanket. The rain fell even harder until Con felt she was standing in the stream, not walking beside it. The warm rain massaged Con's bare back like a forceful shower. It was an exhilarating feeling. The three women arrived at the sheltered camp to find it empty. Like Con, Violet had ceased covering her chest, but Fern still wore her shirt. Now that it was soaked, it clung to her body. Con looked at Fern with surprise, "Fern, are you getting breasts?"

Fern flushed red and looked away.

"Show her, Fern," said Violet. "Con understands these things."

Fern reluctantly removed her shirt. Her nipples were a darker shade than Violet's, and they were swollen, as was the tissue surrounding them. "I have hair, too," said Fern in a miserable voice, "in places it never grew before."

"You're showing. That's all," reassured Con. "It's perfectly normal."

"Normal for you," said Fern. "This isn't supposed to happen to me."

"It's probably something to do with hormones," said Con.

"Will I . . . Will I end up looking like you?" Fern's eyes fixed apprehensively on Con's breasts.

Con smiled self-consciously as she imagined how her modest endowment must appear to the Gaian woman. "I don't think so. I'm sure you'll return to normal after you have the ba . . . after your extraction."

Fern wrung the water from her shirt, then slipped it back on.

"Were you pregnant when you were caught down-when?" asked Con. When Fern hesitated, Con said, "I'm sorry, I don't mean to pry."

"It's all right. I'd like you to know about Medlar. Oak won't talk about him any more than he'll talk about Iris, his own life partner."

"He's a man who hides his wounds," said Violet, "as I'm sure you've noticed."

"Medlar was Iris's brother," said Fern. "He was gentle and understanding. Even in those difficult times, he could make me laugh. As for getting pregnant, I couldn't help myself."

"Like the Kynden women?" asked Con.

Fern's face reddened. "No! It's not like that among us."

Now it was Con's turn to be embarrassed. "I'm sorry, it was just when you said you couldn't help yourself, I thought . . ."

"That Gaians go into heat?" said Fern.

"Fern!" said Violet. "There's no need to be vulgar."

"Ripening. Heat. It means the same thing," said Fern.

"Still, I have friends who would resent that term."

"It wasn't our kind, Violet, that wiped out the other species."

"Samazatarmaku is just one man," said Violet. "You can't condemn all Kyndens because of him."

"As I was saying, Con," Fern continued, pointedly ignoring Violet, "Medlar and I bonded. You Sapenes call it 'falling in love,' but we only do it once. Every trip upwhen was risky, and I wanted to be . . . to be . . ."

"Intimate?" suggested Con.

"Yes," said Fern. "I wanted to be intimate with him while I still could. You must think I was a fool to do it."

"You've behaved no more foolishly than I," said Con.

"Which isn't saying much," said Violet.

IT RAINED THROUGH most of the night, but the following morning was clear, sunny, and humid. Con and Rick hunted by the stream and observed the changes the rain had wrought. The first of these was in the watercourse itself, which flowed more broadly and vigorously. The spots where turtles sunned themselves were submerged, and the reptiles were scarce. The little crocodiles that frequented the river had become rare also, and Con had to walk much farther than usual before she speared one.

It rained in the afternoon, and it rained most afternoons. Often the water came down in torrents and flowed over the ground in sheets. Mating frogs filled the nights with their choruses. Mosquitoes appeared. Leaves sprouted on bare trees, and fiddleheads uncoiled, providing Con's first taste of vegetables, other than pine nuts, since she fled the thirty-first century. The brown plain turned green, and sunlight reflected off distant pools of water.

With each day, the journey Con dreaded came closer. Rick had come to dread it also, though he knew it was necessary. The burden of deciding when it would start rested on his shoulders, and it began to oppress him. Finally, he sought some assurance they weren't throwing their lives away. As with most discussions at camp, it took place after dinner. Rick gazed at the sheet of water cascading over the shelter's edge and said, "We'll be spending our nights out in that. Will it be worth it?"

"Samazatarmaku will least expect us in this weather," said Violet. "This is our best chance."

"Why don't just Oak and I go?" said Rick. "We'll steal the time machine and come back here."

"No," said Con firmly. "We're in this together."

"Con's right," said Violet. "It'll take everyone to succeed."

Rick gazed dismally at the watery curtain. "Then we should start tomorrow."

"Good," said Violet.

Con rose. "I'm going for a walk. Rick, do you want to come?"

"Sure."

The hidden sun was setting, and the light was soft. Beneath the trees, the rain was gentle, making the dusk warm and moist. Con walked only a short distance from the shelter before she pulled off her loincloth. She stretched her lithe body in a way she knew Rick would find impossible to ignore. "I'm tired of walking," she said. "Don't worry. We won't make a baby tonight. This may be our last time."

"Our last time?" said Rick.

"Before we do it in your dorm room," said Con. "Do you keep it neat?"

Rick thought of his room, which resembled a fossil preparation lab in its rocky clutter. "Do you want me to lie?"

"Are you saying it needs a woman's touch?"

"Yeah. That and a shovel."

Con laughed. "I know you're a slob. You forget we were married for almost a year."

The smile faded from Con's face, and for a moment, Rick saw a haunted expression. It made his heart ache to see it. He pulled her close and tried to kiss it away. Soon, he succeeded.

They found a mossy spot beneath a yew where it was not muddy, if not dry. They made love, and it seemed to Con that Rick was especially tender. It made her feel that he, too, feared this might be their last time. Lying on the wet moss afterward, Con wondered if she would ever feel dry linens beneath her again. She doubted it. That thought made her glad she had been reckless.

THE FOLLOWING MORNING, the time travelers ate a hasty breakfast before heading down the valley. The woods were misty in the early-morning sunlight, and, as the five walked, they resembled a band of aborigines. Violet carried the tarp and short poles that would be their tent. Fern and Oak were laden with coils of bark rope. Rick marched in front, toting their small store of food wrapped in rags from his togla. Con brought up the rear with the water jars. Everyone carried a spear.

The path along the stream was underwater, and Rick had to find a way through the surrounding plants. Often, the going was difficult. The wet ground was slippery, and the foliage was luxuriant in the first growth of the season. Thus engaged, he failed to notice when Con dropped behind. Only Fern saw her slip away, and she said nothing.

Con knelt in the undergrowth and listened to the fading sounds of Rick and the others. She was not worried about catching up; their trail over the damp soil would be easy to follow. What worried her was adding to Rick's burdens. Thus, Con fought her morning nausea until she felt sure he would not hear her throwing up.

39

THE FIVE TRAVELERS FOLLOWED THE RIVER'S BANK until they were past the hills that enclosed the valley. Then they turned north. In a world before grass, mud was a problem in wet weather. Although small plants covered the plain with new greenery, their roots were not tenacious, and in the wetter spots, everyone sank ankle deep into the red earth. The ground was so uniformly flat the difference between the high and low spots was often a matter of inches, but eventually Rick became skilled at noting the subtle distinctions that marked the drier areas, and they made better progress.

Temporary streams crisscrossed the plain, so drinking water was not a problem. Finding game was another matter, for all the animals they encountered were too large to hunt. Hunting was especially on Con's mind since she had lost her breakfast. She scanned the landscape as thoroughly as any hungry predator. When a herd of Dryosauruses passed nearby, she approached them to investigate. The smallest animal was five times her size. Discouraged, Con rejoined the others.

By unspoken consensus, they walked as far as possible the first day. Since the only measure of progress was exhaustion, they pushed themselves harder than they should have. Though Rick realized this, he was gripped by the same compulsion. Moving kept his anxiety at bay.

When the sun had nearly set, they halted at a small grove of trees. After scanning the cloudless sky, they chose to sleep upon the tarp rather than under it. Rick rationed out the food. The Gaians insisted he and Con take larger shares, and Con got the most. Even so, her dinner only consisted of three and a half strips of dried crocodile meat and a handful of pine nuts. She ate with meticulous slowness, afraid she might throw them up. Afterward, she quickly fell asleep curled up next to Rick.

The following day was similar to the first, except that the travelers did not push themselves as hard. Con killed a pterosaur with a pajaro, but once its wings were trimmed off, there was not much to it. Nevertheless, Rick built a fire when they camped and cooked the reptile. The stringy breast was quail-sized, but not as tasty. They divided it up to supplement the pine nuts and dried meat not knowing it would be the last cooked meal they would have for days.

On the dawn of the third day, the southern sky was filled with clouds. They steadily darkened, and by midmorning, a curtain of rain advanced across the plain. The travelers heard its roar just before it engulfed and drenched them. The mountains disappeared and even closer things became faint, gray silhouettes. The rain fell so heavily that, within a few minutes, the flat ground was covered with an inch of water. As the water continued to rise and cover the low-growing plants, it appeared as if they were standing in the middle of an endless lake. Still, they slogged onward.

The rain fell all day. As dusk approached, the water was calf high. Rick spotted a grove of dead trees and headed in its direction. One of the trees had fallen over, and it served as their refuge. They huddled upon its trunk like rats on a piece of flotsam and covered themselves with the tarp. They sat numbly, too tired to talk, and shared the last of their rations. Then they tried to rest sitting up. Sometime in the night, the rain stopped. Con blearily crawled from under the tarp to assume a more prone position. It was so dark she could barely see. She stepped into the water and groped along the trunk until she found a place to lie down.

The dark grove made Con recall her dream of Sam. He was not lurking among the shadows, but she sensed his presence all the same. Sam was dry and comfortable, while she suffered privations to reach him. The situation was so one-sided that their journey seemed more like a scheme of his than any plan she had devised. That idea was disturbing. Once again, Con's options had been reduced to one, just as they had been outside Mergonita. She tried to dismiss the idea that Sam was aware of events and benefiting from them, but could not. Only fitful sleep freed her from the troubling thought.

THE SUN ROSE in a clear sky, but it revealed a discouraging sight. The five had wandered into the midst of a shallow, seasonal lake. Muddy water extended around them on all sides. More disheartening was the view of the mountains. Disoriented by the rain, they had wandered into the plain and circled south. All their efforts had taken them farther from their goal. Fern burst into tears, and Con quickly followed her. Rick looked at the two sobbing women, feeling incompetent.

Without breakfast to delay them, they waded through the muddy lake toward the mountains. By early afternoon, the sky promised another downpour, and Rick resolved not to repeat the previous day's mistake. "If we can't see the

mountains," he said, "we'll have to stop. It's better to make
no progress at all than to hike in the wrong direction."

When the rains came down in the afternoon as furiously
as they had the day before, Rick looked for a place to stop.
A grove of trees was barely visible in the distance. As he
headed in its direction, it became more defined. Some of
the "tree trunks" were actually massive legs supporting
huge bodies. A herd of sauropods was browsing the canopy.
As impressive as the Apatosauruses had been, these creatures were even more astounding.

"Brachiosaurus," said Rick in an awed voice.

There was much to inspire awe. The heads of these tree-
top browsers appeared to tower over fifty feet above the
ground. The animals were twice as massive as an
Apatosaurus, with bodies built for verticality, like those of
giraffes. The front legs were longer than the rear ones, giving the torso an upward slant. The neck was longer than the
tail and held upright.

Con could not believe anything so large could actually
be alive. She forgot her weariness and hunger as she stood
in dumb amazement. There were six individuals in the
grove, slowly reducing the trees to leafless skeletons. Not
all were full-grown, but even the smallest was much larger
than an elephant. Without warning, two of the Bra-
chiosauruses reared upward on their hind legs. The effect of
something so tall, suddenly growing taller, was amazing and
terrifying.

The reason for their behavior became clear when a pack
of Allosauruses rounded the grove. They were not running
in panic; this was a familiar game to them. They had looked
for an opportunity, found none, and were moving on. The
five travelers stood in their path, armed only with sharpened
sticks.

"Don't move!" Rick said, as the predators advanced. He
realized if the Allosauruses decided they were food, they
would become food. Their spears would be no more protection than toothpicks for cocktail sausages.

The Allosauruses did not stop. The travelers were
treated as part of the landscape—objects unworthy of

notice. Only the smallest of the pack turned its head as it
trotted by. For a moment, it slowed its pace. Then it caught
up with the others and faded into the rainy grayness.

Rick hiked in another direction until trees became visible. "We'll stop there until we can see where we're going,"
he said, trying not to sound discouraged. In fact, Rick was
profoundly discouraged. Not only was traveling harder
than he expected, he feared he had made another miscalcu-
lation, one that could prove fatal. The greening of the plain
had indeed filled it with game—game that only an Allosaurus
or a Ceratosaurus could easily handle. Rick knew that
remains of smaller animals were rare in the Morrison Formation. There were a number of possible explanations for it,
including the hypothesis that such animals were scarce. Now,
he saw that was the correct one. The seasonal vegetation supported only large, migratory herbivores and their predators.
He and his companions would be hard-pressed to find creatures they could catch and eat. Rick feared they would starve
before they reached the sea. If that were to happen, he was
certain Con would die first.

The trees in the grove were spiky conifers, and though
their tops had been heavily browsed, there was still enough
foliage to break the force of the rain. The ground was covered by an inch of water, so everyone had to rest sitting up
beneath the tarp. Rick leaned against a tree trunk and
wrapped his arms around Con, who rested against his chest.
Soon, she slept within his embrace. Rick continued to cradle
her though his own back ached with stiffness. In his love
and despair, he felt it was the only thing he could do for her.

THE FOLLOWING MORNING was clear. Tired and bedraggled,
the travelers headed off, hampered by the muddy ground.
They slogged though muck until the ground rose and
became drier. There, ferns sent forth fronds to produce a
vast green prairie. They waded through the knee-high plants
until they spotted a herd of bipedal herbivores grazing upon
the new growth. The way the feeding dinosaurs bobbed up
and down marked them as Dryosauruses.

"Who wants to go hunting?" asked Rick.

Everyone volunteered.

"These animals are swift," said Rick. "We can't outrun them, so I'm counting on their ignoring us. Con, you and Violet go after the smallest one while I circle around. Move slowly and stab at the belly. With luck, that will drive it toward me. Fern and Oak, your job is to finish it off. Stab at the chest or neck, but watch out for the feet. I'm sure these things can kick."

Everyone walked toward the grazing Dryosauruses, which seemed aware of their presence but undisturbed by it. As Con neared the herd, her heart pounded with nervous excitement. There were eleven dinosaurs in all, and most were about thirteen feet long. The smallest animal in the group stood as tall as she and weighed considerably more. The beast dwarfed Violet, who didn't even reach Con's shoulder.

Their intended quarry moved as it cropped the vegetation, and Con and Violet moved with it. Con began to worry they were making their prey uneasy. "Maybe we should stop moving," she whispered to Violet. Both women froze, and the tactic worked. Eventually, the small Dryosaurus wandered within spear range. "Now!" whispered Con. The two huntresses stabbed simultaneously, piercing the creature's belly. It gave a hoarse, high-pitched shriek and twisted around, wrenching the spear from Violet's grasp. The shriek panicked the herd, and it bolted. The injured animal took off also. Though a spear still dangled from its abdomen, it ran as swiftly as the others. The herd dashed directly toward Rick and flowed around him as if he were inanimate. However, the wounded dinosaur behaved differently and tried to evade his spear. Rick managed to inflict only a minor wound as it dashed past him.

Con ran up to Rick. "Now what?" she said, the frustration clear in her voice.

"It's wounded, and as it moves, Violet's spear will do further damage. We'll just have to follow it."

The herd ran about half a mile before settling down to graze again. The five hunters approached it as carefully as before, but the wounded Dryosaurus was now wary of spears. It dashed off when it saw them, spooking the herd. That set a pattern that continued for hours, wearing down both the hunters and the hunted. Finally, the wounded dinosaur straggled behind when the herd took off. As Con and the others chased after it, they occasionally found blood on the ferns.

For Con, the chase took on a personal nature. Hunger made her fierce. When the animal began to falter and stumble, she raced after it, determined to push her quarry to its limit and end its life. She was pushing herself to the limit also, but at the moment, she didn't care. She left Rick and the Gaians behind in her single-minded pursuit.

The Dryosaurus's gait betrayed a weakness that caught the attention of other eyes. Con was unaware there was another runner on the plain until she heard the others screaming her name. She paused and saw a Ceratosaurus striding after the wounded Dryosaurus. The eighteen-foot carnivore was a picture of grace and power, and it quickly closed the distance. Con stood still, sweat-soaked and panting, as the Ceratosaurus dispatched the object of her hunt. The carnivore made it look effortless—a snap of the jaws, a few shakes, and the Dryosaurus hung limp in its jaws. The Ceratosaurus dropped it and bent to feed.

Con wept with disappointment and impotent rage. The chase had been costly and netted her nothing. She dried her eyes and walked back to the others. No one said anything, for everyone was too exhausted and discouraged. As they headed north, it began to rain.

As long as Rick could see the mountains, he led the slow march onward. The openness of the fern prairie was disconcerting, and its monotonous expanse provided no shelter. They walked for an hour in the rain until a line of trees became visible in the distance like a green fence. They reached the trees to find they marked the banks of an eastward-flowing river. Swollen with rain, it was a serious barrier. "We'll stop here for the night," said Rick, "and cross the river when we're rested."

Everyone threw down their burdens and went looking

for food. The fern prairie had been filled with fiddleheads, but their astringent bitterness made them inedible. Everyone was hungry. A termite mound would have been a welcome sight, but none was to be found. When they gathered later, only Con had been successful in her foraging. She had killed a three-foot lizard. Despite this, she was distraught. "One of my knives fell into the river," she said. "It's gone."

Rick took the lizard that had cost so dearly, saying, "This is a beauty."

"Yeah," said Con in a dull tone. "I'm sure it'll taste just like chicken."

THE LIZARD DID taste like chicken. Raw chicken. Since cooking was impossible in the rain, Rick butchered the reptile to make it appear as appetizing as possible. He cut the muscle into fillets, then made them into bite-sized morsels. The only objectionable aspect of the bland-flavored meat was its slimy texture. Con had eaten worse fare on her previous adventure, but after she finished eating, she was gripped by nausea. She wandered away from the campsite and was relieved when Rick did not follow her. Only when she was out of earshot did she succumb to her churning stomach and throw up. For the second time that day, she wept in frustration. She was still on her knees and crying when Violet quietly approached. "Does he know?" asked Violet.

Con stifled her sobs. "Know what?"

"I watched what happened to Fern. You termed it 'morning sickness,' as I recall."

"It's not morning," retorted Con.

"No, but Gaian women have the same cycles as Sapene women. Don't you think Rick has noticed you've missed your period?"

"Rick's a man," said Con. "Men don't pay attention to such things."

"So you haven't told him?"

"What's the point?"

"It's a significant development," said Violet. It seemed to Con that Violet was considering saying more, but decided against it.

"If we make it, I'll tell Rick. He'll be glad. He was once before. Otherwise . . . I . . . I'd rather he never knew." Con began to weep again.

"You don't think you're going to make it, do you?"

"I keep remembering Montana," said Con. "I can't get it out of my mind."

"What happened in Montana was Samazatarmaku's doing," said Violet. "Help put an end to his schemes. You must, Con. You're the key to restoring history. You're humanity's only hope."

The intensity in Violet's voice surprised Con. As she gazed at Violet, the Gaian woman did not seem diminutive at all. The look on her face was compelling, and her eyes bored into Con's, pleading and commanding at once. "I'll do anything," said Violet. "*Anything* to help you."

Con knew it was true. She was never more certain of anything in her life. "Don't tell Rick," she said. "And don't worry. I haven't given up. I got weepy the last time I was pregnant, too. It'll pass, just like the sickness."

IT WAS SUNNY the following morning when, tethered to a rope, Rick barely managed to swim the river. Once the line was in place, the Gaians used it to cross. Afterward, Con tied the rope to her waist and let the current swing her over. She was relieved she did not have to fight the river, for she was already weak from lack of food.

Following the crossing, the trudge across the plain was eventless. Hunger slowed them, and evening found them in the open with nothing to eat. It was raining when they set up the tent to sleep huddled together. The ground was wet, and everyone woke up stiff and muddy. Their progress was even slower the following day. Rick kept a worried eye on Con. Her ribs were already beginning to show, and she stumbled along with a dazed expression. In the afternoon, their path merged with the trail left by a herd of sauropods.

The animals were heading north, also, marking their passage with trampled ground, fibrous manure, and cropped vegetation. Toward evening, the travelers spied a group of creatures in the distance. The huge body of an Apatosaurus lay motionless upon the ground, and a pack of Allosauruses was feeding on it.

Rick swerved the line of march, but only slightly.

"Aren't we getting too close to those things?" asked Oak.

"They have tons of meat," said Rick. "They won't bother us."

To Oak's discomfort, Rick led them even nearer to the huge carnivores. At the closest point, they were less than a quarter of a mile away. The predators seemed peaceful enough. The three largest were resting near their kill, having gorged themselves. The smaller pack members were feeding. A grove of trees stood nearby, and Rick headed in that direction. When they reached it, he halted for the night. Everyone was too tired to question Rick's choice of campsite. They pitched the tent and made a fruitless search for food within the grove. When it began to rain, everyone crawled into the tent, not waiting for darkness to sleep.

Rick awoke to crawl into the rainy night. It was very dark, and he moved carefully. He walked barefoot to help feel his way and avoid the sound of his flip-flops striking his heels. Leaving the grove, he was glad he had taken care to orient himself while there was still light; otherwise, he might not have spotted the Apatosaurus's carcass. In the darkness, it was a mere shadow in the distance. He moved in its direction as quietly as he could, but fear amplified every sound he made. Night was the domain of mammals in this world. As one, Rick hoped it would be his also, allowing him to rob the Allosauruses. It was only a theory that he would be safe. Lions hunted at night, and perhaps these carnivores did also. If that were the case, no one would ever know what happened to him.

The world was a nebulous monochrome of dark grays and blacks. Strain as he might, Rick could see little. His situation would have been hopeless if the plain hadn't been so empty or its creatures so large. When he finally approached the huge body, his ears told him as much as his eyes about the nearness of the Allosauruses. He could hear them breathing. That, his footsteps, and the soft sound of rain were the only noises in the night.

The sauropod filled the air with the odor of blood and entrails. Rick strained to discern the details of the immense shadowy form before him. Exposed ribs showed as dim gray lines against an empty cavity. Rick felt something slippery underfoot and suspected he had stepped on a half-eaten organ. He headed to the rear of the animal, then groped along a gnawed hind leg. He wanted to cut loose a slab of meat, hopefully one not yet fouled by a fetid mouth. In the darkness, touch was more useful than sight for the task. He had to climb onto the corpse, using raw flesh as handholds and footholds. He scrambled up the grisly mound until he found an intact spot.

The butchery was hard, bloody work. Rick interrupted it for several terrified minutes when one of the Allosauruses stirred. When the creature settled down, Rick resumed his work. After a quarter of an hour, he had cut away a twenty-pound hunk of muscle. He lugged it back to the grove and hung it in a tree far from the tent. Taking off his loincloth, he used leaves and the falling rain to wash the blood from his body. Only when he felt free of its scent did he grope his way back to the tent and crawl inside.

Only Fern was aware of Rick's return. She said nothing, for she was concentrating on not crying out from the pains in her abdomen. *They're just hunger pangs*, Fern told herself. She gasped as another hit. After it passed, she listened for some indication that Rick had heard her. The only sound was the breathing of exhausted sleepers. When her pains eventually ceased, Fern also slept.

WHEN THE SUN rose in a cloudless sky, Rick produced the meat and astonished everyone with his story. With difficulty, he made a fire to cook some of the stolen food and preserve the rest. The Apatosaurus tasted like stringy beef, and everyone agreed it was delicious. Con was able to keep her portion down. Once her belly was full, she became more optimistic. Con gazed at Rick lovingly, feeling he had become as brave and resourceful as he had been in the Cretaceous.

Meanwhile, the predators Rick had robbed lazed in the sun. Their kill had attracted other scavengers, also. The Allosauruses jealously guarded their bounty, and so far, only pterosaurs and flies had dared approach the mound of meat. The sweet odor of its decay tainted the air. The Allosauruses did not mind the smell and would not mind when it grew even stronger. They were satisfied. Even the youngest was free to gorge itself. Sated, it felt no need to follow the strange odor leading to the grove—the one it associated with blood.

40

THE TRAVELERS COVERED MORE DISTANCE IN AN afternoon on full stomachs than they had the entire previous day. Con, in particular, was transformed by the food. As nutrients entered her bloodstream, the dullness left her eyes, and her step became lively again. She was walking beside Fern when the bark rope the Gaian carried inspired an idea. "Rick," she said, "how would you make a bola?"

"I think you tie rocks to three cords and tie the cords together at the other end," he said.

"What's a bola?" asked Fern.

"Something you throw at an animal to trip it," said Con. "The rocks wrap the cords around its legs. If I could make one, hunting would be easy."

For the rest of the day, Con kept an eye peeled for suitable rocks. When they settled for the night, she assembled her first bola. It proved difficult to use, and her throws came nowhere near the target. Nevertheless, she continued practicing in the rainy evening until it was too dark to see. The following day, Con tried hunting with the bola without success. The next day proved equally fruitless.

After three damp days, the Apatosaurus meat spoiled. Hunger loomed again and desperation sharpened Con's throwing skills. In a heavy downpour, she tripped a full-grown Dryosaurus and slew the helpless beast even before Rick or Violet arrived. It was so large that Rick butchered only a single haunch. They ate it raw beneath the tarp, sitting in an inch of water.

CLOSER TO THE sea, the plains were wetter. The rainy season created temporary, shallow lakes. They became numerous, forcing detours. The soil here was gray with organic matter, and trees were more common. Ginkgoes with their fan-shaped leaves were numerous, as were their relatives. They were all in full foliage, along with the palmettolike cycads. Tree ferns were common in the damp areas.

The march of the travelers matched that of the sauropods, which followed the rains northward and the new growth they brought. The trails left by the giant dinosaurs became a common sight. Early notions of sauropods being swamp dwellers were erroneous; like the humans, the huge creatures preferred firm ground. Still, the dinosaurs visited the shallow lakes to drink. Nineteen days after Rick, Con, and the Gaians left the valley, an old Apatosaurus waded out into the waters of one such lake with fateful consequences.

The water was not deep, but the mud beneath it was. The lake covered an old riverbed that had silted up. During the rainy months, the silt in the former river became a deep morass of soft clay that looked no different than the rest of the lake bed. The Apatosaurus detected it only when its forelegs began to sink into the ooze. When it continued to move forward, it committed a fatal error. The clay had its first victim of the season. The dinosaur was incapable of realizing it was doomed. Neither would a casual observer, for the animal appeared to be merely wading in the water. The powerful legs that frantically churned the muck were invisible, and only the creature's anguished cries indicated it was in distress.

The sauropod was much too large to sink beneath the surface. It struggled all day to free itself, but succeeded only in making the silt looser and deeper. The dinosaur faced a fate of slow starvation, but it would affect other fates as well. Helpless, it served as the bait in a natural trap—the first link in a chain of deaths.

The Allosaurus pack provided the trap's next victims. The same seven animals that Con and Rick had encountered in the valley had followed the sauropods north. Now, they saw an opportunity and rushed into the grip of the wet, brown killer. The large female actually made it as far as the Apatosaurus's rump before she became mired. She was the only one to taste blood. The four other adults and the older of the two juveniles were trapped before they even reached their intended prey. Only the youngest of the pack escaped, for it delayed its attack. All the signs it waited for never came. Instead, the prey remained upright, and the pack was immobilized. The youngster's instincts provided no guidance in this situation, nor could the creature reason. The young Allosaurus watched as the powerful pack it relied upon disappeared into the brown morass. After an hour, only the heads were still visible. The pack's snarls at its unhearing and uncaring foe had diminished to feeble gasps, and the animals stared silently until, at last, the mud swallowed them whole.

For the first time in its life, the ten-foot Allosaurus would have to hunt alone—a pack hunter without a pack. The huge dinosaurs upon which it fed were safe from a small, solitary attacker. If the Allosaurus were to survive, it would have to find different prey.

THREE WEEKS AFTER leaving the valley, Con made a determined effort to break through Oak's shell. Initially, he rebuffed her questions with terse, opaque answers. Oak would not discuss his personal life nor life in the thirty-eighth century. His tongue loosened only when Con asked what he was doing in the past.

"We were researching temporal phenomena," said Oak in the most complete response he had given all morning.

"So you traveled to the past to study *time?*" asked Con. "Why?"

"We were measuring timestream fluctuations, to put it more precisely," replied Oak.

From the animation in Oak's voice, Con deduced he was a person more comfortable discussing ideas than himself. Hoping to draw him out, she pursued the topic. "Does that have something to do with history's varying slightly?"

"Exactly. It concerns the dynamics of free will and the constraining forces of the optimal path."

"Wow," said Con, "That's a mouthful."

"We were investigating how history remains virtually static when, at every point in time, people are free to act. There must be forces at work that limit their actions and make certain choices inevitable."

"Then along comes Sam and blows everything to hell," said Con.

"My research uncovered the very phenomenon Samazatarmaku represents. I think time travel is destabilizing time itself."

"How could you investigate something like that?"

"We used miniprobes to return to the same point in time and measure changes. I believe they were increasing in magnitude even before Samazatarmaku began his manipulations. Every trip to the past, especially those in the human era, introduces random elements. Those elements weaken the restraining forces."

"What do you mean by random elements?" asked Con.

"They can be little things—someone spotting a time machine, a piece of information about the future, a belief out of context . . ."

"And someone like me?" asked Con.

"You're not a random element," said Oak. "Far from it."

"I'm just a person who's been jerked around."

Oak didn't respond, and Con feared she had ventured into forbidden territory again. She tried to restart the conversation. "So Sam's the product of time travel screwing things up?"

"That's putting it inelegantly," replied Oak, "but I think you're correct."

"The people who found me in the Cretaceous said time travel had been banned in their era."

"They'd be from a different reality from my own," said Oak.

"Did I wipe them out when I exploded that bomb in Mergona?"

"The people you saw still exist downwhen in the Cretaceous, but not upwhen from your change."

Con shook her head in puzzlement. "This gets very confusing."

"It does."

"So you understand all this? The changes and all the alternate realities replacing one another and leaving scraps behind?"

"Not without a computer and data from miniprobes," said Oak. "Right now, my technology consists of some bark rope and a bone knife."

"If we reach the island and outfox Sam, do you really think we can set things right?"

"You should be able to undo the damage you caused."

"And then what happens to me?"

"Why then," said Oak in a tone Con thought too glib, "you'll live happily ever after."

EVENTUALLY, THE TRAVELERS reached the banks of a broad river. Its muddy waters flowed swiftly and turbulently. "How are we going to cross that?" asked Violet.

"We don't need to," said Rick. "We've been traveling three weeks, so we should be close to the Sundance Sea. We'll follow the river to its shores, then turn east," said Rick.

Violet gazed at the angry river. "It'll be nice to do something easy for a change."

The riverine environment supported more trees, and within their shelter, a different kind of dinosaur dwelled. These were small bipedal herbivores of the hypsilophodontid family. They resembled the larger Dryosaurus except their necks were more flexible, and they held their heads high above their torsos. At four and a half feet from snout to tail tip, they were the perfect-sized game. As soon as Con spotted one of the green animals, she wanted to go hunting.

Now that Con used the bola, Violet had become her hunting partner. After Con entangled the prey, Violet would rush in to finish it off. They made a good team, and Con came to admire Violet's energy and stamina. After Rick stopped for the day, Violet and Con took off in search of dinner, moving quietly and efficiently along the outskirts of the woods. Violet tapped Con's arm and silently pointed to three green animals browsing on some saplings. Con advanced stealthily, and once her prey was within range, she set down her spear to whirl the bola over her head. When the stones circled rapidly, Con let go of the cord, and the three tethered rocks flew toward their target. The weighted cords struck the animal's legs and wrapped around them almost instantly. Before Con could pick up her spear, Violet flashed past her and slew the helpless dinosaur.

Con grinned. "Pretty fast for a granny."

"Good shot for a child."

"A child!" said Con in mock petulance as she went over to the dead dinosaur. Con unwound the bola from its legs then hefted the four-foot creature upon her shoulder. "Rick will love to see this."

Violet grabbed Con's spear and bola, and the two women headed back to camp. "I saw you and Oak talking today," said Violet. "That was a first."

"Yes," said Con. "He's a hard person to get to know."

"He's grieving. Also, he doesn't believe people from different eras should interact," said Violet. "It has something to do with his theory about random elements."

"Yes, he told me about it. Do you think he's right?"

"I don't know," said Violet.

Con detected evasiveness in Violet's response, and that worried her. As they approached camp, she voiced her concerns. "Violet, what's going to happen to Rick and me? I mean, assuming we survive."

"I wouldn't worry about that," said Violet.

"I may not completely understand Oak's theory," said Con, "but I understand enough of it to know that Rick and I represent . . ."

"Rick," Violet called out. "Con's caught a new dinosaur."

Rick came dashing over with an excited look. "I'll carry that, Con," he said. "I should butcher it away from camp."

Violet hurried away, and Con ended up following Rick. He walked a fair distance before he set down the animal. Based on the primitive leaf-shaped teeth, he decided the animal was an *Othnielia*. Con watched as Rick happily examined, then dissected, the animal. "One would think you were in heaven," said Con. "Dinosaurs and sex, what more could a guy want?"

Rick smiled, then grew serious. "You mean a lot more to me than sex," he said. "You're smart, resourceful, tough—heck—you're even pretty."

"Well, aren't you the sweet talker."

"I mean it, Con. Every word."

"I know. I think we should sneak off tonight, so you can repeat it."

WHILE CON ROASTED the Othnielia, Rick visited the river to view the sunset. The water reflected the sky's pink glow, while the far bank was nearly a silhouette. The scene looked beautiful and serene. As Rick gazed at it appreciatively, he noticed something odd. A stretch of trees on the far shore reminded him of one of those pictures that, when viewed correctly, revealed a hidden image. As Rick stared at the trees, he thought he discerned such an image. It resembled a man-made object. *Can it be Sam's time machine, camouflaged somehow?* The idea was alarming, and Rick attempted to reassure himself. *Time machines are ovoid-shaped, while this looks more like a flying saucer.* He rubbed his eyes. When he stopped, the image was gone. *Did I imagine it?* Before Rick returned to camp, he convinced himself he had.

WITH THE RIVER to guide them, the travelers did not halt when a downpour arrived the following noon. They paused only to catch rainwater with the tarp and refill their water jars. Then they moved on as the warm rain washed away the sweat from the steamy morning.

Later that afternoon, the young Allosaurus found the head, feet, and entrails of the butchered Othnielia. It bolted them down, but not before noting the unusual scent accompanying it. It had encountered it before, mingled with the smell of blood. The scavenged meat was the carnivore's first food since its former pack abandoned the gnawed bones of its final kill. The youngster had gone hungry because its adaptations worked against it. An Allosaurus pack relied on size and numbers to achieve its kills, and the lone youngster found smaller prey too swift to catch. It was wracked by hunger as it headed down the river.

ANOTHER DOWNPOUR PRECLUDED hunting that evening, and the travelers dined on leftover Othnielia. There was no breakfast the following morning. By afternoon, Con's appetite bedeviled her, and she convinced Rick to stop early so Violet and she could hunt. They were at the outskirts of the coastal forest, and game was harder to spot in the less open landscape. Con was worrying how she would hunt in a forest when she heard a rustle a short distance behind her. She whirled about, expecting to find prey, and saw the Allosaurus instead. "Violet!" she whispered. Her warning was unnecessary. Violet had also seen the beast.

Con gazed at the dinosaur, and it returned her stare. The impression she had on their first encounter returned. Then, the creature had regarded her differently than did the others in its pack. It regarded her the same way now. *It under-stands I'm food!*

Con dropped her bola to grab her spear with both hands. The spear confused the Allosaurus, as did the strangeness of the creatures it confronted. It hesitated. Con regarded the killer with perception heightened by fear. Its ten-foot length made it small by dinosaur standards, and its head was the same height as Con's. Yet no full-grown tiger or grizzly bear ever possessed such a large and cruel mouth. Con's entire head would fit inside those jaws. She watched the striped body tense, as she prepared to sell her life dearly.

From the corner of her eye, Con caught a flash of move-ment. Violet sprinted the short distance to the Allosaurus and drove her spear deep into the creature's chest. The dinosaur shrieked with a loud, hoarse voice, then snapped at Violet and seized her shoulder. Con heard a crunch as Violet released the spear. The Allosaurus raised its head and pulled Violet off her feet.

The world slowed down so that it seemed to Con she could count each pulse of her pounding heart; each step of her race toward the Allosaurus; and each violent shake of Violet's body. Con watched in slow motion as her spear entered the creature's neck and blood spurted. The power-ful neck muscles nearly wrenched the spear from her grasp as she dodged the slashing claws. If the dinosaur had let go of Violet, Con would surely have died, but the creature did not. Warm blood filled its hungry mouth, and it would not ease its grip even as its own life ebbed.

As Con held on to her spear, she heard someone scream-ing over and over, "Rick! Rick! Rick! Rick!" Only the raw-ness of her throat told her that the someone was herself. She saw Rick racing toward her with a wild look in his eyes just as the Allosaurus slumped to the ground. Rick savagely stabbed its body as it collapsed and continued even after there was no need to do so.

"Stop!" yelled Con. "We have to help Violet!"

Even in death, the Allosaurus stubbornly gripped the woman. She lay facedown on the ground, her shoulder and upper chest engulfed by the hideous mouth. Rick had to use his spear to pry open the jaws. Only then, was he able to gently turn Violet over.

She was still alive. Violet looked at Con, but not at her ghastly wound. The bite had not only gouged a deep, bloody semicircle, it had crushed her as well. Violet's breath came in gurgling gasps, and blood poured forth in rhythm with her heart. Con averted her gaze from the terrible sight and looked instead into Violet's eyes. She saw pain there, but not fear. There was calmness in Violet's expression, an acceptance that had nothing to do with surrender.

"You saved my life," said Con, as her own eyes welled with tears.

"Stop him, Con," whispered Violet through the pink froth on her lips. "He must not . . ." Violet gathered her strength. ". . . not prevail."

"I will, Violet. I will with all my being."

A smile came to the dying woman's lips and remained there as her eyes turned sightless. Con became aware of Fern and Oak. Fern was sobbing, along with Rick. Oak stood silent, tears streaming down his face.

41

STUNNED AND SORROWFUL, THE FOUR SURROUNDED Violet's body. Although Con was the youngest, she was the most acquainted with death. As harrowing recollections of Rick's corpse filled her mind, she called the others to action. "We can't leave Violet here," she said. "Fern, what would she want us to do?"

"What?" asked the woman, as if roused from a nightmare. Con thought that, at the moment, Fern looked very much like a child.

"We have to take care of Violet's body," said Con. "What are your customs?"

Fern began to sob again, but eventually said Violet should be buried. The four dug a shallow grave with their bone knives. It was sunset when they placed Violet in the earth and pushed dirt over her. Fern spoke over the grave in the Gaian tongue. Afterward she said, "We believe a person's spirit endures in the hearts of others. We can honor Violet through our deeds." Con bowed her head and resolved to do just that.

As the sky darkened, Con and the Gaians silently returned to camp, each alone in their thoughts. Rick returned after hastily butchering the Allosaurus. He lit a fire, for, regardless of their grief, they needed nourishment. Rick had brought back the heart of the Allosaurus. They ate it beneath a starry sky.

THE TRAVELERS LEFT Violet's grave behind. As if to reflect their somber mood, the landscape darkened. The trees no longer clustered around the riverbank, but extended in all directions. They had entered the coastal forest, and its dark green canopy blotted out the sky, making the pathway gloomy. Ferns and other plants that thrived in low light grew thickly around the tree trunks. It did not take long for everyone to miss the openness of the plain.

A hot, steamy morning gave way to a downpour in the afternoon. The four stuck close together the entire day. Rick had brought a haunch from the Allosaurus, so hunting was unnecessary. The meat tasted foul, and Con had a reoccurrence of her nausea. That was the one time she strayed from Rick's presence. Memories of his death had returned to haunt her, and she could not bear to have him out of sight.

The following day, Con overcame her fears and resumed hunting. Her bola was useless in the tangled forest, so she stalked the crocodiles that basked on the riverbank. Fern accompanied her on the hunt and helped slay the wounded reptile and butcher it. Subsequently, she became Con's regular hunting partner. This surprised Con because Fern struck her as the timid type.

Since hunting required silence, they never talked until after a kill. Even then, they avoided one obvious subject—Fern's expanding belly. It had grown so much that Fern had been forced to slit the back of her shirt and modify her pants. Yet neither woman discussed these changes until Fern broke the quiet of a hunt with a sudden moan. Con turned to see the Gaian drop her spear and clasp her abdomen.

"What's the matter?" asked Con, afraid she knew the answer.

"Just a cramp," gasped Fern. "That's all."

"Lie down. Lie down now!"

Fern turned pale as she complied. "What's happening?"

Con glanced to see if Fern's water had broken, but her pants were dry. "Where does it hurt?"

"Down low, near my back. Con, tell me *please,* what's happening?"

"I think you're having false labor pains."

"They feel real to me. They hurt!"

"Just lie still and try to relax." Con unscrewed the top of the water jar. "Here, take a long drink. It's supposed to help." Fern drank. Afterward, Con held her hand and gently rubbed her rounded belly. Fern's small size and the baby's large one made her look well advanced into her pregnancy. "This will pass," murmured Con. "You're going to be all right."

"How will I know when it's the real thing?"

Con did not tell her real labor would hurt much worse. Instead, she replied, "Don't worry about that. It's still a long way off."

Fern smiled faintly, pretending she believed her.

TRAVELING IN THE dense, steamy forest was arduous. They stayed close to the river, though the growth was thickest there and the tangled vegetation slowed them down. It seemed the safest path; it would be too easy to get lost in the maze of trees. Their trunks extended seemingly without end—columns in a vast, dark cathedral. Monkey puzzle trees, dawn redwoods, and other conifers dominated, and they grew to great heights. Noises from unseen animals echoed through the forest, making everyone jumpy.

After five days, the ground turned swampy, and it became hard to tell where the forest ended and the river began. The trees and plants seemed strange and primitive. Con, Rick, Fern, and Oak often slogged through foul-smelling, black muck that would be coal someday. The treacherous ground slowed them down even further. Rick lost his flip-flops in the ooze, and everyone was filthy. They spent two hungry, miserable nights huddled on decaying tree trunks surrounded by stagnant water. The third day promised no better. They were pushing their way through thick growths of horsetails when they heard the sound of breakers. It spurred them on, and soon the muck grew firmer. The vegetation diminished, and a sandy beach came into view.

Con dashed to the shore, feeling like a child set loose on summer vacation. She waded into the surf to wash her black legs and was joined by the others. Yet once Con had cleaned the muck away, she retreated to the sand. Her experience in the Cretaceous made her wary of swimming in a sea with prehistoric predators. Some of the crocodiles she had seen had been frightening enough.

Still, the beach delighted Con. Its seashells quickly caught her eye. The Sundance Sea swarmed with ammonites, relatives of the chambered nautilus that would disappear with the dinosaurs. Their shells were particularly abundant, and Con wandered along the shore picking up one after another. Most were spiral-shaped, though a few had unwound coils. Some were smooth, while others had ridges, bumps, or spiky projections. They ranged in size from smaller than a dime to larger than an automobile tire. Their colors and patterns varied as widely. When Rick caught up with Con, she clutched an armload of shells to her chest. He was glad to see her smiling again.

"That's a quite a collection," he said.

Con showed him a perfect shell that gleamed with the soft iridescence of mother-of-pearl. "I'm saving this for Tom. Do you think he'll like it?"

Rick was both surprised and touched that she had thought of his older brother, despite never having met him. Rick took the shell and admired it. "Like it?" he said. "He'll treasure it!"

"Do you think he'll like me, too?"

"It'd be impossible not to." Rick became thoughtful. "It'll feel strange to be back."

"Yeah," said Con, her voice suddenly melancholy.

"What's the matter?"

"In the twenty-first century, I won't even be an orphan. Orphans at least *had* parents. I'll have never been born. It'll be as if I fell out of the sky."

"Your father will have never existed," said Rick, "but your mother will."

"She won't have given birth to me."

"But you'll still have her DNA. You can prove you're her daughter."

"*That* would be an interesting conversation. 'Hello, I never existed before, but I'm your daughter.' I know my mother; that talk wouldn't go well."

"The Gaians will help."

Con recalled Oak's theories about "random elements" and worried they might not. "Yeah, maybe."

"You'll have me."

Con smiled and glanced at Rick. He seemed very nervous. "What is it, Rick?"

"You'll always have me. That is, if . . . if you . . ." He stared at his feet. "You'd think this'd be easy."

"What?"

Rick lifted his eyes to look into Con's. "Con, will you . . . will you marry me?"

"I already have," she teased. "In 1879."

"Is that a yes?"

Con dropped the shells as she threw her arms around Rick and kissed him. "Yes."

HAVING REACHED THE sea, the four travelers began hiking eastward. The shore was sandy in most places, and usually the forest did not encroach upon the sand. The only dinosaurs that ventured on the beach were the tiny Compsognathuses that came to scavenge the creatures washed up by the waves. Pterosaurs were numerous, both the long-tailed and short-tailed varieties. Some fed on the sea's leavings, but most plucked fish from the water like seagulls. All the pterosaurs were new to Rick, since the rocks of the Morrison Formation did not favor their preservation.

That afternoon, they encountered a rocky stretch that provided shellfish and a kind of lobster for dinner. Everyone helped gather them, and Con did not have to hunt. They steamed the seafood in seaweed over a driftwood fire. After traveling in the swamp, it was a feast. When Con had eaten her fill, she wandered to the surf to clean her face and hands. Fern joined her by the water.

"If we can find places like this every day," said Con, "our hunting days will be over."

"That would be nice," said Fern. "I was terrified every second."

"Then why did you come along?"

"I'm not brave like you or Violet. I thought some practice might help."

"Did it?"

"I'm still scared, Con."

"So am I, Fern. We'd be crazy if we weren't."

"It was all supposed to be so easy. Plant the bomb, and he'd disappear."

"Once we get to the island," said Con, "it'll still be easy. All Oak has to do is take us upwhen, and Sam will be dead."

"Nothing's been easy so far, why should things change now?"

"Because we're due for some luck."

"Con, if we get to the island, and the time machine's not there . . ."

"It'll be there," said Con.

"But if it's not, or if my next pains aren't false ones, I want you to promise me something. Promise you'll try to save my baby."

"Fern, it won't . . ."

"Take Rick's knife and save my baby. Promise you'll do that. Don't wait until I'm dead to try."

"Fern, I don't know if I could do that."

"You have to. Promise. You must promise me."

Fern was grasping Con's arm so hard it hurt. Con looked into Fern's anguished, earnest face and knew she had no choice. "I promise."

Fern let go of Con's arm and took a deep breath. Her face grew calmer, though dread still lingered there. "Thank you," she said. "Now you know why I must practice being brave."

THE TREK DOWN the coast was long, tiring, and uneventful. Occasionally, they could see the long necks of plesiosaurs as they basked on offshore sandbars. Twice, the travelers came across the body of an *Ichthyosaurus*. The first one they found was eight feet long, and Con thought the black-and-white creature was a dolphin. Rick pointed out that its fishlike tail was vertical, not horizontal like a dolphin's, and said the animal was a reptile. Con examined the sea creature in wonder, for it contradicted all her assumptions about reptiles. It was streamlined and fish-shaped with a dorsal fin similar to that of a shark. It had a long, toothy snout and large, golden eyes. Even in death, it looked fast and graceful. The second *Ichthyosaurus* looked like it had been larger than the first, but only the rear third had washed ashore. Rick examined the tooth marks on the remains. "This was done in one bite," he said.

"What could do that?" asked Fern.

"A pliosaur, the Jurassic equivalent of a sperm whale. Big, fast, and predatory."

Fern shivered and glanced at the restless sea.

After five days of walking, the travelers spied faint gray shapes offshore. Over the course of the day, they became more defined until their rocky profiles left no doubt these were the islands they sought. Oak pointed to the rightmost island. "That's the one the time machine was on." It was too far away to make out more than the largest features, and a low island blocked the view of its beaches.

"How far out do you think it is?" asked Con.

"I have no idea," said Oak.

"Me neither," said Rick, "but it doesn't look close."

"How are we ever going to get there?" asked Fern.

It was a problem to which they had given little thought, for the island had always been a distant goal. Now that it lay within view, they questioned if it also lay within reach.

"I guess we'll build a log raft," said Con.

"Small logs have been scarce," said Rick. "And they'll be hard to cut with only a hunting knife."

"Then maybe a raft isn't a good idea," said Con. She recalled the dugout canoes she had studied in anthropology class, but remembered the effort and skill required to make them. She thought of other ancient watercraft. Birch bark canoes. Hide boats. "A reed boat!" she exclaimed.

"Reeds are grasses," said Rick. "Grass hasn't evolved yet."

"How could you make a boat out of reeds?" asked Fern.

"They're hollow," said Con. "They float."

"Horsetails!" exclaimed Rick, "They're hollow, too. Con, what do you know about reed boats?"

"The ancient Egyptians made them. There are paintings of them in tombs. They were sort of like pontoons."

"Maybe we could rig two together in a kind of catamaran," said Rick.

"We could use the tarp as a sail," said Con.

"We'd better make paddles, too," said Rick.

Oak and Fern were unfamiliar with primitive technology, and Con's understanding of such watercraft went no further than her recollection of a few images of the boats. Clearly, they would have to improvise. They found a stream flanked by a thick growth of horsetails and looked at the plants surrounding it with new interest. Horsetails were ancient plants. They had once grown to the size of trees, though by the Jurassic, they had dwindled in numbers and size. Their straight, branchless stalks were jointed like bamboo, and each node was encircled by a whorl of flat, narrow leaves. Some of the stalks were tipped with a spore-producing cone. This species grew taller than any in the twenty-first century, and the largest stalks were sixteen feet high. Rick cut one down. Its inch-thick hollow stem was tough and gritty, but not woody. "I think this will float," he said, tossing it into the stream. The current swept it away.

"Dried and stripped of leaves, it should float even better," said Con.

"So what did this reed boat look like?" asked Rick.

"Sort of canoe-shaped," said Con. "You know, tapered at both ends. And the front and the back curved up like a Persian slipper."

"For decoration?"

"Maybe, but I'm not sure."

"Then let's curve our boat to be safe," said Rick.

"I'd feel safer," said Fern, "if we worked out of sight from the island."

Con recalled the police officer's bodiless legs standing upright after Sam had blasted her, and she was suddenly covered with goose bumps. "I'm with Fern," she said. "We've come too far to get caught."

"He won't be looking for us," said Rick.

"You don't know Sam," said Con. She gazed at the distant, misty island, which had acquired an air of menace. "I do. He's hard to second-guess." *For all we know,* she thought, *he could be watching us right now.*

42

LIFE ON THE BEACH WOULD HAVE BEEN PLEASANT IF IT were not for thoughts of the desperate voyage ahead. Building the boat was slow, but interesting work. Food was abundant and easily obtained. Con and Rick had time together. Though Oak had become even more withdrawn since Violet's death, Fern and Con grew closer. Whenever they were together, Fern freely spoke about her life. She told of her childhood and family, her bonding with Medlar, and her society.

The thirty-seventh century Fern described seemed a wonderful time to live. Humanity had solved many of the problems that had troubled it in the past. In Fern's world, unlike the version of the future Con had experienced, there was harmony among the different human species and within them as well. Technology was used wisely, and the environment was being restored. Thanks to time travel, elms and chestnuts were no longer extinct, whales and sea turtles swam the oceans, and songbirds filled the air. People lived on Mars and would soon breathe freely beneath its open sky. This knowledge made Sam's changes to history seem especially depraved.

"I don't understand it," said Con to Fern one afternoon. "If people are so content in the future, why would Sam want to change things?"

"There are maladjusted persons in every society," said Fern.

"Does anyone know what time Sam came from?"

"Sometime before the fortieth century. That's about all we know."

"The Kyndens I've encountered were pretty cold," said Con. Then she added, thinking of Kat, "But not all of them."

"They're not numerous in our time," said Fern, "and many are aloof."

"I wonder if it has something to do with the Ripening. It sets them apart."

"It does," said Fern.

"I know the trait's intentional," said Con, "but it's hard to understand why."

"Historians think Dr. Kynden did it to simplify the relations between the sexes."

"From what I saw, it doesn't," said Con.

"The version of the thirty-first century you visited is severely distorted," said Fern. "I'd suspect anything you learned there."

"Soon, it won't matter. We'll fix everything." Con hoped she sounded more positive than she felt, for as she gazed at the island, it seemed as far away as the future she hoped to change.

AS THE BOAT neared completion, Fern's condition spurred the work. She had three more episodes of abdominal pain. The last was so severe, she asked Con to have Rick get his knife. The two stood an anxious vigil over the frightened woman until the rhythmic pains subsided. Afterward, Con forced Fern to rest, while she, Oak, and Rick toiled with heightened urgency.

Finally, the craft was ready. The two reed pontoons measured ten feet each from the curved prow to the equally curved stern. Stout poles connected the two floats so they were eight feet apart. A lightweight platform made of branches and horsetail stalks rested on the poles. The tarp was attached to a pole, but there was no mast. Rick and Con planned to hold it up to catch the wind. Additionally, Rick had laboriously carved two wooden paddles.

The launch took place at evening. The plan was to sail, or paddle if necessary, to Sam's island under the cover of darkness. They rested all day, then dragged their craft to the shore at sunset. No one had ever handled a boat before, and the voyagers' understanding of seafaring was sketchy and theoretical. Getting the boat past the breakers was the first test, and it showed how ill prepared they were. Once the craft was in the water, Rick and Con pushed it seaward, hopped on, and began paddling furiously. The first wave turned the boat sideways, and the following waves quickly stranded it on the sands. This drill was repeated several times before Con and Rick gave up and dragged the boat by brute force beyond the breakers.

Once they achieved that small victory, Con and Rick began to paddle because there was no wind. Most of their efforts were directed at keeping the boat aimed in the correct direction, and progress was excruciatingly slow. After two hours of effort, the beach was only a mile off, and the islands seemed no closer at all. "This isn't working," said Rick. "Here, Fern, you paddle, and I'll push."

When Rick slipped into the water, Con cried out, "What are you doing? That isn't safe!"

"Nothing's safe," said Rick, as he grabbed the platform and started to kick. Without Rick's weight and with his pushing, the boat began to make more progress.

Oak joined him in the water. "I can't paddle," he said, "but I still have two legs."

Con and Fern paddled until their backs and arms ached. Then they, too, slipped into the water to push the craft. Con reflected on the irony of working so hard to build a boat, then swimming to the island anyway. They pushed the catamaran until everyone reached the point of exhaustion. Then they climbed back on the platform and collapsed with fatigue. The shore was distant, but the islands seemed little closer. As they rested, the sun rose.

Although Rick had no experience judging distances at sea, he suspected the tall cliffs made the islands seem closer than they actually were. The morning sun shone fiercely, and he realized drinking water would soon become a serious problem. A breeze picked up from the west. As it started to push the boat off course, Rick had the sinking feeling the voyage itself might be fatal. The faces of his companions told him they were thinking the same thing.

"Should we head back or keep on?" asked Rick.

Con gazed toward the shore that had taken so much effort to leave, then looked at the still-distant islands. "I don't know," she said.

"Will things be any better if we start out again tomorrow or next week?" asked Oak. "Will we be stronger, or our boat faster? Will we have more water jars?"

"I'm for going on," said Fern.

Glancing at Fern's distended belly, Con said, "Me, too."

"Okay," said Rick, "We'll rest for a while, then paddle in shifts."

"I can't paddle, so I'll push," said Oak.

"That's not a good idea," said Rick. "Swimming in daylight is riskier. Marine reptiles probably hunt by sight."

"I thought we were invisible," countered Oak.

Rick almost brought up Violet, but instead said, "The rules may be different at sea."

"That's all theory," said Oak. "We need to get to the island, and sooner is safer."

"Then save your strength for tonight," said Rick. Soon afterward, he disregarded his own advice and started paddling. Con joined in, and together, they prevented the breeze from blowing them off course. If they had not been so tired, they would have enjoyed the sights the sunlight revealed. The Sundance Sea was not deep, and away from the shore, the water was crystal clear. Often, they could see the bottom, or at least peer far into the sea's blue depths. A school of ammonites swam underneath them, their shells shining like pearls in the morning light. Fish sped through the waters, singly or in schools. Most exciting were the *Ichthyosaurs* that pursued them. Even in her exhaustion, Con thrilled at the sight of them.

Eventually, Rick and Con had to stop and get some sleep. They crawled under the tarp and dozed. Unknown to them, Fern and Oak slipped into the water and pushed the raft while they slept. When Rick began to stir, Fern climbed on board and pulled Oak in after her. Rick glanced at the islands, which were closer, and then at his wet companions. He was not fooled.

Rain fell in the afternoon, and they caught it with the tarp and refilled the water jars. After the jars were filled, they drank as much rainwater as they could. Then, since the weather hid the islands, they all crawled under the tarp and slept. The rain stopped as night fell, and everyone entered the water and pushed the boat. When dawn arrived, they wearily crawled back on board and slept beneath the tarp.

Con awoke first. When she peered out from under the tarp, the sun was already in the western sky. She gazed toward the islands, and to her dismay, saw that they were farther away than before. "Rick! Fern! Oak! Wake up! We're drifting away from the islands."

Rick pushed the tarp away. "Shit!"

"There's no wind," said Con. "We must be in a current."

The water beneath the boat was dark, and no bottom was visible. Rick jumped into the sea, grabbed the boat, and started kicking. Con was about to join him when Rick yelled, "You and Fern paddle." As the two women grabbed the paddles, Oak slipped into the water beside Rick.

Having rested, they were able to make progress against the current. Slowly, the distance they had lost was regained. Con and Fern were paddling hard when they were diverted by a school of five-foot *Ichthyosaurs* leaping out of the water in graceful arches. It was an enchanting sight. Then Fern noticed something in the water beneath the leapers. She pointed in its direction. "Did you see that, Con?"

"See what?"

"Something big in the water." Fern stared into the blue depths. "It's gone now. No . . . wait . . ." She stopped paddling and strained to see past the reflections on the waves. She screamed, "Get out! Get out of the water!"

Rick and Oak peered down into the depths and saw a huge shape rising beneath them. Four flippers beat like two pairs of wings propelling an immense gaping mouth. Rick was only partway on the platform when Oak uttered a startled cry and was jerked beneath the surface. Rick caught a fleeting glimpse of huge, toothy jaws closed around Oak's legs, pulling him under. The boat rose on water displaced by the creature swimming beneath it. Fern saw a dark shape with something pale in its jaws fading into the depths.

That was it. No trace of Oak remained. He had been erased as completely and casually as a figure on a chalkboard. The suddenness of his death felt even more terrifying than Violet's, and its consequences were more dire. Only Oak could navigate a time machine.

Con, Rick, and Fern huddled on the flimsy platform of their makeshift boat, expecting the pliosaur to return any moment. Only a few horsetails and branches were in its way, a piddling barrier to so powerful a creature. They held each other and waited to die, but nothing happened. Anxious minutes passed, and there was no sign of the predator. Eventually, they realized they might live awhile longer.

"What now?" asked Rick.

"We must stop Sam," said Con. "He can't go on changing history."

"Do you think we can destroy his time machine?" asked Rick.

"That won't be necessary," said Fern. "I can probably take the time machine upwhen."

"I thought you couldn't navigate," said Con.

"I can't," said Fern. "I'll arrive upwhen at the same point in space."

"But nothing will be there," said Rick. "The Earth, the solar system, the entire galaxy are constantly moving."

"I know," said Fern. "I'll end up far beyond the solar system. I'm going to die anyway. I hear when you run out of air, you just go to sleep. And if I want to end it quickly, I can always open the door."

"Fern . . ."

"The only choice left for me is the manner of my death," said Fern. "I'd like to make it count. Get me to the time machine, then go."

"We can't leave you," said Rick.

"No," added Con.

"Don't make it harder for me by throwing your lives away," said Fern. "If anyone can survive here, it's you two."

Rick turned to Con. "I'll be by your side, whatever you choose."

"We must make sure Fern can steal Sam's machine," said Con. "After that . . . Well, I'm not ready to give up. Maybe we can live here."

"It'll be hard," said Rick, "but perhaps we can find an island where it will be safe."

"Rick, there's something you should know," said Con.

"What?"

"I'm . . . I'm . . ." She hesitated, wracked with indecision. "I'm madly in love with you." Con sighed at her cowardice. *I have to tell him about the baby!* Yet she could not bring herself to do it.

"That's good," said Rick with a smile, "because you'll be stuck with me."

Con decided she would let fate decide her future. Of all

the possible outcomes, living in the Jurassic with Rick seemed the most unlikely. There remained major obstacles to a safe return to the mainland, and Con decided to worry about those first. She grabbed a paddle and started rowing. Rick did likewise.

Con and Rick paddled until it grew dark. Then the three of them slipped into the water to push the boat. The wind shifted and helped them for the first time since they had put to sea. They swam all night, spurred by desperation and the feeling this would be their final chance. As the first light came to the eastern sky, they heard the sound of breakers. In the dim light, they could see a low, wooded island ahead. With the last of their energy, they made it through the surf and to the beach, where they barely had the strength to pull the boat onto the sand. They staggered up to the trees and collapsed.

THE SUN WAS high in the sky when Con awoke. Rick was leaning against a tree, gazing at her. When he saw she was awake, he forced a smile on his melancholy face. "How long have you been up?" asked Con.

"Awhile."

"Did you look at the other island?"

"Yeah. The time machine's there." His voice sounded unexcited. The discovery no longer meant a chance to escape, only further danger and Fern's certain death.

"Then there's still hope for *Homo sapiens*."

"I guess so," said Rick. "I don't feel good about Fern dying alone."

"Me neither." Con gazed tenderly at Fern as she slept. "It's funny how she thinks she isn't brave. She's a lot braver than I am."

Rick sighed. "I suppose we should do it tonight. The channel between the islands isn't wide. I think we can swim it without much trouble."

"What about pliosaurs?"

"I'm more worried about Sam's particle gun."

* * *

WHEN FERN AWOKE a little later, the three sneaked a look at the time machine and planned their crossing. Then they retreated to the far side of the island. Con found some shellfish, which they ate raw. It was their last meal together, and it was solemn. Afterward, there was nothing to do but wait for night to fall. When it was dark enough, they entered the sea and swam the channel.

After they reached Sam's island, they climbed the low cliff to where the time machine stood with its stairway extended. Not far behind, a rough, rectangular opening had been cut with a particle gun into the sheer cliff. The opening was completely black. "I'm glad we don't have to wait for Sam to go to bed," whispered Rick. "Shall we go?"

Fern and Con nodded, and the three crept to the time machine. As soon as their feet touched its stairs, the craft's lights turned on. To their eyes, which had adjusted to the darkness, the illumination was nearly blinding. Squinting, Fern entered the machine, rushed over to its controls, and began to study them. She frowned. "They're all different."

"Can you figure them out?" asked Rick.

"I think so."

"Just in case you can't," said Rick, "I'm going to find a very big rock." He hurried down the stairway.

Fern bent over the control panel, muttering. "Temporal destabilizer . . . power modulator . . . Ah, there's the phase integrator . . . transducer . . . transducer . . . There it is." She began flicking switches. Displays appeared on the viewscreen, and Fern looked satisfied. "I think I got it, Con."

Con heard footsteps on the stairway. "The rock's not necessary, Rick. Fern's figured it out."

Fern adjusted a few more controls as she watched the viewscreen. "Con, you should leave now. I'm ready to . . ." She cried out and slumped over the control panel.

"Fern!" Con turned toward the stairway, expecting to see Rick. Sam stood there instead, pointing an object at Con.

"I am pleased to see you," Sam said in a cold voice, "even though I am not surprised. You are, after all, my creation."

Con felt a jolt of pain as darkness overcame her.

43

CON REGAINED CONSCIOUSNESS ON A STONE FLOOR.
Her wrists were bound behind her back. Her ankles were
also bound by a plastic material that had no knots. Con
raised her head and peered about. She was alone in a chamber, roughly five feet wide by eight feet deep, carved from
solid stone. The front of the chamber was open, but a plane
of swirling colors sealed it. *A pain barrier,* thought Con.
The only illumination filtered dimly through the barrier.
There were no light fixtures, and the only feature in the
chamber was a hole in its floor, which Con supposed was a
toilet. Three food squares lay by a shallow dish of water.

Con wiggled across the stone to reach the food and
water. They had been placed close enough to the pain field
that her face tingled unpleasantly as she ate and drank like
an animal. The colors that moved like the hues of an oil
slick barred her escape and made bindings unnecessary.
Con supposed she was bound for discomfort's sake. Sam
had once deceived her with kindness. That ploy would no
longer work, and Con feared he would use different tactics
this time.

The field that sealed the chamber also veiled what lay
beyond it, and Con saw the room outside her cell only
vaguely. It was large and filled with equipment. Occasionally, she could discern two figures moving about, figures
she assumed were Sam and Kat. The swirling colors muffled all sound, so she could not hear any conversation. Con
suspected Sam knew she was conscious and also suspected
he would keep her waiting. Many long, uncomfortable
hours passed before the pain barrier vanished and Sam

stood at the chamber's entrance. He wore a long shimmering robe of bluish gray and a sardonic smile.

"You," said Con, filling the pronoun with the sound of her loathing.

Sam's smile became more pronounced, and a hint of amusement entered it. "You seem less than glad to see me. Yet be assured, I am delighted to see you."

"I saw what you did to history. You're sick and twisted."

"You saw what *we* did," corrected Sam. "You played a vital role in my improvements."

"Improvements? You ruined civilization!"

"Lectures on civilization from a sape? It would be humorous if it were not so ridiculous."

"I have nothing more to say to you," said Con.

"Good. Then we can proceed quickly. You must undo the damage you created with that bomb."

Con forced herself to laugh. "You're even crazier than I thought. I'll never help you."

"Never? It may take you a while, but you will want to assist me."

"I'd rather die first."

"You do not have that option. Others may die, but not you." Sam turned and yelled out his daughter's name in the Kynden tongue. Kat appeared from behind some large instruments. Her expression was wooden, her eyes downcast. "Refill the sape's water dish," said her father, "and toss it a few food squares."

Kat left meekly. "You were a bad influence on her," said Sam, "but she has come around. Just as you will."

Kat returned to refill Con's water dish and set food squares beside it. "Next time," said Sam, "just toss the food squares down. It will find them."

"Yes, Father," said Kat as she left the chamber.

"Since you want my cooperation," said Con, "why don't you unbind me? I'm not going anywhere."

"Your kind arrogantly calls itself *Homo sapiens*— thinking man. Try to live up to your namesake and think about what I have said. Perhaps later, I will release you from your bonds." Sam left the chamber, and the pain field sealed its entrance.

Con did not allow herself to cry. She would not give Sam that satisfaction in the first round of their game. It was a contest where, once again, her sole advantage lay in Sam's need for her cooperation. *If he could do without me,* she thought, *he would.* Why he expected her to cooperate was unclear, but his confidence was ominous. Con was certain of only one thing—she must not trust Sam. She had seen madness in his eyes. *Was that look always there?* she wondered. *Did I just fail to see it?* Regardless, it was there now. Con understood that Sam would not keep his promises. He would only fulfill his threats.

WHEN THE LIGHT ceased coming through the pain barrier, Con assumed night had arrived. She tried to sleep, but the rough stone floor was cold, and her bonds made it impossible to get comfortable. Yet, even if she had lain unfettered on a downy bed, she would not have rested. Her thoughts dwelled on Rick and Fern. *Sam will hurt them to break me.* Con's dilemma was simply put, but not easily solved. She would have to witness the suffering and death of the two people dearest to her or cause the suffering and deaths of millions she would never see. The numbers doomed Rick and Fern, and Con's love doomed the millions. She would deeply regret either choice.

Con was hungry and thirsty when Sam returned late the following day. He glanced at the empty water dish and the dried food on Con's chin. "You should have rationed yourself," he said. "That was meant to last all day. Perhaps, if you prove sensible, I may prove generous."

"Murder is never sensible."

"I have come to bandy words."

Sam called out in the Kynden tongue, telling his daughter to bring the releasing stick. Kat appeared with a small metal cylinder that had a crystalline hemisphere at one end. She handed it to her father and left. Sam touched the hemisphere against the bonds around Con's ankles. They became loose and rubbery. Con had no difficulty slipping them off.

By the time Con freed her legs and stretched them, Sam held the device he had used to render her unconscious. "This is a nerve gun," he said. "It can stun, but it serves other functions." He made some adjustments to the device, pointed it at Con, and pulled the trigger. Con screamed when her kneecap felt as if struck by a hammer. The pain was excruciating, but faded quickly. "That was one of the milder settings," said Sam.

"So you plan to torture me?"

"Of course not," said Sam. "I want you fully functional. That was to demonstrate you must behave. Now, get up."

Con rose shakily to her feet, surprised her knee still worked. "What's going to happen?"

"Another demonstration. Leave this cell, but remember, the nerve gun is pointed at you."

Con entered the large hall-like room she had seen through the pain barrier. It was illuminated by artificial lights and the sunlight that filtered from a hallway at its far end. Con recognized some of the devices in the room from her stay on Montana Isle. Clearly, this was Sam's new base of operations.

"Katulumamana!" Sam called out in the Kynden tongue. "Stop skulking and come here."

Kat appeared, and, as before, she avoided making eye contact with Con. Con pretended not to understand what had been said, thinking she might gain some advantage if Sam was unaware she knew his language. "Set up the apparatus," said Sam in Kynden, "I need to watch the sape. It is rebellious and stubborn."

"Yes, Father," Kat answered in their language. She briefly disappeared behind the jumbled equipment, to return pushing a tray-sized platform that levitated off the floor. Upon it was a cube with some controls on its top. Kat attached a long wire to the cube, then commanded the tray to lower to the floor. "May I go now, Father?"

"No," replied Sam in Kynden. "Stick around. Remember who you are. I won't abide squeamishness."

"Please, Father . . ."

"You will obey me!" said Sam in a hard voice. "Now, stop your whining."

Con watched Kat grow pale, and she feared some atrocity would take place. Sam turned to Con and switched to English as he spoke, using the same compassionate tone Con recalled from when they first met. Only his smile betrayed his mockery. "There are people here I am sure you are anxious to see."

Sam spoke in Kynden to his daughter. "Katulumamana, let down the barriers."

Two openings, sealed by pain fields, flanked Con's cell. Kat touched the cube, and the swirling colors disappeared. Fern and Rick were revealed. They lay bound, as Con had been, upon the floor. Sam spoke to Con in the caring tone he had employed previously. "Your mate lies safe and sound." Then Sam's voice lost its warmth. "I have seen that sape before. It suffered as it died."

Con knew Sam was waiting for her to show distress, and she fought to hide it.

"The runt is new to me," said Sam.

"I'm sorry, Con," said Fern. "I should have entered the time machine alone. If I hadn't . . ." Fern's scream cut her short as Sam fired the nerve gun.

"You will speak when I permit it," barked Sam. He turned to Con. "I know you have feelings for that runt. If you persist in your stubbornness, you will share its cell when it tries to give birth."

Con bit her lip and did not respond.

"I believe that time is near," said Sam. "Still, I have more immediate inducements." He spoke to Kat, who took the wire attached to the cube and clipped its end to form a loop.

"You once felt the full force of a pain field when you tried to escape in the Cretaceous," said Sam. "I know that memory is vivid. Katulumamana, activate the wire." Kat touched the cube and colors filled the space inside the loop. "Good," said Sam, "Turn off the field and place the loop around the male's abdomen." When Kat hesitated and looked apologetically at Con, Sam barked, "Now!" in Kynden.

Kat obeyed and pulled the wire over to Rick's cell. She lifted him up to pass the wire beneath him, then clipped it around his stomach.

"No!" cried Con. "Don't do it!"

"It's all right," said Rick. "Don't give in."

Desperate to buy time, Con said, "Okay, okay! I'll do what you want."

"Am I supposed to believe you?" asked Sam.

"Yes! Yes! I promise," said Con.

"I doubt you are sincere," said Sam. "Anyway, you must truly *want* to help me." In Kynden he said, "Katulumamana, a full second."

Kat touched the cube and Rick's howl echoed through the chamber. It was a cry of pure, animal agony. The searing pain stripped him of his humanity as he writhed and convulsed in his own excrement. There was no room for thought, dignity, or bravery in a body that simultaneously felt on fire, crushed to splintered bone, and torn into bloody shreds. Although Rick was unscathed, every nerve continued to pulse with agony even after the pain field was shut off. Con wailed as he suffered, and Sam had to shoot her five times with the nerve gun to prevent her from reaching Rick.

Finally, Sam told Kat to end Rick's agony. She went over and touched a flattened cylinder to Rick's neck. His convulsions stopped, and his contorted face looked human again. Pain haunted his features, but it was the shame and humiliation in his eyes that Con found most heartrending. She sat up from where she had fallen after the final shot from the nerve gun, her eyes on Rick. He shook as if gripped by a fever, and Kat raised his head to bring a vial of liquid to his lips. "Don't give him that," said Sam in Kynden.

"Rick," said Sam in a voice filled with solicitude. "That could not have been easy. I regret I had to do it, but Con is a stubborn girl. I must hurt you again, and this time you will suffer longer. Perhaps you have something to say to her that will change her mind."

Threads of drool clung to Rick's mouth as he lifted his trembling head from the stone floor. "Con," he said hoarsely, "don't . . . don't . . ." He burst into sobs that wracked his trembling body. It was almost as hard for Con to see Rick this way as it was to watch his physical torment. Rick laid his head on the floor and wept uncontrollably.

"Your mate is not very articulate," said Sam. "Another round with the pain field may render him more eloquent, though I doubt it."

Sam told Kat in Kynden to fetch Con's bonds and bind her ankles again. Kat retrieved the loops from the cell, then knelt next to Con. "Please, Constance," she said in a small voice, "put your ankles together."

Con didn't move. "You're as bad as he is."

"Constance," said Kat. "I did not know."

"Don't make excuses," said Con. "How can you do this?"

"He is . . . he is my father," said Kat, her eyes now downcast.

"And you're Daddy's Little Girl."

"Please . . ."

In her grief and rage, Con wanted to hurt Kat. Suddenly, an inspiration came to her, and she spoke softly to the kneeling woman in the Kynden tongue. "I've lived among the Kyndens, and I understand your ways. Your father took you from everything, even from your own kind. Once, you told me it was to shelter you. I believed that, but no longer."

Con's voice became a whisper only Kat could hear. "I know all about the Ripening. I've heard Kynden women speak of its power . . . of its compulsion. Katulumamana, when the urges come and overwhelm you, to whom do you turn? To whom *must* you turn? I know, so don't pretend your father hasn't used you."

Con struck a nerve, and she exulted in Kat's shame. Yet when she saw the full effect of her words, the abject misery in Kat's face dampened her anger.

Kat slowly rose and composed her features before she turned around. In a calm voice she said, "Father, may I use the nerve gun?"

Sam grinned as he handed it to his daughter. "You may want to increase the settings," he said. "The higher ones are more painful."

"Yes," said Kat, "I think I will."

Kat made some adjustments to the nerve gun and pointed it at Con with an unsteady hand. Con gazed into Kat's wet, tormented eyes and braced for a surge of pain. Then, Kat swerved and fired. Sam gave a startled cry and fell unconscious to the floor. His daughter stood over his inert body. Her face colored as years of repressed shame and rage boiled to the surface. "Never again!" she shouted in Kynden. "Never! Never!" Then Kat dropped the gun and ran weeping to embrace Con.

IT SEEMED LIKE a dream. For a minute or two, Con was unable to believe what had taken place. Kat released Con's wrists, then quickly tended Rick. She removed his bonds and gave him a drink from the vial. The liquid eased his lingering pain and soothed his mind as well. Kat freed Fern, and when the Gaian and Kynden women returned, Con and Rick were embracing. Con left Rick's arms to hug Kat. "Thank you, thank you," she said tearfully. "I'm sorry about what I said."

"Do not be," said Kat. "You spoke the truth. I was his prisoner as much as you."

"What are you going to do?" asked Con.

"My father wants to live only among his own kind," said Kat. "I will leave him on Montana Isle. There, he will get his wish. The only person in the world will be a Kynden."

While Rick cleansed himself, Con helped Kat carry Sam to the time machine. Fern brought the food-square maker, for Kat did not want her father to starve. Then, Kat departed in the time machine. Con never found out if Kat said farewell to her father, or simply left him unconscious on the desert island. When Kat returned, she brought the food-square maker with her. The machine, which seemed new when Kat departed, now bore the marks of many years of use.

"What happened to the food-square maker?" asked Con.

"After I left him," said Kat, "I traveled upwhen to the time when he no longer needed it." She set down the machine. It was her only reference to her father's death. Con imagined Sam alone on Montana Isle, living in the ruined rooms and surrounded by an empty world. Judging from the condition of the machine Kat retrieved, he had lived there for a long time. *She must have found his bones,* thought Con. She gazed at Kat, looking for some signs of grief. She found none, for in this, Kat was her father's daughter.

44

THE CAVES SAM HAD CREATED TO SERVE HIS NEEDS were crude, and the amenities were few. Yet there were toilets, baths, two bedrooms, and a ready supply of food squares. These seemed luxurious to travelers who had lived in the open and ate whatever they could catch. Rick and Con shared one bed, and Fern and Kat shared the other. The Gaian and Kynden women plunged into researching how to undo Sam's changes, and the work bonded them. When Con saw the two together, she thought they looked like a pair of school-aged playmates, mismatched only in size. Con now wore a robe, though she often left it behind in favor of her loincloth when she and Rick explored the island. For them, the Jurassic became the perfect spot for an exotic honeymoon, and they soon found a sandy beach to walk upon.

"I wish they still had beaches in the twenty-first century," said Rick.

"Maybe we should just stay here," teased Con.

"It's tempting," said Rick, "but this is no place to raise our child."

"Our child?"

"Come on, Con. I'm a biologist."

"You knew?"

"Let's say I guessed."

"I didn't want you to worry," said Con, "so I didn't tell you."

"Then why don't you tell me now?"

Con kissed Rick. "Darling, we're going to have another baby."

Rick saw a shadow of grief pass over Con's face when she said "another," and he hugged her close. They walked silently until Rick said, "I guess my brother's right, I should complete my degree."

"You mean finally take the required courses?"

"Yeah, it's the responsible thing. See what love does? For you, I'll even read Jane Austen."

"How are you going to feel, being married with a baby on the way?" asked Con.

"Lucky," said Rick. "But what about you? Weren't you supposed to go to Harvard?"

"Con Greighton was accepted there, and her billionaire daddy was going to foot the tuition. Con Clements hasn't even graduated from kindergarten."

Rick looked concerned. "How's that going to be for you?"

"After my travels, art history seems less interesting than paleontology. I won't need a degree to do field work."

"Con, you're the perfect woman."

Con smiled. "You're just finding that out?"

* * *

"THE KEY TO research," said Kat, "is to do it upwhen from the event you are studying. Even the deepest secrets end up in books. It usually takes only twenty to fifty years."

Con thought of her history courses and knew that was true. People liked to talk, though they waited until it was safe to do so.

"Take the matter of Roberto Peters Senior," said Kat.

"You mean the developer of the virus?" asked Con.

"No, that was his son," said Fern.

"We will use the father, to get the son," said Kat. "It turns out the senior Roberto built his mansion using misappropriated funds. By the time that was public knowledge, his son was the corporate head, so it did not matter."

"It would've mattered a lot," said Fern, "if that information had leaked out earlier."

"Roberto Junior never would have become a manager," said Kat. "The virus project never would have commenced. I am certain. I have done the calculations."

"Calculations?" said Con.

"My father developed a system for calculating the effects of changes on the timestream."

"So, I have to go upwhen and become someone new?" asked Con with trepidation.

"All you will have to do is misdirect a few documents," said Kat. "It should be a day's work at most."

CON'S MISSION IN the twenty-seventh century was as easy as Kat said it would be. Most of her time was spent walking to and from the time machine. She leaked documents electronically. It seemed like something anyone could do; yet Kat assured her that was not the case—only Con's actions would radically alter the timestream. Once Con executed the change, she and Kat made a short hop upwhen. This visit was for pleasure, not business. While Kat remained in the time machine, Con took the mass transport to the Mergonic Corporate Complex.

Con found her way with little difficulty, though it was

years before her previous visit. She arrived outside the mansion at the time Kat said she should and joined the crowd gathered there. Many who milled about upon the manicured lawn with the reporters were simply curious. Con imagined there were a few in the throng who, like her, held a grudge. The front door opened, and a man emerged, flanked by two officials. For an instant, Con thought he was Roberto. Then she saw differences in his face and knew she was looking at Roberto's father. He behaved like guilty men had for centuries, walking quickly and trying to shield his face from eyes and cameras.

Con's attention fixed on the pair that followed the three men. A woman led a whiney boy of about ten by the hand. The boy was resisting, and the woman had to pull him along. Con focused on the boy. She had seen his petulant look before.

"I don't want to go, Mama!" shouted the boy. "Why do we have to leave?"

"This is not our home now," said his mother. "Only managers can live here."

"Papa's not a manager?"

"Not now."

"Will I be a manager?"

"You'll do other work, dear."

Roberto Junior suddenly became aware of Con. "Mama, why's that lady looking at me?"

"Lots of people are looking. Just ignore her."

"But she's smiling. Make her stop."

Roberto's mother impatiently jerked her son's hand and dragged him to a waiting vehicle. Con watched them speed away. Then she headed to the mass transport station.

THE TRIP DOWNWHEN wore Con out, and she slept late. When she awoke, Kat greeted her with a smile. "History has been restored," she said. "Fern has a world to which she can return."

Con looked at Fern. "You're leaving, aren't you?"

"Yes, I have to," said Fern, reflexively touching her rounded belly. "I'll never forget you, Con. I'm so glad you and Rick are back together."

"I have you and the others to thank for that," said Con. "When are you going?"

"This morning. The pains have returned."

"I'll miss you," said Con.

"When I get back," said Kat, "I will start to work on your new identity, so you and Rick can return to your own time."

"Then, what will you do?" asked Con.

"I will destroy all evidence of this place," said Kat, "and go to live in the thirty-seventh century. Fern is going to help me adjust."

"I guess there's no way to use your time machine to save Violet and Oak," said Con.

"I cannot revisit the times in which they died," replied Kat. "It is impossible."

Con sighed. "I thought so."

RICK AND CON said good-bye to Fern. After all their adventures together, the idea of sixteen centuries separating their lives was sad to contemplate. Con and Fern embraced for the last time. "Take care of yourself," Con said, choking back tears.

"It'll be easy after what I've been through." Fern turned to hug Rick. "I'll never forget how you carried me."

Rick lifted her with his embrace. "You're still light as a feather."

Soon, Con and Rick stood on the rocky shelf, watching the time machine rise into the sky. "Well," said Rick, "we have the whole world to ourselves. What do you want to do?"

"I don't know about you," replied Con, "but I'm taking off my clothes."

RICK AND CON spent an idyllic day on the island. They played in a waterfall, watched pterosaurs dive for fish, collected seashells, and viewed the sun setting on the Sun-dance Sea. Afterward, Con said, "Let's drag out the sleeping mat. We can make love under the stars one last time."

"And what if Kat arrives and finds us?" asked Rick.

"She won't," said Con. "It's already been arranged. No matter how long she spends in the future, she'll return an hour after sunrise tomorrow morning."

Rick smiled and kissed Con. "Ain't time travel wonderful."

Con and Rick watched the sunrise in each other's arms, then returned the sleeping mat and dressed for Kat's arrival. As they stood on the rocky shelf, Rick smiled. "I'm glad we're not Kyndens. I'd hate it if last night came only once a year."

Con laughed. "Think of all we'd accomplish with that extra time."

"Oh, we'd just waste it improving our minds."

Con pointed upward. "There's the time machine."

Rick gazed up and saw the time machine's silvery underside against the blue sky. As he watched, a second silvery dot winked into existence. It was joined by another dot that was completely black. More followed, until Rick and Con lost count after three dozen. As the flotilla of time machines descended toward the island, Con grabbed Rick's hand. "What's happening?"

Rick frowned. "It seems we have visitors. And something tells me they're not bringing good news."

45

ONLY KAT'S TIME MACHINE LANDED. THE OTHER CRAFT hovered silent and motionless over the sea. Their forms varied from saucer-shaped to ovoid to spherical, but most were the same size as Kat's machine. With one exception, their colors were either silver, absolute black, or a combination of the two. The uniquely colored time machine hovered directly behind Kat's. It reminded Con of mother-of-pearl. Brilliant hues shimmered on its bluish silver surface as it floated in the air.

A panel on the underside of Kat's time machine transformed into a stairway. Kat descended it alone. She was smiling, but her eyes seemed sad. They were also old. With a shock, Con realized her friend had spent many decades upwhen. "I have returned," said Kat, "exactly when I said I would."

"What's happening?" asked Con.

"You and Rick are not in any danger. They wanted me to tell you that right away."

"And who are they?" asked Rick.

"Humanity's representatives."

Con glanced at the orderly rows of silent crafts. "There must be a lot of them."

"You will be dealing with only one person," said Kat. "She speaks for all."

Kat's statement seemed to be a cue, for an opening appeared in the side of the mother-of-pearl time machine. A woman appeared. She stood on a silver disk that transported her through the air until she alighted a few feet from Con and Rick. The woman looked like a *Homo sapiens,* but one taken to such heights of perfection that she transcended the species. Her finely sculpted features were perfectly symmetrical. Her smooth skin was a velvety shade of blue-black that set off her turquoise eyes. These regarded Con with such intelligence and compassion, she felt at ease under their gaze. The woman was no taller than Con, and she wore layers of gauzy robes so that the graceful body beneath them appeared like an elegant shadow.

"Hello, my name is Nivreeta. I come from the forty-sixth century," said the woman in melodic English. "I extend our gratitude and good wishes to you both. May I embrace you? It is our custom."

"Sure," said Con awkwardly.

Nivreeta hugged Con warmly and did the same to Rick. "You must have many questions and many concerns. I will try to put these to rest as quickly as possible."

"Why are you here?" asked Con.

"We have discovered that time travel has the potential to destabilize the entire timestream. The incident with Samazatarmaku is a perfect example of that disruption. We have gathered here to formulate means to prevent a reoccurrence of such an event."

"And what does that have to do with us?" asked Rick.

"Very little, actually," replied Nivreeta. "We have come here to establish policies, but we also will aid your friend's efforts to return you to your own century."

"It will be much easier," said Kat, "now that I have so many resources at my disposal."

"I am concerned," said Nivreeta, "that you may have been infected with the virus. It was released before you departed the twenty-seventh century."

Con grew pale. "You mean our child could be dependent on kana?"

"We'll treat you both to prevent that. Additionally, we will give Rick an implant. He will need it later."

"Why?" asked Con.

"It will aid his return to the twenty-first century," said Nivreeta.

"This version is an improvement over the one you got,"

Kat said to Con. "He will not get headaches, and he will be able to access it immediately."

"I would like to accomplish the treatment as soon as possible," said Nivreeta. "If you have no objections, we will do it now."

"Why not?" said Con.

"I have no problems with that," said Rick, suspecting it would make no difference if he had.

Two disks floated out of Nivreeta's time machine and landed at Rick's and Con's feet. "Step onto the disks," said Nivreeta, "and they will transport you to my craft. Do not worry, it is impossible to fall off."

When Con floated into the waiting craft, she made the disconcerting discovery that its interior was many times larger than its exterior. She looked about in confusion, and saw that Rick was equally astonished. Nivreeta said, "If time is relative, so is space." Then she led them down a corridor, passing several people on the way. The men and women who politely greeted Con and Rick resembled Nivreeta in their perfection, but their skin and eye shades varied considerably.

Eventually, Con and Rick were separated. Rick departed with a golden-skinned man, while Con proceeded with Nivreeta. They entered a small chamber featuring a large transparent tube that ran from floor to ceiling. Although the cylinder's walls appeared to be made of glass or plastic, they parted like a fabric curtain as Con came into the room. "Please step inside the tube," said Nivreeta.

Con complied, and when she did, the opening closed. She touched the clear walls that surrounded her, and they felt hard. Nivreeta appeared to be saying something, but Con could hear no sound. Then Con had the sensation that she was traveling through time, although the effect was milder and less disorienting. The sensation passed, and the walls of the tube parted.

Con stepped out into the chamber. "Did I have the virus?"

"Your body is free of it now," said Nivreeta.

"So my child's safe."

"Con," said Nivreeta in a gentle tone, "you do not have a child."

"No, you're wrong," said Con, her voice rising in pitch. "I've been pregnant before. I know how it feels."

"You were pregnant, but your body underwent extreme stress."

Con's eyes glistened with tears. "You're telling me I lost it?"

"It was not meant to be." Nivreeta reached out and softly touched Con's arm. "Millennia separate us, yet I understand your grief."

Nivreeta escorted Con back to the opening in the time machine. She stood at the entrance and watched Con float on a disk down to the island. Rick was standing there, and Nivreeta saw Con run to embrace him. She imagined Con was crying.

The golden-skinned man came up to Nivreeta. "Is the child safe?" he asked.

The woman sighed. "Yes, Tovra, I have her. Yet, I do not approve of this deception, on both moral and scientific grounds."

"Neither do I," replied Tovra, "but we were overruled."

"The council is governed by fear, and fear is an intemperate master."

"Still, you accomplished much. They will live."

"Yes," said Nivreeta. "In a manner, they will."

WHILE RICK AND Con were gone, Kat had unloaded a series of containers and instruments into the caves. She watched while Rick consoled Con and put on a smile when they approached. "I have twenty-first-century food," she said. "Sandwiches, chips, fruit, and pastries. Even champagne."

Con smiled, but only slightly. "That will be nice."

"Would you like some lunch? It's past noon."

Con looked at the sun and was surprised to see Kat was right. "Sure," she said. "We have a lot of catching up to do. You spent a long time upwhen, didn't you?"

"Yes, I did. Shall we eat? As I recall, you are always hungry."

Con sensed she was being put off, and she feared not all Kat's news would be good. Kat had set up a table with a view of the sea. It also had a view of the hovering time machines, and for Con, that diminished its charm. Still, she wolfed down two sandwiches. "So how's Fern?" she asked when she was finished. "Did she have a boy or a girl?"

"A boy."

"And what's Fern doing? Tell me all about her son."

Kat looked uncomfortable. "I have not seen Fern for over fifty years."

"You were friends. What happened?"

"She does not remember me. She does not remember the trip."

"Well, how does she explain her son?"

"Con, she does not know she had a son."

Con stared at Kat in stunned silence. As that silence dragged on, Rick tried to divert everyone from the uncomfortable situation. "Hey look," he said, pointing to an open container, "blue jeans." He walked over to them and lifted them up. "Pretty ratty. I'd have thought you'd bring a new pair. Hey, I remembered this shirt. I was wearing it . . ."

". . . the night you disappeared," said Con.

"How did you know?"

"Don't you see, Rick?" said Con. "When you return to the twenty-first century, you'll arrive just an instant after you departed. Isn't that right, Kat? Rick got that implant so they can erase his memories. He'll never know any of this happened."

"That is correct," Kat said in a quiet voice.

For a moment, Con seemed perfectly calm. Then she crumpled under the weight of her despair.

IT WAS A long while before Con could compose herself. Rick did not weep, but he avoided tears only through great effort. He felt his heart would break, and Con's sorrow redoubled his own. Kat, also, seemed profoundly sad, though she had prepared for this moment.

"It is hard to imagine you will ever be happy, yet you will," said Kat. "Your grief will cease to exist. You cannot long for someone you cannot recall."

"That sounds logical," said Con. "But you said yourself, logic only goes so far in understanding the universe. There will be a hole, and, somehow, I will know it's there."

Con expected Kat to argue with her, but she did not. "Rick will return to Missoula, Montana," said Kat. "He will wake up in his room, thinking that he got intoxicated the previous night. From that point, his life will proceed as before."

"And what about me?" asked Con.

"We will create a new identity for you, and ensure that you easily fit into society. You will be an orphan with an inheritance. You will have a personal history that will seem absolutely real to you. There will be corroborating evidence. People will recall you. Con, an immense effort will go into this, aided by extremely sophisticated technology. People are grateful for what you did, and this is how they are showing it."

"By turning me into someone else?"

"Your essential personality will remain intact, and I have leeway in establishing the particulars of your new identity. You will have a say in who you become. In the end, you will still be yourself, under a different guise."

"But why is this necessary? Why can't Rick and I go back together?"

"In the thirty-eighth century, scientists discovered that random elements introduced by time travel were disrupting the forces keeping the timestream stable."

"I know about that theory," said Con. "Oak explained it to me."

"Then you understand how anachronistic knowledge disrupts the natural order. Con, you would have a particularly strong influence."

"We won't tell anybody," said Con.

"How could a paleontologist who has seen dinosaurs fail to behave differently? Both of you would destabilize history, whether you intended to or not."

"Isn't that a little hypocritical?" said Con. "What's any better about paleontologists from the future seeing dinosaurs? They should ban time travel if they're so concerned about it."

"They probably should," said Kat, "but their realities are now the products of time travel. Their worlds are forested with trees that were once extinct. Their cultures have been altered by time travel's discoveries. Having unleashed the technology, they must learn to tame it."

"How come you're able to tell me this?" asked Con. "Why wasn't your memory erased like Fern's?"

"There are people engaged in caring for the timestream, and I have become one of them," said Kat. "The council has decreed that your memories threaten history's stability. Con, if it were up to me, no one would alter your life. Yet, since someone must, I want to be the one who helps you."

Con sighed. "How much time do Rick and I have left?"

"He must go to Nivreeta's time machine at sunset. All the preparations for his return will be done there."

Con glanced at Rick's new implant. "Kat, could you uncover my implant? I think you know why."

"Yes, I do," said Kat.

A few minutes later, the metallic disk on Con's forehead was exposed. "You can access your implant now," Kat said. "When it is time for Rick to leave, a flying disk will come to pick him up."

Con stood up. "I'm . . . I'm not going to cry. Rick, let's go to the beach. We kissed for the first time on a beach. It'll be a good place for our . . . our last . . . I'm not going to cry. I'm not."

When they reached the beach, Rick kissed Con and held her close, as tears streamed down his face. Con looked up at him with a sad smile. "I've seen people share memories through their implants, and I'd like to try. Just touch your dot to mine."

Rick bent down and touched his forehead to Con's. At

first, there was only a vague sensation of another presence. Then new images, sounds, and emotions filled his mind. Initially, they were ephemeral and dreamlike, but they gradually grew in substance and clarity. With the impressions came the understanding that he was experiencing Con's time with him in a reality he could not recall.

Rick saw himself on Montana Isle, watching sea turtles lay eggs on a moonlit beach. He watched the entire sky fill with fire and falling meteors. He surveyed an ashen and desolate landscape as snow fell from a black sky. He saw Joe Burns laughing, wrapped in a cape of Tyrannosaurus hide. He gazed at himself placing a log on the wall of a half-built cabin. He viewed the rapture in his face as he held his newborn son by firelight in that same cabin. It was the most vivid and intimate communication in his life. He saw and heard and felt it all—the joy, the terror, the sorrow, the wonder, and the love. Locked in this most intimate of embraces, Rick and Con forgot about time.

Then the disk arrived, and the spell was broken. Rick reluctantly stepped onto the silver platform after a parting kiss. He rose into the air, feeling that half of him had been torn away and left to wave forlornly from the beach. Con's figure grew smaller until it was finally blocked from sight. Nivreeta's time machine came into view. She was standing at its entrance. As she met him, she made no effort to hide her melancholy. "Soon," she said, "this grief will end."

CON SLOWLY WALKED back to the cave, arriving at dusk. Kat was waiting. She embraced Con saying, "I know that was hard."

"It was," said Con. "It wasn't as bad as when Joey died or when Rick was shot, but it was hard all the same. I can't believe I've lost him twice." Con looked as though she was about to cry, but she did not. "I want to talk about my new identity. You said you had some leeway with it."

"I do," replied Kat, feeling encouraged by Con's outward calmness.

"Could this person still be named Con? I'd like that."

"That is easy to arrange."

"And she'll know stuff, even things I don't know now?"

"Yes, she will have to."

"Maybe she'll even have different interests."

"You could still pursue art history," said Kat. "We can leave that intact."

"I'd rather she be interested in paleontology. More than interested. Devoted would be a better word."

Kat got a slight smile on her face. "She would probably want to pursue a degree in the field."

"Yes, I imagine she would."

"The University of Montana has a good program."

Con smiled. "Yes, I've heard it does."

"Everything you have mentioned lies within the scope of my authority. As long as you have no recollection of your past, history should unfold in a natural manner."

"Along what you call the optimal path."

"Correct," said Kat.

"I think another word for the optimal path is destiny," said Con.

Epilogue

THE COOL MORNING HAD TURNED BLAZING HOT BY late afternoon, but Rick was used to Montana summers. He paused from chiseling rock only briefly to wipe sweat from his brow. He was happy to be working the Hell Creek Formation again. It was his first week in the field, and so far, his luck had not been particularly good. He had found dozens of teeth, some partial bones, and a lot of turtle shell fragments, but nothing exciting. Today, he thought his luck might change. Perhaps the fossil femur he was uncovering would lead to further bones. He chipped steadily at the rock, trying to determine if he was working on a dead end or the beginnings of a skeleton.

The girl was barefoot, so he didn't hear her coming. He became aware of her presence only when she spoke. "Have you seen Professor Clements?"

Rick turned to see a young, athletic-looking woman dressed in cutoffs, a tee shirt, and a wide-brimmed hat. The tee shirt featured an old Ray Troll cartoon captioned "It's Never Too Late to Mutate." Rick owned one just like it. The girl had a broad grin, and her hazel eyes sparkled with excitement.

"I think Tom went to pick up some supplies," said Rick.

"Do his students call him by his first name?" asked the girl. "I'm new here, so I don't know."

"He's my brother, so it's natural for me," said Rick. "But most of the paleo majors call him Tom."

"Then you must be Rick. I've heard about you. I'm Con. Con Davidson." Her eyes went down to the ground, and she casually bent over to pick up a chip of gray rock. She automatically touched it to her tongue to see if it was fossilized bone. When it stuck, her eyes shifted to the fossil Rick was uncovering. Con stooped and inserted the chip into the bone as if she were working on a jigsaw puzzle.

Rick looked up at her, impressed. "You have a good eye."

"The result of a warped childhood," said Con. "As a little girl, I played with rocks, not dolls."

"I used to sleep with an ammonite," said Rick, "instead of a teddy bear."

"You're kidding! With me it was a trilobite, an *Olenellus armatus*. Only then, I called it Trilly." Con laughed, and Rick noticed how pretty she was.

"Why did you want to see Tom?"

"Look!" said Con, extending her palm. She held a small tooth that was sharp and curved.

Rick examined it. "Looks like it came from a small predator."

"See how the serrations are only on the posterior edges? It's got to be from a *Saurornithoidid*."

"That would be a first for here."

"I know," said Con, unable to contain her excitement. "And, Rick, there's a skull! I saw some vertebrae and metatarsals, so I'm thinking there might be a skeleton in the rock. It'd be a lot more work than I could handle alone."

"I'll help," said Rick.

"What about your find?"

"I'll mark it. Can I see your discovery?"

"Sure."

"Why haven't I met you before?" asked Rick.

"I'm transferring to UM this fall," replied Con. "I did all the core requirement crap at a community college. I'm taking your brother's Phylogeny and Cladistics seminar this fall."

"That's a graduate-level course."

"He thought I could handle it."

Rick followed Con as she bounded over the rugged terrain. Usually, he was reserved around women, but today his shyness evaporated. "Don't you believe in shoes?" he teased.

"Not until September; then I wear them out from the inside."

"You must be tough."

"I work like a horse and eat like a pig."

Rick laughed. As he watched Con gracefully scamper up the slope, he doubted the latter was true. He hurried along after her, anxious to see the fossil and eager to get to know the intriguing woman who had found it.